CW01572943

MEMORY BONES

Mike Stone

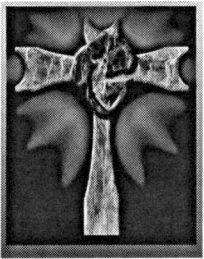

Graveside Tales

MEMORY BONES

Published by Graveside Tales

All rights reserved. No part of this book may be used or reproduced in any manner whatsoever without written permission except in the case of brief quotations embodied in critical articles and reviews. For information address Graveside Tales, P.O. Box
487 Lakeside, AZ 85929, USA
www.gravesidetales.com

This is a work of fiction. Names, characters, and incidents are used fictitiously, and any resemblance to actual persons, living or dead, or events is entirely coincidental.

Copyright © 2012 Mike Stone
Cover Art and Interior Illustrations © 2012 Mark Cartlidge

FIRST EDITION

ISBN: 10 098331411X
ISBN: 13 978-0-9833141-8-9

MEMORY BONES

Mike Stone

For Charles W. Nelson
Who said I should

CONTENTS

Foreword

I first encountered Mike Stone at the Graveside Tales forum almost three years ago. When I heard Mike's first collection of short stories was forthcoming from that same publisher, I was delighted. In my opinion, it's been too long between books. The world needs more Stone-tinged fiction. Once you've read this book (assuming you're not already a fan), you'll think the same.

My first taste of Mike's writing was his collection of four novellas, *Fourtold*, published in early 2008. If you haven't read the book yet, you must pick it up after you've finished *Memory Bones*. It's a surreal, magical treat of monsters new and old.

Mike's writing has a down-to-earth, humorous spirit. Although the humour appears effortless — I suspect there isn't a sensible bone in his body — I've no doubt Mike slaves to make each word perfect. His characters are often ordinary folk enduring bizarre events and they do so matter-of-factly. I imagine Mike would react much the same if a monster rode by on a motorbike or if his wife invited goblins for tea. In fact, even his monsters and angels seem the sort to grab a pie and a swift pint at the local pub before causing havoc.

Lurking within the pages of *Memory Bones* we find sinful angels, organic clones, soap operas, monsters, pentagrams on Frisbees, gamers, time travelling porn stars, dead frogs, and Hitler. We discover that sometimes wolves and sheep need to co-exist, that gargoyles make excellent pets, that some parents are cruel and others willing to sacrifice, that a brass bottle is not necessarily an ideal way to travel, that you should fight back when crab-like creatures crawl up your nose.

Delightful images pepper this book. One of my favourites lines is "*My backbone was a wet thread of cotton.*" Mike's descriptions are evocative, yet not in the least flowery. His words leave a delicious feeling in your mouth. The above line appears in one of the Clob tales — *Lonely Heart Clob*. If you haven't met our pesky hero before (well, Clob would say he was the hero of the tale but others may think Leonard the true hero), you are going to adore his adventures in the aforementioned story and in *Japanese Motorcycle Clob*. If you have read them before, then you're already nodding your head in agreement. I defy anyone to dislike Clob. Even Leonard.

When I read a Clob story, I'm convinced he's my favourite character (as in of all fiction and not just contained here) and then I read about the exploits of Mike's two unfortunate angels Azaliel and Lorcas. If there is a Heaven, then I pray it's crowded with angels such as these dudes and let sin have touched them all. Without doubt, Mike keeps his funny bone sharpened.

But it's not all humour. There are poignant moments such as in *The Arbitrator* with a father's sacrifice, and sick moments, like in *The Damage Done*. In his afterword, Mike tells us a dream inspired the latter story. I'm a little scared of his subconscious. The story is astounding, shocking and perhaps more so because it's told in Mike's matter-of-fact voice.

Mike likes to leave some things to our imaginations. Many of the stories are open-ended. Take my advice: something bad always happens after Mike's left the page. He's just allowing you to dangle on that tiny thread of hope.

When you reach the end of the fiction in this book, don't think you're done. Don't be downhearted and think the humour finished. Mike's afterwords are hilarious. He just can't cease storytelling, and that's why I (and I'm sure you will too, dear reader) love this book and the many others to come. There are big things in Mike's future. This is only the beginning.

Cate Gardner
Liverpool, 2011

Sacred Skin

Hodges' gaze rested on a box at Rider's feet. It was the size of a man's head. They had sat facing each other at the fireside for nearly an hour while waiting for the earl, yet she had made no effort to explain what the box contained and Hodges was too much of a gentleman to ask. Occasionally he would catch a whiff of something rotten.

The light was fading, the small talk petering out. To stymie Derryth Rider's growing impatience, Hodges fished a deck of cards from his waistcoat pocket.

"Sit back, miss, and take a card. No, don't let me see it. Memorise it. That's it, now place it back in the pack. Anywhere, it doesn't matter."

Simon Hodges grinned as he scooped up the playing cards and cut them using only the fingers of his left hand. He shuffled them one-handed and finished his display of dexterity with a flourish, flicking the cards in a blurred arc to settle in his right palm.

"Keep thinking about your card. Here it comes. There!"

A single card jutted from the pack.

"Your card, miss?"

Rider picked it up and laughed, her green eyes sparkling in the firelight. "The queen of hearts, yes. I'm impressed, Simon."

A blush warmed his cheeks. "I learned to do magic after I lost the proper use of my right hand. I was flying on a night raid over Dresden when up popped a fritz in a Messerschmitt Bf 110, raking our fuselage. We dropped our cache and limped home. Our tail-gunner was killed so I guess I got off lightly." Hodges gripped the chair arm with the fingers of his right hand. "There's no real strength on this side from the shoulder down. I took up magic to train my left hand to be as good as my right."

Derryth's lips formed a cautionary moue. "They are merely tricks, Simon, not magic."

Hodges blushed again. "Right you are, miss."

"I'm sorry, I didn't mean to sound uppity. And call me Derryth, please."

The bedroom was darkening by the minute, the setting sun painting the walls a deep sullen red. The mullion and transom cast a crucifix on the four-poster bed. Shadows pooled on the aged floorboards.

Outside, at long last, they heard a car approaching up the gravelled drive. Hodges stood and moved to the window. It was his master in his new Rolls-Royce Silver Ghost. Copper-hued cockchafers bounced off the windscreen.

~

Twenty minutes later the earl, in his tweed three-piece and dark tan brogues, stamped into his bedroom.

"So. It's to be tonight, is it?"

"Yes, it is, Lord Heatherstone," Rider said, handing the parcel to the earl.

She had addressed the earl correctly, but her tone was far from obsequious. This troubled Hodges. His master prized his status above most things. Hodges said a silent prayer that she would not be overfamiliar.

He cleared his throat. "I have told the rest of your staff we are not to be disturbed, sir."

"Very well, Hodges. Close the door."

Heatherstone placed the parcel on his desk and tugged on the twine that bound it. It slithered loose, allowing the stiff paper to spring open. He waved his liver-spotted hands at the foul smell.

"Take over, Hodges."

Hodges stepped forward and removed two plugged jars and what appeared to be a collection of small animal skins from the parcel. He gingerly carried the crinkled mass to the bed where he unfolded it to its full length. It was a patchwork of uncured pelts. Smoothing it out revealed it to be human-shaped. Hodges felt a lurch in the pit of his stomach.

Rider said, "Your sacred skin, my lord."

Heatherstone's nose wrinkled in disgust. From the corner of his eye, Hodges saw Rider's cheeks dimple in mischievous pleasure.

"What are the meaning of these?" Heatherstone ran a pink fingertip over the archaic symbols that flowed over the skin. Branded runes, inked lines and engraved script swirled and combined in complicated patterns.

Rider moved between the two men.

"The Lord's Prayer is branded over the breast, my lord, and here you see it is repeated in Latin. These—" she indicated script inked on the left arm and shoulder —"are sacred Hebrew texts from the Phylacteries. The Muslim Throne verse, the *Ayat al-Kursi*, is branded down here on the legs."

Heatherstone pointed at the right arm. "And this?"

"That is Sanskrit, my lord. It—"

"And that?"

Hodges interjected. "If I may say so, sir, that looks like a Tau. A symbol originating from Egypt and the Middle East that guards against—"

"Yes, yes, I get the bloody picture." Heatherstone worked loose the knot in his tie. "No need to show off! Miss Rider, you've clearly worked very hard. I approve."

Hodges expected Rider to bask in the earl's rare praise, but the mystic merely gave a curt nod and politely faced away as Hodges helped his master undress.

Hodges' eye was drawn back to the bizarre ensemble on the bed. Besides the dangling crescents, silver wheels and rosary beads were the crushed eggshells, mashed leaves, animal bones and seashells crammed into the seams. Fancy feathers jutted at odd angles.

As a loyal manservant, Hodges was privy to many of his master's secrets — he was, in a manner of speaking, invisible — but this strange suit was something he knew little about. He pushed the matter from his mind and concentrated on shaking the creases from a shirt. His mother, a chambermaid to the current earl's father, had instructed him that in service, one was not paid to opine, but to *do*; although that, in Hodges' experience, was easier said than done.

~

Gossip was rife among the staff of the manor.

Since his father's death, the earl of Heatherstone had taken to awaking in the small hours of the morning and demanding his servants dress and feed him before leaving the house on a nocturnal jaunt. He would return home in the grey light of dawn, dirty and dishevelled with a ravaged cast to his eye. Hodges had once observed a smear of blood glistening on the earl's high forehead, but dared not mention it; his master was always unapproachable on these occasions, insisting on bathing himself and given to snapping at any intrusion.

Someone had cut the horses several months ago, their beautifully groomed flanks criss-crossed with wicked slashes from a craft knife. A police enquiry, solicited by the farrier, had drawn a blank, namely because none of the house staff would voice their suspicions. No one wanted to lose their job, and the earl's influence spread far and wide in these parts.

The previous winter, the earl had invited a priest to the manor to conduct an exorcism. Bells and candles, prayers and chants, the shutting and barring of windows; it had been like something out of the Middle Ages and ill-suited to the modern day. The servants had been terribly unsettled. The ritual must have failed, for the earl recalled the priest who had performed the ceremony. Hodges was not privy to their conversation, but he was on chauffeur duty the bright spring day the earl wanted driving fifty miles to a village near Shrewsbury, in Shropshire. Hodges had hoped they could tarry a while at Shrewsbury — he found the wide river and overhanging willows soothing — but the earl was disinclined to stop.

The Rolls halted outside a whitewashed cottage at the end of a narrow dirt track. Black windows peered from under thick thatch.

Hodges stayed in the car as Heatherstone strolled up the path to the front door. The garden was well kept and redolent with lavender, rosemary and chives. Uniform rows of vegetables and canes stood proud, flanked by a hedgerow that rustled crisply in the breeze. Dead leaves crunched underfoot. Hodges cringed and glanced away as the imperious earl rapped his walking cane on the door. When he looked again, it was to see Heatherstone being ushered inside and the door closing behind him.

Later, he awoke to a knocking on the driver's window. He sat up and squinted bleary-eyed as an attractive woman beckoned him to wind down the window. Complying, he was rewarded with the cloying smell of honey. She offered him a plate of sugary cakes and a glass of ginger ale.

"Hello. I'm Derryth. You must be Hodges, although I'm sure you have a first name as well. Your boss is having a lie down in my kitchen." Her eyes twinkled as though she was sharing a joke. "I thought you might like to take a look around my garden with me? Seems a shame to sit in that stuffy car all day."

After removing his cap and coat, Hodges linked her arm and allowed himself to be led around the back of the cottage. The air was alive with the contented buzz of bees. Four hives stood like exotic pagodas under cherry blossoms, the bright sunshine filtered pink by the trees' myriad flowers. Rider told him about the bees — the queen, the drone and the worker — and how they produced different flavoured honeys depending on which flowers they visited. She pointed out the plants in her wild garden and explained the medicinal uses of yarrow, St John's wort and houseleeks.

And she listened as he told her, around a mouthful of cake, how the war had left him unfit for manual labour and — seeing as his left-handed writing was illegible — a future as a clerk had looked unlikely. So he had contacted his late mother's employer and been pleasantly surprised to find the current occupant of Heatherstone Manor wanted him. Hodges related with some pride that he was now the youngest personal manservant ever employed by an earl of Heatherstone.

Rider had touched his damaged shoulder with a concerned frown.

Hodges' palms were sweating and his mouth was dry. He had known love before, he recognised the symptoms, but the sudden onset left him shy and embarrassed.

The spell was only broken when he glanced through the open doorway of Rider's kitchen and saw something spread out across the heavy oak table. All of Lord Heatherstone's body, with the exception of his sweat-slicked, beetroot-red face, was encased in a solidified shroud of plaster.

~

From that day to this — thirty-six, he'd counted — Derryth Rider had played a leading role in Simon Hodges' erotic reveries.

Stripped to his underwear, Heatherstone crawled on to the bed.

Rider said, "I'm afraid you will need to remove everything, my lord. If you'd rather I left?"

"Damn and blast! Isn't a gentleman afforded any dignity in these matters?" The earl slid his silk shorts down over his blotchy white thighs and kicked them across the floor. Hodges stooped to pick them up. "Leave them, damn it. Come and help me pull this bloody thing on."

Hodges, aware that Heatherstone was dangerously humiliated, hastened to his master's side. He lifted the skin and gestured for Heatherstone to sit down on the edge of the bed. He looked to Rider for help.

She laid the skin along the floor at Heatherstone's feet so that it resembled the old man's shadow. Lifting Heatherstone's left foot, she looped the ankle of the skin over it.

"It's like a bloody French letter! It'll be inside out."

Hodges blushed at the earl's casual reference to preventatives.

Derryth explained, "The skin works by augmenting your own natural protection, my lord. The protective charms and verses have to be against your skin to work."

Hodges threaded the other foot into the skin and eased it up over Heatherstone's shins. It was a tight fit. Hodges was surprised at his master's tolerance. He bore the scratches from the rough seams, bones and shells without complaint. This was a man who threw a tantrum if his bath water was one degree above his preferred temperature, or the butler arrived a minute late with his pudding. No one had ever accused Lord Heatherstone of bearing discomfort stoically.

When the skin reached halfway up his thighs, Heatherstone stood and tugged it over his privates. He sat down again gingerly to allow Hodges to thread his arms through and fasten the skin at the back with laces of black sinew. Hodges began to tighten the straps at the ankles, working quickly in the dim light. Lord Heatherstone plucked indelicately at the crotch.

"Is my lord all right?" asked Rider.

"Why should I be defending myself against something that could be repelled by the, er . . ."

"The *Ayat al-Kursi*? The Phylacteries?"

"Yes. Those."

"The creature will be a creation of a belief system. The belief system may be a valid one to you or it may not be, but what matters is that some people believe the creature exists. What *you* believe is irrelevant. The creature is a construct of belief and will behave as it is believed to behave. Ergo, the creature will believe itself unable to penetrate the holy texts and charms present in the sacred skin."

Creature? Hodges sought invisibility.

Once the skin was secured at the ankles, wrists and neck, Hodges bid his master to lie back. Heatherstone stiffly acquiesced.

Rider unplugged one of the two jars that came with the skin and passed it to Hodges. It contained a thick, black ointment that smelt strongly of honey, of lavender, and of barely glimpsed herbs on a spring day.

Heatherstone glowered. "What in the blue blazes are you thinking about, Hodges?"

Hodges felt his cheeks burn.

"I—I do apologise sir. I was just awaiting Miss Rider's instructions."

"Get on with it. We haven't all day."

Rider pushed her fingers into the ooze and liberally spread it over the seams of the sacred skin. The stuff quickly hardened when exposed to the air to form an effective seal. Hodges smeared the cuffs at wrists, ankles and neck. He dabbed it between each toe and finger and under the nails. Rider finger-painted an ancient design on the earl's head. She paused in her work to explain they would stopper his nose, ears and eyes with the preparation and that he would need to breathe through his mouth.

As Hodges pressed a dollop of the ointment into his master's ears and nostrils he saw his florid complexion turn ashen. Heatherstone's chest rose and fell rapidly. The thin dry pelts creaked.

"Sir. I am going to seal your eyes now." Hodges could scarcely believe what he was saying or doing.

The earl's voice was unnaturally loud and toneless. "You have been a good servant, m'boy. A loyal one and a good . . . well, whatever. I just wanted you to know that, Simon."

Hodges blinked. *Simon?* He could not recall a single occasion when the earl had used his forename.

Rider interrupted his thoughts with cool fingers on his wrist.

"My lord, I have to tell you about this." She held up the other jar. She tipped it up and a rubbery off-white piece of root fell into her palm. Making sure she had the old man's attention, Rider enunciated clearly:

"You have to chew on this. It won't taste very nice, but you must under no circumstances spit it out. The creature cannot penetrate the sacred skin, and the black ointment will protect the thin membranes on your face, hands and feet, as well as your ears, nose and eyes. This root, when chewed, will prevent the creature from passing through your mouth. Once it has turned to a mash, slip it under your tongue."

Heatherstone nodded and closed his eyes. Hodges wiped the last residue of the black preparation over the eyelids, sealing them tight. Tenderly, like a mother bird feeding a chick, and thankful that the earl couldn't see his hand shaking, he took up the fragment of root and dropped it into his master's mouth.

Heatherstone coughed and spluttered. His saliva turned vivid purple and frothed over his chin.

Hodges wiped his fingers clean on a handkerchief and let out a deep breath. He patted the earl on the shoulder. The simple show of solidarity, which Heatherstone would never have permitted under normal circumstances, left him feeling strangely treacherous.

"Sir," he said loudly, "do you wish me to stay? Or check on you later?"

Heatherstone made a sideways chop with his hand. *No!*

Rider patted Hodges' arm. Leading him away from the bed, she whispered, "I wish to stay."

"Actually, I didn't intend to leave. In case he chokes." Hodges quietly drew a heavy drape across one half of the window, shutting out the feeble light of a sucked rib moon. As he moved to the second drape, Hodges saw Rider's reflection in the glass. Doubt clouded her fine features. She had wanted to be in the room alone, he was sure of it. He snatched the drape closed and turned to face her.

"Yes," she said. "He could choke, I suppose. The root will have a paralysing effect on him. His face will be numb already, and when it gets into his bloodstream he will be completely immobilised."

"Immob— You never said anything about that! Is there anything else I should know?"

"Please, Simon, don't be angry with me. The earl asked me not to say anything to anybody. I had to respect his wishes."

Hodges looked at the frail figure stretched out on the bed. The skin was ugly, obscene. "He can be very persuasive when he wants to be."

They lowered themselves into the armchairs by the fireside and made themselves comfortable. Hodges tried gamely to make quiet conversation, but it was hard work. The talk of night creatures and possession had left him chilled and vulnerable. He did not believe in such fantasies, and as he recalled the evening's progress, it became less and less real and more like a fever dream. What was there to protect Miss Rider and himself if there really were such beings abroad? He found himself starting at shadows cast by the guttering of the fire. He threw on another log to keep it burning evenly.

Derryth spoke suddenly. "Did I tell you where I got those pelts to make the skin?"

She didn't need to. He knew the pelts came from the desiccated corpses of weasels, stoats and moles that fluttered from the barbed wire fences of the earl of Heatherstone's estate. He wondered what her point was. He said, "He has his gamekeeper setting leg traps and snares all over the place. It's not pretty, I know, but he's a countryman. His father was a keen hunter—"

"So if it moves, shoot it, club it, or chase it into the ground and set your hounds on it. That's what being a countryman is all about, is it?" There was no rancour in her voice, but Hodges felt as though he was being challenged.

She said, "Are you aware of any of your employer's other peccadilloes?"

Hodges experienced a chill. What had his master told her?

Since the attacks on the horses, sheep on the hills had been mauled and lambs ripped limb from limb. Someone had put fox terriers in with a local farmer's newborn piglets. Most alarming of all, a young boy had recently gone missing from an outlying village. No one had vocalised their concerns, but unease was tangible on the Heatherstone estate.

Hodges looked at Rider, gauging how much she knew. His ruminations were interrupted by a drawn out, anxious squeal. It was not a noise that Hodges would have associated with a human throat. It came from the bed. Lord Heatherstone's head was tipped back, his spine arched like a bow.

Within two strides Hodges was at his master's side and forcing his fingers into the earl's mouth. He could feel the hard knotted clump of root wedged in the throat. Derryth's hand clapped down on his. He looked up into eyes alive with fear.

She spat, "What the hell are you doing? Don't meddle with things you don't understand."

"But he's choking, can't you see? Move your hand!"

"He is not choking. It's the creature, it's trying to escape." As she spoke, a rune flared at the earl's shoulder. The old man's body began to vibrate like a jar full of angry wasps. Acrid smoke rose from between his toes. The design on his forehead crackled and his heels drummed on the bed.

Hodges fell back. "Escape? What do you mean?"

"Let me see your hands!"

"Not until you tell me—"

"Show me your hands, damn it!" Her eyes were wide.

Hodges showed his empty palms. His left forefinger was stained purple from contact with the earl's mouth.

Derryth sagged. "Dear God. That was close. I'm sorry, Simon."

Hodges gazed down on Heatherstone who had fallen deadly quiet.

"It is too late for him," she said. "Simon?" She took his arm, dragged him away.

Hodges sat on the edge of his chair and stared at the embers in the grate while his mind searched for normalcy. He made a mental note to tell the chambermaid to empty the ash pan before retiring for the night.

Derryth sighed. "When Lord Heatherstone came to me, he was already a doomed man. The creature is not seeking a way in; it is seeking a way out. The lord was already possessed."

Hodges felt dull and stupid. "Of course. That's why you wanted the inscriptions on the inside. I never thought to question that."

"Listen to me. It's in there. The creature is caged within the sacred skin. It will perish in a few hours. It's a family curse, Simon. When a creature takes over, it does so to feed off the host's emotions. Its ways are subtle. In Lord Heatherstone it was able to sate its lust for bloodsports and cruelty. Heatherstone was not aware for a long time of his actions being guided, but they were. Its thoughts and his became entwined, do you see? But as the earl became old and frail, the creature became restless. It was goading him to commit excessive—"

"Why would it allow him to put the sacred skin on?"

"It's all about control. It *guided* him, but it could not *force* him anymore than—" she waved a hand in the air, seeking a metaphor —

"than sexual desire can force a man to sate his lust on a woman. Although that lust will need to find some outlet."

Hodges could not meet her eyes.

"It wanted a new body; youthful, powerful, and full of desires. *But it can only dispossess Lord Heatherstone when he dies.*" Derryth flicked a stray hair off her face. Her breathing had quickened. "Lord Heatherstone wanted to die wearing the sacred skin because he knew the creature would possess the next in line, and the cycle continue."

"So you deliberately set out to kill the earl?"

"No! He knew what he was doing. He didn't want the creature to pass on to any of his children. He has spent the latter years of his life despising his father for being too weak to do what he did tonight."

Hodges laughed, pityingly. "Children? Oh dear, miss. I think you've been sadly misled. You see, Lady Heatherstone passed away childless."

Derryth looked weary. "I think the expression is 'grabbing a bit of petticoat under the stairs'."

"You mean he . . . with a maid?"

"That's what he told me, yes." She reached behind her neck and undid a clasp on a chain. A key dangled from it. "He asked me to give you this."

Hodges took the key, warm from contact with her breast. It was the key to a desk.

"I'm not sure I understand."

Rider sighed. "My payment is in a desk drawer, the earl said, and there's something for you too. I've told you all I know, Simon."

"What about the police?"

Derryth smiled uneasily. "I thought maybe I'd remove the skin and destroy it, wash the earl down, flush his mouth out, put him to bed as normal and let you find him dead in the morning. He was an old man."

Hodges picked up a poker and stabbed the husk of a log. It crumbled into black shards, sending a shower of sparks up the chimney.

"All right, Derryth," he breathed. "We'll do as you say. But I shall remove the skin and destroy it, not you."

She made as if to touch him, but Hodges moved away. He went back to stirring the fire. From the corner of his eye, he saw her settle back into her chair, scrutinising him.

The stuck-up trollop.

But, he realised, a stuck-up trollop beholden to him. His for the taking. The sacred skin was irrefutable evidence. One phone call to the police, and she would hang. Hodges imagined the hemp noose around that graceful neck, the knot cutting into the delicate flesh behind the left ear. If the rope was too long she would be decapitated; too short and it would take several agonised minutes for her miserable life to end. Hodges' mouth watered. He fancied the latter, imagining her kicking at the air in vain. It was a shame that executions were no longer public.

Hodges felt the heat of the fire on his face.

We used to burn witches.

Before he turned her in, he would have his own sport. He thrust the poker deeper into the hot embers, mesmerised by the bright coals and the smell of cinders. As he leaned forward a deck of playing cards dug into his side. Nestling next to it in his waistcoat pocket, there by sleight of hand, was the half-chewed, purple remains of a poisonous root.

Memory Bones

The sickly butcher's shop smell got stronger as he ascended the stairs. The carpet stuck to his feet.

"It be the bedroom on the left, Doctor."

Messinger turned to acknowledge the speaker, but he had already ducked from view. He muttered his thanks and continued up the stairs, his Gladstone bag bumping against his leg. A dust-dimmed window let in just enough light for him to make out two doors, one on either side of the tiny landing. He pushed open the door to the left.

The room stank of open wounds and wet bandages. Wrinkling his nose, Messinger peered myopically into the darkness, trying to discern edges and corners in the flat greyness.

"You must be the doctor."

Messinger faced the voice and a bed coalesced in the gloom. "Ah, Mr Lode, I presume. Would you mind if I draw back the curtains. I need to see you if I'm to examine you."

"Aye." The speaker sounded hoarse. "If you must. It's just that my eyes are very sensitive at present."

"I shall take a look at them in a moment, Mr Lode." He parted the heavy drapes to let in a chink of light.

"That's enough! No more than that."

There was just enough sunlight for Messinger to see a man propped by pillows, his body hidden by a high-collared, ankle-length nightshirt. The doctor smiled wanly. The nightshirt looked to be the source of the bad smell that pervaded the room. The patient's age was difficult to determine: his hair was as thin and colourless as melting snow, but his long face was unlined, the skin around his jaw smooth and tight. Lode's pupils were pinpricks in pools of baby blue.

Messinger sidled to the bed and eased himself down, placing his Gladstone bag between his feet where it clanked on a bedpan. It was then he noticed the scratches in the wall behind the bed. Reminiscent of a prison cell, hundreds of short vertical strokes with a diagonal slash denoting groups of five covered an area larger than the bed's headboard.

"So what seems to be the problem, Mr Lode?"

"It's not me you've come to see, Doctor."

"Oh! I do apologise. I was told the patient was in this room. By your brother, would it be?"

Lode nodded. "Aye, he weren't having you on." Lode reached out and gripped Messinger's wrist. "You've taken over old Dimmock's practice, yes? Did he mention me?"

"No, but I didn't actually have the pleasure of meeting Dr Dimmock. I was appointed by a selection committee after he retired."

"Pity. He was a good man was Dimmock. Open-minded. Are you a broad-minded sort of lad?"

"I like to think I am." Messinger tried to smile.

"Good, because I want you to listen to me. Right?"

Messinger nodded, although he felt things were far from right. Lode's grip was surprisingly strong.

The grip lessened and Lode settled back on the pillow, his blue eyes never leaving Messinger's. "How old do you think I am, lad? You won't find the answer in your notes so don't bother looking."

Messinger straightened up. "And why won't I find any mention of it in my notes?"

"Because your predecessor made up a name and date of birth for me, that's why. Like I said, he was a good doctor. I'm hoping you'll be the same. Now answer the question: How old do you think I am?"

Messinger considered arguing that Dimmock wouldn't have falsified Lode's details because of the minefield of National Insurance, NHS records, vaccination programs and the like, but decided to humour the man. Maybe that's what Dimmock had done; humoured him. It was a fact that consultations went smoother once one had gained the patient's confidence.

Messinger's eyes were becoming adjusted to the dim and dusty light now, giving him a better opportunity to observe the unlined face and clear blue eyes that contrasted sharply with the thin hair and liver-spotted hands. "If I had to guess, I'd venture that you're somewhere in your early fifties."

Lode laughed. "Way off, lad, way off. Actually, I'm 149!" He laughed again, throwing his head back.

Messinger noticed Lode's teeth were unusually small, very white and even.

Lode's laughter snapped off suddenly. He looked squarely at the doctor. "You think I'm mad?"

Messinger gave a non-committal smile. "That's not within my remit," he said smoothly. "However, I'm a busy man with a lot of patients to see this morning so can we stop playing around?"

"You ought to show some respect for your elders!"

The bed squeaked as Messinger pushed himself to his feet. He heard a corresponding creak on the landing.

Lode shouted. "It's all right, Eustace, the young man is not going anywhere!"

Messinger heard footsteps retreating down the stairs. Disquieted, he sat down.

"I *am* 149 years old. When I was born, Victoria was on the throne and Britain was at war with Russia. Just accept that. I could verify it by telling you loads of historical details but you would dismiss them as mere fancies learned from books. My bones are as full of memories as yours are of marrow jelly, lad.

"When I was in my mid-forties — I forget exactly how old I was — something strange happened. I fell under a carriage. It ran straight over my arm." Lode indicated a point just below his left shoulder. "Severed it completely.

I picked it up and ran home to my wife. Screamed my bloody head off, I did!" Lode chuckled before fixing Messinger with a searching stare. He shook his head. "Regular little doubting Thomas, aren't we, lad?" He rolled up the left sleeve of his nightshirt up to reveal a thick, ropey scar that circumscribed his bicep.

Messinger peered closer. "There's no way they could have stitched your arm back on in the 1890s," he said. "They didn't have the know-how."

"Nobody stitched it on. It grew back."

"Of course." Messinger sighed. "Silly me. It grew back."

"Don't get sarcastic, lad, I'm warning you."

"And what became of the arm? Did that grow into a pet?"

"I buried it in the compost heap."

"Pity, you could have hand-reared it."

Lode's lips tightened.

Messinger sighed. "You were saying, Mr Lode?"

By way of answer, Lode leaned forward and raised the hem of his nightshirt to reveal his knees.

Messinger recoiled. "Jesus Harry— who did that?"

"Eustace."

"The bastard must have used a lump hammer!"

"A sledgehammer, actually. Every other Thursday. He seems to think I might run away." Lode sucked on his teeth. "There are times when he might be right."

Messinger jumped to his feet, took his cell phone from his jacket pocket. He saw again the scratches on the wall behind the bed, and again he thought of a prisoner counting the interminable days of incarceration. The fives were arranged in columns of ten, and there were fourteen completed columns . . . making over 700. But 700 what? Days, weeks? Surely not months?

"If that's what I think it is, put it away, lad."

Messinger put the phone to his ear.

"If you don't put it away, I shall call in Eustace." Lode let the threat hang in the air.

Messinger shot a nervous glance at the door as a floorboard creaked, and felt the fight in him drain away. He disconnected before anyone answered.

"Now come and sit down." Lode patted the side of the bed. "Come on, lad."

He sat down. "But why . . .?"

Lode held up a hand. "All in good time, lad."

"This is crazy."

Lode's face softened. "Aye, lad, I know I'm asking a lot of you." He looked at the doctor from under lowered eyelids and chuckled. "The best is yet to come."

"I can't wait."

"I'll ignore that. Anyway, Bessie and me, we kept the arm incident a secret. I lay low, hardly venturing out while the arm and hand were growing back. We nearly starved to death, with me not being able to go to work. Times were different then. That's when we started the vegetable garden, all the way back then."

Lode's eyes clouded over. "Bess died in 1919 of 'flu. Bloody terrible that was. You young 'uns don't know you're born, I swear. We weren't any more able to cope with grief then as you are now, you know? Just because folks lost babies to disease and brothers and husbands to war, it don't mean we became immune. I was one of twelve children. Only eight of us reached adulthood. My mother used to keep daisies in four little jam jars. 'One for each of my poor mites in Heaven,' she used to say.

"But when Bessie died, I don't know, I just couldn't cope with it. I was an old man, what did I have to live for? In the end, I went down to the Cotton End Bridge." Lode indicated behind him with a thumb. Messinger realised the man was referring to a bridge over a railway line that had served the local collieries. The track was long gone. He hadn't even known before now that it had a name.

"And?"

"I threw myself under a goods train. When I came to, I couldn't see. I was blind." He looked at Messinger, checking he was paying attention. "I staggered for a short distance and then gave up and lay down where I was. I could tell by my sense of touch that I was among those tall weeds, the ones with the pink flowers."

"Rosebay willow herbs," supplied Messinger automatically.

"Right. And I could also tell by touch that my head was missing."

Messinger blinked, then slumped and covered his eyes. "Jesus Christ! You had me sucked into your crazy little world then. For a moment, I actually *believed*."

"And so you should," said Lode. "It's all true."

Messinger shook his head. "Oh no. You're not catching me out again. I'm off." He started to rise.

Lode grabbed his wrist.

"You're leaving without examining your patient? What sort of doctor are you, eh?"

"A sane one," he retorted.

"You think I'm insane? I've been crippled and bedridden since 1952, what d'yer expect? My only contact with the outside world is through Eustace." Lode's eyes flicked meaningfully at the bedroom door. He sat back, breathing heavily. "Please, lad. Stay a little longer."

Messinger sagged. He hated himself for it, but he wanted to hear the end of the story. He knew that all he had to do was peel back that high collar and examine Lode's neck, but he wouldn't — it would be an admission of gullibility. And on a deeper, more primitive level, he *couldn't*. "Okay, but it's against my better judgment."

"Good boy." Lode patted the side of the bed again.

Messinger sat down obediently.

"My head grew back," Lode continued, "just as my arm had. I had no idea how long I lay there among them pink weed things."

"Rosebay willow herbs."

Lode took the correction graciously. "I recovered enough to find my way here and recuperated over a period of several months."

"Forgetting for the moment the sheer implausibility of you surviving decapitation and any subsequent regeneration . . ." Messinger allowed himself a smile. "If what you are saying is true, you wouldn't have any memories. You had grown a completely new brain from scratch. You would, mentally, have been like a newborn. Your story has a plot hole I could drive a bus through."

"We pondered long and hard on that one, me and Dr Dimmock. He suggested that as cerebral fluid surrounds the spinal cord, it could act as a repository of memories." Lode shrugged and spread his gnarled hands as if he really didn't care. "Anyway, while my body was growing a new head, my old head had been busy growing a new body. Eustace turned up. Eustace, like all my brothers, is *me*. A clone. It was Eustace that started to call me Mr Lode. It's a joke, you see — I *was* Eustace Orr but now he is and I'm the lode. He keeps me crippled and when he wants another brother—"

"He removes your head and grows another. Brilliant! Can I go now please?"

"You are being very rude, Dr Messinger."

26

"Frankly Mr Lode, Mr Orr, whoever you are, I think I'm entitled to be rude after all the crap I've had to take from you." Messinger grabbed his bag and stood. "I shall be sending for an ambulance as soon as I have left here, thereby discharging my obligations to you."

Lode raised a shoulder and let it fall, a one-shouldered shrug that said it was Messinger's loss if he left now. "Before you go, take a look out of that window, lad. Tell me what you see."

"What's out there, the tooth fairy?"

"Just look, will you?"

Messinger rested his hands on the windowsill and gazed out, blinking at the change of light. "There are a few old guys at the bottom of the garden. Weeding by the looks of it."

"They'll be tending the vegetables. We grow our own as much as we can. Look closer at them. Notice anything unusual?"

Messinger narrowed his eyes. He turned back to the man in the bed. He did a double take out of the window and then back at Lode.

Lode's smile was that of the cat that has found the cream. He indicated the scratches on the wall. "I have spawned 738 of us so far, with another on the way. And some of them have become lodes too, I daresay."

Messinger licked his lips with a dry tongue. "Why?"

"Why what?"

"Why would you want to create so many clones of yourself?" Messinger thought about what he had just said, and added: "That's assuming your story had a single grain of truth in it, which it doesn't, of course."

Lode barked that bitter laugh of his. "Haven't you ever dreamed of a world without divides? A world where everyone agreed with one another? One religion, one government, one mind; everyone living in harmony? Eustace has watched the world go to hell in a handcart, watched history repeat its mistakes — correction, he's watched *people* repeat their mistakes. He's taking steps to put things right."

Messinger rubbed his eyes. "My predecessor must have been a gullible old fool if he went along with this lunacy. I'm leaving now, and when I get back to my surgery I shall remove the names Lode and Eustace Orr from my panel. As from this moment you are no longer my patient."

"I've told you, it's not me you've come to see."

Messinger made a show of scanning the room. "So, where's my patient?"

Lode motioned with his chin at a deep chest of drawers. "Top drawer," he said. "He's a slow developer, this one. We're a bit worried about him."

Messinger dropped the bag carelessly and crossed to the drawer in question. Glaring angrily at the heavy-looking brass handles, he gripped them tightly to still the quivering in his hands, his nostrils full of the almost overpowering stench of blood and disinfectant. On the limit of hearing he could hear a gentle sighing, a sound like a damp paper bag being slowly inflated. Was it the soft swish of his own blood pulsing in his ears, or the rhythmic rasp of raw, embryonic lungs pulling air? He whipped his head round and glared at Lode . . . who grinned right back at him expectantly, his teeth a string of pearls in a peach-fuzzy face.

I have spawned 738 of us so far, with another on the way.

"Bullshit," Messinger growled. Annoyed with himself for even hesitating, he snatched open the drawer . . .

Lonely Heart Clob

This is a story about how I found faith — faith as opposed to belief — and like many stories, it begins with boy meets girl.

With her auburn hair and smooth, pale skin, her rosebud lips and deep expressive eyes, Catherine Hewson could have sat for Titian's *La Bella*, or perhaps his *Venus with a Mirror*. She reminds me of Jennifer Aniston before she got too skinny. She is what my father, Leonard Stromboldt senior, calls a dolly bird. He also refers to the music charts as the Hit Parade and his jeans as action slacks. Dad is a model train enthusiast. But I digress.

Catherine is a nurse at St Chad's and I your humble porter. We often see each other in passing. She all trim and neat in her crisp white uniform with her long hair tied back, sensible shoes clicking on the polished floors; me hauling trains of dirty laundry or wheeling some old geezer outside for a surreptitious smoke.

Aye, you know how it is. You're lonely and a pretty girl smiles at you. You begin to compare the smiles she gives other guys with the smile she graces you. Did the raised eyebrows and half-smile she gave to Dr Murray the ENT specialist rate more than the nodding smile to the Security man who carefully watched her reverse her little Fiat Uno in every morning? And how did the "Good morning" and accompanying beam she flashed at me compare to the admonishing smirk she invariably posed to Dr Capdeville, St Chad's dental surgeon?

I made the mistake of asking Clob.

"You want to get into this bird's knickers?"

I drew a sharp breath. "There's more to it than that. Why do you have to be so base?"

"It's what I am." Clob shifted his weight on the pepper pot and fixed me with a lopsided grin. We were having this discussion in the staff canteen. (It's a very small canteen — just sixteen chairs at four tables.)

"She is a nice girl," I said. "Decent and respectable I know for a fact she doesn't put it about."

"Oh, right. You mean frigid. I can see why she appeals to you then. All your hang-ups about sex." His small eyes glinted with pure malice. "Virgin."

Little bastard.

I can't remember precisely how old I was when Clob first put in an appearance, but it would be when I was about fourteen or fifteen. To begin with he wasn't a pig but a blue fish with a goggle-mask and a tank of water on his back. I remember telling Mum about him.

"I see," she said slowly. "And what does he say exactly, this Clob?"

Which was also the first question Dad, the family doctor and finally the child psychiatrist asked me. The latter, a Doctor Wilson, was a splendid black guy with a warrior build and a beautiful mellifluous voice. He is the only person I've ever met who actually had leather elbow patches on his tweed sports jacket. I looked into his noble, high-cheekboned face and began the usual question dodging. He indulged me for a while, before turning to my mother who was sitting beside me in this green wool coat she always wore for important occasions like Sunday worship and hospital appointments, and asked if she would leave just the two of us together? I felt nervous myself, sure, but Mum . . . she looked panic-stricken. It was in that moment I realised something that I — with my childish self-centredness — had somehow failed to see before. Mum was weighed down with worry. No, more than worried, she was afraid.

"So we can have a nice friendly chat, Mrs Stromboldt. Man to man, so to speak."

She mouthed the words silently — *Man to man?* — and frowned. "But he's just a boy." Then, capitulating in the face of authority, she shuffled out. It made me terribly sad.

When the door clicked behind her, Dr Wilson moved his chair from behind the desk so he was sitting directly in front of me, our knees almost touching. "Right then, Leonard. Now that Mum is out of the room, perhaps you can tell me what this is all about." He smiled a friendly smile, the effect being slightly marred by the overhead lights reflecting on his small round glasses.

"Clob," I said helplessly.

"Clob, indeed. You said a moment ago that you can see him right now?"

I nodded.

"And what is he telling you? I want to know. I won't be angry, I promise."

I cleared my throat. "He—he says . . ."

"Go on."

"He's wondering if you've got a big . . . wotsit. A big doodah." A hole yawned in front of me; I rushed to fill it with chatter. "Only he says he's heard that your sort, black men, you know, have big—"

He laid a gentle hand on my knee. "Okay, that's okay."

He tipped his head back and addressed the ceiling. "It is perfectly natural for young men to compare themselves, especially when things are beginning to develop. If a young man was to come to me concerned about the size of his penis, afraid that somehow he didn't measure up, then I would assure him that, although there is wide variation in the size of flaccid penises, most erect penises are of similar size."

"I didn't mean—" I swallowed the rest of the sentence. In my dealings with adults, a denial had always seemed to be taken as proof of guilt. I sat very, very still. My cheeks were hot enough to fry an egg.

"That may or may not be of interest to you," he said to the room in general.

I didn't move a muscle.

He flashed me the winning smile again. "Relax, Lenny. Can I call you that? Good. Tell me, have you ever seen anyone else with something like Clob?"

I shook my head.

"And has anyone else ever seen Clob?"

"No." I knew where this was going. "So he's a figment of my imagination and that's why I'm here."

"In our own time. Don't

let's jump to conclusions. Let me try something else. Have you ever heard of Sigmund Freud, Lenny? A bit before your time, before mine come to that, but he had a lot to say about people and the way the mind works. Old Siggy believed that the psychic structure—" he held up three fingers —"comprised the super-ego, the ego and the id. The super-ego is your conscience: all those values that you inherit from society and your parents. The id is your basic drives, your instincts for hunger, desire, revenge, pleasure, et cetera. And finally, we have your ego in the middle, the part of you that strives to balance out the one against the other, the id versus the super-ego."

I frowned with concentration. "You mean like, I might want to do something that I'll enjoy, but if I know it's wrong I won't do it?"

"Because of feeling guilty. That would be one example, yes. Well done, Lenny." He removed his glasses and gave them a cursory polish on his jacket lapel before replacing them. "I'm wondering, Lenny, I'm wondering if Clob is a manifestation of your id. Suppose that you find many of the things you think about, or like to do, make you feel guilty. I'm wondering whether the natural prurience of a young man has become a burden of guilt. If so, might you not find it convenient to disassociate yourself from that voice? Food for thought, Lenny. Food for thought." He clapped me on the knee and looked at the heavy gold watch on his wrist. "We shall talk about this more next Thursday, young man. Let's call your mum back in, shall we?"

He stood and replaced his chair behind the desk.

"What will you be missing in school?"

"Maths," I said.

"We can make it another time, if you want?"

"No thanks. Thursday's fine."

~

"Hey! Penny for your thoughts, Leo." Clob waved a little piggy trotter.

Dr Wesley Wilson never did get rid of Clob. He did warn me that the idea was not to dispel Clob but to integrate him, make him a part of my natural thought processes. Much to my shame, I lied to him in the end, telling both him and my parents that Clob was no more. I should be so lucky: two years of therapy and I've still got this abusive little swine following me around more than ten years on.

"I hope you are not ignoring me, Leo."

I know he's out to rile me when he calls me Leo. I hate the way he flips it off his tongue, putting a spin on the word so that it hangs in the air long after it's uttered.

"Thinking about the fridge?"

I fumed in silence. The trouble with arguing with a manifestation of your id is that they know every chink in your armour. "She is probably old-fashioned, and that makes a refreshing change these days." I was aware as I said it how crass it sounded.

He pursed his lips and peered over the lip of my tray.

"Didn't know you liked tomato soup?"

"Um. I don't."

"Then why, my lionhearted Leo, have you got a steaming great bowl of the stuff in front of you, hmm?"

I braced myself for further ridicule. "I've, um, I've heard Catherine is a vegetarian."

Clob sucked his fat cheeks in. "Eating that stuff will really impress her, yeah?" He made a choking sound and put a trotter to his snout. "Now I would have thought you'd prefer a girl that likes the taste of meat, if you get my drift."

He licked his lips salaciously.

"You really are a complete bastard."

"I know," he said, and sniggered. He broke off mid-snort and said, "Hey. The ice-maiden cometh."

I swallowed hard. If my careful planning came off, Catherine would sit next to me. I knew she didn't like the company of Jason Connelly, a nurse himself, and his two friends who frequented the next table, and that the tables behind me were already full. I tried to look cool.

"Hello. It's Leonard, isn't it? Do you mind if I . . .?"

"Not at all," I said, grinning. Clob shot me a warning glance and I relaxed the face muscles slightly. "Well," I said as she sat down to my left. "Well, well."

Clob slapped his forehead and groaned.

I went to spoon some soup up to my mouth. It ran through the tines of the fork I'd picked up by mistake.

Catherine looked away.

As I dabbed my shirtfront with a paper napkin, I glanced at her plate and saw what looked suspiciously like a ham salad.

"So much for that line of seduction, Leo."

I sub-vocalised something extremely rude.

"Hey, come on, Leonard." Clob smiled ruefully. "Let's work at this together. I'm sorry I rubbed you up the wrong way." He looked repentant, or as repentant as a little red pig with wraparound shades, horns and a pointed tail can. "She is quite something, isn't she?"

I risked a glance at Catherine. She was daintily folding a lettuce leaf up into a compact parcel. She caught me looking at her as she popped it in her mouth, her storm-grey eyes twinkling as though she could hear my thoughts. Her complexion was like silk. "She certainly is, Clob," I said silently. "She certainly is."

A machine-gun laugh came from the next table. Stage whispering, lewd gestures and more guffawing followed it. One of the male nurses was candidly bragging to the others about his bedroom exploits by the look of things. I saw Catherine's eyes flash in annoyance. I caught her eye and tried to make it clear with a shake of the head that I too shared her disgust. I couldn't tell if she got the message.

Clob said mildly, "If you had any balls, Leonard, you'd tell those louts there was a young lady present."

I kept my head down and cursed inwardly, knowing what Clob said was true. But I hate to cause a scene, and I knew that the three lads would easily put me in my place if I dared caution them. I can come up with all manner of witty repartee and smouldering put-downs, but only long after the event. Anyway, I'd procrastinated too long. The moment had passed. Maybe next time. I sipped on a spoonful of soup and wished Clob would give me some useful advice.

"Hey! I'm doing my best."

Someone scraped back a chair at the table. "Is there anyone sitting here?"

"Does it look like there's anyone sitting there, you garlic-crunching pillock?" said Clob, aka Mr Tact.

"Um. No," I said, looking up into the tanned features of Dr Xavier Capdeville. He gave me an easy smile and sat down. I saw with dismay that he had a ham salad like Catherine. It seemed terribly important.

"We've had it now, Leonard." Clob tipped his head at Catherine. "I think she's got something on with the frog."

I followed his gesture and, I must confess, I didn't like what I saw. The handsome Capdeville was clearly garnering all her attention. I took a sip of my soup. It tasted bitter.

There was raucous laughter from the next table again. Jason Connelly made a ring with a thumb and forefinger and collapsed into a fit of giggles. I didn't catch what was said but Catherine was crunching a radish with unnecessary vigour. Dr Capdeville took in the scene instantly and, carefully putting down his knife and fork, rose from his seat. For a brief moment it looked like Catherine would object, but Xavier had raised a placatory hand: I am in charge here, it said. He calmly went to the next table and placed the masterful hand on the shoulder of the nearest nurse. He spoke quietly in his ear, motioned to Catherine and then gently patted the shoulder again. He straightened and returned to his seat. One of the lads, looking supremely embarrassed, gave Catherine an apologetic grin before turning away. You could have heard a pin drop.

Catherine's smile was enigmatic.

"Thank you, Dr Capdeville."

"Oh please, it's Xavier."

"You've got to hand it to the frog, Leonard. That *was* slick."

Xavier spoke in his heavily accented English. "The problem with English men is that they have no romance in their soul."

Clob jumped up and paced across the table. "You aren't going to let the French git get away with that are you, Leonard? C'mon, stick up for yourself!"

Xavier carried on as though he hadn't heard — because, of course, he hadn't.

"Love is reduced by them—" he motioned to the next table —"to jokes about the meat and two vegetables, the cream horns, the wedding tackle. There is no tenderness. In France, love is an art."

I should have taken Xavier to task over his stereotyping of English manhood, but instead I busied myself with my soup, pretending I hadn't heard. Catherine, on the other hand, was more than happy to volunteer me.

"I don't think Leonard's like that. I've never heard him talking crude, and I bet he knows how to treat a woman. Flowers and chocolate, stuff like that. Leonard?"

"Mm, yes, well—" I began.

35

Thankfully, Xavier was quicker off the mark. "I was nineteen and was dating my first English girlfriend. My family had just moved here. She was named Maria. She had this beautiful raven-black hair. I used to tell her I could see the stars reflected in it."

"Tell him if he doesn't stop waving his fork around he'll have someone's eye out."

"She was coming up to her eighteenth birthday," Xavier continued, "a magical time in life and I wanted to get her something special."

She should be so lucky. When I was eighteen, Mum, belatedly acting on Dr Wilson's advice to get me out socialising and interacting with others, enrolled me in the local youth club. (Dad suggested his model railway club.) Run by the local vicar, this youth club consisted of a Ping-Pong table and a crappy little pool table with no bounce in the cushions. Fat lot of use that was. Few girls and all the lads as screwed up and repressive as me. I went to satisfy my mum's conscience for two months before I made any number of excuses to get out of it. At least I came away with a good forehand-smash.

"My search for a suitable present for Maria began in the local library. I looked up the foreign language dictionaries. I remembered something about the word Maria from my Latin studies. I found it; Maria in Latin was a plural of mare. This was no help. I knew that my girlfriend loved horses but there was no way my finances could stretch that far."

"The berk! The Latin mare won't be a female horse like it is in English." Clob stumped across the table and farted in Xavier's salad.

"*Mon dieu*! I slapped my head! What was I thinking? Mare will not have the same meaning in Latin as it does in English."

"Oh, he's quick, this one. Ho hum."

"I quickly looked the word up and there it was, the answer to my prayers. I began to look through other sections of the library. I now knew what I would buy my beautiful Maria. It would be perfect. Can you guess?"

"Bog off, we're not interested," said Clob.

Xavier told us anyway . . . and this is how it went.

~

Xavier helped Maria over the stile. "I wish you'd told me we were going bloody hiking, Xav. These shoes will be ruined."

"Only a little farther now, my dove."

"And it's pitch dark. Where's your torch? My dad's going to kill me if he finds out."

"Hush. We don't need a torch." A full moon bathed the hills in pools of cool limpid blues. Evening dew was forming on spider webs, leaving strings of glistening pearls draped over the heather. It was ideal. He put an arm around Maria's waist and shivered with anticipation. They followed the sandy path that wound its way up the hillside through gorse and bracken until it began to level out at the crest.

"When am I going to get my surprise, Xav?"

Xavier looked at the ground around them and then up into the clear starry sky.

"Here will do."

"Here? Oh, okay. If you say so. This had better be worth it. If you've dragged me all the way up here for . . . for something else."

Xavier looked up at her standing there in her white stockings, pencil skirt and padded bomber jacket. She smiled and her cheeks dimpled. He raised a hand. "Come sit here beside me, Maria. I want to show you something." Maria lowered herself and patted her skirt, tugging at the hem. He guided her hands in the dark. "Here."

Maria felt at something long and slim placed in her palms. It had the feeling of leatherette and made a hollow rattling sound when she shook it.

"It's still in its case, the zip is at the top end."

"What the heck is it, Xav?" Her earlier nervousness was evaporating. The end cap came away and something cold and metal slid out. Light glinted on a glass lens. "A telescope? Lovely! Thanks. That's just what I've always wanted. This will come in useful."

Xavier laughed. "That isn't your present, Maria. You can keep it, it is for you, but it is not your present."

Maria looked at him, puzzled now. All she would see in the darkness were his even white teeth and they weren't giving anything away. "I don't follow."

"Lie back, I want to show you something."

Lying side by side he pointed at the moon. "Use your telescope on that. You may have to turn the ring near the eyepiece to fine focus."

Maria extended the telescope and gave a small gasp as the yellow lunar disc leapt into clearer definition.

"Wow. I can see everything."

He laughed. "That is the idea. Are you looking at the grey plains?" He snuggled closer so that his lips were near her ear. "They are called *maria*."

"Maria? But why? I mean, what does it mean?"

"Early astronomers thought the laval plains were water and so named them as seas, or *maria* in Latin. It's the plural of *mare* (he pronounced it muh-ray). Many have these beautiful romantic names. Do you see the large one on the left? That is *Mare Tranquillitatis*, or the Sea of Tranquility. Slightly above is the Sea of Serenity and below is the Sea of Nectar. There are also Seas of Clouds, Showers, Moisture, Vapours . . ." He had to stop there because Maria had covered his mouth with her own. He kissed her back, deeply and slowly before gently pulling away. "All *maria* are quite wonderful and unique in their own way," he said softly. "As are you."

He looked into eyes shiny with reflected moonlight.

~

Catherine's eyes were shining, too. "Oh, Xavier. You gave her the moon!"

Xavier Capdeville sipped at his coffee and shrugged nonchalantly. "It was nothing," he said, his smarmy smile adding ". . . for a Frenchman".

"Huh, big deal. I mean, it isn't like he actually gave her anything, is it? Apart from a cheesy telescope that probably cost a couple of quid from a junk shop." Clob was trying his best, but I could tell his little heart wasn't in it. I had to hand it to Xavier, there aren't many teenagers who would think of doing something like that. They tend to be more direct.

Catherine gazed at the debonair dentist over the rim of her teacup as she sipped at her drink. She put it down with a small frown. "I'd enjoy this more if I'd remembered to put sugar in."

"I'll go and get you some," I volunteered, half out of my seat.

"It's all right, Leonard," she said, placing a hand over mine, "I'm going to get myself a pudding while I'm there." She giggled conspiratorially as she rose and left the table. My hand felt warm as though indelibly imprinted by the slight pressure of her fingers.

I looked at Xavier who acknowledged me with a raised eyebrow. Our glances bounced off each other like marbles. I stared down at my soiled shirt, adjusting the lie of my tie so that it covered most of the soup stains. So much for the tomato soup gambit, I thought miserably.

"Did you really expect that to work?" It took me a second to realise it was Clob's voice berating me.

"No," I subvocalised. I looked across to where he was sitting on the edge of the table, his chubby legs swinging to and fro. Suddenly he stood up, staring. (And when Clob stares, it's quite an event. His eyes shoot out restrained only by coiled springs that pull them back inside his head with an almighty twang. Too many wasted Saturday mornings watching cartoons, I suppose.)

"What's up? What are you looking at?" I followed his eyeballs but I could see nothing remarkable.

Clob waved a fat trotter. "That!" He looked at me, his eyebrows oscillating wildly two inches above his head. "You can't see it?"

"What?" I was starting to feel unnerved. Clob had never behaved like this before. He had never seen anything or told me anything that I, at some level, didn't already know about. This new development did not bode well.

"It's—It's his id!"

"You mean loverboy here? His actual id?"

Clob nodded, still staring at any empty patch of Formica.

I had to ask. "So, what's it look like?"

"It's a camel wearing a silver foil fez."

"A camel wearing . . ." That, surprisingly, didn't seem too weird. I've always associated France with Camel cigarettes ever since my Uncle George brought loads of them back from a trip to Calais. They are, I suspect, an American brand, but the association is there and the cigarettes come in soft foil packets with pyramids in the background. All this seemed to flit through my mind in a split second. I felt quite pleased at my analysis and subsequent denial.

"You are seeing no such thing, Clob."

"What d'you mean I ain't seeing no such thing? Ah, we're playing that game, are we? Ignore me and I'll go away? You never learn, do you Lenny? You gotta trust your instincts sometimes. Dr Wilson told you that. Look, I know you don't believe in me. I'm just some kind of projection, right? But once, just once, it'd be nice if you put some faith in me."

Catherine was settling herself down. She had chosen a strawberry cheesecake.

"Ooh, I love strawberry cheesecake," I told her.

I could faintly hear Clob protesting in the background.

"Hmm?" she said. "Oh yes, it is nice, isn't it. So, Xavier. You and Maria. Did you go out with each other for long?"

"I beg your pardon, Catherine? Oh! No. Only a matter of a few weeks."

I let my mind wander at that point. I was torn between wanting to excuse myself from the table where I had become a spare part, and staying just to be near Catherine. I chose the latter as it meant doing nothing — something I'm very good at. I watched her from the corner of my eye, her perfect lips parting as she took elegant bites from her dessert with her perfect teeth. Something in her expression made me follow her gaze to Xavier. He looked distracted, the usual easy charm and casual patter missing.

Catherine asked, "How come you parted so soon after her birthday, Xavier? I'd have thought she was very much in love with you after a gift like that." She scowled. "Some girls are so ungrateful."

The dentist shifted uncomfortably in his seat. "No Catherine, you misunderstand. It was I that finished with Maria."

He hung his head, gazing at the tabletop between his outstretched fingers. He made as if to scratch his head, paused, rubbed his eyes instead, and ended up worrying at a thumbnail with his teeth.

I glanced at Catherine, who looked at me as if she expected me to say something. I looked at Xavier to find that he too was studying me from under his fringe. I felt like an insect under a magnifying glass. I cast my eyes down to see a very smug-looking Clob.

"Watch this," he said.

Xavier cleared his throat. "The point of the exercise, with the telescope and the moon, Catherine . . ." He paused to scratch a sideburn. "The point is, I only did it to get into the bird's knickers." A spasm crossed his face as though he wanted to bite his tongue off and spit it out.

Then he dragged himself to his feet and left the table, giving me a heavy pat on the shoulder as he passed me by. His departure was as abrupt as his sordid admission.

I looked down at Clob, stunned. "You?"

He nodded enthusiastically. "Good, eh? I had a word with Humpy. Explained the situation with you and Catherine, and he had a word with the boss there. Not a bad sort, considering he's French. Go on sunshine, the way's clear now." He tipped me a wink and popped like a soap bubble.

My eyes swivelled to take in the delectable nurse at my side. It wrung my heart to see her so. She looked like someone who had emerged unscathed from a road accident, but only by the narrowest of margins. My head was full of candy floss with the implications of Clob and Xavier, or Xavier's id. And I was supposed to come the Casanova with Catherine? My tongue swelled to thrice its normal size and tied itself in a knot for good measure.

But I did something incredibly brave. I reached over and covered Catherine's hand with mine. She blinked, and for an awful second I thought she might snatch it away. But she didn't. Way to go, Lenny!

Panic began to reassert itself. I had this vision of us sitting there all afternoon unable to break the impasse.

She said, "I really thought he was different, you know?" I gave the hand a gentle squeeze and turned my reassuring smile up a notch. "I know he has something of a reputation but, you'll laugh at me now, I thought he was honourable. I'm sick of boors like Jason Connelly. You go out with somebody like that and they are just after one thing, and after that you're just a trophy. I thought Dr Capdeville was above that. How wrong can you be?" She indicated her plate where a lonely slice of ham was sweating. "I ordered this yucky ham salad even though I'm a vegetarian, just to have something in common with him. How sad is that?" She gave a brittle laugh and brushed a stray hair off her forehead.

"Very sad," I agreed. And then told her about the detested tomato soup. I figured it would make her feel better if nothing else.

"And here's me thinking you like the soup so much you want to take it home with you." She motioned at the stains on my shirt with her dainty chin. "So you only had soup because you thought I'd be having it? You are sweet. God, we're a pair together, aren't we?"

"Yes, we are. A pair together." The silence stretched. I still had her hand under mine. It was getting hot.

She checked the watch pinned to her breast pocket. "Oh my goodness." She pulled her hand away and made to leave. "I'm going to be in trouble with Matron if I don't get a move on."

She paused as if she was about to say something — or waiting for me to say something — changed her mind, stood up and walked away. It happened so quickly I hadn't screwed up the courage to say my piece. I had been on the verge of asking her out. I had! I'd been so close — so bloody close — but now the moment was past and I knew with horrible certainty that I had blown my one and only chance. No! I would go after her. *Go on, Leonard.*

My traitor legs remained firmly rooted under the table. My backbone was a wet thread of cotton. Aw, who was I kidding? I slumped over the table, feeling more lonely and dejected than I could ever remember. Clob was going to give me an absolute dressing down and I would deserve every acid-coated barb he flung at me.

A voice spoke quietly at my shoulder. "My shift ends at five today."

Lay off, Clob, you little—I sat up sharply and spun round just in time to see Catherine leaving the canteen, the scent of her perfume a lingering ghost. She popped her head round the doorframe and gave a small wave.

I think I might have waved back.

The Damage Done

Katherine Harper turned to face the camera, her eyes half-closed against the rain. "And here, at last, the cottage I grew up in. Whenever I experience those niggling doubts that occasionally beset us all, I come and spend time here. A fine house in what is, I'm sure you will agree, a very fine part of the country. When my father — a veterinary surgeon to all the local farms — passed away, I refused to sell it. This programme is as much about my father as it is about me."

Katherine pushed open the rickety gate, limped up the overgrown path and grasped the doorknob. Her hands, encased in her trademark leather gloves, struggled to find purchase. But she persisted and the door swung inwards. The producer signed *okay* with his thumb and forefinger and she stepped over the threshold.

"Cut!" the producer shouted. "Okay, Gavin, a panoramic if you please while I discuss the finer details with Mr Beaumont." The cameraman swept his camera in a wide arc to take in the sodden heather-capped moors while the soundman struggled with the wind and driving rain.

Katherine discretely kissed and wiggled her fingers at Ashley Beaumont, her *very* Personal Assistant. Ashley turned to the producer, smiled his winsome smile, said something placatory and then joined Katherine. The shiny material of his windcheater rustled against the bleached doorframe.

"Problems?" Katherine asked.

"He keeps badgering me for the script."

"You told him he couldn't have it, of course?"

"Of course. My brief to them is that we're shooting a promo to demonstrate your humble background to the general populace." He waved an arm at the surrounding desolation. "To relive your rise from obscurity to found the mighty Harper Cybernetics, blah blah blah. Did you really live out here until you were twenty-three?"

"I did."

"And is it always this cold and wet?"

"This is just fresh. A bracing dampness to the air."

"Bloody hell." Ashley huddled inside his jacket. "Anyway, I've told him that if Ms Harper wishes to write her own script and keep it to herself, she bloody well can do. And if he wants it that badly, he can come over here and get it himself." He placed his hands around hers. "Are you sure about this, Katherine?"

She glanced down at the open display of affection. "Quite sure."

"But I'm your PA—"

"You're more to me than that, Ash."

"So you can't blame me for being concerned. These things have to be presented in the best possible light. You've never even told *me* how you . . ."

She shushed him with a chaste kiss and nodded towards the producer. "Tell him I wish to do a piece to the camera in the kitchen, then the living room, which is just through that door on the left. And finally, I'd like to do a piece in my old bedroom upstairs. Maybe the back garden if there's time."

Ashley took the dismissal with good grace. She watched the exchange between him and the producer. "Fine, fine," she heard the other man say. "Yeah, that's fine. Thanks. Okay lads, let's get a light reading in here."

~

Katherine sensed things were going well. She had rehearsed her lines for weeks in front of a mirror, at pains to make them sound natural and relaxed. It was all coming together. This house always brought out the best in her.

Sauntering into the living room, she spoke of helping her widower father do the household chores from an early age: "While most children of four or five can look forward to going to school and making new friends, I was busy helping my father by blacking the grate in the kitchen or scrubbing the floor tiles. Or feeding the pigs. And if I ever complained, my father would wag his finger and say to me, 'Fortitude, my little Kate. Fortitude.' And I knew what he meant. He was making a better person of me, a more resilient person." Her gaze rested on the thick brown leather strap hanging behind the door; her buttocks tingled with the associated memories. Then she looked squarely into the camera, checked her reflection in the large lens, and patted her hair to the accompaniment of a whine from a small electronic servo.

"Cut!"

~

The sparsely furnished bedroom produced echoes. It would take a few minutes for the soundman to get the recording levels to his satisfaction. Katherine studied the white walls covered in a child's handprints and then caught Ashley's eye and smiled. Finally the soundman announced his satisfaction, the cameraman nodded his, and the producer gave Katherine the signal to go.

"Imagine me as a six-year-old and watching my father. He's busy in here, painting the walls with a huge brush. I complained, I think, that I hated the bare white walls. 'Can I not have a nice colour instead, Daddy?' He just ignored me so I took matters into my own hands: my first ever act of rebellion. I went downstairs and fetched several pots of bright and colourful paint. Then I crept back in here, and while his back was turned, dipped my hands in the paint and slapped them all over the pristine white walls. If you look down here, those are the first prints I made. They are the sharpest. I don't know if you can see those?"

She looked uncertainly at the producer who gave her a thumbs-up. Ashley was beaming, obviously enjoying this story of a six-year-old showing the characteristic gutsiness of the woman she would become.

"Anyway, my father turned and saw what I was up to. Now, I expected him to be angry. Very angry. And at first I thought he was, for he frowned like this — *Grrrr!* — a ferocious scowl that turned my very blood cold. But then, to my utter amazement, he smiled. He laughed and said, 'Come here my little Kate. You need to learn fortitude.' He picked me up under one arm, carried me downstairs and put me down on the kitchen table, right next to his veterinary bag."

Katherine paused as she noticed the soundman's raised eyebrows. She moved swiftly on, realising that she had made it sound as if her father was about to commit an impropriety. She forced a laugh, peeling off the thin leather gloves.

"The next thing I know is, I'm waking up in this room with these wonderful handprints covering the entire room. My father had completed the job himself."

She held up her prosthetic hands for the camera to see, flexed her plastic fingers. The servos made a small whirring noise as they extended, contracted, extended. "My father had amputated my hands, you see. He was punishing me, but more importantly he was teaching me fortitude, for even without my hands I still had all my household chores to do every day. He really was the most marvellous man. Very farsighted. Without him, I would never have achieved anything, let alone founded Harper Cybernetics."

Katherine saw horror on the faces of the men. But Ashley had known all about her prosthetics; loved her in spite of them. This big reveal shouldn't have shocked him.

"Did I fluff my lines? I can do it again. But we need to be quick; it's going dark and I want to go into the back garden and show you where my father fed one of my legs to the pigs."

Sheep

Laura had spent seven days in the Waldviertel, Austria's 'Woodquarter', without seeing a single facet of the old ways her grandfather had spoken of. She sighed as she rode past a sign advertising a picnic area. Yet another indicator that despite all her efforts to the contrary, she was still well and truly on the beaten track. A small misty patch bloomed on her helmet visor.

Something registered out of the corner of her eye. She braked and did a U-turn to where a metal signpost marked a junction with a side road.

Strapped to the signpost was a two-metre long spear. Laura dismounted to get a closer look. She stroked the grain of the haft and tested the sharpness of the pitted iron head with the ball of her thumb. The point cut the top layer of her thick leather gloves. This was not some mock weapon pointing to a lame tourist attraction. This was the real deal.

"You were right, *Grosspapa*," she murmured, experiencing a sudden lightening of the spirits. "The old ways do die hard."

She remounted her Yamaha and scanned the western horizon. She figured she had less than an hour of daylight. Shivering inside her leathers, Laura pointed the motorcycle down the narrow side road and headed into a sky streaked with salmon-pink.

~

She would have missed the red-stone farmhouse if it hadn't been for the smoke coiling between the trees. Leaving the metalled road for an overgrown muddy track, Laura brought the bike to a halt at a five-bar gate. A spear was clipped to the diagonal spar. The thatched farmhouse squatted about two hundred metres farther along the track, glowing like a tarnished ruby in the last rays of the sun. The remains of a small fire smouldered in the yard.

Laura removed her helmet and shook out her long hair, scanning the immediate area for signs of life.

The engine noise and wind turbulence had dulled her hearing; it took her a second to realise a German shepherd dog barked at her from behind the gate. Leaving the bike on its sidestand she reached over and allowed the dog to sniff her open palm. "Sshhh. Quieten down, boy." The huge shaggy dog turned tail and ran, likely taking exception to the scent of leather.

A blonde woman appeared at a doorway. "Can I help you?"

Laura was startled to hear an American accent. The woman approached — Laura could see she was a teenager now she got closer — wiping her hands on a towel.

"Do you speak English?" she asked Laura. "Or German? *Sprechen sie Deutsch?*"

"I'm English. I'm touring the area and I saw the spear on the signpost and, well, this place looked interesting." Laura removed her gloves and extended a hand. "Laura Dinniman."

"Candice Asberg. Call me Candy. Are you looking for somewhere to stay?"

"Maybe."

"Well come on in. I'll fix us coffee." Candy dragged the gate open. "It'll be nice to have someone new to talk to."

Presently, Laura faced Candy across a wide pine table with a mug of coffee warming her hands. On entering the building she had expected to find a black pot-bellied stove sitting in the corner of a bare plastered room with a rough plank table dominating the central floor space, with maybe a couple of dead rabbits hanging from the ceiling for good measure. Instead she'd blinked at spotlights spangling off a new AGA, all stainless steel surfaces and chrome attachments; Zanussi white goods rubbed shoulders with those from AEG and Neff. Shiny ceramic tiles covered the walls from floor to ceiling. Laura felt strangely disappointed at what she perceived as a lack of authenticity, then chided herself for wishing others a lower standard of living than she afforded herself at home.

Candy's nasal voice cut through her musings: "My Dad and Grandma are out tending to their flock."

"Your father's a shepherd? Or do you mean he's a man of the cloth?"

Candy giggled. "Neither. There are a lot of people resettling the area, and Dad and Grandma have taken it on themselves to bring them all together as a community. They have these meetings and shit. *Boring!* So, what brings you here?"

"The Waldviertel is somewhere I've always wanted to see," said Laura. "I'm kind of interested in the folklore. I wanted to see for myself if the old traditions are still remembered. My grandfather was born somewhere around here, but he left in the 1930s. He lived on a farm with six brothers and two sisters until he fled the country. Like many, he sensed the coming Nazi persecutions. Grandfather always said I have the Waldviertel in my veins. I've felt, I don't know, energised these last few days. All my adult life it's been like a magnet drawing me here."

"You're thinking of getting a place out here?"

"Unfortunately, no. I'm starting back for England tomorrow."

"Oh." Candy glanced out the window. "I don't blame you. If I had a motorcycle I'd be away from here like a shot. Wouldn't stop till I was back home."

"Home?"

"San Diego. We only came out here last year. Mom died of breast cancer two years ago."

"I'm sorry to hear that."

Candy shrugged. "Since then, Grandma has been filling Dad's head with all this shit about how life was wonderful living out here when she was like, you know, still a little girl. How I'd grow up straighter in the old country. Seems plenty of people got the same idea. Every single one of the new families hereabouts have ancestral links. Freakin' primitives."

Laura looked around the modern, well-appointed kitchen. A bit clinical, perhaps, but primitive?

Candy followed Laura's gaze. "I meant primitive up here," she said, and tapped the side of her head.

"But that's what I came out here to find. People here were raised on superstition. Grandfather said the villagers blamed mist-spirits for anything from a broken hoe to a miscarriage, tied spears to signposts for travellers to fend off marauding wolves, and the shepherd always sacrificed his first lamb so the pack would leave his flock alone. That kind of thing fascinates me." She trailed off as she saw Candy shaking her head.

"Did your grandpa tell you how the priest deflowered the virgin before her wedding night to save her future husband the chore? Not that I have to worry about that." Candy dropped her voice to a conspiratorial whisper. "I got myself deflowered plenty back home."

"Oh. I see." Laura shifted in her seat and gazed out the window at the gathering darkness. A milky mist swirled among the black pines that hid the farm from the road. She heard the dog barking.

"I mean, look at this," Candy said. "This is the kind of shit I'm talking about."

Laura followed Candy's impatient gesture. "The table? What about it?" Laura ran a hand over the pine table, unable to feel the cuts and grooves that scarred the surface through the clear Perspex sheet laid over the top.

"They bought this crummy old table, when they could've bought a new one, and then put a piece of Perspex over it. To protect it! Can you believe that? Just look at all the damn marks on it, and they want to keep it like that."

Laura swept the smooth surface with the flat of her hand. "Yes, I suppose it does seem an odd thing to do, but antique collectors often look for a few knocks. It shows the object's been used. Gives it history. Think about it: they've bought a piece of the past to enjoy all the prettiness and the ugliness and they want to preserve both. Sometimes you need one to know you have the other. You can't visit the past but only choose the smooth; you have to take the rough with it to validate it."

"You sound like Grandma."

Laura sensed this was not meant as a compliment.

The door swung open and a bearded man in a brown leather coat ducked under the low lintel. The dog followed, raising its hackles and snarling at Laura. The man stooped to gently cuff its head.

Candy's chair scraped as she stood, her back ramrod straight. "Dad, this is Laura. Can she stay for a little while, please?"

"Well . . ." Asberg's dark brown eyes appraised Laura in an unhurried fashion. "I think we'd better see what Grandma has to say first. That your motorcycle out front, Miz Laura?"

"Yes. I'm sorry, is it in the way?"

"No, it's fine where it is."

"Hey, Dad, Laura's travelling the area on her own. She's interested in local traditions and folklore and stuff."

Laura couldn't help noticing that Candy's earlier irreverence had been replaced with respectful deference. No, thought Laura. It's more than that. She sounds afraid. She looked at Asberg to see his eyes boring into hers.

"Is that so?" said Asberg, talking to Candy while staring at Laura. His smile revealed even, white teeth. "She'll have plenty to talk about with Grandma, won't she? Maybe she'll want to stay even longer than she originally planned."

"Look," said Laura, "I'm sorry to trouble you, but I really think I should be on my way. Thanks for the coffee, Candy."

"You're leaving?" said Candy. "But I thought you said—"

Laura flinched as a hand rested on her arm. She turned and looked down into a tiny round face as wrinkled as old brown paper. The elderly woman's eyes glittered.

"You made me jump," Laura said, and tried to laugh, but the sound clogged somewhere deep in her throat.

"*En wulf,*" said Grandma Asberg.

"I beg your pardon."

"She said you're a wolf."

"Dad, please . . ."

"Sit down, Candy."

"No, Dad. Leave her alone. You're crazy. Both of y—"

Asberg's hand cracked across his daughter's cheek.

Candy hung her head. Laura's stomach churned at the sight of blood smeared across perfect white teeth.

"*Wulf.*" Grandma stepped back and nodded. "*En wulf.*"

Asberg reached inside his coat and pulled out a knife. Laura threw her empty mug into the man's face and dashed through the open door. She felt the dog's jaws close round her ankle, getting a mouthful of steel buckles for its trouble. Her night vision was excellent despite the bright kitchen and she could see the five-bar gate and her bike in moon-silvered outlines. The leather suit was heavy but she forced her legs to keep pumping. She could hear Asberg yelling at the dog to get after her. She fumbled for the ignition key in her right jacket pocket. Then tried the left.

She vaulted the gate.

She was at the side of the bike slapping pockets when Asberg dragged the gate open. The dog stayed in the farmyard licking a tear in its jowls.

Asberg dangled the bike keys on the tip of his index finger. "Careless, Miz Laura. Never leave the key in the ignition. Someone might steal it."

"What do you want from me?" Laura circled her bike, desperate to keep it between her and this maniac. Fear-sweat chilled her skin. "Just let me leave, okay? Whatever you think I am . . ." She gestured at the farmhouse where a small figure was framed by the light of doorway. "Whatever your mother thinks I am, I am *not* some kind of wolf. So just give me the key, I'll get on my bike, and ride out of here." She held out a hand.

"You're not in any position to make demands." Asberg grinned and sidled around the bike towards her.

They had swapped places now. Laura stood with her back to the gate. She swivelled and snatched up the spear clipped to the diagonal spar. She brought it up to within inches of Asberg's eyes. The point trembled like a leaf.

She stabbed the air. "I'm warning you."

Asberg dropped the key. Laura watched it fall to the ground, then felt the spear wrenched out of her hands.

"Wolf!" He rammed the point at her thigh only for it to be turned aside by her leather trousers. Laura gripped the haft in both hands and tried to snatch it from his grasp. He was too strong. The spear slid through her fingers and punched into her midriff where her jacket met her trousers.

Iron bit into flesh, glanced off bone.

Asberg growled in triumph, raised the spear high and clubbed her across the forehead. Straw-yellow sparks edged her vision. She made to lean on the gate. The world tilted and struck her in the face.

~

"Laura? Laura? Can you hear me? Oh God, I should never have asked you in."

Keeping her eyes closed, Laura raised a hand to a gauze dressing on her forehead. She fingered it gently and then pushed the hand back inside the bed for warmth. Another dressing covered her left hip. She had the worst headache she could ever remember. Nauseating waves of pain rose behind her eyeballs then crashed down into her cheekbones and teeth.

She opened one eye experimentally. A single overhead light burned like the noonday sun until it was eclipsed by Candy's anxious face. A purple swelling marred the girl's cheek.

"Laura? It's me! Can you see all right?"

Laura raised a finger to her lips.

"I'm sorry. I'll try and be quiet. Can I get you anything?"

"No," Laura said, then changed her mind. To her surprise she wanted a cup of sweet tea.

She sat up and swung her legs over the side of the bed while Candy busied herself filling a kettle. Laura shivered in her bra and panties. "Where am I?"

"An empty cottage about four miles out from the farm. Grandma and Dad brought us here."

"And my clothes?"

"They're here." Candy passed Laura her tee-shirt and leather two-piece. Laura placed them on the bed beside her.

"I'm not going back," Candy said. "Dad's dangerous."

"You don't say?" Laura pelted at the dressing on her hip. Blood had oozed through the gauze to stain it a dark earthy colour. "Did you put these dressings on?"

"Grandma said I was to take good care of you."

"Her concern is touching," Laura said, mystified by the Asbergs' behaviour. If they expected to get away with this because they'd tended to her wounds, they could think again. Laura pushed herself to her feet, steadying herself on the brass bedstead.

"Wouldn't you be better sitting down? I think you need to rest."

Laura shook her head and regretted it; it took several seconds for the room to stop spinning. A framed picture hung on the hewn-timber wall. She unhooked it and held it to the light.

"Grandma hung that up. She says it's the people that lived here when she was a little girl. But she's crazy, so—"

Laura raised a hand for silence.

"What is it, Laura?"

"This picture . . ."

Cracks marred the faded image, and a scorch mark obscured one corner, but the photograph was clear enough for Laura to discern a family grouping of seven men and three women. Her gaze fell on the young man kneeling at the front, his hand playing with a fistful of dirt. She observed the cruel curl to the lips and the mocking eyes, the squared shoulders and broad chest, and recognised Peter Dinniman, the man who would one day become her grandfather.

"You said they lived here, in this cottage?"

"So my grandma says."

Laura looked back at the photograph and compared the kneeling youth with her memories of an elderly man, blue-veined and wrinkled, telling her stories of the old ways and declaring that the Waldviertel ran in their blood. Laura ran a finger around the picture frame. She was beginning to understand. "I share your pride, *Grosspapa*, and I share your blood." The instant the words left her mouth she knew them to be true, felt them stir the marrow in her bones.

She lifted her head. The hissing she had thought to be water boiling in the kettle was rain hitting the wooden shingles on the roof.

"It's always raining out here," Candy said. "Another reason to hate the place."

Laura opened the door and looked out. The moon blazed through the clouds and turned the rain to beads of quicksilver. Arrow-straight trees made vertical bars against the blue-grey sky.

"Hey, Laura, you okay? It's freezing out there! At least put some clothes on."

Laura stepped outside. Old pine needles crunched under her bare feet. She tilted her head back and exulted in the tingle of rain hitting her tongue. The water plastered her hair to her scalp and tracked between her breasts and down her back. She unclipped and removed her bra, then slid her panties down and stepped out of their clinging embrace.

The rain increased in intensity, fell like slivers of glass onto her naked skin. Laura raised her arms to welcome the baptismal downpour. She removed the stained dressings on her head and hip to find the skin smooth and unbroken.

She wanted to run through the forests, feel the lash of pine needles on her soles and gulp down the resinous air until it made her heady.

"I—I have your clothes here, Laura," Candy shouted from the doorway. Her voice quavered with uncertainty.

Laura ignored her. The Waldviertel had called and she had responded. And now she was *awake*. Her heritage had claimed her and she no longer needed a sheep's disguise. The shepherd had his spear, the *wulf* her strength and cunning.

She pressed the tip of her tongue to the roof of her mouth and sniffed: she could taste the huddled prey. Their fear was a rancid tone that excited and appalled her in equal measures. And she knew they in turn could sense her. Her presence made them restive; *alive*.

They'd bought into a piece of the past, for the prettiness and the ugliness. Sometimes you need one to know you have the other.

"Laura?"

Laura narrowed her eyes at the intrusion. The shepherd had left a sacrificial offering. His firstborn. It would be rude to ignore it.

"Laura? Laura, are you okay?"

Laura ran a tongue over her teeth, turned slowly to face the young girl framed in the rectangle of yellow light, and smiled. "Coming, my lamb."

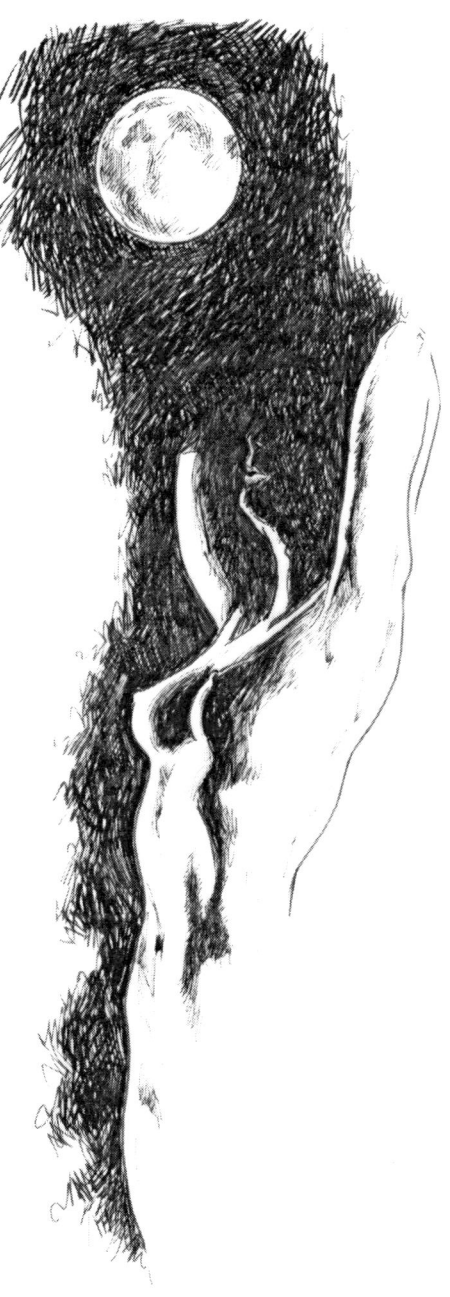

The Fall of Azaliel and Lorcas

"Hell is no place for angels," whimpers Lorcas as the *Bottle*'s wheels judder over churned ice. Claws rake our brass-panelled flanks and rocks bounce off the glass portholes.

"We are quite safe in here, brother." I utter an incantation, the holy fire in the centre of the curved floor flickers and the *Bottle* surges forward. "The warding prayers of the Principalities will keep us from harm."

Despite the heat that forces us to wear nothing more than loincloths, Lorcas' teeth are chattering. "I—I'm sorry, Azaliel. It's just that—"

"It's your first reconnaissance, I know."

We are careering down the snowy slopes of Hell in a small brass cylinder mounted horizontally on wagon wheels. The view through the fore porthole is of a frozen wasteland under a blood-red sky. Through the aft porthole the tracks of the *Bottle* curve to the near horizon.

"It can be daunting," I say.

I am, however, untroubled. Our Divine Duty is to patrol the borderlands and occasionally, like now, penetrate the outskirts of Hell to gather information. This is my thirteenth mission and the *Bottle* — designed by seraphim, assembled by cherubim, blessed by principalities and crewed by two angels — is more than a match for the teeth and talons of our opposite number. The enemy horde could impede our progress in any number of ways, but these are stupid creatures, with strange protuberances and obscene dangly bits. They do naught but throw

themselves at our landship, then howl and shake in our wake.

Wishing to take advantage of a gentler gradient to our right, I close my eyes and say the Prayer of Realignment. Even through my eyelids I detect a change in the holy fire.

"Azaliel?"

"One moment, I need to say the Prayer of Recalibration."

"Azaliel!"

I open my eyes. "Really, Lorcas, I—" The reproach sticks in my throat when I see his raised hand. His fingers and nails have turned a deep cherry red.

His voice wavers. "What does it mean?"

I scan the welds and joints of our vessel, searching for a crack or fault. "We've been breached, Lorcas. Sin has touched you."

He moans, curls up and hugs his knees.

I shout the incantation for the *Bottle* to reverse at full tilt. "I will get us back to the Celestial City before the contamination takes hold." As the *Bottle* jounces over the uneven ground I examine myself for changes, and find none.

Without, bodies impact and demon bones crack on the hull. Within, the incandescent flame throws hard shadows on the cylinder walls.

Just as we are nearing the crest (I can see blades of grass poking through the snow!) Lorcas shoots into a standing position. Arms spread, he stares at his midriff. His breathing is ragged. "I—I felt something down there." Before I can reply his loincloth falls away to reveal something growing in the fork of his legs.

"Sin has touched you!" It is all I can say, so profound is my shock. But my shock is nothing compared to when a thin stream of yellow fluid courses from the wyrm.

"Aaaggghh!" he cries. "What is it doing?"

The peal of a thousand tiny bells caresses my ears as the fluid rings on brass panels. In another time and place I might have relished the sweet tinkling sound, but here and now my mind is on other things. "You're putting out the holy fire!"

I grab his loincloth and try to stem the flow from the demon appendage, but to no avail: the flame is extinguished.

The *Bottle* slows, creaks to a standstill.

The wind whistles through the chassis.

Neither of us dares to breathe.

Then Lorcas points to the fore porthole, to a scaly horde storming towards us. A new word pops into my head. I haven't heard it before and I wonder if it signals that, like Lorcas, I have been contaminated.

"Oh, bugger," I utter miserably.

The demons pound on the hull and soon we are freewheeling into Hell.

Lorcas and I are sealed in the *Bottle* until rescue arrives, but I fear it may be too late for him. There is a sly cast to his eye and the angle of his hips is all wrong when he tries to stand in the rocking, bouncing cylinder. The fattening wyrm between his legs appears to hold a deep fascination for him, and when I tell him to leave it alone he regards my body with a crooked smile.

I don't understand.

My poor brother Lorcas.

Like Cat and Dog

Jade was coming on to Graham like a porn queen. Her seduction was just so artless, from the false yawn that displayed her canine extensions to the stretch that nearly toppled her breasts out of her low-cut dress. But so long as Graham was in on the joke, what harm could it do? Charley cast a proprietary glance over the dimly-lit bar and, seeing no one dying of thirst, settled for giving the counter a wipe with a beer towel. Murphy's tended to be quiet until much later in the evening, when most Cats became active.

She fought to suppress a giggle as Jade groaned in ecstasy and pressed her lips to Graham's ear. He pushed her away, tiring of the charade.

"Come on, lover boy, let's raise the ante." Jade removed a brooch from her dress and pricked her thumb with the pin. A bead of blood trembled on her skin.

Charley's heart began to race.

"Plenty more where this came from," Jade said, "if you'll make me your queen pussy."

"Bitch," Graham hissed. His stool clattered to the floor as he stood.

Charley shouted, "Graham, why don't—"

He wasn't listening. He spun out of Murphy's elegant glass frontage in a whirl of leather and lace to be devoured by the night.

Charley watched him go with a mixture of envy and pride. Panthers did everything with style. They even ran away from girls with panache.

She didn't know how and when Murphy's had become a place where mundane humans and Cats rubbed shoulders, but she did know it was the promise of keeping company with her own kind that brought her here; that and eight quid an hour plus tips, which wasn't bad for this side of the river. Unfortunately, having Cats as clientele also brought in gawkers like Jade.

Jade lit a cigarette and giggled. "Some guys don't know what they're missing."

Charley pitched her voice low. "You're a regular here, surely you know better than to do something that stupid?"

"Obviously I don't. I thought you Cats went crazy over a drop of blood."

"It's not a good kind of crazy, you—" *Stupid mundane!* Charley's annoyance increased as Jade tipped her head back and aimed a thin stream of smoke at the ceiling.

"Ahem."

"What now?"

She pointed to one of two signs hanging over the bar. Beneath the one that read "No Dogs Allowed" was one that forbade smoking.

"God, what is with you, tonight?" Jade sighed and ground the cigarette out in an empty glass. "Another bottle of red wine please, Charley, my little kitten. Make it a Beaujolais."

Charley set down a full bottle in front of the girl and then lifted the hinged portion of the counter. She walked through to pick up Graham's fallen stool. His glass lay on its side, the remnants of the grape juice soaking into the carpet. Non-alcoholic grape juice because Cats didn't have a head for the strong stuff.

Jade tipped half a glass back and swallowed. "A good-looking guy like Graham going to waste, it's criminal." She drained the glass in a titanic second gulp and poured another.

Charley mused that the only thing wasted around here was quality red wine. She had often considered ordering in cheap rubbish for Jade.

"The thing is, Jade, the lust for blood is like . . . oh, I don't know, sex and love. You can live without sex—"

"Speak for yourself!"

"—but you can't live without love. Love is something much deeper, a vital energy that binds. A state of being. I'm probably not explaining this very well, but to us the hunger for blood is as much spiritual as physical. There are medications, but they only go so far to suppress the physical longing. The rest is down to willpower. And then you come along and try to get Graham sampling your blood . . ." She shook her head. "Would you blow smoke in the face of someone trying to quit the weed, or offer a recovering alcoholic a whisky? You were mocking him, Jade. We suffer the pain of abstinence so that we can dwell among you without fear of persecution. You just asked Graham to throw that away for—for nothing."

Jade wriggled her hips and looked down at herself. "I'd hardly call *this* nothing."

Charley tried to relax her neck muscles. It had been three years and two months since she adopted her true-form of a clouded leopard and hunted down her own food. Three years of constantly warring against her instincts, going domestic and shopping for carrion in supermarkets.

"It's a dangerous game you're playing," she said.

"So the predator has become the prey. Big deal."

"Graham was right, you really are a bitch." Charley didn't need to make an excuse to leave Jade alone for a moment; an occasional visitor to Murphy's named Owen, a large guy with a puckered scar that ran from his top lip up to his forehead, swaggered up to the bar and ordered a pint of warm milk sweetened with honey.

Charley served him in silence, not speaking even as she took his money and returned his change. His eyes crinkled with amusement.

Jade banged her empty glass on the counter and beckoned Charley over. "Hey," she whispered. "What's that one? Lion? Cougar?"

Charley hesitated before muttering, "Timber wolf."

"*A Dog*? What's he doing in here?"

"Keep your voice down." Charley's cheeks reddened with shame. "He's provoking us. It'd take a determined lion to face down a timber wolf the size of Owen, and he likes to rub our noses in it." The arrogant bastard, she thought. One day . . .

Charley saw the gleam in Jade's eyes. "Don't even think about it."

"Oh, come on. I'll bet he'll play with me."

"Stop it. Let him drink his milk and go."

"What's with the scar?" Jade gestured clumsily at her face.

"It's a duelling scar. He's a pack leader, the *alpha*."

Jade slurred. "A pack leader. Whoa! One or all, bring 'em on!"

"You can't possibly mean that."

"Oh no? Just watch me." Jade slid the bottle of wine along the bar. "Hi, big guy. Where are all your friends tonight?"

Owen curled his fingers around the bottle, grinned, and then stiffened. He raised a finger to his nose and sniffed, his mouth slightly open, his tongue pressed behind his incisors. "Something tells me you'd better watch your step, young lady." He sloped away to a dark corner to nurse his milk.

"Condescending git. What's with everyone tonight?"

Charley ground her teeth. "For God's sake, Jade, take a hint. I'm telling you now, another peep out of you tonight and you're barred for life."

Jade rolled her eyes and made an uncoordinated grab for the bottle.

Charley swept the bottle up and placed it down behind the counter. "I think you've had enough." She frowned as something tacky on the label transferred itself to her palm. She brought it to her nose, and smelt Jade's blood; fresh, sweet and heady.

Just one taste, she thought, where's the harm? She closed her eyes and touched the tip of her tongue to her hand—

—Juices flooded her mouth. A pounding heat started in her temples. It flowed down over her breasts and belly. She became aware of the sharpness of her teeth, the rending power in her jaws. She could pad over treacherous rocky slopes for mile after mile, day after day, without missing a beat. Tracking the prey, experiencing cold satisfaction in the kill. Hot blood staining her muzzle, spraying over virgin snow. *Gorging . . .*

Charley surfaced from the racial memory. Her eyes fell on Owen. His yellow eyes bored through her stupor. Did he feel this way after smell-tasting Jade's blood?

A sardonic smile appeared on his lips. He rose from his seat and reached inside his leather greatcoat.

"Jade." Charley raised the hinged portion of the counter. "Jade, come through."

"What's wrong?"

Charley grabbed Jade's hand and half-dragged her through the counter, through the stockroom and out the loading bay door. The night air wrapped frigid arms around them.

"Jade, listen to me, this is no time for questions. These are the keys to my car, a green Mondeo. It's in the next block. Turn right at the end of this alley, left and then left again to Battersea Bridge Road. Now run!"

Charley pulled her blouse off over her head and shoved it into a dustbin. Her shoes, tight jeans and panties followed. "Jade, did you hear me? You have to get running!"

"I can't see," the girl wailed. "It's too dark!"

"Give me strength. Right, just stand there and don't move."

All over Charley's near-naked body, hair follicles went into overdrive and sprouted dense white-gold fur. Under her skin, muscles and tendons relaxed, flowed and hardened into compact knots. The skin on her palms and soles thickened into pads of tough leather and her backbone lengthened into a proud tail. Charley shut her eyes as her eyeballs made a sucking *pop* and then blinked rapidly to clear the noisome sensation.

But super-nature could not ignore the law of physics. Charley's mass could not be increased, only shifted. Her strapless bra dropped around her waist, for a clouded leopard has no use for breasts. She unclipped this final item of clothing with black-clawed fingers and shoved it into the dustbin.

The door opened and Owen's face appeared. Mercifully he hadn't changed. Charley smashed her fist into his nose and he slumped to the ground, crimson arcs of blood spraying from his nostrils. She raised her fist to deliver another blow and then thought better of it. To stand and fight a changed alpha wolf would be foolhardy, and there was no doubt that Owen *would* change. He'd underestimated her once; he wouldn't make the same mistake twice. She heaved Jade over her shoulder and padded down the alleyway towards the road.

She dragged a dumpster across the path, overturned another to spill a mountain of mouldy paper and damp cardboard. A howl rose behind her, traversed the streets and soared above the rooftops. All over the neighbourhood doors would be slammed shut and bolted against the night.

"Why is he coming after me?" Jade asked plaintively. "I never did anything to harm him."

"He's blood crazy. He—He *tasted* your blood on the wine bottle. Imagine heroin to a junkie, only ten times stronger."

"I never realised it was so bad."

"Yeah, well, it's a bit late for that now."

Charley quickened her pace, not even slowing when she reached the well-lit carriageway. Two men spilled out of a pub less than a hundred metres away. Pale eyes glowered from under bony foreheads. She spun to see a man and a woman approaching from the other direction. All four Dogs wore long coats similar to Owen's.

"Pack mentality. No individual sense of style," Charley muttered, shrugging Jade into a more comfortable position on her shoulder.

The young woman whimpered, "Oh my God I'm gonna—" and puked down Charley's back.

Charley wrinkled her nose in disgust.

Owen moved alongside the female. Made confident by their numbers, and by the presence of their alpha, the Dogs remained in human form. No doubt they were expecting Charley to drop Jade and surrender. Arrogant Dogs. Just because they outnumbered her five-to-one. Charley sprang at a male and slashed his head before bounding to a first-floor window ledge. She hissed and held aloft a tattered scalp. Her victim lay motionless in a pool of blood. Adrenaline dissolved any regret she might have felt.

Jade stuttered. "Duh-duh-don't duh-drop—"

"I won't," Charley reassured her.

The remaining two males and the female joined Owen in adopting their man-wolf forms.

A siren sounded in the distance, growing louder by the second.

Owen dispatched two Eurasian wolves to Charley's left and a creamy-coated Arctic to her right. Then he dropped to his knees and sniffed the inert body on the tarmac. He raised his muzzle and howled a long, forlorn note before turning a baleful yellow gaze on Charley. "You made a grave error, Cat," he snarled. "I wanted only the girl."

In the window behind Charley drapes were pulled back. A sleepy mundane peered out. Charley roared and he fell back from the spittle-flecked pane.

When she turned back to the street below, Owen had disappeared. Flashing blue lights bathed the walls.

"Jade, where did he go?"

"I duh, I duh—"

"Forget it," she snapped. "Do you still have the car keys I gave you?"

"Yuh-yuh—"

"Good. Don't lose them." Charley adjusted the blubbering mundane's weight on her shoulder and scaled the building exterior. Bounding from ledge to sill, she exploited her phenomenal balance and strength to reach the top of the four-story tenement in seconds. A series of rising and falling pitched roofs greeted her eyes. Dim light filtered up through skylights filmed with bird shit and moss.

"Why not let the police deal with it?" Jade whimpered.

"And be taken down by a trigger-happy police marksman? No thanks."

She spun at a clangour to her right: slid into shadow, ducked behind a small forest of aerials to let the angular shadows and stripes break up her outline. She let Jade slump to the rooftop. A dark-pelted wolf peered over the wall surrounding the rooftop. He had come up a fire escape.

Jade whispered: "What can you see?"

Charley clamped a hand over her mouth and gave it a warning squeeze before letting go. She closed her eyes to slits. The wolf scanned the rooftop then came over the wall. Another followed close behind. The two Eurasian males.

Moving with infinite care, Charley grasped a single-pronged aerial. It was fastened to a chimney, but the mortar was old and crumbly. The corroded aluminium tubing came away with a single, sharp tug. Brick and dust pattered to the tarpaper roof. The lead wolf pricked his ears and sped straight towards her. Charley straightened, raised an arm and shouted, "Fetch, boy!" The Dog hesitated for a split second, long enough for Charley to step aside and lash it across the face with the metal rod. She followed up with a kick to the gut. Her claws raked soft belly skin, and the wolf dropped to its knees.

Jade screamed: "Watch out!"

Charley dropped to all-fours just as the second wolf launched itself at her. It landed on her back but was unable to halt its momentum and slid off. Jaws snapped inches from her left foot. She pirouetted, flailed with the rod and whacked the wolf across the muzzle. The pliable metal rod bent double. Leaving the creature blinded with agony, she turned on the first wolf and rammed the two ends of the bent aerial deep into its throat. Bright arterial blood bubbled and frothed over its chest.

Charley grabbed the second wolf by the scruff of the neck and the belt of his pants. Before it could gather its wits, she hoisted it above her head and staggered under its weight to the parapet.

"Please," it screeched. "I yield."

"This isn't a competition, mutt." Below, a policeman was attempting to hold back a crowd gathered around the Dog she had scalped. "It was you or me, we both know that." Charley grunted and heaved the frantic Dog to the street.

It paddled uselessly in the air before landing headfirst on the road with a muffled, pulpy splat.

Onlookers screamed and fell back. Charley ducked away before anyone looked up and regarded with distaste the specks of blood marring the fine white fur of her chest and belly. Unlike a prey animal's blood which ignited fireworks on the tongue, the blood of a fellow predator smelled and tasted rancid.

She stepped over the fast-expiring, wheezing Dog on the ground and stared at the spot where she'd left the girl. "Jade, where are you?"

A muffled cry came from the other end of the roof. Charley sprinted across the tarpaper and slates just in time to see Jade being dragged through a door leading onto an unlit staircase. She glimpsed a creamy white pelt.

"Leave her or I'll kill you," Charley snarled, moving into the doorway.

The female Arctic wolf stood on the lower landing, one hand around Jade's wrist, the other clamping her mouth. The girl's eyes bulged with terror.

Charley flicked casually at the bloodstains on her pelt. "Not mine," she said, and peeled back her lips in a savage grin.

"Owen said the girl had to be brought to him. You want her, you come and get her."

Charley scanned the narrow concrete staircase less than two yards wide. She leapt, but halfway down changed her angle of descent by springing off the wall to her right, then the left; right, left, right, zigzagging like a rubber ball. The confused wolf shoved Jade away and raised its hands to defend itself.

Charley landed squarely on the wolf's shoulders and bore it down under her weight. She bit hard on its neck, and then wriggled her jaws to work her canines over the back of the skull.

The wolf yelped and flattened its ears. "I yield!"

Charley considered her options. She could spare this creature; convince her to mislead Owen into believing Charley and Jade had escaped. But that relied on trust. A Cat trust a Dog?

The wolf squirmed and looked at Jade. "Run, girl! She's—"

Charley bit down, her canines punching through skin and bone.

CRACK!

The wolf jerked once, then lay still.

Charley rocked back onto her haunches and ran her tongue over the clean fur of her arms to rid her tongue of the revolting taste of cerebral fluid.

Jade collapsed on the steps and buried her face in her hands. Charley shook her by the shoulders. "Hey, come on. You've got to hold it together for me, you hear?"

Jade looked up, her face a mess of running mascara and smudged lip-gloss. "I can't. I can't stand it anymore. I'm going to go down to the police. Owen won't dare—"

"And what about me? I just wiped out four members of his pack. Do you think he's going to let me walk away from this? He's likely calling for reinforcements right now. You have to help me, Jade. I saved your life several times over tonight. You owe me."

"I'll go in Murphy's, tell your Cat friends. They'll help."

"Cats, help?" Charley laughed bitterly. "We are not known for our spirit of cooperation."

Jade shrugged helplessly. "Then what can I do?"

Charley allowed herself a small smile of satisfaction. "You still have my car keys?"

The girl opened her clenched fist to reveal a set of bloodied keys. She had gripped them so tightly they'd cut her palm. The sweet scent rose like smoke, filling Charley's muzzle with aromatic temptation.

"Go down to the next block and find my car. The dark green Ford, remember? The cops will be swarming all over the place, rounding up any stray Cats and Dogs. You'll be quite safe. Get in and start the engine."

"Then what?"

"Good question," Charley muttered to herself. How had she let herself get into this situation? "Damn animal instincts."

"What?"

"Nothing. Wait for two minutes then bring the car round to the entrance at the bottom of these stairs. Got that? Wait two minutes."

Jade stood and swayed. Charley reached out to steady her. "I knew I shouldn't have served you that wine. Are you up to this?"

The girl swept stray hair off her face and nodded.

"I'm counting on you, Jade."

"I know." She took a deep breath. "I won't let you down, Charley."

Charley watched her feel her way down the unlit stairs and open a door onto a carpeted hallway. Light blazed briefly then dimmed as the door closed behind her. With Jade gone she turned the Dog corpse over and unzipped its voluminous quilted jacket. The collar had a gruesome stain but that hardly mattered. She slipped the jacket on and huddled down in the corner of the landing.

When she stood again it was in human form.

Moonlight shining through the open doorway silvered the steps. Her senses were still better than those of a mundane's, but even so they paled into insignificance compared to what she enjoyed in her leopard form. The night lacked texture and depth.

She trotted up the steps, out onto the roof, and headed for the parapet overlooking the road. Down below, two cops strode along the pavement. They carried sidearms and looked jumpy with them.

The click of high heels preceded Jade's appearance. Charley swore under her breath when one of the cops interrupted his patrol to approach her.

"Are you okay, Miss?"

"I'm, uh, fine, thank you."

"You don't look it, if you'll forgive me for saying so."

"I—I've had a bad night. Did you see those poor men on the street back there?"

"Spare your tears, Miss, they were only Dogs."

"They were *changed men*, Officer."

"Of course. Changed men. Um, we're looking for a young woman named Jade Golightly: Caucasian, mid-twenties, long black hair, last seen wearing a low cut black dress . . ." He looked at her expectantly.

"I haven't seen anyone fitting that description tonight, Officer. I hope you find her. Would you walk me to my car?"

Charley grinned. Who ever would have thought Jade could be so resourceful under pressure?

A deep voice rumbled behind her: "You've brought down a shitstorm, Cat."

She turned slowly. Owen towered over her. Six-foot-six of packed muscle draped in a dense grey pelt. The white scar on his brow glowed in the moonlight. He moved between her and the door to the stairs.

"Where's the girl?" he asked.

"Back down on the street."

"You gave her up?"

"Not exactly."

When Charley didn't elaborate he asked: "Do you realise what you have done? For the sake of one girl?"

Charley folded her arms across her chest and shrugged. "She whetted my appetite."

"Does she realise?"

"That I've abducted her? No. She thinks I rescued her from you. It's a facet of prey animals, you see — docile stupidity."

"For years we've lobbied for equal rights and freedom of movement. We leave the mundanes alone, and they leave us alone. You've jeopardised all that."

"Surely you felt it too, Owen — when you tasted her blood on your tongue — the feeling that you're living a lie. We are not domestic animals, to be watched and mocked like some twenty-first century freak show. Especially by the likes of Jade. 'Ooh, Graham, make me your queen pussy.' He should have ripped her face off."

"So you'd rather we return to the Dark Ages, when the changed were driven from their homes and hunted to near extinction? We are legally protected now and—"

"No, I don't want a return to the Dark Ages, but nor do I want to be a tame exhibit in a zoo." She heard a car door slam and seconds later the quiet purr of an engine. She had two minutes to get down there. "So, Dog. What are you going to do with me? Carry me off and bury me alongside your squeaky toy and water bowl?"

Owen smiled slyly and reached inside his leather greatcoat. Charley recalled seeing him perform the same action in the bar, just before she'd taken Jade. She backed off. The rough coping stones of the parapet jutted into the small of her back.

He pulled out a wallet and flipped it open to reveal a silver badge. "You're under arrest."

"*What*?"

"Don't think for one second I'd rather not rip your throat out."

"Like I did with one of your precious pack? I crunched through the female's skull. Hope you didn't have the hots for her. Was she your mate? Did you hump behind the dustbins and howl at the moon, or chase cars together? That's what you Dogs do, isn't it?"

Owen's breathing came short and choppy. Specks of foam mottled his lower lip. "We are *wolves*, Cat."

"Yeah, the Big Bad Wolf who came strutting into Murphy's every so often to scare us little pussy cats. You're a *Dog*, Owen, a wolf tamed and domesticated." She sneered at the police badge shining in the moonlight. "And you're terrified the hand of the master might turn against you. Well, as much as I'd like to stay and goad you all night long . . ." She climbed onto the parapet, cupped her hands to the side of her mouth and screamed.

Owen dashed forward. "What are you doing?"

"Help me," she yelled. "The wolfman's trying to eat me!" Charley launched herself backwards as if pushed. She saw Owen's anger turn to shock. Frozen in time with his hand reaching for her.

The cold air whistling past her ears raised the hair on her hackles.

Muscles reconfigured and her bones snapped into a feline posture. Charley's spine started to twist. Without volition her shoulders rotated, and her hips swivelled to bring her around to land four-square. She didn't have the time to properly brace herself: the impact slammed her body full-length into the tarmac. Her chin hit the ground, and for a long second she hovered on the edge of unconsciousness.

Her pupils sprang into slits with a revolting pop, marking the completion of her transformation. "Jeez . . ." she groaned.

One of the cops pulled his sidearm and aimed at the rooftop. High above Owen raged incoherently.

A hand touched Charley's wrist. A concerned policeman's voice by her ear said, "Don't move; an ambulance is on the way." He gasped. "You're a—"

She rolled over — "Correct" — and headbutted him senseless.

Jade tugged at her arm. "Charley! Come on." The world tilted crazily as Charley got to her feet and staggered to her waiting car. Jade threw open the driver's door and shuffled over into the passenger seat. Charley slid into human form, dropped gratefully behind the wheel, and gunned the engine.

She checked her mirror to see Owen drop into the road. He rose and came after her. Bullets zinged off the tarmac as confused police officers continued to fire on him. Yellow sparks burned briefly like incandescent fireflies. For a moment he was gaining ground on the car, then he stiffened suddenly, clutched his thigh and began to limp.

He threw his head back and began a pain-ridden howling.

A police marksman's bullet ended it.

Charley quick-shifted through the gears. The lights of the city streaked across the windscreen as they sped across the Thames. She darted a glance at the girl in the passenger seat.

"It's been a wild night. I think it's best if you come home with me."

Jade was wide-eyed and trembling. "I'm just so cold."

"We'll soon get you warmed up. I'll fix us some dinner. I thought a nice Steak Diane would go down well."

Jade frowned. "But that's got red wine in it and you hate alcohol."

Charley engaged the central locking system. She took a hand off the wheel and squeezed one of Jade's beautiful plump thighs. Saliva filled her mouth. She had to swallow before she could answer. "That's okay. All the alcohol is burned out of the meat if you cook it thoroughly."

The Exchange

The soft plash of wood on water brings to mind a quote. "There is nothing, absolutely nothing, half so much worth doing as simply messing about in boats!" My fake English accent stirs Grace to sit up in the bow.

"*Wind in the Willows*, Daddy?"

"You betcha, honey."

She flashes an impish grin, her pale face dappled by the sunlight on the water. I ship the oars and inhale the tang of leaf carrying from the wooded shoreline. Spring in the Appalachians is never less than glorious. It makes you want to fill your lungs and shout.

A cold wind comes out of nowhere to tease spume from the glittering wavelets. I reach over to make sure Grace's yellow lifejacket is secure. She bats my hand away.

"Bad child!" I tweak her chin playfully and she giggles.

"I can see the moon." I follow her pointing finger, ready to argue that she must be mistaken. But the moon's there all right, round and chalky in the daytime sky. It's a strange sight.

A louring cloud moves across the sun.

A large black bird beats its wings overhead.

The stirring of the peach-fuzz hairs on the back of my neck has nothing to do with the plummeting temperature.

It's my grandmother's fault. Every Sunday afternoon she'd sit me down by the hearth and tell me New England legends of hobgoblins and changelings, of werebeasts and ghosts that prowled woods and shorelines, intent on devouring humans too stupid to realise they'd strayed over otherworldly borders.

I'm a rational man, not given to superstition: nevertheless I slip the oars into the rowlocks and turn the boat to shore. Grace doesn't argue. It's been fun, but you can have too much of a good thing. Kenneth Grahame probably said that, too.

"Daddy?"

"Not now, Grace. Let Daddy concentrate." Her brow creases. I force a smile. "Sorry. You wanted to tell me something?"

She points to the water at the side of the boat. "I saw something down there."

I flick my gaze to the dark depths and for a split second see something inchoate and white. "The moon's reflection," I say without conviction.

Grace leans over the gunwale.

"Sit back!"

Something thumps the underside of the boat. My daughter's eyes grow wide.

"Driftwood," I spit through gritted teeth.

She is still resting her hands on the gunwale. I stop rowing to rub a sleeve over my brow. "Grace, I've told you once before to sit—"

She's not there.

I blink stupidly and widen my eyes like a drunk, scan the wooden seats as though she's playing hide-and-seek.

Her lifejacket bobs on the water.

"GRACE!" Her name comes out red and raw. I stand up and the boat rocks dangerously. One of the oars floats away.

I remove my lifejacket, take a deep breath and jump in.

The water is colder than I could have imagined. The blue-white shock behind my squeezed-shut eyes is like lightning in its intensity. I force them open and the world is bottle green, which gives way to black with terrifying swiftness as my clothes drag me down.

My feet touch the bottom of the lake. I sink to my knees in the soft silt. In the darkness I sweep my hands like a blind man. My arms feel like I'm carrying hundred-pound weights. I try to take a step forward and I fall in slow motion. My hands touch slick and slimy weeds. Already the cold is sapping my energy.

Grace! I'm haunted by her face, dappled by sunlight and framed by auburn curls.

Something brushes my hand, closes over my thumb and holds tight. I recognise the grip and latch on. With Grace's tiny hand in mine I find a strength I didn't know I possessed. I kick for the surface with strong, even strokes.

But my tortured lungs have had enough. Silver bubbles erupt from my mouth. Water rushes in. Nothing has ever looked so beautiful or unattainable as that bright shimmering ceiling. I fall away. Then a silhouette comes into view, like an angel. It's Grace. She grabs my collar and pulls me up the last few yards.

My head breaks the surface, but I'm spent.

It's Grace, my marvellous Grace, who loops a lifejacket around my shoulders and strikes out for the shore. Together we scramble onto a spit of shingle jutting into the lake. A young man is running towards us.

I drop to my knees. A small fist pounds between my shoulder blades until I puke up a bellyful of green water.

The guy squats on his haunches and regards me with concern. "Are you okay, mister?"

I wipe a string of snot from my chin and then roll onto my back. A child looks down on me.

She wears Grace's sodden clothes, and smiles Grace's impish smile.

"Are you OK, Daddy?"

She even has Grace's voice.

But she's not Grace. She's a changeling. A fairy child in exchange for my own.

"There is nothing," I whisper, "absolutely nothing, half so much worth doing as simply messing about in boats."

I wait for her answer.

She shrugs and arches hers eyebrows. "If you say so."

The young man mistakes my sobs for tears of relief and claps me on the shoulder. I rise to my knees and the child hugs me, whispers in my ear. "Take me home, *Daddy*."

I gaze over her shoulder, weeping uncontrollably for my daughter among the waves.

Soapocryphal

In just a moment we'll be paying a visit to Jubilee Square, *where there is more trouble in store for our favourite married couple.* An avuncular chuckle. *That's* Jubilee Square, *coming up right after the break.*

Philip Crowgutter looked up from his *Skinflick* long enough to notice Molly had fixed her eyelids a vivid blue.

"Say something, rose petal?"

When Molly didn't answer, he returned to his left wrist where he had a 400dpi screen tattooed. A *Skinflick*. With that and the audio receiver chipped into his jawbone he could watch and listen to TV anywhere, anytime. Thousands of epitaxial microprocessors blasted into his skin, tuned to realign 60 times a second as they received digital transmissions. He'd heard they pushed the resolution up to 620dpi on the later models. Incredible. Molly even had epitaxial processors tattooed on her eyelids and lips so she could effortlessly test various colours at the touch of a button.

Philip felt the movement of air as Molly busied herself with her coat and scarf. The front door opened and slammed shut, the sound echoing in the tiled hallway.

"Touchy," he said, and wriggled deeper into his armchair. The familiar opening strains of *Jubilee Square* filled his head. Philip would put the kettle on during the break. He could do it now, of course, without missing a thing, but old habits died hard.

The opening credits ended. Onscreen, the soap-goddess Cassie Taylor put the finishing touches to her make-up.

Philip brought the tattoo closer to his eyes.

We never go out anymore, Jase. Not as a couple, anyway. Cassie swept a remote control over her face and examined the results in a mirror. *You're more interested in that TV than me.*

The illumination from a *Skinflick* lit Jason's features. *I can't miss it tonight. It's going to be a cracker.*

The camera lingered on Cassie's unreadable expression before the scene changed to that of a noisy pub interior.

Philip blinked. Was he watching a repeat? Something sparked in his brain but fizzled before making a connection. He sighed. He didn't know how Jason could neglect Cassie. When Philip made love to Molly, it was Cassie he imagined lying beneath him, her skin flushed and perspiring.

In *Jubilee Square* Jason continued to push his luck: *Where are you off to?* he asked, his voice flat and bored.

Bingo, she said and flounced off-screen, tossing her famous red hair, the sway of her hips mesmerising.

Jason hollered after her.

She stormed back into the dimly lit front room. *What's up now, Jase?*

He waggled his mug. *My tea. It's stone cold.* His eyes narrowed. *And where do you think you're going?*

Don't you ever listen to a word I say? I said I'm off to the bingo. I'll be back about ten, okay?

Jason pulled a face.

You can come if you like.

Jason said he'd prefer a fresh mug of tea.

Cassie visibly puffed up - the actress Sonia Hart-Morse made these scenes her own. *No, I won't make you another cup of tea before I go, you know where the kettle is. You do know where the kettle is, don't you? It's in that room called the kitchen.*

Jason looked up from his *Skinflick* with a blank expression. *Say something, rose petal?*

Cassie's eyes flashed, the close-up of her face lasting a record four seconds before she whirled out of the room.

Touchy, said Jason, and the scene changed to a neighbour's little girl miming pop-stardom with a hairbrush.

The spell broke. Philip's mouth hung open. He shook and tapped his left wrist, fearing he was the victim of a practical joke. What the hell happened there? The show had just replayed his last conversation with Molly — the bickering over bingo and a cup of tea — word for word.

Philip turned his attention back to the *Skinflick*. Jason brooded in an armchair, his own *Skinflick* reflecting in eyes narrowed to slits, his mouth grim. The expression had served Des Newman well. He had played Jason for two decades and the narrowed eyes and grim mouth were all he ever needed. It had become a trademark. Sad or elated, angry, suspicious or maudlin, Des gave it the same expression. It won him awards.

Jason rose and moved to a window.

Philip placed his mug of cold tea on the floor, crossed to the window and parted the curtains. Light reflecting on the glass obscured his view outside so he went to switch it off. He gave a small yelp as he saw Jason doing the same. A small vein began to pulse in Philip's neck.

He watched the screen as Cassie, beautifully lit as always, folded away a black umbrella and boarded a bus.

Philip stepped back to the window, minding his step in the darkened room, and twitched the curtains to peer outside. Dead leaves performed cartwheels across the lawn and blocked the gutters. Rain lashed the deserted street. Holding his breath, Philip pressed his cheek to the icy-cold windowpane and looked down the length of the street to the uncovered bus stop at the end. There was no sign of Molly. He had missed her. He clucked and shook his head. Anyone with an ounce of common sense would stay in on such a filthy night.

He continued to watch *Jubilee Square* while waiting for the kettle to boil: Jason, acting on some unspoken suspicion, was waiting at the bus stop for the next bus.

Philip sat down and hugged himself, torn by indecision. Everything had gone out of kilter. Like having déjà vu. Yeah, that was exactly what it was like — déjà vu. He must be having some sort of prolonged episode of the stuff. He clung to the explanation, found it comforting if utterly unconvincing. He rolled his sleeves down and pressed a small stud under the skin of his jaw, experiencing a semblance of calm as the noise and light abated.

Molly often reprimanded him for his apathy. He never acted on anything until it was too late. But it wasn't his fault — he had a slow metabolism. Or a fast one. Something like that, anyway. But tonight he would act.

Philip reached out and switched the kettle off, strode to the front door, pulled his coat from the hook and stepped out into a squall. He let himself back in a moment later, realising he had no small change for the bus. That, he rued, was more like real life.

Invigorated by the cold rain that streamed over his face, Philip was nevertheless grateful for the red double-decker that pulled up at the kerbside within seconds of him reaching the bus stop. He paid his fare, sat down and tugged up his left sleeve to watch *Jubilee Square*. Everyone else on the bus, he noted, was likewise preoccupied, their listless heads bobbing like ripe corn as the bus swayed down the road. Cassie Taylor was walking down a cul-de-sac towards a smart detached bungalow, the rain surrounding her as a mist. The scene cut to Jason, his broad shoulders hunched against the elements, watching her from the roadside. A departing double-decker growled in the background.

Philip Crowgutter studied the door as Cassie knocked and waited. Classical music played inside. The door opened. *Hello Clark.* Arms reached out and hugged her, lips kissed her proffered cheek. She shot one last guilty look over her shoulder and entered the bungalow.

Jason's face — all narrowed eyes and grim mouth — filled the screen as *Jubilee Square* gave way to a commercial break.

Philip pondered. The number of the bungalow Cassie entered was 27. That was also the number of one of Molly's workmates, a homosexual named Tim Andrews. He lived in a bungalow and, more importantly, it was on this bus route. Philip stood and motioned to the driver that he needed to get off. He didn't trust himself to speak.

Careless of his open coat Philip walked up the dead end road. His body felt airy and intangible as though he walked in a dreamscape.

He recalled Molly telling him about Tim's supposed homosexuality. Philip had shrugged and said something trite like, "Every man must have his little hobby." It occurred to him now that such a lie would be a perfect cover if she was . . . having an affair. Oh, God. To think he had swallowed her lies hook, line and bloody sinker. How they must have laughed at their cleverness as they played him for a gullible fool.

Phillip skipped over Tim Andrews' wall and cut across the garden, deliberately crushing the daffodils and snowdrops. He hesitated at the door and wiped the rain from his eyes. Could he be jumping to the wrong conclusion? He checked his video tattoo, and felt an indescribable rush of pleasure to see Jason standing at Clark Atherton's door. Clark was the soap's token homosexual.

Philip felt there was a *rightness* to this, as though it was scripted. And he wasn't just a bit-part player, either. His was the lead role. He hammered on the door with the flat of his hand and rehearsed what he would say. Oh, there would be denials and excuses, explanations and counter-accusations, but he could handle it. Phillip was all keyed-up for the big scene. His eyes narrowed and his mouth formed a grim line. The loud classical music from the other side of the door failed to drown the buzzing of the hornets that raged inside his head. He began to kick at the door until the crashing notes snuffed into silence. Philip fumed impotently, clenched and unclenched his fists.

The hornets began to sting.

A deadbolt clacked. Light spilled across the path. Tim Andrew's face appeared in the narrow gap. He looked flushed from exertion. "Oh my," he panted. "We weren't expecting you."

~

Philip sat on the stationary bus, his hair wet and plastered to his forehead and cheeks. Sodden leaves clung to the muddy soles of his shoes and rainwater coursed down the sleeves of his coat to drip on rubber mats. His tongue was sore and swollen where he had bitten it. He passed the back of his hand over his eyes as the roiling clouds finally thinned and dispersed. When he had first entered the bungalow at the end of the cul-de-sac, a storm had blown up, blinding him to everything bar the duplicity of the two people he went to confront. The high pressure sustained itself until the last killing blow landed, the force of it twisting a heavy bronze figurine from his slippery hands. He had only freeze-frame images of Molly — a disjointed montage, a dramatic edit.

Molly wearing a garish gown, eye and lip tattoos turned up full.

Molly standing with hands raised to ward off the blows.

Molly with her head at a strange angle and long hair stiffly fanned.

Molly sprawled across the body of her lover.

Molly lying motionless on the floor with spit-bubbles on the mottled skin of her neck.

Molly's eyes meeting Philip's in a glass-eyed stare . . .

No doubt there would be complaints that *Jubilee Square* had become too violent in a blatant bid for ratings. But Philip thought it made sense for soaps to reflect real life, it being a moral obligation of the studio to depict society in all its evils. And anyway, the violence was more suggested than actual. It had been creatively and artfully depicted without resorting to gore.

The bus he boarded remained stationary. The driver was probably ahead of his timetable and so taking a timeout — smoking a cigarette and watching his *Skinflick*.

Philip thumbed the audio receiver on his jaw and rolled his left sleeve up.

Jason slouched on a bus, his skin the colour and texture of grey cardboard. The garish light of a *Skinflick* flickered artistically in the water that dripped over his face. His eyes crinkled, his face crumpled, and he began to sob, his shoulders shaking. It looked hammy, but Philip forlornly followed suit, burying his face in his hands as he shared the man's grief.

The camera angle rotated to look down the gangway. A sexy redhead boarded the bus and strode purposely towards Jason, the neon strips playing delicately over her black plastic raincoat.

Cassie!

Philip pinched the skin on his wrist. "No!"

Jason started in his seat. *Darling, I am so sorry!*

Cassie brushed him aside as she swung in beside him. *Forget it, Jase! What the hell did you think you were doing barging in like that? I have never been so humiliated in my entire life! And God knows what poor Clark must think.*

Jason looked wretched. *I am so, so sorry, sweetheart. I don't know what I was thinking.*

I mean, it's not like you didn't know Clark is gay! So why? He's been a real sweetie giving me the ballroom dancing lessons and this is what he gets: you barging in and accusing him of having an affair with me. The poor man was beside himself.

You said you was going to the bingo.

You wouldn't have said anything if I'd said I was going to the bleedin' moon! Just look at you, Jase, and all these other people — living in their own squalid little worlds with that crummy thing on their arms.

Please, Cassie, give me another—

Philip's eyes swivelled to the front of the bus as the concertina door flapped open. A broken hand gripped the handrail, smearing watery blood on the chrome. Molly heaved herself up to face him. A shattered mannequin, with a damson-coloured smile that twisted to reveal a gap where there should have been front teeth. Her eyelid implants had crashed, cycling through red, yellow and purple above spider legs of running mascara.

Philip found himself standing in the gangway. "Darling," he croaked. "I didn't, I mean—" He glanced at the other passengers in mute appeal, but their heads were bowed, filled with voices from the ether. Philip backed away as Molly jerked towards him. "I am so, so sorry sweetheart. I don't know—" Molly's cold blue fingertips rested on his lips. A shard of bone jutted through the matted hair at her temple.

She stood on tiptoe so that her lips were next to his ear. She whispered, "Personally, I think the script stinks."

"Molly, I—I'll get the tattoo removed first thing. I promise."

"There's no need." She stepped back and placed her hands on either side of his head. He felt her thumbs dig into his eyes. He wrenched at her wrists but she was too fast. There was a silent pop and a sticky viscous fluid oozed down his cheeks.

"There's no need," he heard her whisper.

The Uinta Incident

Spotlights roved over the shuttles' silver hulls. Danny Feinberg stood in the shadows and noted the names of the *Polo*, *Magellan* and *Boone*.

"The cold, mechanical edge of man's ingenuity whisking away the cream of humanity."

Danny turned the phrasing over in his mind.

"The cream of humanity will smother the dust of the Red Planet."

He shook his head. That last sounded awful.

Danny was struggling to find his journalistic objectivity, for although the stationary behemoths inspired a spine-tingling awe that verged on the spiritual, he loathed the sight of them and everything they had come to represent. Then Karen Kitson was at his side and thoughts of bylines fled from his mind.

"Karen, it's not too late. Please."

She sighed and adjusted the bulky green flightsuit. "We've been given a few minutes to say our goodbyes. Don't let's waste them going over the same old ground as always."

"What do I have to say to make you change your mind? Don't leave me, Karen. I don't think I can live without you."

Her gaze locked onto his. "And what's that supposed to mean?"

Danny stared at the tops of his shoes. "Don't worry. I wasn't saying I'd do something stupid."

He turned to watch protesters throwing themselves at the four-metre-high barricade in the distance. Their sibilant hissing raised the hairs on the nape of his neck. Karen placed smooth fingers on his cheek, turned him to face her.

"I don't understand why you won't come with us."

Us? Did she mean her and their unborn baby, or the other passengers who comprised the vanguard to Mars?

"Come on, Danny, you must realise by now that you will never play a full role in Tiffany's life. But you *can* be a part of ours."

He turned away.

"Danny?" She tugged his forearm, as though she had been about to raise his hand to her swollen belly before thinking better of it. "Aren't we enough for you?"

"If you stayed, I'd have everything I ever wanted right here." He gritted his teeth, fighting the tears. "And I'm staying because running away isn't the answer to our problems."

He took a shallow breath: she knew that by "our" he meant the whole goddamn world and his uncle Joe.

Her voice was sharp. "Save that for the press, Danny. I was talking to my man Danny not Mr. Daniel Feinberg, spokesman for the—"

"I am *not* anti-Salvationist!"

"Then stop sounding like one. No one's running, Danny. Colonising a new world is not the same as running away."

"Until we fix the mistakes we made with this one, we don't have the right to screw up another."

"Oh for God's sake! That's the kind of bullshit those primitives over there are spouting. Look what happened when they tried to fix the problem. They gave us a new sub-continent. And where are you going to be standing when Yellowstone goes up, Danny? We are just . . ." She gestured at the phalanx of gleaming shuttles behind her. "We are just being realistic."

A light on her flightsuit cuff flashed. It was the signal for all departing personnel to wrap up their goodbyes.

Danny looked at her in horror. "They didn't give us enough time."

"Enough time for what? To settle our differences? No, they didn't. They'd have to delay the mission for several years for us to do that." Her smile was bittersweet.

"I didn't mean all that crap about . . . I can't believe we argued. I just want you to stay."

"And I want to go." She kissed him chastely, her lips barely brushing his. "Goodbye, Danny. You really wouldn't be deserting Tiffany, you know."

He shook his head, hardly trusting himself to speak. "She's my daughter. Even if she grows up hardly knowing who I am, she is still my daughter and I will not put all those millions of miles between us. Right now she is indifferent to me, but if I went with you she'd have every right to hate me. One day, you might appreciate how I feel."

"So," she sighed. "That's that, then."

He watched her walk away, to fade into the crepuscular light.

"Don't go," he whispered. "Just . . . aw, fuck it." He kicked angrily at the asphalt before turning for the transporters laid on for the relatives of the departing colonists. He would not accompany them to the observation compound, though. He would not — could not — watch the staggered take-offs.

He had an appointment with a beer. Several beers.

~

As she reached a circle of brightly illuminated asphalt, Karen Kitson turned, hoping to see Danny one last time. She had been harsher with him than she intended. She had meant to be composed, but the Ice Queen side of her nature had taken over. A defence mechanism she had rued on more than one occasion and would doubtless rue again. She shielded her eyes against the glare of floodlights and saw a silhouette slouching away. Oh Danny, she thought. My love. She wiped the back of her hand across her eyes. It came away wet.

"Ms Kitson!"

She turned and managed a weak smile for the benefit of the cameras lined up to record the departure of the Project Salvation pioneers.

"Over here, Ms Kitson."

"Could you give us a wave?"

"Lovely. Thank you."

She gratefully accepted the intervention of a steward, who bustled her past the throng and onto the boarding platform. She grabbed a rail as it rose into the air on hydraulic pillars towards the massive bulk of the *Magellan*.

"Your baby will need to be FED before you take up your position," the steward said.

Karen dipped her head, mechanically acknowledging the man's instruction.

She wasn't comfortable with the idea of becoming a mother. She even suspected Danny of deliberately forgetting his pill, getting her pregnant to jeapordise her eligibility for the trip, but the Project Salvation directors had assured her a pregnancy was no barrier to being a pioneer. Not any more. The baby would be FED, injected with a

Forced Embryonic Diapause agent, the three-month-old foetus' normal growth resuming when it was deemed safe to do so. There were alternatives, even then. She could terminate the pregnancy, on Mars, if that was what she wanted.

Perhaps she should have told Danny that, used it as lever?

She shook her head. Get thee behind me, Ice Queen.

"Medical officer Stevens is waiting for you aboard the *Magellan*," the steward said, stooping to meet her eyes. "Ms Kitson?"

"Yes, I understand," she said.

"You okay?"

"Yes, I'm just . . ."

"Pre-launch nerves. You'll be fine once you're underway." He squeezed her shoulder. "Just fine."

Karen half-turned and squinted into the darkness. No sign at all of Danny now. She had always prided herself on her independence, but without him by her side she felt small and alone. She recalled her first meeting with him. When a relationship ended one's mind invariably returned to the beginning, as if — blessed with hindsight — one might see the warning signs.

Karen smiled to herself. It had been an inauspicious one.

~

Karen had been smoothing a bead of cream into the back of her neck when some clumsy fool nudged her in the ribs. They were sitting on an uncovered press platform, crowded by dozens of journalists and broiling under a desert sun. Struggling to jostle his notepad from his hip pocket, the idiot jolted her again. She smeared cream on her collar.

She said, "Watch out!"

"Sorry."

He was an unprepossessing sight. A thirty-something with cut-off denims, patchy facial hair and a peeling nose. He offered his hand. "Danny Feinberg, *Cincinnati Chronicler*."

She looked at the hand, then away.

His smile widened at the calculated slight. "What d'you think Doc Dinosaur has planned for us today?"

"Doc Dinosaur?" Karen raised an eyebrow.

"That's what we call him on our paper. Oscar Levine is—"

"Doc Dinosaur. Yes, you said. Very droll."

"I'm sorry, I didn't catch your name."

She pushed her Ray-Bans higher up her nose and smiled.

Undaunted, he squinted at the laminated press pass clipped to her safari jacket. "Karen Kitson, *London eTelegraph*. You've come a long way, Karen."

"I'm hoping it'll be worth it." She gestured with her stylus at the curtained-off dais before them. "Whatever it is, it's not very big, is it?"

"It all looks kinda familiar, actually." Feinberg checked the battery indicator on his notepad and opened a new file.

A man in a Stetson strode onto the stage. The beeps of notepads powering up punctuated a polite round of applause for Dr Oscar Levine, founder and president of Saurbac Technologies. Powerfully built and in his late fifties, he looked comfortable in his trademark check shirt and denim jeans. He held his hands up to acknowledge the applause. "Afternoon, ladies and gentlemen." The thick Texan drawl was unmistakeable. "Glad y'all could make it."

He turned to the dais and nodded to an operative. The curtain fell to reveal a two-metre long marine tank. Sediment stirred as sunlight fell on the blue-green water.

Levine rolled up a sleeve, thrust his hand into the tank and calmly plucked out a 320 million-year-old trilobite. Glistening legs thrashed around a wet, segmented body. "You ever seen one of these before?" he crowed.

A grumble rose from the crowded press platform.

"Goddamit, Doc."

"Who hasn't?"

"Is this your idea of a joke?"

"You've dragged us all the way out here to see one of them dime-a-dozen dickies?"

Levine nodded. "See, that's the trouble. Less than ten years ago this little fella would have been a celebrity. Now?" He gently lowered the trilobite back into the tank and walked away wiping his hands on his shirtfront, leaving a disbelieving gaggle of reporters honking after him.

"What the hell was all that about?"

"He's lost it!"

"Dime-a-dozen dickies, I'm telling ya."

Feinberg laughed. Karen glared at him. "What's so funny?"

"Didn't you see what he just did? That was a perfect re-enactment of when he unveiled the first recovered trilobite back in '38. Only then, of course, we all fell over ourselves to get pictures."

"Meaning?"

Danny shut down the notepad and slid it into a hip pocket. "Meaning, Karen, that the show ain't over yet. Not by a long way."

~

After Levine's presentation, the reporters and photographers had stewed in their self-righteous ire for several minutes before two Saurbac operatives corralled them all into four air-conditioned, balloon-tyred coaches. The vehicles featured cool, orange-tinted glass sides to afford the passengers an all round view while filtering out the hostile glare. Karen removed her Ray-Bans and flicked her fringe off her forehead. Her long hair might be unfashionable, but it covered the unsightly patches on her skin.

She spread her belongings out to discourage anyone from taking the adjacent seat and smoothed more cream into her neck. The tinea, which led to round patches of skin becoming inflamed on her scalp and down the back of her neck, had been driving her to distraction in the unaccustomed heat. Anyone looking would assume her fair skin had not predisposed her to the Utah desert sun, and that's how she wanted it. At least it was cooler on the coach than it had been out there on the press platform.

Damn that mangy dog, she thought for the millionth time. And damn the feature editor that thought readers of the e*Telegraph* would be charmed by a top journalist becoming a veterinary nurse for a week. She had contracted tinea just two days before leaving for this desert assignment.

She dipped a finger in the cream and dabbed a little more on her hairline. She kept the anti-fungal cream in an old moisturiser tub to ward off embarrassing questions. Or rather questions that demanded embarrassing answers.

"Can I have some of your moisturiser?" said a voice from behind her. "For my nose?"

"Mr Feinberg, again." She hesitated, then passed the anti-fungal cream back though the gap in the seats. He scooped a dollop out of the tub and plastered it over his sunburnt nose.

"Thanks, Karen."

She took back the tub and smiled. "You're welcome. By the way, I found these. Are they yours?" She held up two photographs.

Feinberg snatched at them.

"Where did you find them?"

"On the press platform."

"Hell, they must have fell out of my pocket when I was getting my notepad out."

"She's very pretty," Karen said. "Who is she, a niece?"

"My daughter. I'm estranged from her mom, but . . . you know how it is. They moved out to Washington Heights last year." He carefully replaced the photographs in a billfold. His movements were almost tender.

After they had been travelling for twenty minutes, the coaches veered off the road into the open desert, the intelligent suspension and balloon-tyres soaking up the jolts without loss of speed. They were now aligned with a distant mountain range.

"The Uinta mountains," Feinberg said.

"I knew that." She applied stylus to notepad.

"Of course you did."

Her search for 'winter mountains' drew a blank.

"It's spelt u-i-n-t-a."

"Thank you." Karen waited for the telltale creak of leather that told her he'd sat back in his seat, then touched her stylus to the info icon of her notepad. Info on the Uinta mountains scrolled up the screen. She let the statistical data on average rainfalls and highest peaks slide by before pausing at Native American settlements:

The Uinta cave carvings (illus. iii) *are being analysed. The circle seems to have had mystical significance for them. A common artefact is a highly polished stone* (illus. iv) *with a hole bored through the middle. Archaeologists have noted the circular artefacts compare closely with those of primitive tribes in Scandinavia, Southern Europe, East Africa, and Central and South America, despite there being no evidence of contact between the tribes. Theories proposed thus far to explain the significance of these rings include the circle of life and death, the rotation of the seasons, or astronomy.*

She put the notepad on stand-by and sat back to watch the cacti and Joshua trees roll by her tinted window. Her eyelids were heavy. She heard the clink of glass on glass. Voices were becoming raised.

She closed her eyes and pretended to sleep.

The dryness in her scalp was intensifying. She tried ignoring it, but it spread down her shoulders, onto her arms, and even across her belly. She discreetly lifted the seat belt and parted her blouse, wincing at the angry red weal circumscribing her waist. This is how tinea got its common name of ringworm. The fungal patches, if left untreated or aggravated by scratching, expanded into large unsightly rings. The raised skin on her belly felt crisp and paper-thin.

She swallowed her anxiety and reached for the tub of cream. The movement brought a stab of pain. She glanced down and saw a flicker of movement under her skin.

"Oh my God." She twisted in her seat. "Is there a doctor here?"

Faces stared back, blank and uncomprehending, swaying with the rhythm of the coach.

Ignoring the tenet forbidding it, she raked the infection with her nails. The relief was momentary, then blood oozed as papery skin tore. Something slithered, burrowed deeper into her abdomen.

"Please, somebody help me!"

Feinberg appeared soundlessly, kneeling on the seat in front of her, leaning over the backrest to reassure her. He pressed his hands over the wound, closing the two ragged edges together. His presence calmed the hideous slithering sensation inside her. She took a deep breath and—

—awoke with Feinberg's hand on her shoulder. He was standing over her. The rest of the seats were empty. "Are you okay?" His face radiated concern. "You look kinda shaken."

She tugged self-consciously at the hem of her blouse. "Yes. Yes, I'm fine, thank you. I think I . . . I must have fallen asleep."

Feinberg's face creased into that warm smile he seemed able to switch on at a moment's notice. "Well, if you're okay. We're here."

The Uinta mountains appeared as a solid wall a few metres away. A few seconds of ocular adjustment, however, and her perspective shifted to see that their coach was parked about a kilometre from the foothills. She wiped her mouth with the back of her hand, grimacing at the drool in the corner of her lips. "Can you just give me a couple of minutes to get my act together?" she said.

Feinberg was waiting as she stepped down off the coach. "Impressive, huh?"

The mountains were, she had to admit, very impressive.

"I meant that." Feinberg gestured to behind him, where banks of floodlights played over a three-storey-high block constructed of mesh stretched over steel bars. Karen tried to gauge its length and came up with something like a hundred and fifty metres. An electrified fence surrounded it to keep anyone from getting too close.

"That—" She rubbed sleep-crusted eyes and yawned. "That is some holding cage."

Feinberg smiled. "Yeah, biggest I ever saw. Question is: what has old Doc Dinosaur found that he thinks he's gonna need a cage that big? C'mon, we're being left behind."

They followed the crowd towards a marquee, its walls creaking in a welcome breeze. Inside, Saurbac employees were handing out refreshments and information discs. A bank of hologram projectors in one corner were reciting the history of Saurbac and the heroics of its founding father.

"Headache?" Feinberg asked.

Karen nodded miserably.

"You are probably dehydrated," he said, and took two bottles of Perrier from a passing flunkey. "C'mon, let's go find a seat."

The holograms flickered as they walked through them. They showed an old story: Levine had pioneered the technique whereby live prehistoric animals were brought forward through time; none of that foolish DNA business that captured the public imagination at the end of the last century but proved such a commercial dead end. Get your fossil, potassium-argon date it, let the computers take care of the spatial calculations and reach back through time for one very confused, live animal. Vast amounts of power were required, and it took the advent of portable nuclear fusion plants to make it viable. In 2038, Levine had revealed his trilobite to a world agog.

"I was doing some background reading on the plane," Karen said to Feinberg over her Perrier. "And there was something I didn't understand."

"What was that?"

"Radiometric dating . . ." she glanced at him to check she had used the correct terminology. He nodded for her to continue. "Radiometric dating is far from accurate . . . something to do with only dating rocks formed by volcanic action?"

"It doesn't need to be that accurate. You see, what Saurbac do is send a virtual lasso . . ." He broke off to laugh. "Well, Levine *is* a Texan! This lasso follows the track of the fossil until it encounters something living and expands to encompass it, then just hauls it back in. By roughly dating the fossil they save themselves time and power by knowing approximately where to pitch their lasso."

"So it doesn't even matter whether the fossil is organic or inorganic. That was something else that had me baffled," she admitted.

"It helps if you think of the fossil as merely a tracking device. Reports of resurrection are misleading." He looked at the journalists milling around and taking advantage of Saurbac's hospitality. "But you know, if you want to find the interesting stuff, you have to look for what they're not showing you."

Her face must have betrayed her bafflement for his stubbly cheeks wrinkled in a wide grin.

~

The sun was a red molten ball on the horizon. The cage under the floodlights looked even more impressive in the gathering dusk. Karen squinted at the base and saw caterpillar tracks inching the vast construction across the desert plain. She followed the line of travel and realised the cage was being manoeuvred into a position over a narrow man-made shaft, all of it within the boundaries of the electric fence.

Feinberg said, "That's where the fossil is, I'll bet, down there. I saw Levine going down a couple of minutes ago. C'mon, I want to show you something."

She had assumed the moving cage and shaft had been the object of interest, but Feinberg was striding towards the dark foothills of the Uinta. She ran after him.

"Where are we going?"

"I thought you might like to see where the natives used to hang out." Feinberg ducked under a tape barrier and began to descend terraces cut into the desert floor. An archaeological dig. She glanced over her shoulder. No one seemed to be paying them any heed.

She called after him. "But why do you want to show me something? I mean, aren't we competing for the best story here?"

Feinberg knocked dust off his trousers. He looked genuinely puzzled. "D'you think so? I doubt the *Cincinnati Chronicler* and the *London eTelegraph* are competing for the same readers."

"That's true." But when had that ever mattered. Then she remembered him saving her on the bus and—whoa! She checked herself. That had been a dream. Karen rubbed her neck. She needed to wake up.

He was waiting, wary of them being stopped. "What are you thinking?" he called back.

"I'm thinking . . ." I'm thinking that you are a good man, and if you say it's safe down there, it is. I know I can trust you.

"Nothing," she said, and followed him down.

"You'll need this." Feinberg dug into his satchel and passed her a flashlight. He paused at a cleft in the ground. "Levine's men uncovered this last year. It leads to an underground cave system. But when they found wall carvings they had to back off and find themselves another dig. Archaeologists can get very touchy about these things."

Feinberg sat down and swung his legs over the lip. Karen heard loose stones clatter into the blackness. She switched on her flashlight. Feinberg stood on a narrow ledge a metre below. He scrambled down until his head was below ground level. "I covered this for the *Chronicler*. I expected it to be guarded against nosey journalists, but I guess it's not considered important compared to what's going on over there." He extended a hand for her to follow. When she hesitated he said, "Don't worry, I've been down here many times in an official capacity. It's perfectly safe as long as you don't stray down the wrong path. There are drop-offs that could kill you."

"Oh, good. I really needed to hear that." She wriggled her hips through the crevice and dropped onto the ledge.

Bent double, Karen allowed herself to be led through a passageway in the rock. Someone had provided luminous markers at hazards and junctions. She paused at a drop-off to shine her flashlight down a borehole. The powerful beam did not reach the bottom.

Feinberg's voice echoed. "This system was formed by rainwater coming down off the mountains, eroding away the softer stone." He stood his flashlight on its end and adjusted the beam to give a wide spread of light. He gestured with the air of a proprietor. "Here we are."

Karen raked her beam over the floor of a cave. She gauged it to be about five metres by five, walled on three sides with the fourth side falling away into a precipice. She straightened her back and shuffled cautiously to the edge. The cave they were in was a rough cube on the upper arch of an enormous black cavern. The other side of the cavern was too far away for her to see.

Feinberg asked, "What do you make of those?"

She backed away from the drop and followed his pointing finger. Now that her eyes had adjusted she could see the walls were covered in recessed circles. Shadows pooled in their centres. She reached out to touch the nearest one. The diameter was no bigger than the length of her middle finger. A grid of faded red markings filled the centre.

"Rings," she said. "Hundreds of them."

"More like thousands," said Feinberg. "They extend all the way down the passageway." He bent down to wipe sand away from the lip of the drop. "If you look here, you can see notches worn into the rock."

"Water erosion? It must be like a waterfall when it rains heavy. Speaking of which . . ."

"Relax, there's been no water coming down here for millions of years, probably. It would have washed the paint out of those circles."

Karen felt foolish. "So what caused these notches?"

"Ropes. Someone stood here," he moved to the back of the cave where it joined the entrance, spread his feet and braced himself as though he held a rope. "Look, you can see two indentations in the floor where generations of feet have worn it away. And someone climbed down the rope into that drop for . . . well, the archaeologists haven't worked that out yet."

Karen stood as close to the edge as she dared. She looked from left to right, shining her flashlight in each direction. It reminded her of standing on a platform of the London Underground waiting for a tube. Or how a mouse would feel standing on the platform. "You're saying water erosion created this massive cavern? What came through here, the bloody Mississippi?"

Feinberg joined her.

95

Karen said, "This extends quite a way to the left and right before it peters out into rubble." Her flashlight illuminated scree that sloped down from the ceiling into the abyss.

Feinberg said, "The archaeologists have been doing studies of the terrain and found several faults running north to south. But for now, mentally extend the line of the tunnel and tell me what you see. Where does it go?"

"It goes to . . . it goes to where Levine has sunk that new shaft. What are you implying?"

"Let's consider the facts we have: Levine's party discover this ancient drain and investigate the cave system. They see these rope markings and send someone down, yeah? So what did they find down there before the archaeologists came along with their injunctions? What did they find that they had to break into the tunnel system further along and then invite the world's media along for the party?"

"A new species of dinosaur, obviously. But wait a minute. If this place was a natural cistern millions of years ago, the dinosaur would have to be aquatic to survive down there. But what would an aquatic dinosaur be doing out here in the desert? Or was this area under water 200 million years ago? Or perhaps it'd be a small land dinosaur that got washed down and then grew and evolved. Like those old myths about alligators growing huge in New York sewers. But there'd have to be more than one. A family."

Feinberg had already thought it through. "This whole area was under the Niobrara Sea, so an aquatic dino is not too bad a hypothesis. But Levine's brought a cage, not a fish tank. Your other idea, as crazy as it sounds, is probably nearer the truth. That cleft we came down may not have been the only drain. There would be several places where water drained off the plains and mountains into underground caverns, some of them large enough to let animals in and out again. Supposing some came in and liked it down here? With a trickle of water and mould growing on the walls they might have survived the mass extinction 65 million years ago."

Karen shone her flashlight over the walls and the carved rings. "Where do the Uinta fit into this?"

"I doubt the Uinta actually lived down here. I think this place served some specific purpose."

"An observatory? I read the Uinta may have possessed astronomical knowledge."

"An *underground* observatory . . . when they had mountains?" Feinberg's mouth turned down at the corners. "I think it's more likely something to do with religion."

"Sacrifices to a lizard god, then?" Karen's tongue stuck to the roof of her mouth as she spoke. She needed another drink of water. Her head was starting to pound.

Feinberg smiled. "Now you are fantasising. But I am speculating that if dinosaurs survived underground until recently — relatively speaking — then they would have definitely evolved into something new to science." He swept up his flashlight and adjusted the beam. Shadows swung around the cave. "C'mon, we'd better get back before we're missed."

Karen took one last look at the rings stippling the walls, ran a finger over the faded grids in their centres, and followed Feinberg up the passageway.

~

It was fully dark when they surfaced. Nuclear generators throbbed and whole rows of floodlights punched bright spears through the darkness. Viewed from a short distance the marquee and gigantic cage looked like a circus. Karen found herself revising her earlier, rather haughty opinion of Feinberg's "Doc Dinosaur" tag.

When Oscar Levine recovered the first trilobite back in 2038, he became a billionaire overnight. Zoos and parks worldwide, conditioned by a lethargic public, were always clamouring for something new and exotic, and since 2038 new and exotic meant prehistoric. She had read the week before that the San Diego Zoo had flattened their old polar bear exhibit to make way for a stegosaurus compound. A breeding pair of steggies had cost them 210 million dollars.

No doubt about it, Karen thought, Levine recognised the commercial value of showmanship.

She and Feinberg joined their colleagues on a natural platform that afforded them an eye-level view of the cage. The fenced enclosure below was busy with Saurbac employees. Above and behind them were ranks of film crews primed to catch what everybody had been prepped to believe would be the most spectacular scientific event of the decade. Journalists were placing bets on what they were about to see:

"A giant burrowing mammal, that's my guess."

"Nah, it's some sort of insect. No, I've changed my mind, put me down for a flying lizard. Yeah, a flying lizard I'm telling ya."

"I'll go for the insect then, if he doesn't want it. Or a giant tarantula."

Feinberg held up a hand to the bookmaker. "I bet five hundred that it's a family of blind, long-necked herbivores of a kind hitherto unknown to science."

The banter died away as a well-built figure took the floor before the cage. Levine's voice boomed out of loudspeakers. "Ladies and gentlemen, glad y'all could make it. I hope you forgive my little joke this morning, but I assure y'all that what you are about to witness will more than make up for it. A while back we discovered a site, not far from where y'all are sitting, that showed promise. We found an immense shard of bone that tests proved to be part of a rib."

A quiet voice asked if he could change his mind about the insect.

"However, before we could further investigate we were denied access to the site. The archaeologists were quite right to do so," he said magnanimously, "science before commerce has always been my byword, too."

Feinberg whispered in Karen's ear. "Like hell. He fought like crazy to get the injunction quashed. Hey, aren't you going to hazard a guess at what's down there?"

She started guiltily from scratching her neck. Blood glistened on a fingertip. She swore softly. "No, I just want to check something on my notepad."

Feinberg had scotched her supposition that the Uinta had used the cave as an observatory, but she still felt that the Uinta were recording something. She scrolled back up the page and clicked on a link to pictures of the circular stones recovered from the site. The stones, with their hollowed centres, did look remarkably like the wall carvings she'd seen in the cave. There was also a link on the page to other cultures around the world that placed special emphasis on carved rings. Karen speed-read articles and viewed pictures of ancient artefacts. A chill that had nothing to do with the cold desert night passed down her arms.

"Tonight," Levine shouted, "it all comes together. In less than thirty seconds that cage will hold the most astounding sight in ten years. A species of dinosaur that we have yet to set eyes upon! And as you can see, we're expecting something *big*." A glow emanated from the man-made shaft.

Karen said, "Did he say they found bone, or fossil?"

"Bone, I think. Or maybe he meant an organic fossil, rather than a cast or impression. But either way, my bet's looking good."

Karen muttered. "Ouroboros."

Feinberg leaned closer. "A rubber what?"

"Ouroboros, the world serpent, a symbol of death and regeneration in many cultures." She passed her notepad to Feinberg to let him see the images of a serpent devouring its own tail. In many of the pictures it girdled the earth, a distance of over forty thousand kilometres.

Feinberg shook his head. "How did this thing take a crap?"

"Be serious, Danny."

"I can't be serious, Karen. It's just a stupid myth. A snake big enough to encircle the world?"

The lights dimmed unexpectedly. Levine's whisper carried over the loudspeakers. "Who screwed . . . patch in the auxiliaries. As much as it takes, godammit!"

"Danny, how much power do those fusion generators put out?"

"What?" Feinberg had stood to get a better view of the action. "I've no idea: somewhere between a helluva lot and infinite."

"And they are struggling to lasso this creature and bring it back? Is that normal?"

Feinberg sat down. "Are you feeling okay? I guess you aren't used to this heat."

Everyone around them was chanting: THREE! TWO! ONE!

Levine swivelled theatrically and pointed at the illuminated cage. It remained unmistakeably empty. A muffled crump of imploding machinery came from the shaft. After a few seconds a smattering of applause started up. Someone shouted. "Good one, Doc. Even better than this morning."

Kittson sagged. "I don't think Levine realises what he's got down there. I think the Uinta were measuring the contractions and growth of Ouroboros. Levine found part of a rib. Well, that figures. Then there's the perfect symmetry of the cavern walls: that vast tunnel wasn't caused by water erosion. And those fault lines running north to south you mentioned, and the difficulty lassoing him."

"Karen, I don't know—"

"I bet they couldn't date him. How can you date something that was recycled again and again over thousands of years?"

Feinberg eyes searched her face. "You're serious about this, aren't you?"

The heat and dehydration, the pounding headache and the itching ringworm . . . She felt exhausted. She couldn't focus. "I—I don't know, Danny."

The sarcastic applause petered out as the crowd turned to the drain behind them, where a fountain of sand was erupting twenty metres into the air, the hiss of falling sand a counterpoint to the whistle of expelled air. Karen and Feinberg looked at each other, then turned their attention to the ground. A deep rumble tickled the soles of their feet. Cracks appeared, and dust floated up as something ancient and unimaginably massive flexed in the earth's crust.

~

A wet flagstone betrayed him.

It had taken Danny many attempts to find a bar not screening the take-offs, and afterwards, as he staggered home, he had turned his face from every electrical store window and newscast wall. But here, just metres from their apartment — *his* apartment now — he glimpsed what he had been avoiding all night.

The nearest streetlights had failed and he stood in shadow, gazing in puzzlement at three pinpricks of yellow light wobbling in a puddle. The sidewalk was dry, and Danny realised he was looking at reflections in a dog's piss. He chewed on his cheek linings. Of all the rotten tricks! He threw his head back and nailed the night sky with an angry glare.

There they were, the vast starsails of the shuttles, mocking him with their glorious, ethereal precision. Karen leaving. The three-month-old foetus inside her FED prior to take-off.

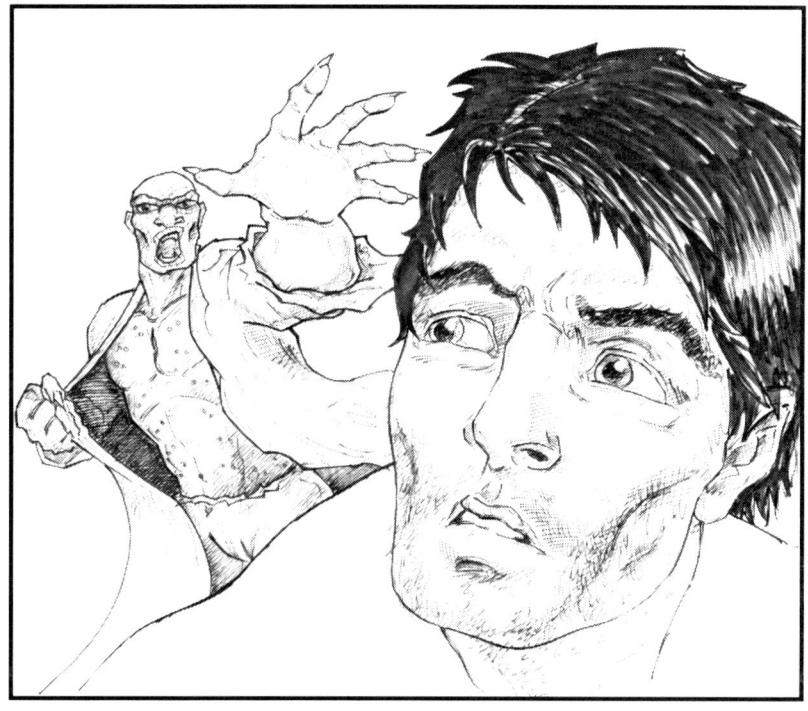

"They are the cursssed!"

Danny jumped. He hadn't noticed the speaker's approach. He looked into a face disfigured with prosthetic scales and wondered whether the man had modified his tongue, too. Many snake cultists did.

"They ssshall fail. Ssso ssspeakss the Ssserpent." The cultist raised a hand, his silken robe falling away to reveal several puncture marks. The more extreme cults offered themselves to snakes. They popped vials of antivenin like Danny popped aspirins.

"Pro- or anti-Sssalvationissst?"

"Neither, but right now I'm *pisssed* so why don't you fuck off." Danny shoved the cultist aside and staggered towards his apartment block.

Karen had become a *cause celebre* for the drive to terraform and colonise Mars. The woman, whose dramatic firsthand account of Levine's folly would forever link her with the Uinta Incident, was seeking salvation on another world. Her communication skills would prove invaluable, and her child would be the first of many on the reborn Mars.

Danny grimaced as he shouldered open the lobby door. The Project Salvation directors had asked him to go (for *his* communication skills presumably). Pleaded, in fact. His stubborn refusal perplexed them. Perplexed Karen. What did he have against Project Salvation?

Apart from luring his lover away and separating him from his teenage daughter? Ha, nothing!

He had written an article for the *Cincinnati Chronicler*, about how mankind should fix its problems before screwing around with other worlds. He had also wondered, in the same article, if there would be a place for the poor and benighted on this glorious new world or just the cream of society (or, as in Karen Kitson's case, people whose inclusion added gloss to the media kit)?

Oh, boy. That was when the arguments really started.

Danny's stomach flipped as the elevator shot upwards. He thought of Karen, strapped into a gel-filled take-off couch, the webbing specially tailored to protect the delicate swelling of her abdomen.

He should have gone. Karen shouldn't be doing this alone. But even as he thought it, the idea of being millions of miles from Tiffany — a daughter he only ever saw once, maybe twice a year — tugged him in the opposite direction. But it was clear now: he should have gone.

He should have gone.

The earth was forever changed: evolving, a scant few said; ruined was how the majority saw it. Much of sub-continental Europe was locked in ice after the Gulf Stream had been switched off by an Atlantic desalinated by a shattered icecap. Central America was a chain of islands. An area in the Yellowstone Caldera had risen three metres in as many years, causing grave concerns over the supervolcano beneath. North Island, New Zealand, was one vast crater after Taupo exploded. Tsunamis, earthquakes: no one knew for sure how many South Sea islands had disappeared.

The human race had become compartmentalised, slowly compressed into smaller and smaller pockets of stable land. Wars broke out as countries rebelled against refugee quotas.

All they could do was wait for Ouroboros to die again, or they could leave Earth.

An attempt to destroy the giant snake with a series of limited nuclear strikes along his length ended in a convulsion that sheared East Africa along the line of the Great Rift Valley to form a new sub-continent. And Ouroboros did not just survive, he healed. Further attempts to destroy him had been iced.

On the landing outside his apartment, his hand raised to the recognition pad, Danny felt a slight tremor through the soles of his feet. He turned, expecting to see the cultist. The landing was deserted. Then he experienced the gentle judder again, and this time he was certain of the direction. Light footsteps were coming from within his apartment. But only two people had access . . . He felt his heart tripping as he spread his right hand and pressed it to the illuminated pad on the doorjamb.

The door field switched off to reveal a room wrapped in darkness. Karen was standing by the window, stargazing. She turned with two mugs of strong, aromatic coffee in her hands. "I thought you might need one to clear your head. That disgusting yeast beer can pack quite a punch."

He took the proffered coffee without a word. So many questions were fighting to escape they formed a logjam in his mouth.

Her voice was a whisper. "I never once stopped loving you, you know?"

Danny nodded. "So, what changed your mind?"

Her smile twisted into something mysterious. "Because of a bad dream I had, a long time ago."

Danny frowned.

"They were just about to inject the embryonic diapause agent when I felt our baby move for the first time. It should have been momentous but instead I felt terrified. This . . . this life stirring inside me. I needed you to be there." She took his hand and placed it on her belly, her eyes turning to gaze out of the window. It seemed to Danny that she was not looking at the street below, but at somewhere else, far, far away.

"You are a good man, Danny. The best. If you say it's safe down here, then I know I can trust you."

Danny wasn't sure he understood, but nevertheless he set his coffee down, wrapped his arms around her waist and held her close. Maybe one day they would both go to Mars. With their baby *and* Tiffany.

Maybe.

For now, the only certainty was that he would not let go of Karen.

Not for a long time.

Speaking in Forked Tongues

Morning sunlight streamed through the kitchen blinds, casting a nimbus around Mrs Nash's frail body. She slid a dinner plate into the sink and began scrubbing. She said, "You're up late this morning. Did you oversleep?"

Jacob Cleeves rubbed his jaw. "Late night. I thought I might take the day off."

"Oh?" Her scrubbing missed a beat. "I hope Mr Halpin isn't working you too hard."

"No, Mr Halpin is a very generous employer."

"Really? I've heard he can be as tight as a duck's arse."

" Not with me he isn't."

She tossed a takeaway carton over her shoulder. It entered the waste bin without touching the sides.

"Nice one, Mrs Nash."

"Easy-peasy, Mr Cleeves. You take a day off. A young man shouldn't spend too much time working. He needs his energy for the bedroom."

Jacob swallowed hard.

"Dear, dear. You young ones think you have a monopoly on the old rumpy-pumpy." Mrs Nash turned her head sharply, her dentures distending her bottom lip. "But it's we oldies that invented it. Why, only last week Mr Nash and I tried doing it . . ."

Jacob downed the coffee in four gulps, said his byes, snatched up his jacket from the back of a chair and ran out of the front door. He shuddered as Mrs Nash shouted something about needing a neck brace for three days afterwards.

He slid a hand into an empty pocket— "Damn and blast!" —spun on his heels and barged into the old woman.

"Silly boy, you forgot these." Mrs Nash handed him a set of car keys. Cloud shadows crossed her cornflower-blue eyes. "Joking aside, Jacob, things are afoot. Be on your guard."

"Have you been reading . . .?"

"What?"

"Nothing. Doesn't matter."

Gravel crunched beneath his expensive leather soles as he wandered over to his car. He paused in the act of spinning the keys around his index finger. Mrs Nash had not only pre-empted him with the keys, but had managed to dry her hands and remove her apron too. He glanced back over his shoulder, but she was gone.

He climbed into his car a troubled man.

~

Mrs Nash watched Jacob leave through the dimpled door window. She grinned, hitched her skirts and took the stairs three at a time.

Jacob's bedroom had an unmistakeably masculine smell to it. Of stale breath and lingering curry farts. She pointed a finger and a casement swung open. A stiff breeze billowed the curtains.

Mrs Nash touched her ear and linen sheets flew off the bed, snapped, folded and tucked their edges under the mattress. Pillows plumped, rotated and settled. She made a circle with her left thumb and a feather duster began to flick over the windowsills.

"Easy-peasy."

She sat at Jacob's desk and gave it a commanding glare. The solid wood shimmered and became insubstantial. Settling into a chair, she plucked Jacob's not-as-secret-as-he-liked-to-think journal from a locked drawer and began to read.

I thought I was awake, and sitting up in bed. Something moved in the darkness, something white. I thought I was seeing a ghost, but then this angel stepped forward. He has the silk gown and feathery wings, a golden halo, the lot. He really is the most striking bloke I have ever seen. He has this pale oval face and startling silver eyes. It's strange, but when he speaks, his lips aren't in synch with the words. It's like watching a dubbed foreign film. He said that this is because he is speaking in tongues and has to be translated for me. Whatever, it's surreal. He said his name's Lucidus. I asked him if he really was an angel but he just smiled, said I must trust him, and disappeared!! I woke up for proper then, sweaty and scared. The weird thing was, I'd swear I could still smell him. I think it's lilies.

Mrs Nash snorted. That had been just the first visit of many from Lucidus.

Lucidus told me last night that he had visited this realm once before. The Lord had given him a flaming sword and a divine edict to stop the terrible carnage that was taking place here on Earth. He manifested at the appointed hour above an immense, crater-pocked field of mud where men were facing each other in combat. He had been told to wave the sword about and make it obvious to the soldiers below that God was angry that they should be taking lives, that He was the One to judge. Each group of soldiers misunderstood Lucidus — they thought he was on their side — and set about each other with even more venom. Lucidus railed at them, threatened to bring down heavenly retribution, but the soldiers just cheered and fought all the harder.

I told Lucidus that it sounded like the Battle of Mons in WWI, where legend has it an angel appeared in the sky to give heart to the British troops as they faced the Germans. He shook his head and said it had all gone horribly wrong. When I said that I thought I was only dreaming this, dredging stuff up from my subconscious, he just asked that I trust him and slowly faded away.

"Lord, what fools these mortals be!" Mrs Nash turned a page.

God was terribly cross with Lucidus. Lucidus told Him and the Archangels that it was hardly his fault that the stupid mortals had not taken the hint. But God laid all the blame on Lucidus. It still upsets him even now, his eyes were filling up as he was telling me and he blew his nose on his gown. The worst part is that he lost his job in the Administration Dept (that translates badly, I think), which is a good gig in the Kingdom of Heaven by all accounts. He is now at the bottom of the career ladder.

I asked him if he would be coming again, because I always felt confused when I woke up. I'm still unsure if these are dreams or not. He said that he was sorry about that, but I had to trust him.

Mrs Nash came to the entry Jacob had penned the previous night.

I awoke in a terrible state again tonight. As usual, I'm writing this as soon as possible so that I can be as accurate as I can. Like before, I 'wake up', sit up, and Lucidus walks to my bedside and sits down. I even feel the bedsprings settle slightly under his weight, the dream is that realistic — if they are dreams. There was some preliminary chat (which I forget now), but he eventually got round to telling me how I could help him. At first I felt really chuffed that he thought I could be of assistance, but when I realised what it entailed, I was less keen.

Basically, Lucidus reckons that he could get me into the Kingdom as a personnel manager. Lucidus tells me this is a very good posting and about as high as a new soul can expect to go. Once there, I could get Lucidus his old job back.

He was really excited about the proposition. But I'm in no rush to see the afterlife. Who is? He accused me of not looking at the bigger picture, then faded away. I expect him back tomorrow. What do I say? The rational part of me knows Lucidus is only a dream, but even so, I am afraid.

Mrs Nash snapped the journal closed and sucked on her dentures. In the same drawer as the journal was a envelope of photographs. She'd seen the pictures enough times already. Or perhaps not. She picked them up again and flicked through them, clicking her tongue. Jacob was such a bad boy.

~

Leaving the staff carpark Jacob strolled towards the hardware shop where he worked as floor manager. As he passed the windows he saw Martin the new boy wrestling with a display of garden forks. *Wotcha mate*, Martin mouthed. He made a chopping gesture across his neck.

Jacob shrugged: *Wanna bet?*

Above the door was a sign proclaiming that he was entering Halpin Hands hardware store. The pun set Jacob's teeth on edge. He wondered if the sign writer had been tempted to add [sic] after Halpin.

A bell dinged as Jacob put his shoulder to the heavy shop door. Claire in gas bottles and paraffin heaters looked up and then quickly away. Roseanne gathered an armful of candles and disappeared into a storeroom. Then Jacob saw Halpin coming down the stairs and relaxed. Halpin would be a fool to cross him.

"Aah, good morning, Mr Cleeves. So good of you to join us." Halpin made a show of looking at his watch. "And to what do we owe the pleasure, hmm?"

Jacob could think of no suitable answer to such an asinine question and so settled for a blank expression. It wasn't difficult in the circumstances.

"Listen here, Cleeves, you are not going to keep sauntering in here as and when it suits you." Halpin leaned in closer; close enough for Jacob to detect the other man had eaten eggs for breakfast. "You are making this impossible!" His voice dropped to a whisper. "It's bad enough that you're holding me to ransom without undermining my standing with the rest of the staff."

Through this one-sided exchange Jacob stared at Halpin's handlebar moustache and the bad acne scarring it was meant to hide. "Finished?" he asked.

Halpin bristled.

"Because of that little tantrum," said Jacob, "I'm knocking a day off. You have only until Friday now." He gazed nonchalantly into Halpin's eyes and gave a knowing wink. "Now, piss off."

Halpin hissed like a burst tyre.

"See you later," murmured Jacob, and strolled away in the direction of the washroom.

Cool, calm and collected.

Inside the washroom Jacob splashed cold water on his face. Damn Halpin. Why couldn't he just acquiesce to Jacob's demands and let them go their separate ways? Surely he realised he couldn't possibly win? Jacob stared at his reflection in the mirror and sighed. Two more days. Two more days of this unbearable tension.

A door swung open behind him. He spun to face it. "Oh. Hi Martin."

"What the hell did you say to Halps? He's going apeshit!" Martin's face shone with admiration. Jacob wondered if he would be so impressed if he knew how he got away with taking such liberties with their employer.

~

Michael Halpin sat behind his desk, staring at the phone and systematically snapping pencils, imagining them to be Jacob Cleeves' neck. He lifted the receiver off its cradle and punched in a number. It was only three digits and the number six figured predominately.

The answer was instantaneous. A sibilant masculine voice: "Customer Liaisons. Who is this?"

"Um." The abruptness always caught him off guard. "It's Halpin. Michael Halpin."

"Your account number?"

Michael gave his number. He could hear keys being tapped as he spoke, accompanied by an unpleasant scratchy sound as though the typist had exceptionally long nails. He started as an ear-splitting shriek emitted from the receiver. It seemed to go on for a long time before being cut off as abruptly as it started.

"Sorry about that. A new arrival. They always act so *surprised.* Now, Mr Halpin, how can I help you?"

"It's Cleeves. I thought you'd have sorted him out by now, this has been dragging on forever."

The line went silent but for the mournful howling of a distant wind blowing through the wires.

"There was no need for that," the voice ground out finally. "May I remind you that we don't use the f-word here."

"I never said fuh—oh, you mean, *forever.*"

"You mortals don't know the meaning of the word. I can illustrate it for you, if you like?"

"No, no, it's okay, thank you. It's just that Cleeves is threatening to deliver those damned photographs to my wife this weekend! I paid him once but he still won't hand them over, the bastard."

"Mr Halpin, as it would no doubt have been explained to you when the contract was drawn up, we have to get Jacob Cleeves' trust. That is the Protocol. Trust is the keystone of our business. Where would we be without trust?"

"Yes, yes, I know all about that, but—"

"But me no buts, Mr Halpin. Our field operative's most recent report suggests that the matter is ready to be brought to a close. He believes that he will get Cleeves' consent this very night as long as there is no interference from the *other* side."

"Tonight?" Michael Halpin let out a breath. "My, that is good news."

The voice sounded mollified. "We run a tight operation here, and don't you forget it."

~

Jacob thumped his pillow, a terrible restlessness building up inside as though his body was a vast pressure cooker. He swung his legs over the side of the bed and paced across to the window to let in some fresh air. Clouds brightened as they raced the moon. Streetlights cast pools of sallow light on the road. A drunkard weaved down the pavement with a traffic cone on his head. A normal suburban scene, a normal night.

Welcoming a yawn, Jacob let the curtains fall back across the window and returned to his bed.

An hour later found him squirming in the darkness, the sheets wrapped around his legs. The room was warm and stuffy despite the open window and he couldn't stop his mind from working overtime. The pillow felt lumpy under his head.

Eventually he must have fallen asleep.

There was a silent rush of air that made his ears pop. Trembling, he stared hard at the corner of the room and watched as a million points of light swirled and coalesced into the familiar figure of Lucidus, a white toga doing little to conceal his hard muscular body. He approached Jacob like a panther stalking its prey: slow, stealthy, feline. The angel radiated light as though he basked in golden evening sun.

"Good evening, Jacob," Lucidus purred, easing himself on to the bed. "Have you given any thought to my proposal?"

Had he given it any thought? It wasn't everyday an angel wished to claim his mortal soul to further his own career. And stated as baldly as that, it wasn't the most attractive of propositions.

"I have thought about it Lucidus, but—"

"You're not going to help me?"

Jacob flinched. "I want to, but—"

"Shut it, you snivelling little turd." Lucidus' eyes flashed silver in the darkness. He twisted his body and forcibly straddled Jacob. "You know something? I'm tempted to screw the Protocol and just take your soul anyway."

"Except you cannot ignore the Protocol, Lucidus. Can you?"

Lucidus' head swivelled at the sound of the new voice and then back at Jacob.

"Who's this old bitch?"

"It sounds like Mrs Nash, my cleaning lady." Feeling that this was somehow an inadequate explanation, Jacob added, "She's very thorough and only charges seven pound an hour."

The angel eased off Jacob's chest and stared hard at the frail old woman in the doorway. "What do you know about the Protocol, hag?"

"The Protocol means you cannot take a mortal's soul without his compliance. You don't trust Lucidus, do you, Jacob?"

Jacob couldn't answer, an icy cold band of fear was restricting his lungs.

Without moving from Jacob's chest. Lucidus lashed out, his arm stretching like warm plasticine. Mrs Nash was backhanded off her feet, the force of the blow knocking her flying through the open door.

Lucidus turned back to Jacob and licked his lips. With a growing sense of unreality Jacob saw the tip of the angel's tongue had a cleft, and that there were altogether too many teeth between those cruel, cherry-red lips. Something warm and heavy pressed on Jacob's chest. His eyes crossed as he struggled to focus on the object. Now *that* definitely hadn't been there before.

Lucidus traced a line over Jacob's throat with a beetle's carapace fingernail. "Where were we?"

Mrs Nash staggered back into the room. "Thou art a foul demon of the pit. I say to thee, Begone!"

"My, is she for real?" Lucidus rolled his eyes. "You don't know when to give up, do you?"

Mrs Nash stood her ground and matched Lucidus' stare. "I'm taking back what doesn't belong to you, Lucidus."

The angel dimmed, as though a cloud had passed over the sun illuminating him. Before, he had looked glorious; now, he looked like a tawdry Christmas tree fairy. "Hey, what the fuck's going on?"

Mrs Nash began to glow. Her wrinkles coursed with photons. Light coalesced in the air around her frail body, and then poured into the corners of her eyes, her mouth and her ears; into the neckline of her cardigan, the cuffs and buttonholes. The light fed her like sherry feeding a dry fruitcake. She began to fill out . . .

"Oh, shit!" Lucidus crawled off the bed and backed away.

Mrs Nash's grey hair receded into an expanding scalp and flaxen tresses issued forth. Her clothes seared on her body and fell as ashes to the bedroom carpet. She shrugged her shoulders in an elaborate reverse orbit. Silver-scaled wings swept the air behind her.

Mrs Nash made an imposing sight as a seven-foot tall angel. She put a finger to an eye and removed a small cornflower-blue contact lens, and then, just as carefully, removed the other. Blinking silver eyes, she placed the lenses on her tongue and swallowed.

Lightning-quick she lashed out and grabbed Lucidus by the throat. Vertebrae crunched and the false angel gargled an oath. He raked her face and light sprayed from four parallel wounds before they sealed. The colossus smiled grimly. A glowing pit of coals opened at Mrs Nash's feet. "Goodbye," she said, and broke Lucidus' back across an immense knee before casting him into the abyss. The hole closed with a whoosh, leaving no trace of its existence but for the faint stench of sulphur lingering in the air.

"Easy peasy." She — Jacob decided to stick with the feminine pronoun despite the bodybuilder muscles — turned slowly and fixed him with a stare. "Do you know why he was after your soul?"

Jacob shivered and cupped his fear-shrivelled genitals.

"Because of these." Mrs Nash plucked a packet of photos from within the desk as though the solid wood was fog. "When you stoop to blackmail, you send out ripples, tremors like a fly in a spider's web. Lucidus was sent to enrol you in Hell's nefarious army."

Jacob wiped away tears. "I didn't know. I thought he was an angel. He told me he was the Angel of Mons, that he had been discredited in Heaven. He lied to me!"

"That is the Lord he serves, Jacob. Just as it is the Lord of Lies you serve when you blackmail people with photographs like these."

Jacob took the proffered photographs. They were of Michael Halpin cavorting with a bondage queen. Screaming erections, studs, leathers, whips and chains featured rather heavily. All arranged and secretly photographed by Jacob. If Halpin didn't dance to his tune, the photographs would go to Mrs Halpin, or be posted on the staff notice board, the Internet or sent to the local newspaper. Whatever it took to get Halpin to part with his cash.

"Halpin paid up the first time, but this time he's being stubborn. Um." Jacob mentally replayed his outburst and realised it lacked for repentance. "I meant I won't do anything like this again." He whimpered like a smacked child and added, "I promise."

Mrs Nash took back the pictures. They glowed briefly before igniting in her palm. She dusted her hands, spilling white ash to the floor.

"I shall wake up in a minute. This is a stupid nightmare."

The angel stood, resolute and immovable. "Then wake up, Jacob."

He screwed shut his eyes and told himself to *Wakeupwakeupwakeup.* When he opened his eyes the angel was staring at him implacably.

"You are on the far shores of dream, beyond any state of sleep or wakefulness. Lucidus brought you here to try and tempt you from your own, more familiar realm."

Jacob smelled smoke. He peeked around the huge body of the Mrs Nash to see yellow wisps curling up from the bedroom carpet. As he watched, a circle of glowing coals widened and burned brighter. A black-clawed hand rose and clamped over the lip of the pit with a muffled thump. Another followed it. *Thwack!*

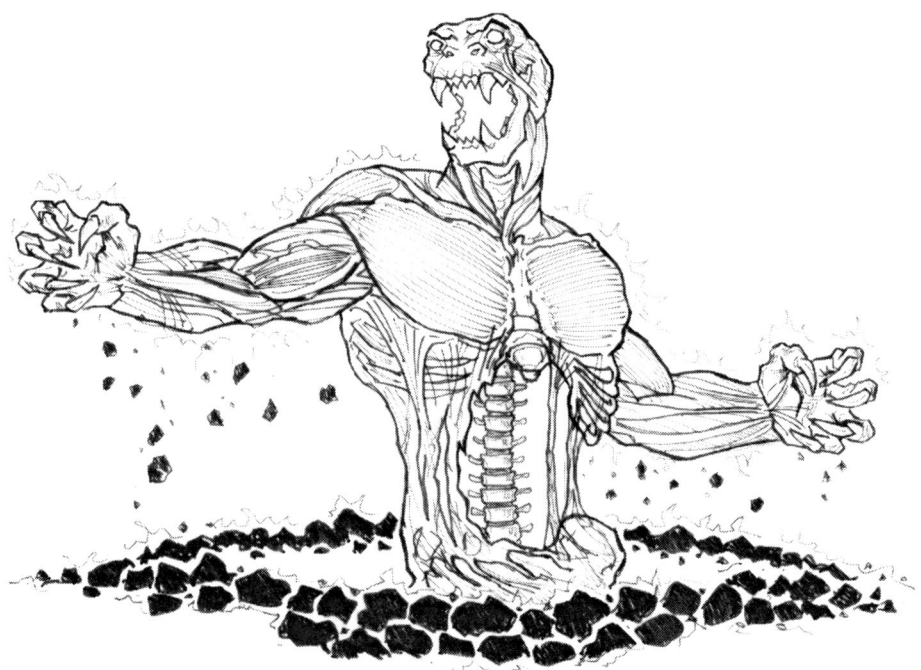

The minion of Hell hauled himself over the lip of the hole. He was halfway to showing his true form. He twisted his head and horrendous grinding noises sounded from tortured vertebrae. His mouth yawned and his lips peeled back to reveal bare jawbones. Writhing ropes of dark pink flesh spewed wetly from his open mouth, anchored themselves to his face, remoulded cheeks and remodelled his brow.

Sinew advanced down his neck and shoulders, building, bonding and reinforcing his slender frame. Jacob winced as bones broke and splintered.

The creature's skull cracked like an egg, and Jacob experienced an unpleasant loosening in his bowels as twisted scimitar horns emerged from Lucidus' head. They gouged lumps out of the frescoed ceiling.

Muscle and skin continued to flow from his maw, criss-crossing his body, giving it immensity and strength. The dark viscera flowed, blackened and solidified.

Lucidus snarled. Fire dripped from his extremities. Small tongues of straw-yellow flame danced over his black-tar hide.

Jacob screamed to Mrs Nash. "Do something about it! Quick,"

"He may be too powerful for me in this form, Jacob. We must take our leave. Please, take my hand."

Jacob placed a hand in a cold white palm. He could see Lucidus approaching on his deformed hind legs, his leather wings flapping spasmodically.

Mrs Nash said, "Jacob, I can't . . ." A hint of worry had crept into her authoritative voice.

"What?"

"You don't trust me!"

"What the hell are you on about? Of course I trust you!"

"Do you?"

Jacob looked beyond Mrs Nash's anxious visage to see Lucidus almost upon them, with a gin trap talon pulled back, ready to decapitate Mrs Nash. "I trust you, all right? I BLOODY TRUST YOU!"

Silence.

Complete and utter darkness.

Then Mrs Nash's voice: "This was all an illusion. I'm just about to put everything back. You may experience a brief moment of nausea."

Reality slurped him up through a bendy straw and belched.

Jacob looked down to see a vast scaly talon dwarfing his hand. His gaze followed a black, pitted arm up into the grinning face of a demon. It shrugged, almost apologetically. "Easy-peasy," it said,

Behind it, lowering his arm as though he had been about to lop the monster's head off was a man with a familiar pockmarked face. The moustache curled up as he smiled.

Jacob's mind meshed mental gears. So Mrs Nash was not a guardian angel, but a demon? And Lucidus had been . . .

"Mike?"

"Hello Jacob," said Michael Halpin. "Surprised?"

~

A snake of blue light writhed in the demon's scaly palm. Michael Halpin peered closely and then drew back. "Is that his you-know-what?"

"His soul? Yes, it is." There was no trace of Mrs Nash's wavering voice, or the angel's dulcet tones. Its voice was now akin to someone gargling with gravel. It tipped its head back and popped the soul into its red maw. It saw Michael's sickly expression. "Just for safekeeping," it said. The red glow in one lidless eye dimmed momentarily in what Michael took to be an approximation of a wink.

Michael nudged Jacob's dead body with the tip of a toe, gingerly, as though he expected it to bite. "It all seems so final."

"Nothing is ever final. There is always a 'next'. When I return to Hell, Jacob Cleeves' soul will enter the Furnace. How long he spends in there is up to him. He could be out in no time at all if he behaves badly. An enterprising young man like him could find himself racing up the career ladder in no time at all."

Michael had a grotesque thought. "So if I was to come to, um—"

"Hell," supplied the demon helpfully.

"Jacob would outrank me, be my superior?"

"That is correct."

"But that's monstrous!"

"That's Hell for you. What did you expect? Despite what you may have heard, Hell is not being locked in a room with your friends. We may use subtle means to get you, but once we have you we prefer a more direct approach. Anyway, time for you to go home to Mrs Halpin. See you *again*, sometime."

Michael was too giddy on adrenalin to register the demon's parting shot. "Just running Halpin Hands will seem quite boring after all this nightly excitement." He noticed Jacob's bedroom becoming indistinct. "I made a good Lucidus, didn't I? I was such a damned good looking angel, too. And playing him as a demon was even more fun. I don't know how you can walk on those hooves, though, I nearly broke my ankle."

There was what might have been an amused hiss.

Michael was hitting his stride. "But for future reference — and I hope you don't mind me saying this — I had a job keeping my face straight with all that, 'Thou art a foul demon' shit. It sounded so passé." He felt a blast of hot breath on his neck. "But that business with the contact lenses on the tongue, that was pure class!"

The Bridge

Manley's boots leave tracks in the frozen snow. *Skrunch*! *Skrunch*! *Skrunch*! It's the same sound chewing dry toast makes in his head.

His breath steams in the pre-dawn darkness as he skips over the shiny cobbles approaching the canal bridge. Ma told him that if it's really cold you can sometimes hear your breath tinkle as it freezes. But not this morning: the slight breeze ruffling the rabbit-fur trim on his collar puts paid to that. He fancies, though, that he catches the occasional glitter of ice in the steam.

He dashes to the stone edifice rising from the mist, a smattering of virgin snow mottling the humped belt of cobbles. But the snow is not virgin, for a single set of footprints have compressed it into ice. They shine silver in the moonlight. Not silver like poets call the stars, because Manley knows the stars are really fire, but silver like the paper around a tube of Polo mints. *Real* silver.

A breath of wind stirs the mist. A shooting star races across the heavens.

He's never seen one before, but Manley knows he is allowed to make a wish now and that it will come true. He wishes he could capture this moment: the air that feels as though it's about to snap like spun sugar, and the scrunch of snow beneath his boots; the glittery steam that probably tinkles, and this single set of silver footprints. Wishes it would last forever.

Manley falls into step, deliberately treading in the shiny tracks. He has to put his feet down flat to avoid skidding on his arse.

Arse is Manley's favourite word as of yesterday. He was making snow angels — lying down in the powdery snow and moving his arms up and down to leave man-shaped impressions with wings — when his dad nudged him with his foot.

"What are thee doin', kiddo?"

"It's a snow angel, Dad. He's goin' to take care o' me."

"Oh aye? Well, you'll need summan to take care o' thee if thee don't get thee up off thy daft arse and 'elp me t' muck cows out."

"Arse," says Manley as he stamps along in the footprints.

He cocks his head. The tracks have petered out, just here, where the snow on the parapet is scuffed. Manley peers over the edge.

"Hello?" The mist over the frozen water swallows his voice. He scans the canal banks where frosted reeds cast blue-white shadows. No sign of disturbance there.

Manley rests his thighs on the stones and wriggles forward. "Hellooo!"

His body seesaws. Vertigo takes a hold, squeezing his chest. He scrabbles, then topples.

The descent is swift.

The mist parts to reveal hard lumpy ice. Manley sees something man-shaped impressed on the thin covering of snow. Man-shaped, but different — arms spread like wings as if to catch him. He braces himself for the impact—

—Manley skips over the shiny cobbles approaching the canal bridge. *Skrunch*! *Skrunch*! *Skrunch*! It's the same sound chewing dry toast makes in his head.

The *Vendetta*

Mycaelis L'Angelo planed the new wheelhouse door, his long smooth strokes producing curls of aromatic white pine. The boat deck rose and fell beneath his bare feet as salty tongues lapped the hull.

He paused in his unhurried labour to sniff the air. When he had been cast out and fallen to the place that would become the Felice Marina, Mycaelis could fill his lungs with the peppery scent of human bodies scrubbed clean with fine sand and olive oil, the acrid smell of animal fat burning on torches, and the pungent scent of resin from the cedars that fringed the hillsides.

He opened and closed the door experimentally.

Now the air hummed with the stink of pizza, toilet disinfectant and diesel. Mycaelis would not understand how this was progress if he lived till Doomsday — or beyond, if repatriation did not come on the Final Day.

He turned at the sound of sandalled feet clopping on warped planks. A family of bored-looking tourists traipsed the jetty: a man, a woman and a young boy. They had that air of listless torpor common to many of those who wound up at the Felice Marina.

Mycaelis unhitched the handrail at the stern, then laid out a boarding plank to make it clear he was open for business. He caught the young boy's eye and winked.

The boy squinted, lifted one hand to shield his eyes against the sun's glare bouncing off the turquoise water. Mycaelis smiled and raised his cap in greeting, his white curls falling to his shoulders.

The boy turned and tugged on his mother's strapless top. She patted his hand away to adjust her clothing, so he cajoled his perspiring father instead.

"I'm telling you, Dad, I saw his eyes shine. They're proper silver!"

"For God's sake, Tony," Mother said. "He'll hear you. Put a lid on it."

English. Not Mycaelis' favourite language, albeit one he knew well. But then Mycaelis understood every language uttered by a mortal tongue.

Father's head came up to regard Mycaelis, vaguely curious and irritated by his son's insistent demands. He tousled the boy's head. "I think you're imagining things, Tony. The sun has addled your brain."

Mycaelis called out, "A warm sticky day, is it not? Much cooler on the water. There's a refreshing sea breeze out there, beyond the headland."

Mother smiled, that brief stretching of the lips and cursory nod the English excel at when they are being polite but not particularly friendly.

The boy said, "Come on, let's go for a ride! Can we?"

"Ask your father," Mother said.

"Can we, Dad?"

"Well, I don't know, it's up to your mother," said Father.

"I have a well-stocked cooler." Mycaelis pointed to a chest in the shade of the wheelhouse. "The first drink is included in the price."

Father licked his lips.

Mother pointed at Mycaelis' hand-painted sign on the jetty. "How long do we get for our euros, and is there a discount for children?"

"Two hours, and your delightful boy sails free of charge. He can earn his keep as my crew."

"It's a deal," Father said.

Mycaelis L'Angelo stepped aside. "All aboard the *Vendetta*!"

~

The mainland was a distant, grey smudge framed by the vee of the boat's wake. Gulls kee-hawed, the engine chugged its hypnotic mantra and the sun blessed the passengers from the blue vault of Heaven.

"For the last time, Tony," Father hissed, "they are not silver. They are just a very light grey."

Mycaelis cut the engine and let the boat drift. Out here, away from the marina, the air was salty clean and the water was unmarred by rainbow slicks of diesel. White horses, their manes festooned with diamonds, cantered on the blue-green waves.

He cleared his throat to catch the attention of his three passengers. "Anyone care for a drink?"

They crowded around the cooler. He had all their favourites. Gordons and Schweppes for Mother, Southern Comfort for Father and Pepsi Max for Tony.

"Anyone want ice with their drinks?" Mycaelis asked.

"No thank you, Cap'n, this G&T is plenty cold enough," said Mother, her icy reserve showing signs of thawing.

"Ditto," said Father, moving away to take a position at the prow. He placed a knotted handkerchief on his head to show he was a fun-loving sort of guy and not above making a fool of himself.

Mother laughed. "Oh, the English abroad."

Mycaelis quietly agreed. "How about you, crewman?" he said to Tony. "Ice or a bendy straw, perhaps?"

"No, thank you." The boy straightened his back. "Any duties, Captain L'Angelo?"

Mycaelis rubbed his chin. "As a matter of fact, there is one duty more pressing than any other. One that only you can perform for me."

A light came in Tony's eyes. "Wow! What's that, Captain?"

"Would you know what I meant if I said we could throw Frisbees?"

"Sure, everyone knows what Frisbees are." Tony gave the length of the boat a calculating look. "But where?"

Mycaelis opened the cooler and slid aside a frosted door to reveal a freezer compartment. "Can you reach those?"

"Sure." Tony set down his Pepsi and pulled out several discs of translucent blue-white ice. He held one up to catch the sun's rays. The disc had a five-pointed star etched into its surface. "Ice Frisbees. Wow!"

"*Disposable* ice Frisbees." Mycaelis pointed over the railings. "Go on, throw it."

The boy carefully drew back the disc, keeping his forefinger along the leading edge to steady it, then launched it. The Frisbee skimmed the wave tops before settling on the surface where it undulated with the sea's swell, a shimmering, translucent spot.

"Aren't you having a go, Captain?"

Mycaelis folded his arms across his chest. There were some things that an angel — even a fallen one — couldn't touch, and a pentagram was one such thing.

He watched as the boy spun several Frisbees out onto the sea. Some broke, but most remained intact.

Mother and Father sauntered over.

"Strange pattern," Father said, tracing the etchings on the discs.

"May I have a go?" Mother asked Mycaelis.

"Be my guest. You too, sir. Help yourself."

The family flipped Frisbees, whooping and hollering, until the sea to starboard was decorated with blue-white dots.

When the freezer compartment was empty, Mycaelis said it was time to be getting back, and entered the wheelhouse. "Help yourself to top-ups," he called over his shoulder.

"Why, that's very decent of you, Cap'n," said Mother.

"Ditto," agreed Father.

Mycaelis pushed the starter button and the engine burst into life.

For many years, misguided souls versed in the arcane arts had used blood, saliva and other more unsavoury bodily fluids in their rites. But humans carried the sea in their veins. Their bodies had been fashioned from it. For a successful summoning one needed only seawater, pentagrams and words. As he turned the boat for the near-distant marina, Mycaelis muttered an ancient spell of summoning few humans understood.

Dark clouds snuffed the sun. The temperature dropped with alarming swiftness.

Mother gave a startled cry as a noisy spume of water erupted to starboard, followed by several founts fore and aft. Sulphuric steam wafted over the deck as malformed creatures spawned on the delicate pentagrams before tipping into the sea. Demons thrashed in shock as the cold water leeched hellish heat from their red scaly bodies. Gargled curses turned the air blue.

Mycaelis L'Angelo regarded their deaths impassively. It was a dirty trick, but this was war.

Mycaelis looked upwards. He didn't expect an acknowledgment from on high, but he knew the Supreme Commander would be pleased. One day, He might even take Mycaelis back.

Within seconds, it was over. The sun punched holes through the clouds and combed the sea with radial spokes of light as a sudden wind whipped away the spindrift. Flocks of marauding gulls descended to pick over the debris.

"What the—" Father nearly dropped his tumbler. He shouted to his wife: "Did you see that?"

Mother turned to Mycaelis. "What on earth was it?" she said, her lips trembling.

"Red snappers."

"I beg your pardon?"

"A shoal of fish."

"Fish?"

"Of course. The ice sometimes draws them to the surface. Why, what did you think they were?"

Mother turned back to her husband, who was nodding slowly. "Fish," they said in unison.

"Of course."

"Ditto."

Their shoulders sagged. Linking arms, they took sips from their glasses.

Mycaelis returned to the wheelhouse, followed by Tony.

"My parents are stupid," the boy declared.

"Folks see only what they want to see."

They stood in silence for a while, before Mycaelis glanced down and said, "I'm sure your mother has taught you that it's rude to stare."

Tony shrugged. "I was just looking at your eyes. They are not light grey, they're silver."

"Aye, that they are, crewman, that they are. But let it be our little secret." Mycaelis winked, and Tony winked back.

Japanese Motorcycle Clob

I scrambled along the highest branch that would bear my weight and gazed down on the heavenly body of Catherine Hewson. Sunlight splintered on the stream, lending a pleasant gauzy quality to the vision. Her auburn hair glowed as if she wore a halo. She lifted the hem of her cotton dress and waded out into the current, the water chuckling as it caressed her knees.

Plucking an acorn, I let it plop into the current. And then another. *Plop*! Soon, a flotilla of nuts bobbed around her thighs. She shielded her eyes and glanced up.

"Leonard, what are you doing up there?"

"Just climbing."

She graced me with a glorious smile before going back to her contemplation of river life.

Courting Catherine had knocked ten years off me. I was like a teenager again. Today, on our country walk, as well as climbing trees I had taken great delight in skimming flat stones across a crystal clear lake, dammed a narrow brook with clods of earth before tearing it down, gathered pine cones for a fire and whittled our names on a fallen tree. Moreover, I performed these acts without a trace of self-consciousness.

A tiny red pig with horns and a pointy tail strutted along the branch above my head and squatted so his eyes were level with mine. He gazed down on my beloved and licked his snout.

"Wow, Lenny. You're one lucky guy."

"You don't have to tell me that, Clob."

"So why haven't you pair got round to doing the horizontal jig-a-jig yet? You're 26 and still a virgin living at home with his mum and dad. Some folks might say that's a bit peculiar."

My sub-vocalising went up an octave. "I'll have you know that this relationship is founded on companionship, mutual respect and friendship and . . . and mutual respect."

"That's all right then. Very important things, those." He held up a trotter. "Seriously, I'm agreeing with you. Especially mutual respect."

I had been fourteen years of age when Clob came into my life. My mum took me to see a child psychiatrist named Dr. Wilson, who simplified the thoughts of Sigmund Freud as thus:

"Old Siggy believed that the psychic structure comprised the super-ego, the ego and the id. The super-ego is your conscience: all those values that you inherit from society and your parents. The id is your basic drives, your instincts for hunger, desire, revenge, pleasure, et cetera. And finally, we have your ego in the middle, the part of the you which strives to balance out the one against the other, the id versus the super-ego."

Wilson the psychiatrist speculated that my id — due to feelings of guilt at natural prurience, perhaps — had manifested itself as a porcine imp. Wilson advised me never to ignore Clob:

"He is a part of you, Lenny. Reason with him. *Argue* with him. But ignore your instincts at your peril."

He needn't have bothered. To my regret, my id was impossible to ignore.

Catherine bent down to examine a shiny pebble. "What a peach," Clob observed.

"Firmer and smoother than a peach, actually. More like a nectarine."

Clob snorted. "Why don't you admit that you are dying to give her one?"

"I don't deny it."

"Gagging for it."

"Yes, I think we've established that."

"Positively dripping, I suspect."

"I'm not sure what you mean," I said miserably. "But yes, I probably am."

"So why haven't you done something about it?"

I looked down on Catherine. "I've dropped one or two subtle hints. We kiss and cuddle, but when things get more serious she goes all coy. We are basically two very shy people. I don't want to push it and risk spoiling what we've got."

"A problem as old as Man, that one. What you need to do is come across as something of a Lothario, and then she'll have the confidence to let you take the lead. Climbing trees is not impressing her, Lenny. I think you're a bit old for that kind of tactic."

"D'you think so? I could write her a poem, I suppose."

We thought about this in silence, gazing out across the vista before us. The sky was an upturned bowl of Wedgwood blue. Over the slopes below and on the hillsides opposite, herds of wych elms grazed with sycamores while the proud Scots pine stood aloof in pairs and threes. And down there, in the green velvet basin of the valley, a river threaded its way through the alders like an errant strand of white cotton.

"Roses are red, violets are blue . . ."

Clob sighed. "Forget it."

"Xavier's just bought a motorbike," I said, as much to change the subject as anything else. I had once considered Xavier Capdeville my major rival for Catherine's affections and still took an insecure interest in his movements. "He's traded his car in for it. He looks a bit silly if you ask me, it's too big for him." My dad had an expression for this kind of thing. He called it looking like a tomtit on a round of beef.

Mum would chide him for using such language in the house, despite all his protests that a tomtit wasn't the naughty kind of tit.

"What sort of bike is it?" Clob asked.

"A Harley Davidson."

"A Harley's a pussy magnet, Lenny. Well known fact. Guys with big choppers are always popular with the chicks." He sat up. "Hey—"

"No," I said. "No way, *Jose*. I know what you're going to say, and the answer's no. Not a chance."

"Why not? You've got a full motorbike license, haven't you?"

"Technically, but I've never ridden anything bigger than a 90cc Honda step-thru."

Clob donned a pair of mirror shades and a black helmet in the style known to motorcyclists the world over as 'pisspot'. He made throttle-twisting motions in the air.

"C'mon, Lenny, my man. We was born to be wild!"

~

"*Wild*, Leo. Take note of what I am saying here." Clob crouched down on the headlamp dish and flipped the collar on his leather jacket. He began to yodel. "Born to Be Mild!"

Leo. He only calls me that when he feels I don't deserve the implied grandeur. It's like when a politician begins a sentence "With all due respect"; you just *know* what he really means is, "You, sir, are an insufferable arse".

"Give me a break, pig." I fluffed another gear change and the bike lurched like a drunken rottweiler.

A bus overtook us. Teenagers made rude noises out of the back window. Clob jabbed a V-sign at them, a cloven hoof being perfectly shaped for that kind of thing.

"Safe and steady wins the race," I said in reply to Clob's baleful glare.

"I'm surprised you didn't say 'They won't get there any quicker.'" He delivered it in a perfect mockery of my mum's voice.

"You talk like I should be ashamed of riding slow. Well I'm not, so there." Although I was. And Clob knew that only too well on account of him being a porcine representation of my id.

Well, maybe I could go a teeny bit quicker . . . I twisted the throttle and the bike surged forward. The bus went past in a blur, as did several cars, a pedestrian crossing and an amber traffic light.

"Yee-haaw!" Clob's ears flapped in the wind. "That's more like it. Heady stuff, eh?"

I eased the throttle off and grinned as the silencers snarled a delinquent *crobba-crobba-crobba*. It was, I agreed, heady stuff. "I think I might be getting the hang of this."

I had bought the bike a little under an hour ago from a small bike shop on the outskirts of the city.

~

"It says here," I'd read off a piece of handwritten card propped on the fuel tank, "that it's the classic water-cooled triple."

The shop-owner, a bald guy with a distinctive trident beard and a leather waistcoat, looked askance; first at me, then at the ancient Kawasaki 750. "Rocking horse shit."

"Pardon?"

"*Rare.*" His grin revealed several gold crowns.

"Yeah, baby!" Clob mounted the bike, making vroom-vroom noises.

Even stationary, the bottle green bike looked menacing. It positively loomed. I couldn't imagine myself controlling anything so big.

"C'mon, baby, lemme whip ya!"

The man said, "One of the most powerful bikes on the road, the Kwacka."

"I wasn't really looking for anything fast."

"In its day, I meant. Now they're considered tame. A pussycat really. Anyone can ride them."

"Really?"

"Oh yeh."

"Never ridden a Kwacka," I said, adopting the lingo. "I was a Honda man." The step-thru Honda 90 had been passed down to me by my dad after he had a scare on it. On his way back from the model train shop one of the tartan panniers came adrift on a roundabout and knocked a sprung buffer off a highly prized Fowler 4-P coach. I'd never seen him so animated.

I slapped the Kawasaki's seat, squeezed the brake lever and kicked the tyres. "Um. It's very nice, isn't it. Solid, like."

The guy spread his hands. "I can see you know your bikes. No wonder you were taking a good look at this beautiful machine. Come into my office, brother. I always relish the opportunity to chat with a fellow diehard."

In his office he introduced himself as Zack. "But you can call me Big Zack." He gave me a can of warm beer and told me he had somebody else interested in the bike. "But if you pay cash I can let you ride it away today. You're not a timewaster, I hope."

Just then Clob came dashing in, skidding on the greasy floor. "Lenny, Lenny! That bike's got a bad oil leak."

A girlie calendar hung behind Big Zack's head. A nurse with infeasible breasts was doing something unorthodox with a stethoscope. I focused my attention on Zack with difficulty. "I have the money," I said, "that's not the hitch."

Clob hopped from trotter to trotter. "Too right that's not the problem. I'm telling you the bike's got a bloody great puddle of oil under it."

Zack's heavy hand clapped my shoulder. "There is no such thing as a problem, Leonard. Only solutions we have yet to find." He nodded slowly, savouring his homebrewed philosophy. "So what is the goddam hitch?" he growled.

"Lenny, listen to me. There's a better bike at the other end of the showroom. A 1000cc monster. Imagine what Catherine will say to that! Grrr, go get 'em, tiger."

I said, "I don't have a helmet or jacket, Mr Big Zack. Or any other protective gear." My voice hardly quavered.

He slammed a helmet and leather jacket on the desk. "All inclusive. Can't say fairer than that, can I?"

Clob cast an eye over the helmet. "This thing's knackered. It's a bleeding liability. And the jacket stinks. Tell the big lummox to shove 'em where the sun don't shine."

I mentioned to Mr Big Zack that, with all respect, I thought the helmet and jacket had seen better days.

"The distressed look is in. The chicks dig it."

Clob went quiet.

I thought of Catherine as a chick for the first time and said, "So how much did you say?"

I stalled the bike six times before I got it out of the garage. I asked Zack what I was doing wrong and he introduced me to the mysterious lever on the left handlebar. This, Big Zack told me with a smile lubricated by the flow of cash, was for operating the clutch. "All bikes have them, discounting those poxy automatic Honda step-thrus. Not that you'd call one of those things a bike, eh?"

How we both laughed.

~

I'd decided to take a ride in the countryside before going to Catherine's house, figuring I needed a little time to get used to the characteristics of the bike. Like addictive acceleration. Just over an hour had passed since leaving the shop and buses trundling past me were a distant memory. I snicked the gear lever up into fourth and whacked the throttle open. The front wheel went light and the handlebars shimmied. My cheeks wobbled. My shoulders strained. Buildings streaked by. Then I noticed a regular blue flash in the periphery of my vision.

"Lenny, it's the Plod. Make a run for it."

I groaned and pulled over.

"You stopped," Clob said in an accusatory tone. "The amount of smoke this thing's chucking out he won't have been able to read your number plate. You should have cleared off."

The double-decker came past to a chorus of laughter and rude gestures through the back window. Clob turned and wobbled his bottom. There was a *phut* sound and a wisp of black smoke curled up behind him.

"Clob," I complained, "stop that."

"Huh. If I wasn't an imaginary pig I'd go and sort the little bastards out."

"Shut up. Now watch and learn."

I'd read a book by a Dr Desmond Morris, and he reckoned you could get away with minor traffic offences by adopting certain body postures that mimic our distant ancestors' non-verbal communication.

130

"Step one, Clob, is to get on the other man's turf so they feel stronger — so I am getting off my bike and walking slowly to the police car. Step two is to make your head lower than his — that is why I am sagging slightly at the knees."

"That's . . . fascinating."

"Thank you. Now step three is to make an appeasement face. So I let my lips sag at the corners, like this, taking care not to reveal my teeth, and scrunch up my eyebrows."

"Afternoon Sergeant," I said aloud, promoting the young constable a stripe or two. "What seems to be the problem?"

The police officer's smile was pure predator. "Been reading Dr Morris have we sir?"

I returned to my motorcycle five minutes later a chastened man, with my pockets thirty pounds lighter and my license three penalty points heavier.

I noticed hot oil dribbling from the Kawasaki's engine casing. I didn't know anything about bikes, but I knew that it wouldn't be wise to start the bike again until the leak had been properly fixed. If the gearbox seized while I was in motion it could throw me off.

"Let's take it back to wotsisname," Clob said.

"You mean *Big* Zack? We are closer to Catherine's house. If I can get it there I can probably fix it myself, or get somebody to come and have a look at it."

"Yeah, like that Zack fella. If he thinks he can rip-off Leonard Stromboldt Junior, he's got another think coming. Right, Lenny?"

"Yeah, right," I said without enthusiasm. "But first things first." I removed my helmet and jacket and hung them over the stricken bike.

"Why not get a tow off somebody? You're never going to push this thing the four or five miles to that frigid bird's house."

Something snapped inside me. I brought my fist down on the tank. "Don't you *ever* call her that, again. Understand? *Ever*. If a beautiful sensitive woman wants to spend time with me without committing herself to . . . then that's fine. There's nothing amiss in that, nothing at all." My anger choked me. I snatched at the handlebars and let the sidestand retract. It clattered against the silencer. "It's your fault that I'm in this sodding mess. Get a motorbike and impress her, you said. Well, it's going to really impress her when I turn up on her doorstep with this clapped-out pile of Jap crap, practically penniless and a conviction for speeding, isn't it?" I leaned against the bike to get it rolling.

Clob wailed. "I was only thinking about you."

"Wrong. You were thinking about instant gratification."

"So?"

"Clob?"

"Yes?"

"Get off the bike."

"But I don't weigh anything, I'm a figment of—"

"GET OFF!"

After only minutes of pushing, damp patches had stained my T-shirt under the arms and across my back. My hair clung to my forehead and sweat dribbled into my eyes. Every slight incline took its toll on my legs. I chopped the journey into increments, mentally checking off landmarks as I passed them to make the journey seem smaller.

Clob kept up a stream of complaints about his aching trotters, but I made him walk all the way.

No less than five motorcyclists stopped to see if I needed assistance. I thanked them all but refused their kind offers of lifts home. A man and his wife offered to come back with their bike trailer. I waved them away politely, my pride intact. I was a man on a mission. Clob declared me insane.

I was less than a mile from Catherine's home when I realised I'd conquered the last major steep bank. This called for a rest. I flipped the sidestand down with my foot and let the bike lean on to it. Only in my exhausted state I never registered the clatter as the stand accidentally retracted back into place under the silencer. Before I knew what was happening, the bike toppled over with me under it, both of us hitting the pavement hard.

Petrol spilled over my jeans. A mirror shattered and a rear indicator broke off to hang by a single red wire.

I kicked the bike off me, scrambled to my feet and stared at the Kawasaki in disgust, experiencing a silent roaring in my head as if I was looking down a wind tunnel. A passing driver honked his amusement. I was too despondent to even throw him a rude gesture. Clob did it for me.

Then the little pig turned round and spun a handle on his hip — unravelling the hosepipe that is his wanger — and began to urinate on the bike.

In a detached unhurried fashion, I unfastened my trousers and joined in. I swivelled my hips for maximum effect, revelling in the hollow ringing sound the yellow jet made on the lacquered metal.

Clob sighed and reeled himself in. "Well, I don't know about you, sunshine, but I feel a lot better for that."

My anger drained away with the last drop of urine. Reaction set in. Sweat on my body turned icy cold as if someone had thrown a bucket of water over me. I began to tremble, teeth chattering.

I picked up the mercifully unsplashed leather jacket and, leaving the bike where it lay, walked to Catherine's house. I hung my head in shame all the way.

~

A worried Catherine met me at the door. "You said you'd be here hours ago. I phoned your mum and dad but they didn't know where you were. That's not like you, Leonard."

"Can I come in, please?"

She moved aside and I traipsed into her living room. She stood in the doorway, watching me as though I was a stranger. Woman's intuition? She sensed something was amiss with me.

"I'll go and put the kettle on." She disappeared into the kitchen.

Clob, now minus the crash helmet, popped up on the back of the settee. "You're not going to tell her the truth, are you? That would be a big, big mistake. She's a classy girl, Lenny."

"And too good for me, Clob."

"Don't talk stupid."

"I *am* stupid. Don't you realise what I've done? I deliberately set out to get the loveliest girl in the world to sleep with me. I even pushed the bike instead of getting a lift because I thought I still had a chance to salvage some pride, or to put it another way, a chance to impress her. All that guff about friendship and mutual respect, it was just so much hot air."

"Don't beat yourself up over it, Lenny. 99 guys out of a hundred would do the same. It's only natural. Probably summat to do with testosterone."

"But Catherine is one in a million, Clob. Don't you see? She deserves better than an average joe. So I'm going to tell her the truth and then walk out of that door."

I stopped sub-vocalising when I noticed Catherine observing me from the lounge doorway.

"Always a million miles away, Leonard. What are you thinking?" She moved to within a foot of me and touched my brow. I committed the touch to memory. So that, like a happy childhood experience, I could bring it out to brighten my skies on a rainy day.

She said, "I bet it's something really deep."

"Catherine, I . . ."

Clob made frantic neck-chopping motions.

"Catherine, I bought a motorbike today."

"A motorbike? You?"

"Uh huh."

She plucked at the jacket. "I wondered why you're wearing this oily old thing."

"Yeah. But the damn thing broke down and I had to push it the last four miles."

When she didn't believe me I showed her the blisters on my palms.

"Oh, Leonard, you poor man."

"Poor man, my arse. You want to see my trotters!"

Clob was jumping up and down, snorting and spitting like a slightly damp firecracker. I ignored him and told Catherine the bike's ultimate fate.

"You urinated on it!" Her hands shot to her face. "In broad daylight, you urinated on it?"

I nodded miserably.

"Oh my God. Did anybody see you?"

"There was a lot of traffic, so yes, I guess so."

"But this is a close-knit community, Leonard. People round here know who you are. They know you're my boyfriend." Two spots of colour had appeared on her cheekbones.

"I'll go now. I'd better arrange for someone to retrieve the bike."

"I can't believe that anyone I know would do such a thing," she said in a small voice.

"Sorry."

"It's just so animalistic."

"Yes. It was pretty animalistic, I suppose."

"Couldn't you control yourself?"

"Seems not. I guess I just lost it."

"Animalistic." She put her arms around my waist and pulled the T-shirt from out of my jeans. "Really, really filthy. You just got your thing out, there and then, in broad daylight, urinated on a motorbike. You're not the man I thought you were."

"Catherine?"

"Leave the jacket on. Mmm. Ooh, God. Don't you just love the smell of leather, and oil and petrol, and honest toil? It's just so . . ."

"Animalistic?"

"Yes!"

"Get a room!" Clob guffawed before disappearinng like a burst soap bubble.

My eyes swivelled to the settee, and then back to Catherine's face before sliding down to where she had pushed her warm, questing hands.

Sometimes I hate Clob. I like to think our intellect can score over our base desires; that careful, considered deliberation is better than gut instinct.

Sometimes I hate Clob . . .

But not always.

Pretty Useless Says

>Dion says: man u suk dik

The message gradually faded from the bottom of the screen, but the words burned bright in Stephanie's brain.

Man, you suck dick!

She knew from spectating that human enemies were not as compliant as those in single-player mode where, despite the supposedly advanced AI routines, they failed to take rudimentary cover or avoid obvious lines of fire (and even then she only succeeded by keeping low and to the shadows, using cunning rather than reflexes), but this was ridiculous. She was being victimised.

Man, you suck dick!

When Stephanie logged on for her first multiplayer experience she chose a conspicuous white-armoured soldier for an avatar and named it Pretty Useless, hoping that the other competitors in the online arena would cut her some slack. She even selected a server where there were only two other players logged on.

And one of those said she sucked dick.

Stephanie typed a reply. It appeared at the bottom of the screen, visible to the other two players logged on.

>Pretty Useless says: Can we just play the game please, Dion?

>Achtung_Baby says: yeah come on

The screen turned fuzzy red. A server message informed her, needlessly:

>Dion kills Pretty Useless

Killed seven times without firing a single shot in reply. Stephanie rotated her shoulders and forced herself to relax. She was a tolerant woman. She had to be; if she reacted instinctively when a patient swore at her, or spat in her face, she would lose her license to practise. Tolerance and understanding were her bywords; the patients were not responsible for their actions. The only gut reaction she permitted herself was to duck thrown chairs. That didn't mean Stephanie couldn't and didn't harbour fantasies, though. Secret, elaborate fantasies of retribution were a safety valve — a release shared by her colleagues, she'd wager.

>Pretty Useless regenerates
>Pretty Useless says: Hey Dion. You must be a BIG man.
>Dion says: u bet i am
>Pretty Useless says: You sure you are not some little squirt talking BIG?

She could see Dion, or rather his avatar — a black-garbed terrorist — kneeling on a rooftop. Black-bellied clouds scudded across the mauve sky behind him. He brandished a long-range crossbow fitted with a 'scope, a weapon he had used to skewer Pretty Useless with consistent ease. She would regenerate only to be pinned to a wall by a crossbow bolt within seconds, before she even got herself oriented.

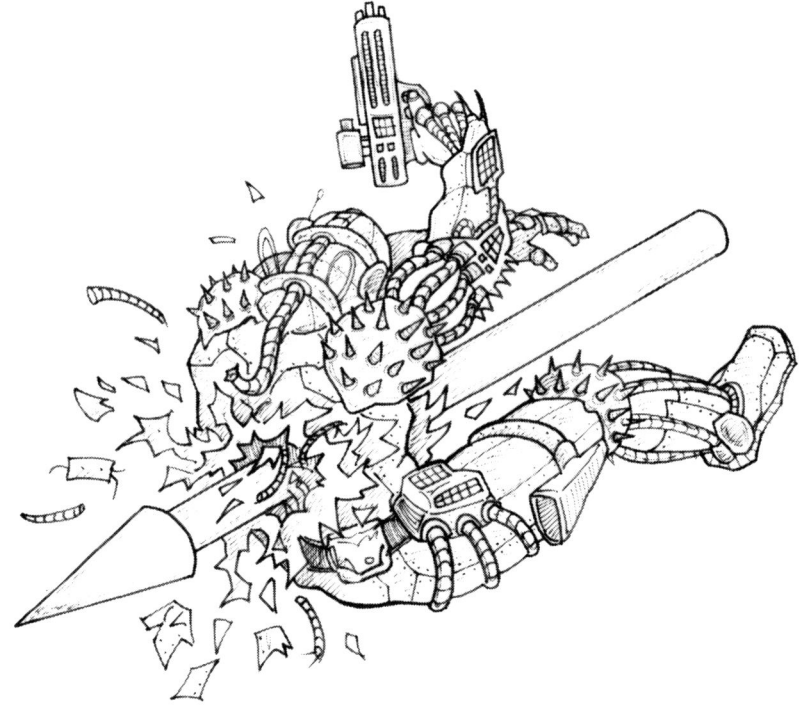

>Dion says: u got 10 secs
>Dion says: 9
>Dion says: 8

Stephanie nudged her mouse so that the view on her monitor displayed a ladder bolted to the side of a red-brick factory. Partway up, it was surrounded by a protective cage of steel hoops. She pressed the W key to move forward.

Dion says: 7

If she could get within that cage of hoops it would provide her with some protection from that deadly crossbow. She could even reply with fire of her own from the Zee Zee Corps plasma rifle in her inventory.

Dion says: 6

Pretty Useless glided up the ladder. Nearly there . . .

>Dion says: 54321

The screen turned red.

"Bastard!" She smacked the keyboard with the flat of her hand. "What's the point of playing if—" The words weren't there. "*Bastard*!"

>Dion kills Pretty Useless

>Pretty Useless regenerates

>Achtung_Baby says: hey cut it out, dion. don't be a spawn-killer.

>Dion says: ya both suk dik

>Achtung_Baby says: f u!!!!

>Dion says: boo hoo cry baby

>Achtung_Baby has logged off.

>Dion says: just me and u total useless

Stephanie's view of the screen went red as her avatar took a crossbow bolt through the neck.

>Dion kills Pretty Useless

Kill number nine. Her anger brought a boiling lump to her throat. Where was the community spirit, the camaraderie?

>Pretty Useless regenerates

Stephanie swallowed with difficulty. Tolerance and understanding might be the order of the day down at the institute, but this was R & R. Rest and recreation. Her own time where there were:

No.

Fucking.

Rules.

Stephanie took a calming breath and typed: Are you set up for vox?

>Dion says: y?

A crossbow bolt thudded into the brickwork above Pretty Useless' head. Stephanie's speakers crackled with the sound of falling dust.

>Pretty Useless says: Because I'm intrigued by this little boy who says he's a BIG man.

She added a cute smiley.

>Dion says: u got 10 secs

>Pretty Useless says: Afraid of a girl?
>Dion says: ur a grrl? gimme a sec
The avatar on the rooftop froze.

Stephanie used the time to scale the ladder. As Pretty Useless hauled herself up the metal rungs, Stephanie cycled through her inventory: a flashlight (non-combative), a serrated dagger (close combat, inflicts low damage) and a Zee Zee Corps plasma rifle (close to mid-range combat, inflicts low-to-medium damage). The crosshair in the centre of the screen flashed green to indicate that an adversary was within range of the rifle. But Stephanie had no intention of using the rifle on Dion now.

Not *just* yet, anyway.

On a flat rooftop punctuated by steaming air shafts, she selected the flashlight, leaving it to automatically cycle through its infra-red, ultra-violet and white light settings.

Stephanie slipped her headphones on and spoke calmly into the microphone.

"Can you hear me? Hello, anyone there?"

"I hear you. Though I don't usually bother with vox in a free-for-all arena. It's not etiquette."

Etiquette? Stephanie nearly choked. She said, "You have a very deep voice."

"That's cos I'm, like, a big guy, y'know."

"Yes, I bet you are. Is Dion your real name?"

"Yeah. I don't hide behind no stupid pseud."

"I can call you Dion, then, can I?"

Pretty Useless sidled to the left of the rooftop. The point of Dion's crossbow followed her.

"Call me what you like, girl."

Stephanie sighed with exaggerated languor. "I'm so comfortable here, in my leather chair. It's important to be comfortable, isn't it?"

A pause, then, "Yeah, I guess so."

"Make yourself comfortable, Dion. Lean back. Let's talk a while."

"Okay, I'm leaning back, but—"

She purred. "What do you think of my voice?"

"Your voice? It's okay, I suppose. Kinda soft."

"Kinda soft? You mean like dreamy?"

"Dreamy, yeah."

"I like talking to you, Dion, it's pleasant. And I hope you find it pleasant listening to me. If you listen to me and watch your screen . . ."

Pretty Useless let the flashlight wash over Dion's face. His amethyst goggles darkened.

"Look at the lens flares on your screen, Dion." Stephanie wet her lips, concentrating on her inflection. "Those lens flares. Circles and rings, circles within rings, within circles, within rings. Moving, shifting. Red and blue and white and red and blue and white and red and blue and white . . . You don't need to point that crossbow at me do you, Dion?"

"I—I guess not."

"After all, we are just having a pleasant conversation, aren't we? Relaxing. Taking pleasure from listening to the sound of another person's voice. I'm your friend. You can trust me."

The crossbow was sheathed with a metallic sound. Dion's avatar stood with its arms loose by its side. The only in-game sound was the thudding of a helicopter patrol a block away.

"That's better. So what do you do when you aren't playing games, Dion?"

"I work in a record store."

"Good, good. I work as a hypnotherapist in an institution, a kind of hospital. I help people that can't help themselves, people with bad problems. Tell me, do you live alone?"

"Yeah."

"You are alone now?"

"Yeah."

"There's no one to disturb us?"

"No."

"Good, good. I like your crossbow, Dion. Will you give me your crossbow?"

Onscreen, the blank-faced avatar in black Kevlar armour unsheathed the crossbow and threw it to the floor. Pretty Useless swept it up and cocked it. She held it up briefly, flaunting her prize before levelling it at her adversary. The weapon thrummed with tension.

"Now, Dion, something has happened to you, something strange. You and your avatar are as one. Whatever happens to your avatar, happens to you. Whatever your avatar experiences, is experienced by you. Hit the space bar if you understand what I have just told you, Dion."

The terrorist jumped in the air.

"Good. Now hit C."

He crouched.

"Do it again, quickly. Keep doing it, again and again."

Stephanie giggled. The sight of the enemy doing bunny hops *was* amusing.

"Okay, Dion, you can stop that now."

Stephanie eased back in her chair and adjusted the mouse so that the luminous green crosshair wandered over her opponent's armoured body. She traced a line from his eyes, his shoulders, belly and hip, all the way down to his padded crotch. She left-clicked, releasing the crossbow bolt into Dion's kneecap. The figure spun across the rooftop, coming to rest in the gutter.

Stephanie smiled. The ragdoll physics programmed into the game engine were truly first class.

There came a strangled hiss through the headphones. She took them off before Dion drew breath and began screaming. She had to tolerate that kind of din at work. This was R & R.

Pretty Useless shot the avatar through the hand, pinning him to the low parapet. If he fell the server would call that a kill.

And Stephanie didn't want Dion to die.

Not *just* yet, anyway.

Marbles

"All rise!"

Curator rose to her feet. She had not been in a courtroom before, and from her elevated position in the dock she had an unobstructed view of the lustrous oak panelling and high casement windows. It reminded her in many ways of home. If all went well she would be returned home before the day was out. If not . . . well, there were always other avenues. She flexed aluminium fingers. Polymer skin creaked over knuckles. One of the two discreetly armed policemen flanking her slid a hand inside his jacket. Other avenues, perhaps, but violence was not one of them. She made eye contact and raised the corners of her mouth; the guard frowned. His hand stayed inside his jacket.

The judge made himself comfortable in his leather chair. He rearranged his robes, shuffled his notes and polished his spectacles. Curator suspected he deliberately made the court wait in a bid to reinforce his authority.

The judge brought down his gavel and the court settled in their seats.

He said, "Good morning, Curator of the British Museum. Before we start the hearing I wish to assure myself that you understand what you are doing here. This is not a trial by jury, but a hearing to decide whether you are suitable to continue in your role as a public servant." He didn't say that if she was deemed unsuitable for public service she would be scrapped, but she was under no illusions.

"I fully understand, Your Honour." She dipped her head once in confirmation.

"You were quite within your rights to elect a defence lawyer, and to call upon expert witnesses, character references and suchlike." He checked his notes. "And yet . . ."

"I decided against it, Your Honour."

"Very well."

During this exchange the Prosecutor had risen from his chair and was hovering expectantly. The judge inclined his head. "Mr Seymour, you may take the floor."

"Thank you, Y'onour." Seymour grasped the lapels of his black worsted suit and elevated his beak-like nose. "Y'onour, members of the public, you will no doubt be familiar with the name of John Silver. The man has achieved the sort of fame that his rivals can only dream of. Of course, he has attracted criticism from certain moral groups, but surely no one here begrudges a man an honest living?"

Curator looked out over the public gallery to see everyone nodding in compliance.

"If I may, I would like to briefly encapsulate his remarkable career for you: John 'Long Prong' Silver worked his way up the pornographic film industry ladder, rising from humble beginnings as a stunt-dick—"

The judge coughed.

"Y'onour has a question?"

There was a lengthy pause, with all eyes on the judge. Curator saw his mouth move. *Stunt-dicker?* He must have decided he really didn't want to know; he motioned for the Prosecutor to continue.

"Y'onour. Pornography has outstripped the mainstream cinema in popularity since early this century, but only in the latter half of this century have its creators truly reaped the spoils. For six years running John Silver was the highest paid movie star *in the world*. But was he content to rest on his laurels? Oh no. He had a burning desire to push the envelope, and so he became the first, and to date the only, time-travelling pornstar.

"He travelled to dangerous locations in the past, always alone, always living on his wits, to ravish the most famous women in history. On the sixth of July this year he embarked on his most ambitious project to date: Mr Silver attempted to seduce no less a personage than a goddess!" Seymour acknowledged the respectful "Aah" from the public gallery. "Sadly, in the course of this performance, Mr Silver suffered a debilitating injury.

"Today, I will demonstrate how Mr Silver suffered needlessly, for his art no less! And you will be left in no doubt that he suffered because of one thing." He pointed at Curator. "And the one thing I speak of is sitting right there."

Curator's voice rang loud in the chamber. "Objection, Your Honour. To call me a 'thing' is only one step removed from such common derogatory terms as 'bot or clank; maybe the Prosecutor would prefer to use these terms to trivialise me?"

"Objection sustained. I will remind the Prosecutor that in my court drones can expect to be treated with grace and dignity. However," the judge turned his attention to Curator, "in legal terms you are an appliance. If you find *that* distasteful then I will remind you that this court is not the place to air your grievances."

He sat back. "Very well, Mr Seymour, continue with all haste. I'm hoping to get this out of the way for lunchtime. Mrs Fingers has packed me a delightful ploughman's pickle." The public tittered. Seymour's mouth merely shrank.

"I wish to question Curator, Y'onour."

Curator took her place in the witness box and declared a legally binding oath. Before the hearing she had been given a booklet with a choice of oaths, depending on her faith. The booklet also outlined court procedure and advised her on appropriate modes of dress. Today she wore the drones' standard clothing of a scarlet second skin that left only the face, hands and neck exposed.

Seymour leaned on the witness box. "I am informed that drones possess faultless powers of recall, Curator. Is my information correct?"

"It is."

"Then perhaps you could tell the court exactly what happened when you met John Silver. Take us back — figuratively speaking — to your home, the British Museum, on the sixth of July."

~

The grey skies over London were always alive with aerial cambots, and John Silver appearing in the flesh was enough of an event to concentrate three hundred and sixty-seven of the pinhead-sized cameras over Great Russell Street alone. The cameras looked like a model of Brownian motion as they quested for images to suck up and squirt into the insatiable e-streams.

Out on the streets a crowd of Keep Time Pure lobbyists exploded in anger as a 'copter touched down inside the security cordon. Curator immediately recognised the first man out. Silver's dusky skin appeared even darker in the wan sunlight filtering through the clouds, though the chain connecting his nose to his ear burned bright gold. He had shaved his head to leave three black stripes from front to nape. The crowd's open hostility seemed to feed the man; he *swelled*. His companion, a slight man with dyed green hair, was dwarfed by the two aluminium suitcases and rucksack he carried. He trotted up the steps like a dog at his master's heels.

She deactivated the museum's inner security field with a thought-pulse. Silver turned at the top step and waved — whether to acknowledge the cameras' interest in him or to antagonise the protesters, Curator couldn't be sure. Probably the latter if his sly smile was anything to go by. She closed the field with a second pulse.

"Welcome to the British Museum, Mr Silver."

Silver looked at her hand as if she'd offered a snake.

She swivelled at the sound of an embarrassed cough. "You'll have to excuse my associate's lack of manners, Miss Curator. He doesn't always realise when introductions are in order. I'm Justin Pilch."

Silver turned from a hologram of Princess Diana. "Hey, Justin. Maybe I should consider going back to bone this babe for my next film?"

Justin shook his head. "I say we stick with the Diana we've chosen, mate. Princess Diana was close to a saint."

"Oh God. I couldn't face another saint after Joan of Arc. What a damn fiasco that was. No one told me she was only thirteen, I swear."

"Excuse me a moment," Curator said, turning her back on the two men. "May I remind you that no unauthorised filming is allowed on these premises." Pilch and Silver stared in bemusement as she waved a hand through the air.

Crack.

"Paparazzi," she explained, and dusted the remains of a cambot off her hands.

"Did you see that, mate?" Pilch said. "If that thing had gone undetected we could have lost billions in revenue to video pirates."

"Yeah, well, I'm not saying drones are without their uses, but why waste manners on one? She's an *it*, not a Miss. A dead machine created to look after dead objects. Then again, you've always been more comfortable with machines than women, haven't you?" He rubbed his hands. "We are wasting time. Where is this poor deprived goddess requiring my attention?"

"Deprived?"

"Hey, drone, a woman who hasn't met me is deprived."

"I see I have much to learn. This way," — she allowed a precise pause — "gentlemen."

Pilch smiled. Silver scowled and strode on ahead.

"I have illuminated the corridors leading to the Ephesus exhibition for your convenience. Please stay in the designated areas for your own safety." Curator paused to allow Pilch to catch up. She took the two aluminium suitcases from him and casually tucked them under one arm. She held out her free hand, palm up. Uncertain of her meaning he slid his hand into hers.

"I meant for you to hand me the nuclear reactor from your back," she said. "It will be quicker if I carry it."

Pilch blushed. "Oh, yes, of course." He hastily removed the rucksack and draped it over her arm. "Thank you."

"Mr Pilch, if women make you uncomfortable I could adopt a more masculine appearance or pitch my voice lower?"

Pilch waved his hands. "No, no, there's absolutely no need. Women don't always make me uncomfortable, despite what John thinks. It's just that most of the women I meet as his technician are, how can I put this—"

Curator subtly remoulded her features — a slight sagginess around the lower jaw and a few crow's feet at the corner of her eyes would suffice. She adjusted her height to three centimetres less than Pilch's and thickened her waist.

"Unapproachable! That's the word I'm looking for. Not like you. Sounds a contradiction, I suppose, porn actresses being unapproachable, but there you go. Life's full of contradictions, isn't it, Miss Curator?"

Silver's voice echoed back up the tiled corridors. "What's keeping you two? I hope you aren't making overtures to that machine, Justin."

"Life is not something I feel qualified to comment on, Mr Pilch."

"Do you have a name other than Curator? No, stupid question. Forget I asked."

She patted his arm. "Actually, I have always liked the name Amy. But let that be our secret."

"Oh, definitely!" Pilch beamed. "Come on, we'd better catch John up before he takes a wrong turning and sets the alarms off."

~

While Judge Claude Fingers admired the Prosecutor for his sharp, legal mind, he didn't actually like the man. He looked altogether too much like a carrion bird for Finger's liking. When he smiled his mouth puckered as if he'd ingested a bitter morsel: a zebra's pancreas, perhaps, or a crocodile's bile duct. Having interrupted Curator's testimony, Horace Seymour was eyeing her as if she was a bloated carcass.

"Are you in the habit of manipulating people?" Seymour asked.

"I don't follow."

Seymour licked his lips. "Your occupational soubriquet is not enough — you really hanker after the name Amy?"

"No, but—"

"I see. So you lied?"

"You are deliberately twisting things: using tact and diplomacy is not the same as lying."

"When I require a lesson in semantics, Curator, I will ask for one. You deny manipulating Mr Pilch, and yet you secretly changed your physical appearance to act on his subconscious will. What is that if it isn't manipulation? It's manipulation in my dictionary, Curator."

"Mr Pilch seemed to be in some distress, due to the presence of the Keep Time Pure protesters. So I acted to put him at his ease, to facilitate a friendlier relationship."

Seymour sneered. "Relationship?"

"In my dictionary it says: Relationship, noun."

"Thank you, Curator. But tell me, have you modified your appearance, or acted in any way, to influence His Honour?"

"No, but you have. It's called body language; humans are transmitting subliminal messages all the time."

"Objection, Y'onour!"

"Objection sustained. Curator, I remind you to confine yourself to answering the questions put to you."

She nodded meekly.

Seymour's eyes glittered. "No further questions, Y'onour."

"Thank you, Curator. You may return to the dock." Fingers checked his notes. "Mr Seymour, you wish to present the court with an exhibit. Perhaps you should introduce that while we are waiting for your next witness to take the stand."

An usher stepped forward bearing a slim box with a certificate of expert verification attached. He passed it to the judge.

Seymour explained. "That is a 1:12 scale model of an alabaster-and-bronze statue that stands in the British Museum. Her name is Diana. She was a Roman goddess, variably known as the huntress, the lunar virgin, the goddess of the moon, of nature, of the beasts, and the Mother of All."

Fingers slid a plain white figurine from the box and rotated it. Whoever had carved the statue got carried away in the breast department. Instead of a single pair, the goddess Diana had rows and rows of breasts extending down to her waist. They looked like an oversized bunch of grapes hanging around her neck. The epithet "Mother of All" was appropriate; she could have suckled half the Roman Empire at a time.

Fingers looked up to see Pilch taking the oath. He wore a sombre olive green suit that complemented his green hair.

The Prosecutor reached the witness box in three impatient strides. "Hello, Mr Pilch. Tell me, how long have you known Mr Silver?"

"Seven years."

"You've been present on all his time jumps, is that correct?"

"I send him on his way, yes."

"Tell me, Mr Pilch, what is Mr Silver's demeanour when he returns from these missions?"

"Ah." Pilch laughed. "I'd have to say bloody irritating. He can be rather full of himself."

"So you are saying that usually his mood is effervescent, ebullient?"

"Yes."

"And how would you describe Mr Silver's demeanour on his return from fourth century Ephesus on the sixth of July?"

"He was angry. Really angry."

"Really?"

"Yes. He hopped off the time machine and made straight for Miss Curator. Said he was going to rip her head off and shit down her neck."

"How interesting. Perhaps you should tell us how Mr Silver prepared for his jump, so we can more clearly understand the events leading up to this singular occurrence."

MARBLES

~

Pilch had been glad of Miss Curator's company as they made their way to the Ephesus exhibition. She explained how the treasures had come from Ephesus in 2048 as a deal between Turkey and Britain. The Parthenon Marbles — stolen by Lord Elgin and brought to England early in the nineteenth century — had been brokered, much to the anger of Greece. They had petitioned for the marbles to be returned to Athens for over two and a half centuries, only to see them handed over to their ancient rivals, the Turks. Pilch didn't much care for the politics, or indeed the ancient artefacts on display in the British Museum, but he listened politely. Miss Curator's soft voice brushed away the silences in the endless corridors.

When they arrived at the Ephesus exhibition. Silver gave a knowing grin. Pilch smiled and mouthed, *Arsehole*.

He took the cases from Miss Curator and quickly assembled the time machine. An imitation marble plinth had been designed to conceal the time machine and its power source from the eyes of fourth century Ephesians.

Pilch placed the assembly in front of a statue and asked her for the nuclear reactor in the rucksack. She examined it with interest before handing it over.

Maybe she was interested because the portable nuclear reactor would be similar to the one powering her. Drones designed to interact with humans were designed humanoid in appearance; not to blend in with humans as was commonly assumed, but because the world was designed for upright bipedal occupants with two arms that ended in hands with opposable thumbs. And once the human design was adopted, the inner anatomy naturally followed the same course — after all, Mother Nature had several million years head start when it came to overcoming design constraints. Miss Curator's fusion plant was lodged in her chest.

Silver stepped around the time machine to scrutinise the statue. A white plate on the plinth read "Diana". The Roman goddess sent out mixed signals; her outstretched arms and raised palms bestowed blessings, whereas her imperious gaze made Pilch feel they were trespassing. Silver gestured at the rows of bulbous appendages hanging from her torso. "Just look at all these gazungas, Justin. I mean, wow!

I've seen some implants — I met a whore with three breasts once — but this babe takes the biscuit."

Miss Curator said, "It is fortunate for you that the statue now resides in Britain. The Turkish authorities would never have permitted you to use their property to film a sexual adventure."

"There will be a real flesh-and-blood representative inside the Temple of Diana, right?"

"Almost certainly," the drone replied.

Silver clapped his hands in delight. "Sex with a goddess, by proxy!"

He unzipped his sweater and pulled it over his head in a languorous movement. He removed his trousers and underpants with the same deliberate care, watching Miss Curator's face for a flicker of emotion. After a pause he shook his head and draped a white toga over his shoulders. "Stupid machine."

"Your charms are wasted on me, Mr Silver. I cannot respond to your maleness any more than I could respond to a flower with an oversized stamen."

Pilch chortled. "Now there's a backhanded compliment for you, mate."

Miss Curator pressed her hands together, the fingers pointing downwards. "I wonder, Mr Silver, if your inability to engage with drones sexually is the root of your antipathy towards us?"

Silver's jaw muscles bunched. "No, it's you that's got the chip on your shoulder cos you can't be sexually motivated. And chew on this," he said, tapping her on the chest. "That reactor powering you was paid for by pure libido: Bob Guccione, the founder of *Penthouse* magazine, invested millions in designing a nuclear reactor small enough to fit in a briefcase. His *own* money, made from fuelling libido! I'm right, aren't I, Justin?"

Pilch didn't look up. "Right so far, mate."

Miss Curator said, "But he didn't succeed, did he? Why do you think that was?"

"Because the stupid machines said it couldn't be done, that's why. The scientists kept putting in all their figures and asking if a reactor could be built small enough to go in a briefcase, and the computers kept saying 'Nope!' The project was shelved eventually, after Guccione nearly bankrupted himself. But years later, someone put in the same data and asked the computer, 'Okay, how about a big suitcase then?' and the dumb machine said, 'Oh yes, that's possible.' And that's why I hate you machines. You're all so literal. So blinkered."

Pilch coughed to break the impasse between impassioned man and passionless drone. "I think Miss Curator has been very generous allowing us access to that—" he nodded at the statue —"as well as a secure environment to work in. Don't you, John?"

Curator said, "Generosity had nothing to do with my decision to permit the use of the premises, Mr Pilch. We have so few visitors these days the museum relies on external fund-raising. Your offer of five percent of the gross from all media distribution for the next three years, paid on a quarterly basis to the British Museum, is the reason you're here."

Silver laughed at Pilch's chagrin. "See? You're wasting your time being tactful with a drone, Justin. A human would know when to tell a lie and save face."

Pilch hung his head. Silver's story had been the lie. A lie that placed the failure of Guccione's dream at the hands of scientists and their computers. People took comfort from knowing that cleverer people than themselves could fail by committing a simple oversight. The fact Guccione had tried to develop a portable *fission* reactor when the technology just didn't exist, and that the portable reactors widely utilised today were fusion units, passed John by.

Pilch felt embarrassed for Miss Curator — for Silver's behaviour towards her — although he knew the sentiment was wasted. He shook his head. It was time to concentrate on the mission.

Silver screwed a translator into his left ear.

Pilch said, "Don't forget that although that's loaded with several ancient languages, accents can still confuse it. Best stick to our story: you're a freed gladiator from afar looking to join the cult of Diana."

Silver had used the "I am a god, obey my every whim!" ruse on Cleopatra to startling effect, and Marie Antoinette had fallen head over heels for a huge foreign amnesiac. But Joan of Arc, the poor child, had screamed for hours after a proudly priapic Silver had appeared to her in a vision. Even the indefatigable 'Long Prong' had admitted defeat with that one.

Silver bent to fasten the last strap on his sandals. Sixteen pinhead cambots clustered above the big man's head. "Time I was on my way," he said, straightening.

"Good luck, mate." It amazed him how relaxed John could be. It also worried him that familiarity was breeding complacency. "No unnecessary risks, remember. Once you go back you're on your own, never lose sight of that fact. And for God's sake make sure you conceal the time machine well. And separate the fusion reactor from it, then at least if—"

"Justin. I have a hot date waiting."

Silver strolled to the raised dais of the time machine. The eyes of Diana regarded him coldly; he tipped her a wink for the benefit of the cameras. He didn't spare Miss Curator so much as a glance. He uttered the word *Lovelace*, which initiated a pre-programmed sequence of commands in the box beneath his feet, and disappeared. The machine would trace the statue's path through time like a bloodhound, jumping off at 370 AD before the path ended in a lump of shapeless stone.

Pilch whispered, "Bon voyage, mate."

~

Pilch asked for a glass of water to ease his dry throat.

"Thank you for that fascinating tale, Mr Pilch." Seymour made circular motions with his hand. "When you are ready to continue . . ."

"Well, John returned and—"

"When?"

"Five seconds after he made the jump."

"You mean the time machine malfunctioned?"

"No. That's how it's supposed to work."

"You've lost me. Mr Silver's mission to fourth century Ephesus could take days — weeks, even — and yet he reappeared in the British Museum only five seconds after he left?"

"The machine was calibrated to return to the present exactly five seconds later than the time it left. So no matter how long he spent in the fourth century, John would only be away from the present for five seconds."

"Y'onour, I think now would be a good time to present exhibit B."

The usher brought forward what looked like a cube of white rock. This was the dummy marble plinth that contained the time machine. The usher placed exhibit B down on the tiled floor and stood to one side with his hands behind his back.

"Is it safe for me to stand on it?" Seymour asked Pilch.

"Yes. It can't go anywhere unless John speaks the password. It's set up to respond to his voice, and to his voice only. That's seventeen billion pounds worth of hardware you're standing next to."

A respectful "Aah" went around the courtroom.

Seymour placed a foot on the dummy marble. It skidded slightly under his weight.

"So Mr Silver returned angry with Curator. What happened next?"

"Well, Miss Curator ran up one of several corridors leading out of the Ephesus exhibition. She had a good head start anyway, and the laser beams winked out just before she reached them, coming on again as soon as she passed through. Of course, as soon as John entered the corridor all the alarms went off. I didn't know what to do. I stood there for a couple of minutes — minding the time machine — then decided I'd better go and find John. I found him in a security cage that had come down from the ceiling."

"Did you attempt to free him?"

"There was no way of getting him out of there, so I made my way to the main entrance where there were eight policemen summoned by the alarms. They were able to bypass the security system and release John from the cage."

"Did you see Curator during this time?"

"No. I was told the police later tracked her down and took her away for questioning."

"You said something about Curator having a head start: could you elaborate on that for us, Mr Pilch?"

"Well, I might be wrong, but to me it seemed she was already running before John reappeared."

"That's interesting. Do you think she knew he would return angry?"

Pilch glanced at Curator. "Yes. On reflection, I think she knew what John was letting himself in for, going to Ephesus."

"Thank you very much, Mr Pilch. No more questions, Y'onour." Seymour stepped cautiously off the dais.

"Curator," Fingers said. "Do you wish to cross examine the witness?"

"No, Your Honour."

"No? Are you sure?"

"Yes, Your Honour."

"In that case, Y'onour, I would like to call Mr John Silver as my next witness. I promise that you shall soon be able to go and enjoy Mrs Fingers' ploughman's pickle."

The doors at the back of the court burst open, ensued by a brief altercation as a large man shook off the attentions of an usher. Buttery sunlight spilled down the central aisle, silhouetting the advancing figure of John Silver. He acknowledged the stares he received with grins, nods, waves and even, for one young lady, a hearty kiss. He inclined his head to Fingers — who nodded back before he had the chance to check himself — and stepped into the witness box. His tiger-skin pants creaked as he sat down.

While Silver took the oath, Fingers suppressed the tom-toms playing in his head. That the man had charisma was indisputable, but this court was Judge Claude Fingers' domain: he would remind himself that the big guy sitting on his left had once been reduced to stunt-dicking for a living; whatever that was.

"Good morning, Mr Silver," Seymour said. "We have just been talking to your friend Mr Justin Pilch, about your journey to Ephesus."

"Hi, Justin." Silver raised a fist to Pilch in the public gallery. Somebody, caught up in the moment, whooped.

Fingers rapped his gavel. "Silence! Mr Silver, I will remind you that this is a court of law, not a film set. Please comport yourself with decorum."

"Hey, man—"

Seymour stepped smartly in. "Mr Silver, as yet the court does not know the nature of your injury, or how Curator is to blame for it."

"That KTP bitch, she set me up."

"By KTP you mean the Keep Time Pure lobbyists. Don't let's be sidetracked, Mr Silver. If you will just—"

"Damn, those KTP freaks have been trying to skewer me for years. She has to be in cahoots with them."

Seymour's annoyance at a witness not keeping to the script was clear for all to see, except maybe Silver. "With respect, Mr Silver, I believe you are wrong. Far from being in cahoots with the KTP, I believe Curator wanted your mission to *succeed*." Murmurs rose from the public gallery. His mouth puckered in a sour smile.

"Now if we can move on, with Y'onour's permission, I would like to present Exhibit C: the film that came back from Ephesus with you."

Silver didn't look happy. "Oh man, d'you have to?"

Seymour said, "If there is anybody in this room prone to sickness when viewing XYZs, I am giving them advanced warning to close their eyes. And anybody squeamish or of a nervous disposition may also want to close their eyes."

Fingers grunted. People closing their eyes during a Silver film premiere? Fat chance. But did it have to be XYZ? "Mr Seymour, I'd like to point out that the court has a perfectly serviceable flat-screen viewer."

Seymour's mouth almost disappeared in amusement. "I'm afraid the film has only been encoded in XYZ, Y'onour. Shall I proceed?"

Fingers nodded and gripped the edge of his chair.

An usher slotted the capsule into a projector and . . .

. . . The court fell away. Fingers found himself in freefall above an ancient city at night. Then the vertical descent slowed and the trajectory flattened as the aerial cambot taking the shot cruised down a roadway.

Fingers remembered to breathe. This wasn't too bad. If he could get through the first few seconds he'd be all right. Then the cambot shot upwards and he nearly passed out.

The view zoomed in on John Silver standing on the steps of one of the seven wonders of the ancient world: the Temple of Diana. He hefted the time machine over to a jumble of marble blocks and disconnected the reactor. The deception wasn't great, but it would suffice.

Before him lay the Roman-occupied city of Ephesus, 370 AD. A spectacular sunset was dyeing the sky a deep crimson. Smoking torches held back the night along the narrow pathways. Crowds roared in the open-air theatre and light blazed from buildings which, in the excavated city of the future, would be bone-white husks.

Entering the Temple of Diana he passed pillars that were wide enough to be embraced by no less than four people; they soared fifty metres to support a vast ceiling of cypress wood. The pillars, like the statue of Diana, were painted in vibrant hues of red, blue and gold.

An aged priest with a wattled neck and dressed in crimson robes approached the big man. He spoke rapidly. Silver raised open hands and shrugged. "I've come to join you, Turkey-neck. Take me to your leader so I can give her a good seeing to."

It was the priest's turn to shrug.

Silver took a handful of his white toga and gestured at Turkey-neck's garment. When this met with a puzzled frown, he pointed at the statue of Diana.

Turkey-neck nodded understanding. He spoke in a gentle, questioning tone. Silver placed a finger to his ear and scowled. Clearly the translator was not up to the task. "Can we quit gabbing and get on with the action?" He cupped an imaginary pair of breasts and slid a hand down to fondle his crotch.

The priest's features melted into a picture of delight. He stepped forward to embrace Silver.

"Ah, we have contact. Damn, I'm good."

The priest led him deeper into the temple. Torches in sconces threw shadows onto the unadorned marble floors and walls. The priest paused outside a pair of ornate cypress doors and gestured for him to enter.

Silver expressed surprise at a sunken bath filled with steaming water. "Man, that's neat, and I guess I am dusty after travelling all the way from wherever it is I'm supposed to have come from." The doors clunked behind him as Turkey-neck left.

Silver addressed a cambot. "Well, guys, look like the show is about to begin. Stay with me, you don't want to miss this." He kept up a commentary as he stripped and slid under the water. Looming over him was yet another statue of Diana. In the British Museum she had been plain white, whereas the statues here were multicoloured. Her skin was accurately rendered in flesh tones.

Silver said, "Look at that; all the details — even the eyes — have been filled in, right? So why miss her nipples out? I mean, you have to wonder about these people. All those titties and not a single nip!"

He stood and stretched, luxuriating as the water ran down his hard, muscled body.

The door swung open and Turkey-neck ambled in. He had a gold chalice cupped in his right hand. "*Bibo!*"

"The name's John." Silver took the chalice and swilled the contents around. "It looks like red wine, and it smells like red wine so . . ." He took the lot in one gulp and thrust the empty cup back at the priest. "Man, that's rough. You want to get yourself the number of a decent wine merchant."

Turkey-neck moved around to his left and placed a hand on his arm. Silver allowed himself to be led, still naked, out of the bath and into the corridor. "Not so fast now, it's a bit dark out here, and chilly. And chilly ain't good in my line of work, if you get my drift."

Deeper into the temple they went. Murmuring priests emerged from cells to either side of the passage, their bare feet slapping on the cold stone floor. They were all clothed in crimson robes. The murmurs became chants and the light grew brighter as they came into an open chamber. At the centre stood a horseshoe-shaped altar.

Silver stumbled, to be caught by the solicitous Turkey-neck.

The chanting stopped. Torches hissed loudly in the silence.

Silver let his head roll on his shoulders to ease his neck muscles. "Come on, lady. Come to Long Prong. Don't be shy."

As if in response, a misshapen figure separated from the shadows at the opposite end of the hall. A look of uncertainty crossed Silver's face as he was urged to approach the altar. Again, he cupped imaginary breasts and fondled his genitals. "We are talking about . . . y'know?"

The priest embraced him as though praising a particularly bright novitiate.

"Well, so long as we're clear on that score." Silver strutted to the altar and rested his weight on it.

"Should never have had that wine," he muttered. If Silver sometimes appeared less intelligent than his fellow man, it was probably because his brain was not the heaviest organ in his body and thus did not get the required blood flow. Right now, though, something seemed to be interfering with his unique plumbing.

Hands grasped him from behind and arched him backwards across the altar. A wad of cloth was stuffed unceremoniously into his mouth.

The priests had removed their robes to stand naked. Silver glanced down to eye the competition and shuddered to see they were all eunuchs.

The goddess Diana gazed from the shadows through haughty, kohl-rimmed eyes. She glided towards him, her gait hampered by the weight of her pendulous breasts. Veins criss-crossed their moon-white surface. They brushed his chest as she leaned over him. His skin flinched at their touch.

Fake. He'd surely known they would be fake. A jacket of fake breasts. But they weren't even meant to be breasts! It had all been a ghastly miscomprehension. The larger, fuller breasts were bull's testicles while the smaller, subsidiary breasts had been taken from her eunuchs.

Her lips parted to reveal yellow teeth. She raised a mallet in her right hand and a chisel in her left.

Silver strained to rise, but his coordination and strength had deserted him. "Oh gorrocks," he said around the gag.

~

The *chink* echoed around the courtroom long after the usher had switched off the projector.

Judge Claude Fingers knew the onus was on him to say something. He uncrossed his legs. "Mr Silver, I appreciate that reliving that episode must have been very distressing for you—"

"And the court shares your distress," Seymour chipped in. "Isn't that right, Y'onour?"

"Yes, thank you, Horace. I mean Mr Seymour. Um, Mr Silver, I'm afraid I closed my eyes at a critical moment. Can you confirm for me that you really are now, um, *sans testes*?"

"She hacked my damn balls off. With a chisel!"

"Oh dear. Mr Seymour, do you have any more questions to put to the witness?"

"No further questions, Y'onour."

"Do you wish to cross examine the witness, Curator?"

"No, Your Honour."

"In that case, Mr Silver, you may take a seat in the public gallery."

"May I present Exhibit D?" Seymour gestured to the usher to bring the relevant item to Fingers. As the usher was about to step back, Seymour spoke quietly to him. "You may take this now, but for God's sake don't drop it." He picked up the fake marble plinth and passed it to the usher, who ferried it away with all due deference.

"What you are holding in your hands, Y'onour, is a fascinating booklet commemorating the arrival of the Ephesus relics from Turkey. You will notice on the cover that it is written by none other than Curator of the British Museum."

Fingers took the tome and gestured to Curator. "Did you write this booklet? It's not by a predecessor?"

"I wrote the book, Your Honour."

"What am I about to read?"

"On page 45 I describe how the goddess Diana was decorated with the testicles of her followers, the more dedicated among them being castrated by their own hand. The symbolism was obvious; their seed would enter her body and fertilise her, the Mother of All."

He let the book fall to the bench. "Mr Seymour, you stated earlier that Curator acted as she did to ensure the success of Mr Silver's mission, rather than its failure. Elucidate, please."

"Certainly, Y'onour. The British Museum is contracted to receive a generous five percent of the gross from all media distribution for the next three years, paid on a quarterly basis. Curator is also quoted as saying, 'We have so few visitors these days the museum relies on external fund-raising.' It is reasonable to assume, therefore, that Curator would act in a manner designed to maximise those profits and thus ensure the longevity of her charge. I have here a figure provided by the court's accountants — a ballpark figure, I must stress — of what the British Museum would have received had the film been made as planned. One point two billions pounds over the next three years is a not unreasonable sum, I'm sure you will agree.

"However, Curator — who I have proved to be an habitual liar and manipulator — decided a film showing the world's highest paid movie star being castrated would be more beneficial to her, than one where he merely ravished a priestess."

"Would it?" Fingers asked.

"All indications are that the film we watched today would gross twice the original estimates, Y'onour. It would appeal to his fans and detractors alike. I rest my case."

Fingers sighed. "Curator. You have heard the case against you. Do you wish to make a statement before I adjourn the court for lunch?"

"Only, Your Honour, that I believe Mr Silver should employ a researcher before he embarks on any more adventures."

"Why, that damn bitch should—"

"And also, Your Honour, I wish to ask what's so bad about losing his testicles? With hormone supplements he can still function, and even if he couldn't he's done it enough times to sit back and reminisce."

A ragged cheer broke out amid cries of, "Switch her off!"

Fingers banged his gavel. "Somebody restrain Mr Silver for his own safety. Court adjourned." He banged the gavel again and rose.

Lunch, at long last. Although in truth he no longer fancied the pickled onions.

"All rise."

Fingers banged the gavel without preamble and addressed Curator.

"The purpose of this hearing was to determine whether you are suitable to continue in public service. The evidence indicates that you are not. It is the court's opinion that you should be returned to the place where you were manufactured to be dismantled. A member of this court will be present to see that its wish is carried out to the letter." So long as it isn't me, he thought.

Curator received her execution order without comment, although the two heavily armed policemen flanking her shifted their weight in readiness for action.

"However, it is also the wish of this court that the film it viewed this morning be made available to the general public in the same manner as the previous John Silver historical adventures." The drone's head came up. "Five percent of the gross takings for the next three years to be paid to the British Museum." No doubt Silver and his backers would appeal against that, but that was a hearing for another day in another court.

Curator looked directly into Fingers' eyes. "Thank you," she said, and vanished.

The courtroom exploded as people panicked. Ushers barred the doors at the back. The two policemen pulled weapons but appeared uncertain as to where to aim them.

Fingers banged the gavel again and again. "Silence in court! No one can leave this courtroom until we determine the whereabouts of Curator!" He saw Justin Pilch forcing his way down the central aisle, against the flow of people fleeing an invisible killer drone.

Fingers shouted, "Can you explain this?"

"I believe so, Your Honour." Pilch crossed to where the usher had left exhibit B and opened it up. "I thought so."

"Thought what?" Seymour stood behind him.

"Empty. Well, the nuclear reactor's in here, but that's all. You and the usher lifted this easily, Mr Prosecutor, which I thought was odd because the complete assembly usually weighs a bloody ton. I guessed then Curator had helped herself to the time machine." Pilch's eyes twinkled. With his green hair and green suit he looked like a mischievous leprechaun.

"Which makes you guilty," Seymour shouted, "of allowing a dangerous felon to escape!"

"Calm down, Horace," Fingers said. "She was, at worst, a faulty appliance. So, Mr Pilch, Curator removed the time machine while you were busy with the police in the British Museum, and implanted it with the reactor in her own chest?"

"Seems like it. She could easily get around the encryption by recording John's voice saying the password when he left for Ephesus. A single thought-pulse and *ping* she's out of here."

"Where?" demanded Seymour.

"It will have been loaded with the coordinates it referenced from the Diana statue. In other words, gentlemen, a place she knows well."

~

Epilogue

The sun cleared the eastern edge of the world. Ephesus was a thin grey smudge on the horizon. Back there an actor wore a drone's scarlet second skin. Curator had traded it for a short, green toga and an elegant black wig. She liked the wig. When she got to Rome, she would get more.

She walked over to a barrel and helped herself to some fresh water to fuel her reactor, and then back to the gunwale to watch dolphins sport the waves.

Leaving the British Museum, her home and charge since her manufacture, had been harder than she realised. It had left her strangely incomplete; bereft, like a parent without a child. She set the cup of water down, lifted her tunic and opened up her chest to expose the time machine.

She was sailing to Rome.

Rome: the seat of a shrinking empire; a super-power torn apart by corruption and civil war. In forty years the Visigoths would sack the city. In eighty years the Vandals would take the outpost of Carthage. The period of peace in the Mediterranean, brought about by Roman might, would be at an end. But that did not bother her. For then she could travel east, where the Empire would live on for another thousand years as the Byzantine Empire. Or she could travel into Asia to see the gathering of the Huns, follow them as they rode into Europe with Attila at their head.

Gulls kee-hawed in annoyance as the time machine narrowly missed them. It flashed black against the pale blue sky before briefly disturbing the aquamarine calm of the ocean swell. She watched the bubbles disperse in the expanding V of the ship's wake.

There was no shortcut home now: only the long way back.

Cutting the Cord

I discovered last year that I can move objects by the power of my mind. Sounds grand, doesn't it, but what I wouldn't give to be able to reach for something with my hands again.

The apple I'm reaching for rolls off the end of the table and hits the floor. Mummy shouts at me. "Lisa! Now look what you've done. I've told you before, leave everything to me."

I close my eyes. Use my remaining energy to levitate the apple. It lifts gently off the carpet and hovers before Mummy's face.

"It's not bruised," she admits.

I lower it into the fruit bowl.

Her gaze goes to the clock on the wall and she wags a finger at me. "No more funny business. The health visitor is coming at three."

I blink slowly. *Okay, Mummy.*

She nods and goes to busy herself in the kitchen of our little one-bedroom flat.

Mummy hates me.

Mummy loves me.

It's complicated.

I'm a vegetable. Is that a politically correct expression? Tell it to someone who gives a shit. Call a cabbage by any other name and it still smells like a cabbage. Mummy has to feed me through a nose tube leading to my stomach. Check my body for bedsores and rub creams into the folds of my skin. Change my waste bags.

I'm twenty-two, but I'm still Mummy's baby.

She can never be free of me, but knows I'll never leave her again.

I'm reliant on her and we accept it.

Except for the telekinesis.

I want to develop my talent. Let others see it. It's a miracle, call in the researchers! But Mummy won't allow it. Not because she fears it, although I suspect she does a little, but because it chips away some of my reliance on her. Sure, you heard right. She wants me to be entirely dependent.

See, Mummy blames herself for my condition. She prayed I'd drop out of university and come home to her, and after an attack of meningitis during first term, she got her wish.

And now Mummy's whole life revolves around me being the way I am. I hear her sometimes, out on the landing, talking to our neighbours. She says things like "My Lisa, she was so young and bright before . . ." and "She could have been a doctor if . . .". She'll start these utterances and then choke off, and they'll hug her shoulders and ask her round for a cup of tea. Which my mummy refuses, of course, on account of her not daring to leave me alone: "Not even for five minutes, in case . . ." Choke.

Last night I heard her tell Mr Barnes that she must have done something wicked in a previous life.

At first I tried to laugh it off. *Gee, thanks, Mummy. So now I'm a punishment, am I?* But the more I thought about it the more it needled me. I can accept being a burden, really I can. I am what I am. But a *punishment*? I'm her daughter, for God's sake.

The health visitor will be here soon. Miss Denham's hands smell of Pond's cold cream, and she gets too emotionally involved with her charges. She overcompensates for this by talking in a crisp no nonsense manner. I like her.

Mummy pops her head round the door. She's adopted a slight stoop for the occasion. She's such a fucking martyr. I swear if I could I'd give her a slap. Her eyes inspect the surfaces for dust — she doesn't want the place to be *too* clean, lest people think she's actually coping — then she ducks back out again.

I've recovered my energy since the aborted attempt to reach an apple for my mummy. I'm able to slide the pillow from under my head and pull it down onto my face. The first hitched breath is terrifying, but I'm nothing if not determined. I force the pillow down with invisible fists, numbing my nose and crushing my head into the mattress. The periphery of my vision fizzes with pale yellow sparks.

It's a gamble. Maybe I'll black out and my mind will release the pressure on the pillow before I'm dead. Then again it might not. Either way I'll be out of here.

And Mummy will *still* be the centre of attention. She'll appreciate that, I'm sure.

The Rise of Azaliel and Lorcas

I perch on a rock rimed with frost and gaze at the distant horizon. When my brother Lorcas and I became stranded during a routine reconnaissance of Hell, we'd expected God's forces to mount a swift rescue operation, and been disappointed when none came.

And so, as the days wore on, we had squatted inside the *Bottle* — a brass cylinder mounted on cartwheels and powered by holy fire — and braced ourselves to have our squashy bits stamped into the earth by the legions of demons waiting impatiently outside. Instead, when the warding prayers finally expired and we were dragged through the aft porthole, the hordes had simply roughed us up a bit: a bite here, a gouge there, and lot of farting in our general direction. Positively a welcome by demon standards. Probably because we'd looked nothing like angels by then; the presence of sin had corrupted our immortal forms.

The frost makes my tail itch. I scratch it as I stare at the mile-high wall cutting me off from Heaven.

"Forget it," a voice grates near my ear. "You're not going back."

I turn on my rock to face the speaker. "Don't bet on it, you spiky-faced—oh! Sorry, Lorcas, I—I didn't recognise you with the, um . . ." I avert my gaze. Lorcas had been such a beautiful angel with his rosebud lips, baby blue eyes and blond curls. Four days in Hell and his face looks like a porcupine is copulating with it.

Copulating. I shake my head. I shouldn't even know words like that. The presence of sin has corrupted us spiritually as well as bodily. I go back to contemplating the far-off wall.

"They'll come for us," I declare with determination.

Lorcas tips his head to the milling demons. "Face it, Azaliel, we are just like them now."

I regard our bodies with sadness. The black scaly skin, stunted wings and the inchoate horns prove his point, and the thing that meets my eyes when I peek under my loincloth isn't something an angel should be packing either. Lorcas, sadly, has been exploring new avenues with his beastly equipment. He even tried to have his wicked way with me. Only a swift prayer and an even swifter raised kneecap deterred him from exploring *my* avenue.

"But I don't *feel* demonic, Lorcas. I miss life in the Celestial City. I miss—wait, what's that?" I point to a star in the blood red sky. It descends and the blurry light concentrates into a golden disc. Only one caste of the nine choirs possesses a non-humanoid form.

Lorcas gasps. "It's a throne!"

"Quick, Lorcas, to the *Bottle*!"

I run and dive through a porthole. The vessel creaks as the throne exerts its influence, and then lifts gently off the ground. Several demons try to follow. I thrust the stowaways out.

Lorcas is still standing where I left him.

The *Bottle* is gaining height.

"Lorcas! Quickly, before it's too late!"

He shakes his head slowly, as one resigned to his fate, then runs and makes a desperate leap. I grab his wrists and haul him inside.

"For a horrible moment there I thought you'd decided to stay."

The quills on his face wobble as he smiles. "It was something you said, about missing the Celestial City."

"Yes, it will be good to get back to the choral singing, the mission briefings, the camaraderie . . ." I trail off when I realise that his smile is a bitter one. "What is it?"

"You think they'll welcome us back when they see us like this?"

I have no answer, for I had given no thought to what sort of homecoming two corrupted angels would receive. Not a pleasant one, I suppose.

"Then why *are* you coming back, Lorcas?"

"Because someone missed his welding classes."

"What?"

He gestures to the battered *Bottle* with a talon. "Sin got in and touched us because someone screwed up the welds. We never stood a chance."

"The cherubim do the welding."

His coal-red eyes narrow to slits. "I know."

We kick out a side panel as we pass over mile-high gates. Overhead, the throne hums a rousing hymn, while far below verdant fields form a pastoral quilt, pierced here and there by pearlescent minarets. There is an uneasy feeling in my throat. I think it is anger or resentment, or something equally foreign.

Lorcas follows my gaze, and the spines on his face rearrange themselves into a malevolent grin. "What say we go kick some cherubic ass, Azaliel?"

I try to hold back the words on my tongue, before succumbing to the uneven struggle.

"Fucking A, brother."

~

Author's note: Azaliel assumed the throne was humming a hymn. It was actually Wagner's *Ride of the Valkyries*.

The Migrant

On the 18th of December, 1918, a young Austrian by the name of Adolf Hitler disembarked from a train in Munich. Snow was falling from darkling skies, curling like ashes in bitter wintry draughts. It coated the stark framework of the steam sheds, glistened like sweat on the engine's black iron flanks.

Adolf stepped onto the platform, his nostrils flaring as he savoured the commingled scents of coal, dung and oil-laden steam. He thumbed the moustache that grew thickly on his cheeks. I thought he appeared calm and appraising, if a little dishevelled after his train journey.

He sauntered past me, the snow squeaking under his boots. He gave no indication he noticed that the snow at my feet was ugly with bloodstained phlegm.

I fell into step behind my quarry.

Presently he stopped outside a *gasthaus*, squares of sallow light leaking from its windows onto the slushy road. *Das Schwarz Wildschwein*. The Black Boar: a drinking hole popular with servicemen. Adolf hitched the rucksack higher on his shoulders, straightened his bonnet cap and ran his fingers through the close-cropped hair above his ears.

He shoved open the door and let the babble of deep male voices wash over him. A badly scarred pine counter ran the length of the opposite wall. Pewter steins hung by their handles from brass hooks. Yellow candlelight flickered on brown bottles. The smell of beer, stale sweat and fresh sawdust combined with the blue-grey miasma of pipe-smoke. A single oil lamp struggled to penetrate the fug. Adolf Hitler placed a coin on the counter then selected a table near the fireplace.

I stood on the pavement outside and watched through fern-frosted glass and condensation as he struggled to remove his wet rucksack and greatcoat. A Christmas tree stood in one corner, decorated with spent cartridges and silver paper, the role of the fairy taken by a crude imitation of Wilhelm II, cruelly complete with a withered left arm.

Placing his cap on the table, Adolf sat down with his back to the fire and stretched his legs. He wasn't made to wait long; a wide-hipped serving-girl threaded skilfully through the clamour carrying a stein and a jug of beer.

I couldn't see what was said, but she laughed at some witticism he made. He took a sip of the cold beer and smacked his lips in appreciation.

My own mouth was a mass of painful sores. My feet were dead from the cold.

I entered the *gasthaus* and ordered myself a drink, although I knew I would be unable to taste it. I stood well back from the fire.

"Won't you join us?" a man at an adjacent table asked Adolf.

Adolf gave the speaker a cursory glance, registering the man's round florid face and gleaming high forehead.

"We were just about to start another game." The man shuffled a deck of cards with the jaunty air of a showman drumming up an audience.

"Room for another at the table," said one of his two companions. "Especially for a comrade back from the war."

Adolf declined and rooted the inside pocket of his greatcoat for a slim, finely etched cigarette case, opening it to reveal two dog-eared cigarettes. He selected the slightly longer one and lit it with a taper from the fire. I have never claimed to be a telepath, but I find I can often judge a man's thoughts by his facial expressions, eye movements, or by subtle changes in his posture. Adolf was thinking: *To welcome one of our boys back from the war? Some welcome*. We had returned from the Western Front to a Fatherland weighed down with disease, poverty and, worst of all, defeatism. Some welcome indeed. In that we were agreed. He settled back with his cigarette, the smoke purging the cold from his bones. He looked at ease. I would soon change that.

"It is very busy tonight," I said. The chair scraped noisily over the stone floor as I sat down at his table. Adolf closed his eyes, blanking my intrusion.

"I remember you, don't I?" I said.

He opened his weary eyes to see me craning forward, scrutinising his face in the dim light. "You were a rider, taking messages to and from the Front. I am right, aren't I? Tch, my manners." I offered a grubby hand. "My name is Hubert."

"Adolf. You are quite right, I sometimes performed despatch rider duties." He shook my hand — I could see it made him uncomfortable

— and moved his head slightly to allow some of the light from the fire to fall on my face. To his credit he suppressed a natural reaction to flinch. I admired him for it; many did not hide their disgust. My face was grim, I knew. Blood and discharge from my ruined lungs crusted in the creases of my lips. My eyes were yellow and crazed by small veins; the pupils looked like black flies trapped in amber.

"I was caught in a gas attack," I said.

"Ah." Adolf relaxed. "Me, too, and blinded. I have just come out of hospital. One eye is still worse than the other. A little fuzzy." He waggled a hand. "But it is improving."

"The Somme?"

He nodded, his expression bleak.

I raised my glass. "To fallen comrades."

"To fallen comrades."

I gasped as the spirits scorched a trail down my gullet. "So, you are a local man?"

"I come from Branau am Inn, Austria, but I was in Munich when the war broke out so I enlisted in the Bavarian infantry. The List Regiment," he said with obvious pride. "I shall be reporting to the adjutant after this drink."

A buxom *fraulein* placed a candle on a saucer in the centre of the table. I imagine I looked even more grotesque by its flickering light.

I said, "The army has dispensed with my services so I have no barracks to welcome me, but there is a dry spot in some cellars not far from here. There are many of us ex-servicemen down there."

I removed a bullet from my breast pocket and slowly turned it in my fingers. It was squashed and misshapen from an impact, but easily recognisable by someone with Adolf's experience as an eight-millimetre round.

"A wartime keepsake?" he asked.

"More than that," I said, but before I could finish my sentence I was taken by a violent spasm. I coughed noisily and raised a rust-red handkerchief to my mouth. Mindless of my surroundings I had to retch and spit into the handkerchief to avoid choking on a blood clot. I folded away the piece of rag and gave myself a moment to recover. Spots floated before my eyes.

Adolf was looking with open distaste at my sleeve cuffs, which were slimed with the same discharge as my handkerchief.

Quietly, I began to tell him my story. "We were sent over the top three times in quick succession, each assault doomed to failure. The enemy's heavy artillery was fierce and unrelenting."

~

I was pinned down behind a dry-stone wall. It provided adequate cover, but the muzzle-flash of my *Muskete* at the interstices gave my position away. I was trapped like a rat cornered by terriers. Despite the numbing cold, I sweated profusely.

I sniffed, then sniffed again. Tin. I could smell something like hot tin, a piercing tang over and above the cooling gun at my side. My eyes were starting to smart too. I blinked away a tear. Quelling the rising panic, I tugged the gas mask from its receptacle webbed to my chest and pulled the bulky hood over my head, taking care to replace my helmet afterwards. I made it just in time, for a corrosive mist had billowed in on the breeze; a dirty, choking cloud of sour green.

I rolled onto my knees and made ready to run. I could see other figures beating hasty retreats, some with their protective masks on and some without, the latter flapping at themselves as though putting out flames. One soldier spun to let loose a grenade before continuing his sprint back to the relative safety of our trench.

Kicking hard, I left the cover of the wall and began to run. Bullets cracked the air like angry lead hornets, kicked up splinters of frosty mud. A grenade exploded behind me, giving me a moment's respite from the withering Allied riposte. The mask made my breathing laboured, a harsh scraping sound in my ears. I struggled to pick out obstacles as the glass eyepieces steamed over. I was terrified that any second would see me pitch headlong into a crater or be cut down by enemy fire.

Ahead, I could discern the grey, blurred outline of a comrade running pell-mell, his legs rising and falling like pistons, his heavy boots thudding on the packed earth.

I hit the ground hard. I struggled to rise but my legs weren't responding. There was a pain high in my belly. My eyes stung fiercely. I put a hand to the respirator box at my chest. There was a small neat hole in the casing, and my coat felt wet and sticky. My head snapped back as scalding gas flowed into my mouth and up my nose. My eyes burned as though they roved in orbits of hot ashes. Blisters erupted on the inside of my cheeks. Wave upon wave of hellfire flooded my body as delicate veins burst and membranes shrivelled. My nose trickled a warm coppery fluid into my mouth. I wept blood as the linings of my eyelids swelled and ruptured.

I retched, and bright red blood cannoned off the inside of the mask.

~

"I had been less than twenty metres from home." I rapped the bullet on the table in a steady rhythm. "This slug hit me here, high in the belly. The surgeon said I was fortunate the respirator box had prevented it from penetrating deeper and causing any real harm."

Adolf smiled his appreciation of the gallows humour. It was, he agreed, a game of chance. "A bullet passed clean through my sleeve during an attack on enemy lines, missing my arm entirely although I don't know how. Your whole life hinges on moments such as those. Our fates were in the lap of the gods."

"You said you were caught in a gas attack, too."

He shrugged. "There is nothing to tell. My unit was resting alongside the artillery, just behind the frontline trenches. A mustard gas shell detonated nearby and we got out of there fast, but not fast enough. Many of us were blinded. We placed our hands on the shoulders of the man in front and were led to safety." He shrugged again and took another sip of his beer. He turned at a tug on his sleeve.

"Look at them," said the first card-player. Adolf followed his gaze to where some newcomers were standing at the bar. Something indefinable — small nuances, their modes of dress — singled them out. An area had cleared around them.

"What of them?" asked Adolf in a reasonable tone.

"Jews. They only call themselves German when it suits them, when they want our money and our homes. But while we fought and died for the Fatherland they came hobbling home in their droves. Stones in their shoes, most likely. Pah!" The round faced man spat on the floor, the spit rolling in sawdust. "Jew boys, I hate them all, every last one of them. The knife takes more than their foreskin, it cuts off their balls too."

Adolf Hitler's jaws clenched. He looked as though he was about to argue with the man but turned away instead. The card player mumbled something inaudible and then returned to his game.

"Do not be troubled," I said. "One becomes immune."

His penetrating gaze roved over my face, trying to work out if I was a full-, half- or quarter-blood Jew.

"I spent much time among your people when I lived in Vienna as a student. I have served with them and, despite that oaf's assertion that they are all cowards, they were good men. In Vienna, before the War, things began to turn ugly and I fear now it will spread. The rampant anti-Semitism in that city always struck me as wrong. Righteous anger at politicians misdirected onto innocent people. I am a patriot. I wear my uniform with pride. I would lay down my life for my countryman, but nationalistic pride does not mean having to hate everyone else."

I felt crusty blood cracking on my lips. "Your sentiments bring you much credit, but I fear that you are in a minority. And also I am thinking you didn't tell me the full story, Herr Hitler."

"What do you mean?"

"The gas attack."

"The what?"

"The gas attack. You didn't tell me everything." I raised the squashed round and rotated it between finger and thumb. He understood. I saw it in his eyes.

He stood and grabbed his greatcoat, putting it on with jerky, uncoordinated movements. His knee bumped the table, causing beer to slop over the rim of the stein.

"Don't forget this." I passed him his cap.

Adolf snatched it up and hurried through the crowd of drinkers, heedless of the dirty looks as he barged them aside. He tugged the door open and staggered outside, gasping as the cold air hit him.

I wiped condensation from the window to watch him. Visibility was poor in the mist that had descended after the snow petered out, but I saw him run across the road. He surprised me by dashing in the opposite direction of the army barracks. His feet skated on the icy cobbles.

I picked his rucksack from under the table and went after him. I gambled on him cutting back to the army barracks once he had regained a cool head.

He had not lied to me about the gas attack on his unit, but he had omitted the truth. When Adolf was temporarily blinded, he had not acted calmly or with bravery. He had been commended for the coveted Iron Cross twice — he was no coward — but unable to see, his eyes and skin burning with the effects of mustard gas, he was temporarily unmanned. He unslung his *Steyr-Mannlicher* rifle and let loose with two shots before someone still in possession of their faculties disarmed and knocked him to the ground. Adolf endured the pressing weight of comrades as they piled on him, held his thrashing limbs until his fear spent itself. He was then dragged unceremoniously to his feet, had his hands placed on the shoulders of a fellow soldier equally blighted and ordered to keep his fool head down.

I had not picked his brain for this information. Have I not already explained I am not a telepath? But it had been surprisingly easy to discover who had opened fire after the order to cease firing during a retreat had been given.

Blind and in considerable pain, that march to safety would have been the longest night of his life. Over the ensuing nights, as he lay in a hospital bed, he would have wept with the fear of being permanently blind. Was the silence behind his bandaged eyes punctuated by those two reports from his rifle, his moment of cowardice? The first shot he had heard ricochet off stone, but the second . . . now he knew the second had winged away into the green mist to strike a fellow infantryman named Hubert.

I found Adolf staggering in an alleyway. The network of fizzing gas lamps did not extend far enough to dispel the swimming mist-wraiths around us. He pressed a hand to his side and leaned against a soot-stained wall, his ragged breath swirling in droplets of moisture. His sodden moustache hung limp.

He stiffened at the sound of my footsteps and peered myopically through the shifting grey curtain of fog. I imagine I looked quite daunting: a silhouetted figure in a long trench coat emerging from the mist. I carried his rucksack. It contained his Iron Cross and several paintings.

Adolf froze. I strode closer, ice-skinned puddles crunching under my heels until we were separated only by an arm's length. My chest heaved. I could feel wet blood on my lips and chin. I wiped it off on my sleeve.

"You left without your rucksack. I thought you would want it." My words sounded as though they had been dredged up from a deep well. I knew my time was near.

Adolf swallowed, his dry throat clicking. "Thank you."

I watched impassively as Adolf put his arms through the straps of the rucksack and cinched them tight.

"I owe you an apology," he said. "I don't know what came over me. Perhaps I could have a word with someone about a room for you, or . . . I don't know. If I had anything to give you, I would. But I don't."

I nearly smiled. "Oh, I wouldn't say that." I took Adolf's unresisting hand and pulled him closer. "You have your body."

Adolf recoiled, his head smacking into the wall in his haste to get away. My head darted forward like a striking cobra. I had done this before. Many times. I pushed my sticky tongue between his lips. It skated over gritted teeth. I kneed him hard in the testicles so that his mouth sagged and let me in.

I made the exchange.

He tried hard to lever me off, but he would be feeling weak now. He would feel his strength dissipate as though every particle of his body was rushing away at impossible speed. I was experiencing the same thing myself. It is like being flipped inside out, as if your insides are being drawn through your navel, your brain tearing from its anchors, the inner ears and optic nerves detaching. The sensation is horrifying, especially the first time, but it is, paradoxically, without pain. I released him, his wheezing breath echoing in my ears.

Adolf stumbled, bereft of sensation; deaf and blind. His knees crumpled, his world spun and the flagstones struck him a vicious blow to the left temple.

While he slept, I absorbed his memories. Sifted, correlated and assimilated them.

He would dream. They always do.

~

The sunlight is blinding, the sky a burning copper bowl over a scorched earth. The heat buckles the ground beneath the watcher's feet. It scorches his nostrils and threatens to hammer him to his knees.

A crowd jostles and shoves at his back. He snarls and shoves back with his elbows, determined to keep his place at the roadside. Shielding his eyes, he squints into the dazzle and watches the ragged procession snaking its way up the rough track. It shimmers in the heat haze. Centurions — tall and lean in their horsehair-plumed helmets, their polished breastplates dulled by dust — jeer and goad their charge as he struggles under the weight of the coarse, unplaned timber.

The watcher sees the bent figure draw closer, close enough for the streaks of dried blood on the victim's face to become apparent, the cruel imitation of a crown on his head and the gouges on his shoulders and legs made by the whip. He is smaller than the watcher expected, this self-proclaimed Son of God, and darker; his skin burned nut-brown by the sun.

The watcher wants to whimper, but instead hostile foreign sounds spill from his throat, the sarcasm unmistakable. He extends a finger and jabs the air. The bent man pauses under his burden and establishes eye contact. And though he speaks quietly, and from a distance, every strange-sounding syllable rings like a bell.

The watcher falls to his knees as if physically struck, the superheated air drawing the moisture out of his lungs.

~

Poor Adolf. I could see his chest burned with every breath as though he drew in flames, a fire not even the freezing fog could quell.

"Open your eyes, Herr Hitler. Come on."

He tried to move, but it took so much effort . . . it was easier to just let oneself liquefy and bleed into the cracks between the flagstones.

"Don't sham me, I know you are awake."

He gingerly opened one eye and gazed unfocused at my feet. "That's better." My voice would be tauntingly familiar . I strode away, keeping my back to him. I wore his greatcoat and rucksack.

"*Thieving bastard*!" he whispered, and spat a string of pink and black mucus that roped his chin to the floor.

I executed a smart about-turn. The tip of the cigarette I smoked glowed in the darkness, illuminating my bushy moustache.

Adolf screwed shut his eyes, but not before I saw the panic in them.

"What did you see in the dream?" I asked. "Tell me."

Adolf's eyes swivelled to face me and looked with horror into his own face, for I wore more than just his clothes.

"Ach. You know who I am? What I am?"

Adolf was silent. His mother would have told him the legend of the Wandering Jew.

I squatted to look my victim squarely in the eye. "The Roman soldiers took Christ, they stripped and whipped him, humiliated him, were about to crucify him . . . Back then, I was simply Ahasue'rus the cobbler. I got caught up in the heat of the moment and I shouted, 'Faster, Jesus, faster!' I still don't understand why I did that; it was so out of character for me. The Son of God said he forgave me, but told me I would roam the earth until he comes among us again.

"I never saw him nailed up. A singular moment in human history, but I had retired to my workshop feeling curiously sick and exhausted. While they were nailing the Nazarene to a cross I was busy cutting leather to repair sandals."

Sparks bounced brightly off the cobbles as I discarded the end of Adolf's last cigarette. "So, then, I had become an eternal. But flesh ages, corrupts and decays. And it can be damaged." I gave him a pointed look. "However, I possess an instinct: I always know when I need to leave a shell and seek out a new one, like a hermit crab finding a new home. For without a shell, I would just be a lost soul, a blind and mewling, intangible thing cast upon the wind.

"I spent the first few centuries making myself a very rich man, bequeathing wealth from shell to shell. Then one day I gave it all to the Church. But God obviously recognised a bribe when He saw one and I remained here on Earth. I spent the next few lives in debauchery thinking, Why bother?

"I became a sheep. Some men become wolves, and others shepherds, but most are content to be sheep."

I squatted on my haunches beside the mortally wounded carcass of Hubert Schmitt, a shell of less than seven years. I felt no sentimental attachment to it.

"This country will rise like a phoenix from the ashes, and I shall be at its head. A wolf in the guise of a shepherd. There will be no weak leaders procrastinating, just a select cabinet of men who will crush all before them with an iron fist. I have observed people for two millennia, I know how to manipulate them; tell them what it is they want and then promise it to them. Give them words like bones to dogs. Words are power.

"You've seen all these disaffected young men, standing around in small knots on street corners. Revolution is in the air. They are waiting for someone to come along and guide them." I pinned a medal to my chest and patted it significantly. "A war hero, perhaps."

He opened his mouth to speak. Nothing came out. I squatted closer. He lifted a hand and beckoned weakly.

I knelt and put an ear to his lips. "It's no use," I said, "I cannot hear what you are saying."

His left arm shot out and clasped me behind the head. He dug his fingers into my neck and gripped tightly. I screeched in pain and surprise as Adolf brought our faces together in a passionate embrace, mouths mashing, tongues entwining. Then he fell back, panting, dark blood bubbling on his lips. His head struck the icy ground.

He must have known then that it was all over. Fingers of ice would be entering his belly; that welcome, numbing coldness that flowers in the chest.

Adolf's amber eyes stared into the milky opaqueness overhead, as though waiting for the enduring chill to overtake him.

I stood sharply and raised a foot to plant a kick, then lowered it and laughed. "My God, but you are a plucky fighter, Herr Hitler. No one has ever tried that before."

I recovered my composure, for he had shaken me.

"I was at a church service, and in the pulpit was a real fire and brimstone preacher as they say in that part of the world. He told his congregation that when they have children, that they were giving God a lever, a hostage, that no matter how much love and devotion they poured into that child its fate was in the hands of One higher. I saw it all then: you threaten someone through their children and you have a terrible power over their heart and soul. And what do I see all around me? Despised and feared wherever they settle? The Jews. The Children of God. Doomed as I to be strangers and migrants and outcasts, forever misplaced. *They* will be my hostages."

"You're mad," Adolf whispered.

"You think so? Maybe I am. But if so, the world is an asylum. I won't be short of volunteers to my cause."

"Burn in hell." Adolf's final breath rattled in his chest.

I nudged the corpse enviously, then looped the rucksack over one shoulder and began the trek back to the *gasthaus*. I knew I would find at least a handful of men there who would listen to my politics.

The Devil's Fauna

'Take us the foxes, the little foxes, that spoil the vine: for our vines have tender grapes.' Chapter two, verse fifteen of The Song of Solomon *proves beyond fair doubt that Reynard, from ancient times to modern, has plagued the god-fearing with his sly and destructive ways. He kills not to feed himself, but because it is in his nature to destroy that which is healthy and to satisfy an unquenchable bloodlust.*

From Haplowe's *The Fauna Satanica* (1876)

Edward scribbled the words *Scooped out by God's hands*, then crossed them out.

Shaped by God's hands?

No, that wasn't quite right either.

In God's cupped hands, then?

Hmm, yes. In God's cupped hands, that sounded promising.

Edward Dempster-Smythe tapped his teeth with a pencil and tried to ignore the damp seeping through his plus-fours. He could see the purple-headed mountains flowing in verdant swoops, and how, dappled by yellow sunlight, the glen below resembled a cloth of watered silk. But how did one go about conveying that image as a romantic metaphor?

He studied his notebook.

What rhymed with hands?

Lands, Scottish Highlands? No, no, far too prosaic. Observe, man, and think!

He rested a hand on the shotgun at his side. Poetry was a lot less rewarding than game. With a Boss & Co twelve bore, one either hit the target or missed. Wordplay was a vague, wishy-washy art by comparison. Damned silly waste of time to be sitting on one's arse in a place this grand. A-ha, *grand*! That had a certain ring to it. It conjured size, awe, immensity.

He scribbled it down then pushed the notebook into the satchel slung around his neck. That was when he noticed the burgundy, pocket-sized book stashed alongside his sandwiches and flask. He allowed himself a wry smile. He didn't need to look at the gilt lettering on its cover to know what it was. Elizabeth must have put it there. Which meant she had her suspicions about this daytrip of his. His smile waned as he realised he would have some explaining to do when he got back to the hotel. But, really! How anyone as intelligent as Elizabeth could claim to empathise with animals — especially game animals — was beyond him.

He had left her poised at her easel overlooking Oban harbour, feverishly sketching outlines; her pencil making large sweeps across the dazzling white paper, her eye and hand impatient to capture the seascape. He'd kissed her chastely on the forehead and she had nodded in return, her pink tongue protruding in concentration. As he walked away, Edward had looked back over his shoulder and his breath had caught in his chest — her white dress, wide-brimmed hat and parasol had glowed with an ethereal brightness, like a vision of an angel amid the dismal, weeping stones of the harbour. It was fanciful, he knew, but Edward endeavoured to fix that beatific image of her in his mind so that he would never forget it. He felt a warm glow now, as he thought of her, and imagined her face illuminated with admiration when he told her that the valley overlooking Glen Orchy looked as though it was in God's cupped hands.

Or cupped in God's hands.

Damn, he needed to shoot something.

Edward thrilled to see a flash of rust-red flicker among the long, green grass. Fox! The beast was approaching him, he was sure of it.

Reynard appeared again, closer now, then veered away. Edward followed the creature's line of sight and saw a crow atop a fallen tree, preening its blue-black feathers. The fox closed on its prey and pounced, taking the luckless bird in a single bite. Edward unfolded himself with care, raised the shotgun to his shoulder and sighted along the barrel.

The crow exploded from the hidden clearing and flew straight towards him. He pulled the trigger, but surprise threw his aim and he missed the bird by a country mile. He swivelled to see it flying up the mountainside. The bird seemed to tumble in the air, nearly colliding with the ground before correcting itself. Edward might have winged it, but he doubted it; more likely the fox had wounded it.

He found the fox lying on its side, panting hard, eyes screwed tight, its legs jerking. A single black feather clung to the creature's sharp muzzle. Edward felt for a cartridge in his satchel and thrust it into the breech of his weapon. Stepping back, he raised the gun to his shoulder and blasted the worthless creature.

~

Two hours later, Edward's legs were aching from the climb. He hugged the stock of his shotgun and appraised his position on the mountainside. Ahead, a long saddle lay slung between two granite peaks. He turned to look again at the valley below. Dark mysterious clefts and crevices ran down the slopes like folds in a sleeping dragon's hide. The temperature had plummeted; the sun was a bleached disc behind banks of glowering cloud. He had been forced to wrap his tweed jacket tighter and pull his cap over his ears. Low cloud obscured the higher slopes.

It would be prudent to turn back now, to descend to the glen and his waiting Bentley, drive back to the town of Oban, and Elizabeth. But, he reprimanded himself, he had set out to ascend this mountain and bag a bird or two. The only thing he had managed to shoot so far was a damned half-dead fox. There must be more out here for the rugged sportsman. He even dared fantasise about bagging a stag. The Highlands were supposed to be teeming with them.

Blowing into his cupped hands, Edward tried to gauge which peak was the closer. The clouds were drifting lazily over the hillside from the right, partially obscuring the view. Turning smartly to his left and whistling 'When the Saints Go Marching In' to raise his spirits, Edward set off at a jaunty pace.

~

Where stalks the Reaper, follows the corby. Foul bird! One of my congregation, who served on the Crimea Peninsula, enquired of me: where in a landscape blasted by cannon and shot did the crows come from to feast upon the carcasses of man and beast? My answer? From the very Gates of Hell, brother!

Ibid

Edward took a sip of whisky from a hip flask, idly running a thumbnail over the delicate etching on the silver case. He sat at the peak of the mountain, a plateau of boggy peat and granite, with the cast off crusts of his devoured sandwiches littering the ground around him. There was a sense of anticlimax in his achievement. The low cloud was so impenetrable he could have been anywhere sitting on a tussock of sharp, wet grass. His thick black hair clung to his forehead and his moustache drooped forlornly. At least by cutting across the mountainside he could get down to the Bentley in a lot less time than it had taken to get up here. It was probably still sunny down there, too.

Edward's hand went to his satchel, where he felt the outline of the book that Elizabeth had covertly placed there. He took it out and hefted it in his hand. *The Fauna Satanica* by the Reverend James Haplowe. Elizabeth bought the book the month before in Charing Cross Road. "A little light reading for you on our holiday, dahling! In case you get bored with me." She had been teasing, of course. She knew only too well his dislike of animals, although indifference summed it up better: he couldn't see the point of them — apart from game, of course. Elizabeth, on the other hand, adored animals, and wanted Edward to share her passion. A condition of her becoming Mrs. Dempster-Smythe had been him giving up guns, a compromise he reluctantly accepted in exchange for her hand in marriage.

He stroked the gun nestling in his lap. He ought to get on with the poem; he needed it all the more now, not just to impress Elizabeth, but to serve as an alibi.

He sighed, his breath stirring the mist. By buying the book Elizabeth had intended to highlight his misconceptions about animals and illustrate how foolish he was by comparing him to Haplowe. She opined that humans were far more dangerous than any animal, which Edward felt was taking things too far and told her so. Haplowe may be a complete nincompoop, he'd said, but so are you.

He should have thrown the book away, the arguments it started.

A harsh rattle interrupted his musing, the sound muffled by the fog. Edward stood and listened.

He heard it again, much closer, the hair on his neck bristling. Was it a stag? Did they make a noise like that in rutting season? He hadn't seen any deer up here though, and the noise had sounded close. Sheep? A goat? Edward sucked moisture out of his moustache and pushed the stock of the shotgun into his armpit. A light breeze stirred the mist and he glimpsed a crow hopping over the uneven ground. Edward despised crows. He had seen them on his estate, feasting on the bodies of lambs, snapping at dead eyes and tearing off slivers of gristle. They squabbled among themselves over juicy carrion before hopping away with some meagre scrap to toss down their throats. He heard a caw and shuddered. A rational part of his mind knew that he was allowing the eeriness of his surroundings to faze him, but he was unable to quell the growing unease.

He flinched as invisible wings parted the air somewhere above. Just a bird, he told himself, you jittery fool. Even so, there would be no more hiking through low clouds for him this day. Edward turned and ducked as something black threw itself at his face. His cap fell from his head. He raised the gun and swung it around, seeking a target.

The grey mist swirled, devoid of shadow or form. Then came the flutter of wings again, accompanied by a harsh, mocking caw. Behind him! Edward spun and brought the muzzle of his gun up. Too late! Claws raked the skin of his cheek.

The crow wheeled away, disappearing once again into the mist. Edward jerked the trigger. The boom echoed around the mountaintop. The recoil stung his shoulder. He quickly dropped to his haunches, fumbled the fastenings on his satchel and ripped open a new box of cartridges, desperate to reload before the mad crow returned. He thumbed the cartridges home, snapped the weapon closed and scanned the mists around him. Blood trickled off his chin.

He whispered. "I will have you for that, you bastard. Just show your ugly beak and I shall blow you to smithereens."

Tense seconds turned into minutes. Edward worked his jaw and shrugged his rigid shoulders, forcing himself to relax. He picked up his cap from where it had fallen, took a swig of whisky from the flask and settled down to wait. This had become personal.

~

I myself have borne horror-struck witness to the mesmeric power of mustelid nivalis. It hypnotised its luckless prey with a crimson gaze, petrifying it, turning it to stone. No one can behold such conduct without partaking of the terror and dread of the victim. The weasel is of the uppermost ranks in Satan's army on Earth!
Ibid

He did not have to wait long before the sound of cawing alerted him to the crow's nearness. The guttural calls seemed to be coming from the east. He stowed the flask in his satchel and began to sidle in the direction of the sounds. He swept the barrel of the gun left and right as he walked, keeping his eyes open for any attack from above.

A black speck swooped in low, following the contours of the land. Edward allowed himself a smile and aimed just in front of the bird. He steadied the gun, took a breath, let it out slowly and squeezed the trigger. The crow's tail feathers exploded and the bird crashed to the ground. But as Edward lowered the gun the crow began to hop away from him, bounding over the purple thickets of heather. Edward thrust another cartridge into the breech and strode after his quarry, determined to finish it off.

He fired and the crow cartwheeled through the air in a riot of black tufts. Edward cheered under his breath and ran to the spot where the bird had landed. He stamped thickets of heather aside and searched the shadowy ground, but all he found was a handful of flight feathers amid a drift of soft down.

Normally he wouldn't have bothered, but this bird had possessed the temerity to attack him; he needed to see it dead. It had to be the same bird that he tagged earlier in the day, the one that survived a fox attack. Edward recalled the fox's attitude when he had first spotted it. First the fox had been stalking him, and then this crow . . . A small part of him admitted disquiet at this, registered the simple fact that such behaviour was somehow unnatural. But he ignored any misgivings and continued the search. He poked the barrel of the gun into stands of prickly gorse and muttered imprecations at the contrariness of nature.

From somewhere to his left came the quietest of sounds. Rhythmic and rasping, as though a paper bag was being slowly inflated and deflated. He scanned the dense thickets for movement, but in his pursuit of the crow Edward had descended several hundred yards down the eastern slope of the mountain. The setting sun's afterglow did not reach down here where the land was painted in the blue-grey shades of twilight.

A dark streak with a white bib flashed through the undergrowth. Either a stoat or a weasel, Edward surmised. He would have been able to identify it close-up, but in this poor light and from a distance of ten yards he couldn't be sure. The creature had scented the crow's blood and homed in to finish it off. An easy kill for an accomplished predator.

Edward perused the louring skies. He should have started the trek down the mountain half an hour ago to make sure of reaching the glen before nightfall. But he desired to see the bird's carcass now, and so edged closer to where the wheezing sound emanated. He found the crow on its belly among a clump of thistles, its wings flapping feebly at a marauding weasel, the mustelid's body no thicker than a man's thumb. Edward's approach disturbed the weasel and it scampered into the undergrowth.

The crow gave Edward a baleful stare and opened its beak wide as if to give a final croak, its slimy brown tongue flexing between the secateurs of its beak. But then Edward noticed a curious thing. What he had thought of as a tongue dropped out of the bird's mouth and scuttled away after the weasel. Edward blinked and stepped back, unsure of what he had just seen.

The crow's movements stopped. Edward nudged it with the toe of his leather brogue. Dead as a Dodo. He wiped the scratches on his cheek and turned to go back the way he came. He had a short climb ahead of him before he could enjoy the relatively easy descent to the glen and his motorcar, and this piqued him. He chastised himself for allowing some mad corby to lead him a merry dance down the wrong side of the mountain.

"What a complete waste of bloody time!" He lopped the head off a thistle with the barrel of his gun.

He reached the mist-shrouded plateau in minutes, and was just about to start the descent down the western flank of the mountain when a chittering sound pulled him up short. His eyes swept the ground and skies, a creeping sense of déjà vu stealing over him.

"Don't be distracted, Edward," he told himself.

He quickened his pace, forcing his way through prickly stands of thistle and gorse, bounding sideways to prevent himself from going head over heels. The scratches he received only heightened his anxiety. In places the mountainside fell away sharply into crevasses and he would have to navigate a tortuous route to avoid them, ever mindful that within half an hour the only light would be from the half moon rising behind him.

After what felt like hours, but may have been less than twenty minutes, he paused to catch his breath, wincing at the soreness in his feet, his ankles, his knees. He bent to massage them and saw a pair of black rapier eyes regarding him with interest. The weasel's body made a sinuous humping motion and those piercing eyes were suddenly scant inches from his own. Edward could smell the creature's foetid breath, read strange, alien thoughts in its unwavering gaze. He felt paralysed. The creature's fearless stance had shocked him into immobility. The animal snickered before dashing into the undergrowth.

Edward straightened, shook his head clear and began to run again, swearing under his breath. The gun was an encumbrance now. The satchel bounced under his right armpit. The poor light rendered the mountainside grey and featureless; distances were deceptive, hard to judge.

A crevasse running longitudinally barred his way. A stream, barely visible, burbled among the tumbled rocks. Edward, scouting the quickest route around it, snarled as something pricked the skin behind his ankle. He rubbed at it briskly, and quailed to see blood glisten blackly on his fingertips.

A quiet snicker. The rustle of heather.

The little bastard had bitten him! Sunk its needle-sharp teeth into his Achilles tendon.

Edward raised the gun to his shoulder, swung the barrel to and fro. Straw yellow sparks edged the periphery of his vision.

Pain flared in his buttock.

He swivelled. Saw nothing. He touched his seat and felt blood through a tear in his plus-fours.

A snicker to his right.

Swivel. Nothing.

Edward bellowed. "Come out where I can see you, damn it!"

The weasel ran up his back and sank fangs into the tender flesh of his exposed neck. Edward squealed, with shock as much as pain, spun and slipped. His foot skidded from under him and he toppled into the rocky crevasse.

~

A Dr. Wilson of Aberdeenshire disclosed information to me of a curious creature indeed, which forms not its own carapace as do others of its kind, but prefers instead to occupy that of its cousin, the whelk, which it takes with godless haste lest its ugly, brown, misshapen body shrivels in God's sunlight.

Ibid

Edward's eyes flickered open.

Dull pain throbbed throughout his body, but the most severe seemed to stem from somewhere in his forehead. It felt like a red hot poker had been inserted up his nose to cauterise his brain.

His body rested at the edge of the stream. He could feel, if not see, ice cold water running over his lower extremities. He tried to raise his knees, to drag his feet out of the water, but it was as though his body had become detached from his brain. He couldn't so much as tilt his head.

Paralysed!

The word slammed into his heart like a hammer blow, robbing him of the very breath in his lungs.

Paralysed. And yet . . . Edward's eyes registered movement. The edge of the crevasse above was slowly sliding across his vision. At first he was at a complete loss to explain this phenomenon, but then he realised that his body was rising, drawing itself into a sitting position. Movement . . . but not of his volition. He would have opened his mouth to scream, but he could no more use his throat as claw down the moon.

Then he tried to stand. Edward looked out of eyes he no longer had any control of and suffered an acute sense of vertigo as his body rose to stand on wobbly legs. It wavered for a second, as though unaccustomed to the act of balancing, before toppling face down into the stream. Water gushed up his nose and into his mouth, making him choke. His hands worked their way under his chest and raised him onto his knees. Slime and bile poured from his gaping mouth. He began to crawl up the sides of the crevasse.

A small furry body lolled among the rocks. Stunned or dead, the weasel no longer figured in Edward's thoughts. He had a new enemy; one within. A possessor. An usurper.

He crested the crevasse on his knees. Edward thought of his motorcar, and the safety it offered earlier. Immediately his head twisted to where, rendered invisible by distance and darkness, the Bentley was parked. The usurper tried to stand again, but again it toppled heavily to the ground. This time though it broke the fall by thrusting out his hands.

Those same hands picked up and squeezed a wad of black peaty soil between them. Edward boggled as they raised the soil to his mouth and pressed it between his lips. His jaws worked up and down before his tongue, registering distaste, laboriously pushed the dirt out.

The creature, the usurper, was testing its new human-shaped vehicle. Undaunted by the fall, it tried again to stand upright, and this time it appeared to master the art. It placed one foot in front of the other, wobbled, fell. Edward felt every bone-jarring jolt. The cuts in his hands and knees hurt like the devil.

Within a few painful minutes, the usurper had mastered bipedal locomotion and was heading down the mountainside, making a beeline for the motorcar.

Edward was a passenger in his own body.

The journey down the mountainside in wan moonlight would have been fraught with difficulty for an adult in full control of his limbs; as a man seemingly commanded by a witless child, the journey swelled to nightmare proportions.

Edward no longer felt the valley deserved the nomenclature God's cupped hands. It had become the Devil's Punchbowl, the Wicked Hollow, the Black Vale. His hands and knees were skinned by the constant stumbles over granite and slate, his face bled from numerous cuts where he had ploughed carelessly through gorse and hawthorn. He wept, swore and hammered at the barriers of his mental prison without effect. And all the while he tried not to think about what the usurper planned once it reached the motorcar. Edward concluded the usurper, picking up on his emotions, had seen the car as some sort of haven. But what would it do when it reached it? Did it have any concept of using a car to travel; would it, sensing Edward's longing for Elizabeth, attempt to drive?

He screamed: What do you want from me!

The creature's march continued unabated.

Edward lapsed into a numb silence, lost and detached from everything around him. Then his gait altered and he realised there was a solid road surface underfoot. A handful of bends and the Bentley would be there, parked on a grass verge at the roadside.

A human form registered briefly in the corner of his eye. Edward began to clamour. Go back! There was someone . . .

Even as he screamed it, he knew it was hopeless, that he and his usurper did not share verbal communication. Yet the creature slowed. Edward's head turned and he dared to hope that all was not lost, that here would be someone who could help him in this desperate hour. But what he had thought to be a fellow human being was merely a ragged scarecrow, swaying like a drunkard in the wind. Disappointment poisoned Edward's thoughts and his head turned away, his legs took up their *metier* and his body continued its determined listing along the road.

Edward began to piece together the day's events. First there had been the stricken fox and the crow's haphazard flight, which he realised now had nothing to do with him winging it and everything to do with the usurper mastering flight. And that odd brown parasite that he mistook for the crow's tongue, just before the weasel started to track him . . . The usurper had targeted him from the beginning, using the fox, crow and weasel as vehicles to capture the ultimate prize; the species which evolution had favoured.

The Bentley hove into view. Sheep milled around its leeward side, sheltering from the chilly breeze sweeping the glen. They looked like indistinct, grey clouds scudding across the grass.

But why had the usurper chosen him? Had it been his gun, his clothes or his posture?

Respect: it chose me because it sensed the animals' fear of me.

With sudden clarity, Edward knew what he needed to do.

~

And so my opus is complete, and if you hearken to my warning then my toil has not been in vain. Heed my words, and heed them well, for if you do not, then you will surely be consumed by those creatures I have labelled herein as Fauna Satanica.

Put your faith in the Lamb of God, my children; for He, and only He, can keep us safe from harm. May the Lord be with you.

Ibid
Edward boiled with fear.

Keep away from the sheep! In the name of God, keep away from the bastards! He imagined being smothered by greasy fleeces infested by blood-gorged ticks.

The usurper paused.

That's it, go on. Take the bait.

The usurper brought his head up and resumed to walk towards the Bentley.

No! The sheep, the sheep, they're . . .

Edward gave his fear full rein, attributing it to a vision of sheep as the new world masters; cities full of sheep, trampling humans underfoot. He imagined satanic sheep, with horns curling around their faces and smoke issuing from their monstrous mouths. Sheep feasting on newborn babies.

The usurper stopped and looked upon these docile-looking beasts surrounding the motorcar as if unsure of what it saw. It reached a hand out to touch the nearest animal, a lamb. It bleated and shied away.

Edward could see his chance slipping away. Then a large ewe came forward and gently butted his thigh; a warning to stay away from its young. The usurper shoved it back and was once again rebuffed.

Edward screeched a mental warning. The ground shook beneath these devils, it smouldered beneath their hooves. They cracked whips over the heads of their human slaves and spat fire into blood-red skies.

A terrible pain shot through Edward's forehead as the usurper shifted. Sinus fluid trickled over his lips.

Something slimy dropped out of his nose.

~

His eyes were open. He was not unconscious. Immobile, but not unconscious; as though he was recovering from a debilitating fever. A spasm shook his legs and he heard the sounds of scattering hooves. He must have scared off a curious sheep.

One of the flock, he knew, would be struggling to master its limbs.

He had to regain control, and quickly.

Overhead the heavens were crystal-clear, revealing the stars in all their glory. Elizabeth had begged him to travel further north in the hope that she would see the Northern Lights. They almost argued over it. Edward's chest tightened at the memory. He screwed shut his eyes and summoned his last sight of her, down at the harbour in Oban. There was a pleasant gauzy quality to the vision. He could see her paintbrushes softening in water, the sun's rays fracturing into splinters of light on the jar.

His mouth gritty, he berated himself to stop dreaming and get moving. Concentrating, he flexed his fingers; rolled a blade of grass between his thumb and forefinger. Then he found he could move his head and flex his shoulders. He rolled over and brought his knees up under his stomach. His head swam with the effort, he wanted nothing more than to lie down and sleep. He forced himself into a kneeling position.

Alone, ignored by the rest of the flock, a lamb was struggling to its feet. It fixed Edward with a yellow stare. He wondered if the usurper realised it had been tricked, or whether it dreamt now of unbridled power. Edward wished for the gun languishing at the bottom of the crevasse. He pressed himself to his feet, limped to where a branch lay and grasped it with both hands, brandishing it like a club. Lichen oozed between his fingers.

The lamb staggered back, its feet splaying, its head lolling drunkenly.

Edward raised the branch over his head, paused and sighed. There was something altogether too brutish striking a tiny domesticated animal like this. He couldn't do it. Not without the distancing effect of a gun. He threw the branch aside and, cursing his weakness, dived into his motorcar.

He smiled as six and a half litres of engine jumped into life. He had never been so glad to hear that throaty roar as he was now. The possessed lamb glowed white in the headlights. Edward engaged first gear, closed his eyes and stamped on the accelerator. He heard the small body slam into the grille before scraping along beneath the chassis. He checked the inert body in his mirrors, engaged reverse gear and smashed into it again.

The mangled animal lay motionless before him, its fleece scraped and bloody. It had to be dead. Had to be. But was the usurper?

Edward got out of the car and approached the carcass. He picked up the fallen branch and poked it, tentatively, as though it might rise and snap at him. Something stirred in the blood glistening around the mouth. He looked closer and caught a glimpse of a slick, spiralled body, fringed by jointed legs and fronted by reddish pincers. It burrowed into the lamb's thin wool. It had looked like a crab without a shell; a misshapen crustacean no bigger than a little fingernail.

Edward stabbed with the branch, jabbing at where he imagined it might be. Then he saw it crawling across the ground towards his feet. He stamped on it, hard, his incomprehension driving him to stamp down again and again and again until all that remained was a damp spot on his heel. He wiped his shoe on the grass, tossed the branch aside and climbed into the idling Bentley.

~

As Glen Orchy and the surrounding mountains became a distant silhouette viewed through the motorcar's mirrors, and the first road signs for Oban appeared, Edward mused that Elizabeth would never accept his excuses for his lateness or, indeed, his appearance. He didn't care. He would get her into the car tonight, by force if necessary, and drive them inland to the safety of the Dempster-Smythe estate.

And there they would stay, surrounded by pits and traps, nets and guns and alert gamekeepers, and if she argued, well then Edward would just sit her down with a copy of *The Fauna Satanica* and damn well make her believe.

Perhaps he should sell the estate and move into the city? But even there he could trust no one, no *thing*.

Edward gripped the wheel tightly. Of only one thing could he be certain: the Reverend James Haplowe had a new convert, and it was his duty to make more.

His headlights picked out the ghostly form of an owl, sailing the night on silent wings. Edward crossed himself and whimpered.

The Arbitrator

White sunlight flashes between the roadside trees. You smack the visor down but it's ineffective: the windscreen looks like the teenager at the traffic lights washed it with milk. It's a migraine waiting to happen. The little bastard short-changed you, too.

But it'll take more than a young waster to put a crimp in your day. You're the man. The arbitrator extraordinaire. Without making concessions to militant union leaders you've averted a strike and saved a company hundreds of thousands of pounds, not to mention a shitload of misery for the workforce. You're in the mood to celebrate. There's a bunch of flowers on the passenger seat and a bottle of white burgundy in the boot. It's just a pity Cherie won't be interested in stories of wily boardroom manoeuvres. This is the woman who feigned disinterest in your bedroom manoeuvres, remember, which goes a long way to explaining why she is now your ex-wife.

The first thing she'll ask is, how come — seeing as you're such a big hotshot — she's raising your kids in a crummy two-bedroom semi? You can see the turned-up lip already. The sneer that launched a thousand heartburns.

This is a bad idea. Go home, look up some old mates and ask them to come out for a celebratory drink. Go out on the tear. Like the old days before life became an interminable blur of negotiation, arbitration and Powerpoint presentations.

You indicate left and turn down a narrow lane. A shortcut. You'll give Cherie the flowers and ask her to share a bottle of wine for old time's sake. If she says no, that's cool. You're not here to fight.

Up ahead there's a guy leaning on a brick parapet, where the road bridges railway lines. He's dressed like you, office casual. White shirt, top button undone, tie loosely knotted and sleeves rolled up. But it's not his appearance so much as where he is: the arse end of nowhere at — you check the clock on the dash — 8.33 in the evening.

There's a notebook and pen in his hands. You picture him writing "Life is a crock of shit", clambering onto the wall and jumping to his death. The vision raises goosepimples on your arms. You ease your foot off the accelerator as you glide past him.

Once he's a receding silhouette in the rear view mirror you rub your jaw and tell yourself to get real. He's probably a waiter or a barman from one of the local pubs, stopping off for a cigarette before clocking on. He could even be a trainspotter, the sad bastard.

So why do you feel this odd squirming in the pit of your belly? Why can't you rationalise away your worries?

Just because.

You slow down and execute a three point turn.

The guy doesn't move as you approach. Nor does he acknowledge your presence as your car mounts the grass verge a few feet away, its ticking hazard lights bathing him in an intermittent orange glow. Your shirt sticks to the seat as you climb out.

When you ask if he's okay your voice betrays your nervousness. You try again, injecting a touch of authority.

His eyes swivel to look at you. He says he's fine, thank you for asking, and uses your name.

You pat your chest, intending to remove your ID badge, but you took it off when you left the office. So now you're trying to figure if you know the guy.

There's a ghost of a smile on his lips as he points out that you thought he was going to jump.

Your face flushes. You root around for a witty reply but nothing comes. You start to back away, but he urges you to stay a moment. He's sketching rapidly in his notepad. He flips a page and then sketches on the one below, then goes on to the one below that, and the one below that . . .

You take a step backwards, reiterating your desire to leave.

He says the flowers are a lie.

You glance at the car, trying to judge whether he can see the bouquet on the passenger seat. From where he's standing? Unlikely. A breeze dries the sweat patches on your shirt.

Without looking up from his notepad, he tells you Cherie doesn't hate you anymore. She's battle weary. What she feels could only be described as indifference. Then he goes on to explain how indifference can be worse than hate in some cases, because at least hate betokens passion.

Betokens? You snort to mask your confusion. What sort of bullshit word is that?

Then confusion gives way to fear as the stranger points out the irony of you making a living by evaluating others' motivations when you persist in this charade of wanting to see Cherie. After all, you hate her. In the privacy of your own head you often refer to her as "the bitch", the worst appellation you can think of for a woman.

He stops drawing and regards you carefully. You rub the muscle at your temple, the one that twitches when you're anxious, and stammer that you don't hate your ex-wife at all. You still love her, damn it.

He's not fooled.

And so he continues. Cherie got a court injunction to stop you seeing Poppy and Stefan. She did many things to hurt you. Maybe some of those things were a matter of carelessness, but depriving you of your children 24/7 was malice. A twisting of the knife. You know she's told them lies about you, poisoned their young minds.

You want to cover your ears as he goes on — in his infuriating, reasonable tone — that you don't want to see Cherie at all, that you're just hoping to catch a glimpse of your children. Maybe a quick "Hi kiddo, how's school?" You need to hear their voices, touch their hair, to hug their little bodies and assure them Daddy is always thinking about them.

Your breathing quickens. You admit to hoping Cherie hasn't put the children to bed yet.

There's no inflection in his voice or expression on his face when he asks if you really want Poppy and Stefan to see you like this. He says your desperation is a sour reek.

Your hands ball into fists as you stumble backwards to your car. Screw you, pal, and the horse you rode in on . . . whoever you are. Then you're in the driver's seat, fumbling for the ignition key.

He gently raps the windscreen with his knuckles and holds up the notepad. He's filled every page with near-identical drawings. Flicking through the pages creates the illusion of movement. The first sketch is of the back of a car. But not just any car, *your* car. And yet he was drawing these pictures before you arrived.

In a heartbeat you're out of the vehicle and snatching the pad from him. He doesn't resist; he wanted you to take it. The second sketch is from an angle, as though the viewer has moved towards the driver's door. In stages, the view pans through 180 degrees until the final pages see the car head on. The movie lasts only a few seconds, but takes your present funk to new heights.

Every detail of the animation is seared onto your brain: the hose snaking from the exhaust pipe to the partly opened rear window on the driver's side, and the shifting image of you, slumped in the driver's seat with your head lolling over your left shoulder. In the last few frames Poppy is revealed as a front passenger, while Stefan, visible though the gap between the front seats, lies across the back. Their mouths are covered with broad strips of tape. The same tape binds their hands to the necks.

Terror and confusion manifest as a physical pressure behind the eyes. There's a keening noise in your ears. You pinch the bridge of your nose between trembling fingers. A rage you can't quell rises like magma in your chest and you grab him by the throat, swing him round and force his back against the parapet. Your thumbs are pressed into his Adam's apple. You shake him, scream: *Who are you? What are you?*

He raises a hand to wipe flecks of spittle from his face. You might as well be throttling a shop dummy. You let go and step back.

He stays where he is, arched backwards over the parapet like a broken doll, and tells you in his reasonable tone that you're both in the same line of work. He ventures no further explanation.

Not trusting your voice, you retrieve the notepad from the ground and thrust it at him.

He takes it from you and for the first time you see what could be a hint of sadness in his eyes. Why did you stop your car here? He puts it to you directly, but before you can speak he answers his own question: Because you have a highly developed sense of empathy, that's why. An arbitrator needs to see every facet of an argument to find the inevitable compromise. Every day you put yourself in other men's shoes. Today you saw a man on a railway bridge and you thought of suicide. Why? Because your life is all peaks and troughs, where the peaks are mere molehills compared to the abyssal depths of the troughs. The one thing that stays your hand on the exit door is the thought of leaving your children behind.

He stands straight, writes something in the notepad, tears out the page and hands it to you. He has written "Life is a crock of shit" in a script remarkably close to your own handwriting.

You're gasping. This is all wrong. What if you were to drive home and swore never to go near your wife and children again? You could do that. You could cheat fate, couldn't you?

He shakes his head. It doesn't work like that.

You plead with him.

He looks away over the railway lines so you don't have to see the pity in his eyes. You realise then how much he hates his job. He has averted a tragedy, but at what cost? You rest a hand on his shoulder, as one professional to another. Arbitration is all about compromise. It's not necessarily the right course of action that wins the day, just the course of action that is least wrong for all the parties concerned.

He appears to appreciate your support.

You ask him again if he's absolutely sure there isn't another way out of this situation. When he assures you there is not, you know it isn't a response lightly considered; he has deliberated long and hard. You thank him for his integrity.

Then you fold the note away into a pocket, heave yourself up onto the parapet and regard the parallel lines of burnished steel curving towards the horizon.

You didn't hear any footsteps, but you know the Arbitrator has left you.

You close your eyes to feel the soothing breeze on your eyelids. You picture Poppy and Stefan, and reclassify what you are about to do as self-sacrifice. It sounds better than suicide. You open your eyes to focus on the far off joining of sky and land, and wonder if you should wait for a train. Or would that would be overkill?

You smile at the phrasing, and let go.

C is for Clear

A thick silence descended over the small tableau. Charity said to Andy, "Just run that one by me again, will you?" Tom the fat tomcat sidled out of the kitchen into the lounge.

Andy wilted under his wife's megawatt stare. "This bloke down the pub said they were all the rage across the Atlantic. That is, until somebody sued the manufacturers and put them out of business. He's got a contact who sends 'em over by the lorry load. On the black market, like. That's why there are no instructions with it, or packaging. Not that you need any, it looks pretty much self-explanatory to me."

"Go on, I'm listening."

"Well, this bloke, he said that they were a great tonic for anybody dazed, or weary. Or if they was just plain jaded. He reckons It works like an emotional back-scrubber. Perks you up, like. You put this plug attachment in your ear—" Andy demonstrated —"enter a number on the keypad, presumably you put in a higher number the more depressed you are, and press the green button here. Only the battery needs recharging first."

"When you say 'green button' do you mean this one here, the one with a phone symbol on it?"

"Yes, that's the one. A phone? I thought that was a C for . . . I dunno. Cheer up? Carefree?" Andy's Adam's apple bobbed up and down. "It does look like a phone though, doesn't it?"

Charity nodded.

There was a long pause.

"D'you think I've been conned?"

Charity let the silence speak for itself.

Andy's shoulders drooped. "Sorry, love. How the bloke was saying, you could wake up all groggy and fed up, and just refresh your brain. He said that's why it's called a *DazeAway*. And I thought to meself, That'd be grand! I'm always a bit dazed and confused first thing."

Charity snorted, opened her mouth to say something and then decided against it.

"And I thought about you and little Robbie and the . . ." They never mentioned Charity's postnatal depression by name.

"Oh, Andy, I know you mean well, but the doctor said it was going to be a long haul. There are no shortcuts. Even if this stupid thing worked." She picked up the *DazeAway*. "It's not as if we haven't already got a mobile phone. I bet this one was nicked. What did you pay for it?"

Andy looked even more wretched.

Charity sighed. "Go on."

"I told him I hadn't got the cash, but he said it was okay, he took all major credit cards."

"And?"

"We-ell, he did. I gave him my card and he took it. Just got up and walked out, like."

"You pillock! Didn't you try and stop him?"

"I couldn't believe it at first. I kept thinking he must've gone to get a pen or summat. Then when he'd been gone a couple of minutes I got suspicious."

"You don't say? Good God! What am I to do with you? You and little Robbie, it's like having twins! Look, get on the phone and give the credit card company our details. Tell them your card has been stolen."

"Isn't it a bit late at night for that?"

"They'll have a 24 hour automated service. Just do as you're told." Charity wiped a hand across her eyes. It *was* late and no doubt Robbie would be awake in a couple of hours. She loved the little blighter but God he was demanding. A bit like her husband really. She smiled. That's it Charity, she thought, keep smiling, and it just might see you through.

"I'm sorry Charity, love. I didn't think."

"No, you never do. Tomorrow, go down the police station and tell them what's happened. If some thug is going around selling what are probably stolen mobile phones, he needs locking up. Would you recognise him if you saw him again?"

"Too true I would! I've a good memory for faces if nowt else."

"Okay." She patted his cheek. "But for now, just phone the credit card company. I'm going to bed."

~

Andy stood in the draughty hallway, frustrated. A pleasant woman's voice, after welcoming him to the Credit Card Customer Careline, told him to test to see if his phone was a touch-tone model. "Press the star button now," the voice advised.

Andy frowned and fumbled with the dial. "What's a bloody star button when it's at home?" He snatched up Charity's mobile off the side of the phone table and saw a button with a * symbol at the bottom right corner. The dial phone had no such provision.

What to do? It'd be expensive making the call on Charity's mobile, but if he waited until morning for customer services to be manned by real live people, the bugger with his credit card would have had all night to rack up a fortune. Andy switched on Charity's mobile and began to punch in the number for the careline. The keypad was locked. "For God's sake!" He shook it ineffectually and considered waking Charity for advice. His sense of self-preservation quickly derailed that train of thought.

Andy trudged back into the kitchen and idly picked up the new phone. Why not? he thought. After a little jiggery-pokery he managed to use Charity's charger to plug it into the mains. A smug smirk plastered itself across his face as a green display lit up. "I ain't so dumb."

He screwed the earpiece into his ear tightly, balanced the phone book on the kitchen table, traced the careline number with his left index finger, and thumbed in the number.

~

Charity's slippered feet slapped the stair rods as she carried little Robbie down to the kitchen. She had spent twenty minutes trying to coax him back to sleep. He was neither too cold nor too warm, he wasn't hungry or thirsty, and his nappy was clean and dry. "So go to sleep you little toad!" Robbie, ignoring his mum's sound advice, continued to grizzle.

She sighed. "Let's get you a drink of milk, eh?"

Charity frowned to see the kitchen light on and the lounge in darkness. She had expected to find her husband watching some late night TV or sulking over a beer. And she was ready to give him some grief over it, too. Why did she have to get up to the baby when her dozy hubby was already awake? "Hush, Robbie." She set her baby down on a mat where he immediately found something crunchy to pop in his mouth. Charity moaned. Robbie had a knack for finding something small, inedible and potentially lethal. She bent down to take it from him when she saw the *DazeAway* smashed apart on the tiled kitchen floor. Poor Andy, she thought. He must have taken it harder than she realized. She prised a shard of black plastic out of Robbie's mouth and gathered together several larger pieces from under the table. She examined them closely. One was the battery compartment lid. On the inside was embossed a logo. A white sticker read: *Memoraze and DaysAway are trademarks of*

Charity frowned and examined another fragment. *Caution! Always consult the manual before using your DaysAway.*

"The manufacturer accepts no responsibility for misuse of portable Memoraze equipment." The words spilled from her lips like bitter cherries. So Andy *had* got it wrong about the *DaysAway*, but then so had she.

"Come here, Robbie!" She gathered the youngster up in her arms and trod slowly to the lounge. "Andy? Andy, are you there?" She flicked the lounge light on. There, curled up between the settee and the wall, was her husband.

"Andy? Are you . . . are you all right?"

He removed a thumb from his mouth. "You aren't my mummy!"

Tom the fat tomcat, sensing he wasn't going to get any peace tonight, got up and sidled back into the kitchen.

"I owe you an apology, Andy."

"Go away!"

Charity thought it again: You and little Robbie, it's like having twins. And then covered her ears when Andy began to wail: "I want my mummy, I want my mummy, I want my mummy . . ."

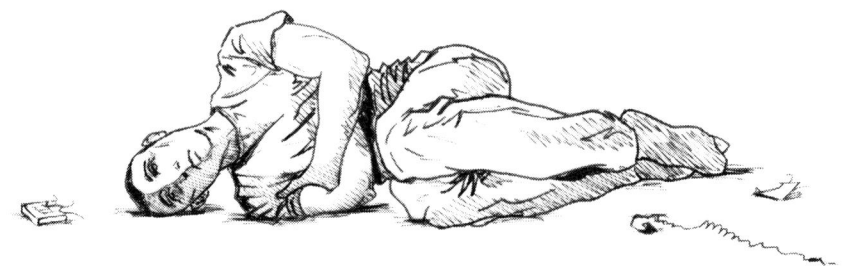

The Colour of Lemons

"*Close.*"

The soundproofed kiosk door slid shut behind Harding as he sat in front the video camera. He checked his image in the monitor, straightened his tie, smoothed the wrinkles out of his lab coat and said, "*Record.*" A steady green LED glowed.

"Date: March 10, 2008. Anthony Harding, chief neuro-psychologist of the Ufology department. Subject: Robert Leese. Date of birth 12/7/61. White British national, age forty-seven, height one point seven eight metres, weight seven two kilos. Distinguishing features: an appendectomy scar and a six-centimetre scar over his left eye."

Harding riffled through the notes on his lap. "The subject was admitted to Re:Search yesterday and samples of his blood, saliva, spinal fluid, urine and stools were taken. Test results appended in enclosed documentation. The subject voluntarily underwent a cranial scan by MRI. No aberrations, lesions or evidence of clots. No history of epilepsy. Investigative material appended in enclosed documentation.

"Subject history: Robert Leese was born to Janet Leese in Buxton, Derbyshire. Father's name was not recorded on the birth certificate. In 1967, when Robert was six years old, his mother rented a small two-bedroom house within the town and began seeing a man named Dennis Black.

"September 8, 1968: Janet Leese was found dead in an area of the Staffordshire moorlands known as the Roaches. She had been strangled. The post-mortem also revealed that she was seven weeks pregnant. Clothes belonging to Robert were found nearby but no body was recovered despite an extensive police search of the area. Dennis Black was arrested when he walked into Buxton police station claiming Janet Leese had stolen his car. He pleaded innocent, but a jury later found him guilty of murder on two counts and he was sentenced to life imprisonment.

"September 9, 1978: Hikers roaming the Roaches found a naked adolescent in a highly distressed state. He was suffering from amnesia and unable to supply a name to the police. A local television and newspaper appeal led to his grandparents coming forward who

205

positively identified him as Robert Leese. Two months later, Dennis Black's case was reviewed. His conviction for the murders was quashed and he was released. This much is Public Record."

Harding mentally reviewed the hundreds of closely typed pages of medical records, all the impenetrable jargon and illegible signatures in Leese's folder. "The subject has undergone extensive medical examinations but despite numerous attempts by various experts in their fields, his childhood and the ten year period between Septembers 1968 and '78 remain a blank." From the corner of his eye Harding saw a shadow hovering on the other side of the glass. "*End record. Open.*" The door hissed open on command. "Yes, Laura?"

"Dr Harding, the patient is in the PHS."

"Thank you Laura, I've nearly finished in here." He watched Laura Chang's wasp-waisted form retreating, her hips swaying under the belted lab coat. A colleague in his student days had once said to him, "Radiographers see everything in black and white," guffawing like it was the funniest thing ever. Harding always recalled the joke when he saw the coldly logical Ms Chang.

"*Close. Record.* The purpose of today's examination by Parkes-Hansen Scanner is to determine the subject's whereabouts during the ten-year period of which he has no recollection. Conclusions to follow. *End rec*—Oh, I almost forgot." Damn! That was going to look great on playback. "The subject informed me during yesterday's preliminaries that he hates yellow. I have not had the opportunity to conduct reactivity tests to find the extent of the subject's problem, but apparently, exposure to the colour brings on dizziness, nausea and can even result in a *petit mal*. It was a condition of his consent to be examined by Parkes-Hansen Scanner that I agree to investigate the origins of his lucidophobia. Conclusions to follow. *End record.*"

~

Cabling snaked overhead and along the floor from a gleaming cylindrical coffin. Harding stood behind radiographers Laura Chang and Alain Petit, and watched Leese through a video-link situated above their heads. The subject lay motionless within the cylinder. Polymer blocks either side of his head steadied him. Harding was thankful that the subject wasn't claustrophobic. The Magnetic Resonance Image scan had required him to undergo a similar procedure so Harding was confident Leese wouldn't freak out.

Wires, fibre optics and filaments traced across Leese's naked upper torso, gummed and suckered to points on his chest, eyelids and scalp. As Harding regarded the foreshortened length of Leese's body, he felt like a Lilliputian watching a bound and secured Gulliver.

"We've put the psychos' and espers' noses out of joint, Anthony." Petit was referring to the Psychic and ESP research teams on the floors below. Interdepartmental rivalry within the institute was intense between the saucer people, the psychos and the espers: a divide between three groups of specialists whose disciplines were so tightly focussed as to exclude overlap. All three departments had petitioned the Administration to be the first to use the new Parkes-Hansen Scanner. The Ufologists won.

"What do they want with this baby, anyway?"

Petit shrugged in his flamboyant Gallic manner. "They were going to stick one of their pet spoon-benders in there, I suppose."

"Well they'll just have to wait their turn. How's it going, Laura?"

"I have a fix on the alphas. It should be completed in a few moments." She was watching streams of data flow across the screen as she rotated and manoeuvred the transmitters and receptors within the shell of the PHS.

Petit said, "The results from the MRI were a bit disappointing, Anthony."

"What did you expect, Alain, a stainless steel implant grafted to his hypothalamus?"

Petit grinned. "It's traditional. Alien abductees should always come back with a neural implant. Or a chip in the neck. And that scar on his forehead; he didn't have it before he went missing according to his grandparents' statements."

Harding smiled. "He will be showing us how he came by it himself in a short while. Won't he, Laura?"

"Nearly there, Dr Harding."

"As a percentage, Anthony," Peiti said, "how confident are you that we have an abductee in there?" He was staring at the bulk of the Parkes-Hansen Scanner. "Possibly the first one ever to be validated under laboratory conditions."

"I'm quietly confident, Alain. That's all I'm saying for now." His heart beat a little faster. Once Chang had a fix on Robert Leese's alpha, beta and theta cycles, and was successfully downloading his aural and visual data, Alain Petit would split the incoming data into what were glibly called the conscious and conceptual streams, which would then be displayed on twin monitors.

A steel door at the rear of the laboratory slid open and excited voices wafted in. A florid executive waddled through, followed by a gaggle of shiny-faced men and women with notebooks. Harding was only slightly mollified to see two security guards flanking the small crowd.

"Laura, Alain, you continue here. I'll deal with this. What's going on, Max? You are not supposed to be in here. And who the hell are all these people? Get them out of here, *now*."

Maxwell Pearson, the institute's chief of media relations, looked surprised. Harding, however, did not need his skills at reading body language to see that the surprise was entirely feigned. Pearson was as subtle as a house brick.

"But Anthony, these are some of the best and most respected journalists in the country. Let me introduce you to—"

Harding ground his teeth. "Get them out of here, Max."

Pearson sighed. "I do apologise, ladies and gentlemen. I need to have a word with my colleague here. If you could return to the hospitality suite, I shall join you shortly. Thank you." He nodded to the security guards. After the group had left, he said, "*Close*," and turned to Harding, he said, "That was most rude, Anthony."

One of the visitors had stood to one side as everyone else left; a hatchet-faced man with close-set eyes that flicked around the laboratory as if gauging its capacity to harm him.

"Max. A private word, please." Harding grabbed a chubby arm and led the bemused executive a few steps from the visitor. He spoke quietly: "This is a scientific endeavour, not a media circus. What does this—" he gestured at the Parkes-Hansen Scanner with a thumb — "have to do with all those clowns you just paraded in here? And who the hell is this?"

Pearson smiled. "Well actually, Anthony, rather a lot. That is none other than Dennis Black. Does the name ring any bells?"

"Of course it does." Harding reappraised the man standing by one of Chang's prized yuccas. He had perused files and downloaded images of Black, all of them from the 1960s and 70s. Vilified or lauded, depending on which paper you read, Black had become a *cause celebre* until the media found another sacrificial lamb to slaughter, chew up and spit out. He was in his sixties now, with grey hair receding at the temples and a heavily lined face. He appeared uncomfortable in his rumpled blue suit.

"Dennis Black? But why?"

Pearson's smile disappeared and his voice became more businesslike. "Because the media like to portray us as a bunch of overpaid eggheads looking for little green men from Mars. This is a golden opportunity to demonstrate that some of the hardware we are developing here has some very practical, real world applications. Dennis Black spent ten years banged up in prison for murdering Janet and Robert Leese. The case was only reviewed when one of the victims turned up alive and well. And now you are going to be able to find out, at long last, who killed Janet Leese. I've put a lot of work into this, Anthony. You have no idea how hard it's been to persuade Black to come here today."

"Expensive was he? Who's he selling his story to?"

"It's an investment. Come on, Anthony, this is sensational stuff. We need the media. We need them on our side or we are not going to get government funding next year."

"Ah." Harding nodded sagely. "Funding. The Holy Grail. I might have known."

"Don't play the high-and-mighty with me you sonofabitch. You aren't the one that has to go begging cap-in-hand. People want to see results, and they want to see them soon. By the way, Anthony, who do you think got you the use of the Parkes-Hansen Scanner? The psychos were before you in the queue. Ask Administration if you don't believe me." Pearson raised an eyebrow, leaned closer. "You owe me this one, Anthony."

Harding knew when he was on a hiding to nothing. "Okay, Max. But I'm warning you. Keep out of the way. And if I order you out of the lab, I want you out *immediately*."

"You're the boss, Anthony."

"Gotcha," Chang hissed.

Leaving Pearson to escort Dennis Black to a seat, Harding returned to his station behind the two radiographers. Chang's screen showed a small black cross flitting around a white polymer surface.

"Excellent work, Laura." She rewarded Harding with a coy smile. He leaned forward and addressed the desk microphone.

"Robert, can you hear me? Robert?"

Petit reached across and switched the microphone on. Harding mumbled his thanks. The Frenchman stared ahead, his expression carefully neutral.

"Hi, Robert, you okay?"

"Still here, Dr Harding."

"Sorry to keep you waiting, but we're nearly there now. I want you to look at the cross, stencilled on the ceiling above your face." The cross on Chang's screen steadied. Harding had Leese rotate his eyes from left to right and the cross moved accordingly. Chang killed the small desk speaker and they listened to Harding's voice filtered through Robert Leese's ears.

Petit downloaded all the information he needed from Chang's console. Squinting at the lines of code he nodded for Harding to continue. "Okay, Robert, we are just waiting for a few final tweaks to be made and then we can begin the scan. I need you to picture something in your mind, something very familiar, as we did during the preliminaries yesterday."

"Okay. I'm picturing my front room at home. That all right?"

"That's fine, Robert. Keep the image focused and try not to let your mind wander. It's not easy, I know."

Alain Petit's fingers raced over his keyboard. An image of a settee flashed on his monitor, then a chair. They were replaced with a bow window, the sunlight highlighting smoky streaks on the glass.

Harding said, "Your windows need cleaning, Robert."

Leese spluttered. "You are seeing my thoughts? I know you said you would but, well, that's . . ." He trailed off, clearly embarrassed and nervous. The view on Petit's monitor became a rapid slideshow of sexual imagery. It was to be expected. Tell someone you could read their mind and they started to think of all the things they didn't want you to see. Harding checked over his shoulder to where Pearson and Black sat in plastic chairs. This wasn't fair on Leese.

"Relax, Robert, it's okay. I want you to look at the cross above your face and concentrate on that. Don't take your eyes off it. I am going to count slowly from one to ten, just like I did in our rehearsal, remember? And as I do so, you will become very relaxed, very drowsy. You'll feel good." He rested his hands on the back of Petit's chair and began to talk steadily. Hypnotism was all about tone and inflection. Within a few heartbeats, Leese was in a deep trance.

"Robert." Harding made a conscious effort to keep his voice level, to suppress his excitement. "Can you still hear me?"

"Yes."

Tentatively, then with more confidence, Harding took Robert Leese back through the years.

Alain Petit clattered away at his keyboard. He would occasionally rail at himself *sotto voce* for some imagined ineptness.

Using gates opened up in previous psychiatric evaluations, Harding was able to reach the gate that he was convinced would be their starting point. No one had been able to persuade the young boy to take them beyond this gate: "You are seven years old and with your mum at the Roaches. Uncle Dennis has taken you there in his car. You are away playing by yourself. What are you thinking, Robert?"

"'Bout a dinosaur. A giant dinosaur. Godzilla!" Robert Leese's voice was small and bashful.

Chang sounded uncharacteristically excited. "It's through." Harding looked over her shoulder and saw on her monitor a memory, pure and untainted: a pair of chubby hands playing with a rubber Tyrannosaurus Rex in long grass. The ground sloped steeply away into a valley. A breathless, squeaky rasp came through the speakers.

"There!" Petit flopped back in his chair. The monitor before him displayed a slightly fuzzy image of a stop-motion T-Rex. *The Valley of the Gwangi* would be Harding's guess. Then it was a man in a rubber suit trampling Tokyo into cardboard ruins, discordant bellows and flames. A flash of four-colour comic panels, a saluting handlebar-moustached general, speech bubbles, whooshing silver-and-yellow jet planes and tanks.

Petit knocked the volume down on the monitor displaying the conceptual imagery. Holding their collective breaths, the three researchers strained their ears. On Chang's monitor, a woman was shouting in the distance.

Harding whispered into the microphone before switching it off. "Your mum's calling you, Robert. You had better go to her. Bye-bye."

Like the licensed voyeurs they were, they watched Robert Leese's memories unfold like a stage magician's fingers.

~

"Bobby! Bo-beee! Where are you? Oi, Bobby! You've got a cup of tea here going cold. C'mon."

Bobby pushed himself to his feet and stuffed his toys into an anorak pocket. "Coming, mum." He ran to his mother with his arms stretched out at right angles to his body.

"Eeeeee-yooooowwwwwwww!" His mother laughed and Bobby felt the blood in his veins turn to warm milk.

"Come on, Airman Leese." She took his hand and together they strolled up the hillside to where a Ford Anglia was parked. A tall man filled the driver's seat.

"Where the bloody hell have you been? Your mother was worried sick about you, ye little—"

"Shut it, Dennis," Janet warned. "He was only a few yards away in the grass." Dennis's face darkened.

Janet hinged the front seat forward to let Bobby clamber into the back before passing him a mug of tea.

"I hope your feet are clean. Keep 'em off the seat." Dennis looked at Janet. "I cleaned the car out yesterday," he explained, "I don't want him muddying it first time out."

Janet gave her boyfriend a slow shake of the head before turning to Bobby. "D'you want a beef sandwich or boiled ham, Bobby? There are some biscuits for later, too. I brought your favourite." Mum was trying so hard to be comforting it brought a lump to Bobby's throat. He knew it wasn't her fault, but . . .

"Nice here, innit?" Dennis was looking at him through the rear-view mirror. Bobby knew better than to ignore Dennis so he agreed that, yes, it was indeed as Dennis said, *nice*.

"That's the trouble with kids his age, they don't appreciate what you do for 'em. Give us a sandwich, Jan. Beef'll do." Dennis gave Bobby a glance through the mirror again and winked as he bit on his sandwich. Bobby wiped a sticky bogey on the back seat and smiled back.

It had been his mum's idea to come out here to the Staffordshire moorlands. What she saw in this desolate and wild expanse of coarse grass and granite was beyond Bobby. But when Dennis pulled his face and moaned about missing the football results on *World of Sport*, Bobby had feigned excitement.

Janet sliced the end off a lemon with a small fruit knife and sucked on the soft, juicy flesh inside. Dennis drew in his cheeks and grimaced. "I dunno how you can do that, Jan, it's disgusting."

Janet laughed. "I had the same craving when I was expecting Bobby."

She was talking quietly now as though he wasn't meant to hear, but Bobby could hear quite plainly. "I've not told him about the baby, yet." She placed a hand on her belly.

"What about us? You told him about us getting wed?"

"No, I haven't. But he's quite mature for his age, I think he'll welcome a little brother or sister."

"But?"

"But what?"

"Come on, Jan, don't pull the wool over my eyes."

Janet lowered her voice further. "He thinks you don't like him."

"I don't particularly." Even Dennis, never the most sensitive of men, must have felt the temperature in the car fall a few degrees. "But—but, I meant like, I want to get to know him better, I suppose. Aw, come on, Jan, he's a right little turd at times. He doesn't make it easy for me." Dennis's voice became a whine. "Look when I set those seeds in your garden for you."

"He was trying to be helpful. And woe betide you if you ever lay a finger on him again."

"Oh! Nice to know where your loyalties lie." Dennis threw his door open and stormed out. "Go and marry some other sucker." He slammed the door so hard the car rocked on its soggy suspension.

The ringing silence he left behind was punctuated by the sound of Janet's sobbing. Bobby passed her a tissue from a box on the rear seat. He didn't know what to say. He wanted to throw his arms around her neck and comfort her but he was held in check by the fact that he wasn't supposed to know what was going on.

Bobby upended the tissue box, plucked a few tissues, and let his mind play.

~

"Hey," Petit said, "I've got this on disc at home." Robert was daydreaming of an old man with his granddaughter, strange twisting wraiths of plasma standing between them and the safety of a blue police box.

Black's triumphant voice cut through the background hum in the laboratory. "See? That's exactly how it happened. Exactly what I told the coppers. I walked off and left 'em there. I shouldn't have done that, I know, but I did. I was angry. And not a day goes by when I don't regret it. I never saw my Janet again. Or little Bobby," he added quickly. "When I did go back for my car, it was gone. An' obviously, I thought Janet had drove off and left me stranded."

Pearson laid a hand on the older man's knee, nodded sombrely. He caught Harding's eye, winked, and gave a surreptitious thumbs-up.

"I might as well go now, hadn't I?" Black moved as if to stand, but when no one answered him, he settled back in his chair. He rubbed a hand over his jaw, kneading his cheek with his fingertips.

Harding wondered if anyone else had noticed Black was wearing the necktie when he left the car. Forensic examination would later show that fibres from Black's tie had been embedded in the wound to her neck. Black's defence stated that he removed the tie while in the car and placed it in the glove compartment. When the car was recovered after being reportedly stolen, the offending article was found scrunched up in the back seat. Harding's gaze met Black's. He'd noticed.

Harding scanned the first page of his notepad where he had written "Loving and loved" and underneath, "Idealised". The boy adored his mother. Her skin was flawless and her features perfectly symmetrical. As she spoke, her face blurred and the mouth sharpened into focus. Then he had checked her eyes, and relaxed when her pupils dilated. Harding found it remarkable, if common, that a seven-year old should be so finely tuned in to his mother's subliminal body language.

On Petit's monitor, Dennis Black had appeared massive and devil-like, his skin sallow and pockmarked, although it appeared quite healthy and smooth on Chang's screen. His pupils were pinpricks, his hair impossibly shiny, wet-looking and midnight-black. His jaw was square, stubbled and oversized. A patch of dry skin on his cheek had been exaggerated into scales.

"Whoa! By the pricking of my thumbs, something wicked this way comes." Petit was gesturing at his monitor.

The devil Black had returned.

~

The car door swung open and Dennis stuck his head in. "Sorry, love, I just lost my rag. I didn't mean to upset you."

Janet dabbed at her eyes and sighed. "'S'okay. Where did you get to?"

"I found a little stream further down the road. I thought maybe Bobby would like a paddle with me?" He was looking at Bobby. "Put them tissues back in the box first, and then d'you fancy getting your feet wet, Bobby?" Dennis looked back at Janet and smiled. "I've been thinking, y'know."

She nodded gratefully, and then looked away.

The stream was a little further than Dennis had made out. He was clumsily trying to make conversation as the pair walked down the grassy banks. "So who's your favourite footballer then, Charlton or Best?"

Bobby pondered before replying. He wanted to make Dennis like him. "I think Bobby Charlton and Dennis Law are my favourites. Bobby and Dennis," he added in case the man had missed his point.

"Oh yeah." Dennis laughed. "Bobby and Dennis, like you and me. An unbeatable partnership, eh?" He roughly tousled Bobby's hair.

Bobby smiled up at Dennis, sensing a change had taken place somewhere along the line and Dennis was going to be pleasant to him from now on.

Presently, they came to a small brook that ran in the shade of an oak grove. Bobby thought it a real treat to be allowed to take his shoes and socks off and to paddle in the cold stream. He giggled as chilly tongues of water lapped at his knees and slippery brown pebbles shifted under his toes.

"Aren't you coming in, Uncle Dennis?" he asked.

Dennis sat brooding at the side of the stream, his black leather sports jacket buttoned to the neck despite the warm sunshine.

"Uncle Dennis?"

Dennis didn't answer. He just continued to stare across the floor of the valley, his jaw muscles bunched.

Bobby shielded his eyes and gazed in the direction they had come. The car was hidden from view by the stand of trees. He couldn't explain it, but Dennis's taciturn expression was unsettling him. He wished his mum were here.

Bobby had never trusted Dennis from the moment that his mum had introduced the dark-eyed, dark-chinned man. The incident in the garden they had so recently rowed over — *again* — confirmed Bobby's fears that Dennis was nothing but a bully. Bobby had been so pleased at the soft, dark, fresh texture of the soil after he'd struggled to drag the unwieldy rake through it, he'd expected, if not gratitude, at least a smile of encouragement. Instead, Dennis, having checked that no-one was watching him, lifted Bobby from his feet by the front of his jersey and threw him bodily into a patch of daffodils, crushing them. Which served to fuel Dennis's rage further. Dennis kicked him until a man walking his dog shouted over the fence. Dennis laughingly picked Bobby up and, dusting the dirt from him, told the man that they were playing rough-and-tumble. Bobby was an unwilling accessory to the lie. As soon as the man had walked away, Dennis punched and shoved him to the ground before striding away. He didn't once look back. Bobby lay with his tears soaking into the soil, snivelling as the narcissi gazed down on him with their jaundiced cyclopean eyes.

His mouth had remained silent but his bruises sang a lament his mother could not ignore. There had been hell to pay. The devil was cast out and Bobby even dared to hope that he would never see him again. But flowers, Milk Tray chocolates and apologies — to *her* — saw Dennis inveigle his way back into their lives.

"Oi! Pass us that branch, kid." Dennis stood and pointed to a heavy bough lying in the water near the far bank.

With no small amount of trepidation, Bobby paddled over and clutched one end of the fallen branch. It was slippery in his grasp and the slimy bark came away in his hands. It took a lot of effort to tug it free of the shingle and drag it against the current towards Dennis.

"That's it, bring it over 'ere."

Bobby heaved it on to the grassy bank and stood with his hands on his knees, panting heavily. "What do you want it for, Uncle Dennis?" There was a small quaver in his voice.

Dennis didn't reply. He picked up the length of wood, weighted it in his hands, and swung it at Bobby's head.

A crack of lightning flared behind Bobby's eyes, his knees buckled and he felt the icy embrace of the water encompass his body. A wisp of blood dispersed in the water before his face like smoke in a winter draught.

~

There was a stunned silence, followed by a bellow from Black. "No way! I never hit 'im. I never saw 'em again. I'm bloody well telling you I never saw 'em again. That machine's lying. That bloody Leese is lying." Pearson's chair scraped across the floor as he moved away from the belligerent Black.

"What a bastard." Coming from Chang's lips it sounded shocking.

"What did she say? What did that slant-eyed cow say?" Thin colourless veins stood proud at Black's temples as he continued to yell abuse. Pearson tried to put a restraining arm around his shoulders.

Harding dropped his notepad to the floor and hurriedly checked Leese on the video-link. Flashing digits in the corner revealed that although his heart rate had risen, he wasn't hyperventilating or showing any serious signs of stress. Harding looked closer at the black and white image and slowly shook his head. He had to be mistaken.

Both Petit and Chang were looking to him for confirmation of their next move. Harding tore his gaze away from the monitor, thinking fast. The correct procedure would be to bring Robert out of his hypnosis. He had been under for — he checked his watch — fifty minutes now and had just relived a traumatic episode. They had seen how the patient had obtained the scar on his forehead and also the origins of his lucidophobia had become more concrete. And it was probably treatable. If only Black would shut up and let him think.

Pearson mentioned the words "inadmissible evidence" and "double jeopardy". Black quietened down. He could not be tried twice for the same crime. The reporters in the room below, though, would jump on him like a pack of wolves.

Harding made his decision, and felt a flush of shame as he did so.

"We continue," he said, and prayed his colleagues wouldn't argue with him. Petit looked grateful and turned eagerly to his monitor; Chang looked at him a second longer than necessary before showing her back. Guiltily, Harding looked back at the video-link. He wouldn't have thought it possible, but there it was, clear and undeniable: fresh blood trickled from the old scar above Robert Leese's left eye.

~

Bobby awoke shivering and nauseous. For a few seconds, disorientated with concussion, he couldn't make sense of the world. He was lying in a stream on his left side, his right arm twisted behind his back. He couldn't feel his legs. Strong sunlight strobed through the whispering treetops, flashed and sparkling on the water. He struggled to his feet, panicking and fighting to free himself from a tangle of tree roots. Water streamed from his hair and clothes, his nose and mouth. He doubled over, vomited slime into the fast running water. His throat felt raw.

Bobby clambered up the bank, gripping the tree roots, and flopped onto his front. Thin blood ran from a painful gash on his forehead. He began to cry, the stinging tears born of ice-cold fear and white-hot frustration. A man — an adult, a grown-up, his mother's boyfriend, his future stepfather — had done this to him and he felt powerless to reply. Then the torch of anger flared bright. Let Uncle *Bastard* Dennis charm his way out of this one.

Pushing himself to his feet, Bobby began the long trek back to the car. It was when the coarse, whip-like grass started to cut his feet that he remembered to return for his socks and shoes.

The climb uphill felt a lot farther than the walk down, and despite the mid-afternoon sun Bobby was shivering as his wet clothes clung to his small frame. He removed his shirt and vest and tied them around his waist, feeling an immediate wave of warmth pass through him as the sun washed his bare skin. Every now and again he ran a hand over his cut forehead. In a perverse way, he hoped that it would be bleeding heavily when he reached the car. More dramatic, he thought, and more condemning.

Finally, Bobby reached the road. He couldn't be sure, but he thought the car was parked in a lay-by further up the lane to his right, beyond a jumble of lichen-covered boulders. He started up the slight incline. He recognised a fallen gate they passed on the way down.

As he rounded the granite outcrop he spotted the gravel lay-by where Dennis had parked the Anglia. The car was gone. He ran to the exact spot where earlier in the day his mum had told him not to wander too far.

Something rolled away from his foot. A lemon. Panic swelled in his chest. He clutched at his head and tugged his hair. Where did they go? It had to be some stupid joke. Perhaps they rolled down the road to hide from him? Or had Dennis told his mum that Bobby liked it so much he wanted to stay? Had she replied "Okay, let's leave him here"? Was she angry at him? Did she love Dennis more than him? Had they brought him here to dispose of him because a new child was taking his place?

Bobby felt he would choke on his heart. He looked down at the lemon and kicked it as hard as he could to send it skipping off the road and into the grass. He stopped dead. And ran to his mother's side. He had not seen her lying in the long grass, with only a single limp hand visible from the road.

She was playing dead. Very convincingly. A purple bruise ringed her throat, the skin puckered and ugly.

Bobby squatted at his mother's side and studied her expression. He waited and waited, for the flicker of an eyelid, a twitch of a lip that would signify the end of the ghastly, morbid joke that they were playing on him. He watched her breast for the giveaway rise and fall of breath. He told her quietly about Dennis and the attack at the stream, told her that this joke was mean and cruel. He told her that he was happy about a new brother or sister and, now that it was getting cooler, he would like to go home. Please. He talked until he grew hoarse.

Bobby gave up. Picking up the lemon, he slouched through the tussocky grass towards the stream at the foot of the hill. The oaks looked black and indistinct. He hadn't gone far when he stepped awkwardly and stumbled. He couldn't be bothered to rise. He lay where he fell.

His pants were cold and clammy and smelt of wee. Removing his plimsolls he cast them away with a scream. His socks, pants and underpants followed with a similar grunt of effort. He sat with his bare bottom to the earth.

The sun neared the hilltops at the opposite side of the valley: warm, yellow and comforting. The shadows lengthened. Bobby lay back and raised the lemon between his thumb and forefinger to block out the sun. If he extended his arm to full stretch and squinted through one eye, the lemon appeared black, framed with a flashing corona of chrome yellow.

He twiddled the fruit between his fingers and imagined the lemon as a large object seen from faraway. Slowly, ever so slowly, he brought the lemon closer to his eye.

~

Petit was in a filthy temper. For some obscure and unfathomable reason, both screens were displaying the boy's conceptual imagery, which was, he assured Harding between gritted teeth, impossible. Diagnostics had turned up nothing. He made a few desultory passes over his keyboard. He was clearly at a loss.

On both screens a lemon hung in the air above the Staffordshire moorlands. Bright yellow framed by a darkening sky.

Harding chewed on a thumbnail. He would have to reassess his previous evaluation regarding Leese's lucidophobia and the incident with the daffodils — the boy was playing with a lemon. Therefore the phobia had put down roots later.

But that was not the main thing bugging him.

"Laura, did you notice anything, um, unusual when Bobby kicked the lemon?"

She looked at Petit before turning to face Harding. "Well, yes, I did actually, but I thought it was a glitch in the machine."

Petit scowled at her.

"What did you see?" Harding prompted.

"His foot missed the lemon completely, but it still moved."

"That's what I saw." Harding knew he was overlooking something. He removed his glasses and pinched the bridge of his nose. Before him were the rounded backs of Chang and Petit in their heavily creased white coats. The realist and the dreamer. For a moment he was reminded of the brain's structure, how the left lobe was connected to the creative right lobe by a dense strand of neural gristle called the corpus callosum. Had Parkes and Hansen, the inventors of the scanner, deliberately mimicked nature when they set the two monitors side by side: the "real world" on the left, the "conceptual world" on the right?

Chang looked at him quizzically. "Dr Harding?"

"If we discount a software or hardware fault—"

"It's neither of those, Anthony, I'm sure."

Harding took a deep breath "Then I think it means Robert may have telekinetic abilities. The blow to the left side of his head or something, I don't know."

Petit's mouth dropped open. "He's a blasted spoon-bender?"

Chang dipped her head. "Yes. This is what we'd see: the subject's creative right overruling his conscious left. Shall I call up an esper or psycho, Dr Harding?"

"No!" chorused Harding and Petit.

"No," Harding breathed. "He's my subject and I don't intend to lose him to a damned esper."

"Whatever you say, Dr Harding."

"Let me get this straight, Anthony. You're telling me that we really are watching a boy make a lemon fly using the power of his mind?"

"Yeah, I think so."

"Cool."

~

It came from out of the sun, rotating along its axis in the washed-out sky. It was accompanied by a low murmur, felt in the throat as much as heard. It came closer, the surface dented and pockmarked by countless meteor impacts absorbed by the flexible epidermis during its interplanetary travels. The bow and stern showed lime-green where the super-furnace heat of entry into the Earth's atmosphere had scorched it.

The organic spaceship continued to descend over the valley; the hum becoming a series of intermittent pulses and clicks. The breeze stiffened and stalks of grass bent as the craft passed close over the hillside.

It halted and hung in the air directly over Bobby, filled his vision. He screwed shut his eyes. A soft swish and metallic click, and a glow illuminated his eyelids, turning them bright scarlet. His body felt a fraction of a degree warmer as a strong light played over his naked skin.

"Robert!" The voice sounded urgent. "Robert, this is Dr Harding. You must listen to me."

Bobby frowned at the intrusion. He kept his eyes firmly closed as the heat intensified and his stomach went inexplicably lighter.

"Dr Harding! Look at the video-link."

"What the hell? Somebody tell me that's a software glitch."

"What software? It's just a camera, Anthony."

"Dr Harding, we're losing contact."

"Oh my God! What's going on? Max, stop him. Put that chair down, Black. Don't be a damned fool."

Bobby thought he heard Uncle Dennis shouting. Uncle *Bastard* Dennis was here? He giggled as he felt the tickle of grass unfurling beneath his back.

~

A brief flash of actinic light threw harsh shadows around the laboratory. A chair bounced harmlessly off the Parkes-Hansen Scanner and clattered to the floor.

An empty blue suit with a white shirt and underwear inside lay in a crumpled heap. A black toecap peeped from beneath the pile.

The monitors burned with a baleful yellow glare for a full seven seconds before blinking out in a crackle of static.

Harding tapped the screen on the overhead video-link. There were discarded wires and fibre optics strewn around the hollow interior of the scanner. Of Leese there was no sign. He had whisked himself and Dennis Black away in a lemon spaceship.

Pearson said, "I'm calling security. Black must be in the building somewhere." He peered at each of them in turn, his pleading eyes avoiding the empty pile of clothes.

Harding rubbed his cheeks with the flat of his hands. He suddenly felt extremely weary.

"*Open.* Close. *Close, you voice-activated piece of crap.*" The recording kiosk door slid to, cutting him off from the laboratory. Harding jabbed the rewind button on the video before falling into the chair. What had they witnessed? His head was full of phrases and terms he had no faith in; mind over matter, matter transference, spatiotemporal loops, dimension slips, parallel universes. He'd wanted to see aliens, but instead he had seen . . .

He ground his fingertips into the corner of his eyes and saw spots.

There was a barely audible clunk as the video hit the stop and began playback. *"Date: March 10, 2008. My name is Anthony Harding . . ."*

Harding puffed his cheeks out and shook his head. *Oh boy.*

The espers and psychos would be petitioning Administration to serve them Harding's head on a plate. He would be spending the next thirty years pushing a broom up and down the corridors if he didn't come up with something plausible in the next five minutes. But that was the problem: there *was* no plausible explanation. Two men had disappeared into a mind-construct. He contemplated what an abused young boy's mind would do to the bullying adult that had killed his mother and attempted to kill him. It didn't bear thinking about.

". . . hikers roaming the Roaches found a naked adolescent in a highly distressed state. He was suffering . . ."

There was a sharp rap of knuckles on the soundproofed door. Harding lifted an eyebrow enough to see it was Alain Petit. He was pressing his face up close to the glass and mouthing something.

"Open. What is it Alain, are they back?"

Alain grimaced. "No such luck, Anthony. But Laura just—"

He didn't get any further. Harding had closed the door in his face.

". . . examined by Parkes-Hansen Scanner that I agree to investigate the origins of his lucidophobia. Conclusions to follow."

The video paused. A red LED began to flash on the camera. Harding wet his lips and mentally composed what would effectively be his resignation. He glanced up in irritation as Chang's silhouette joined Petit's. She rapped on the glass door. Damn. He could never be rude to Laura.

"Open. Laura, we're finished."

"No we are not, Dr Harding. We merely have to wait ten years." She raised an eyebrow and waited for him to catch up. Harding's mouth hung open in admiration.

"Good God," he said. "But can we be sure Robert Leese will do the same again?"

Petit laughed. "We don't need to be sure, Anthony. So long as Admin can be convinced."

But what of Dennis Black and the assembled media bodies in the building? Tough, thought Harding. Maxwell Pearson's problem now. Harding swivelled to face the camera, hardly able to believe he had the audacity to say what he was about to say. But then, a radiographer who saw things in black and white — God bless her — had probably handed him a ten-year reprieve.

"*Record.*" A green LED came on. "Phase one of the experiment has been a resounding success! Conditions were perfectly recreated and the subject subsequently vanished in a controlled manner. We are now preparing for phase two," he intoned, "when the subject returns."

He grinned wolfishly.

"*End record.*"

The Light Knight Returns

A bedside lamp cast a diffused glow over the boys' bedroom. Tommy Knight, perched on a box wadded with comics, studied his older brother's sketch. "It's good, Billy," he said, "but can I make a suggestion?" He waited for Billy to say yes. The seven-year age gap between them meant Tommy never took his brother's agreement for granted.

"Go on . . ."

"The facemask is too fearsome." Tommy twiddled the hem of his pyjama jacket. "If he was a supervillain then it'd be okay, but my guy's a hero. And can you make him a bit thinner? And I didn't want those sort of boots, I wanted boots like Captain America wears."

Billy's mouth quirked. "But apart from that you really like it, huh?"

Tommy thought this might be sarcasm. He nodded and hoped for the best.

Billy sighed. "Pass me another piece of paper." He crouched over their shared desk. "So you don't want the head fully covered." He sketched a man's broad face, all sharp angles and planes. "His forehead, cheeks and nose are covered by a mask, but we can see his hair and mouth."

He drew a lantern jaw, but Tommy objected. Billy drew a slimmer one and sneaked in a cleft chin. Tommy let it pass.

"Dark and wavy hair, like yours?" Billy asked.

"Please."

"Body not overly muscled, but powerful-looking. One-piece suit of—" Billy picked a coloured pencil —"dark blue leather. No underpants over girlie tights for our man. Silver hoops around his chest. How many?"

"Three."

"Okay. Hands in gauntlets, feet in swashbuckling knee-high boots that fold over at the top. Just like Captain America's. What colour?"

"White."

"White? Bit impractical for boots. You sure?"

"Uh huh."

Billy shrugged. "You're the boss. Anything else?"

"Yes, a white cloak fastened by a gold brooch."

"What's the magic word?"

"Please."

"One cloak coming up. Does he need a belt or holster?"

"I haven't decided yet. I don't want him to have a gun or knife, or anything like that. They're too . . ."

"Villainish?" Billy prompted.

"Exactly," Tommy said, delighted his brother was taking the creation seriously.

"Okay." Billy slid the drawing across the desktop. "How's that?"

Tommy held the picture aloft. He couldn't stop beaming. "Perfect. I'm going to call him the Light Knight!"

"Your alter ego, huh? He looks a bit of a faggot if you ask me."

"William Knight!" Mom glared at him from the doorway. "What have I told you about saying that? Now come on, it's bedtime."

Tommy suppressed a giggle as he crawled into bed. Mom propped him up on pillows and unscrewed the lid on a bottle. "You okay tonight, hon?" She popped a spoonful of medicine into his mouth.

He clamped his lips around the spoon and nodded. Some nights he felt his chest was full of treacle and he was breathing through cheesecloth, but tonight it wasn't so bad. The medicine helped to alleviate the symptoms of cystic fibrosis a lot. Even if it did taste disgusting. He stuck his tongue out and scowled. Mom smiled and kissed his forehead. "Bang on the wall if you need me," she murmured in his ear.

Billy clambered onto the top bunk and Mom straightened his blanket. "Goodnight, boys."

The brothers chorused: "Goodnight, Mom."

She switched off the bedside lamp and pulled the door closed. It took a minute or two for Tommy's eyes to adjust to the darkness.

"Billy?"

"Hmm?"

"Can you make me a badge tomorrow? One that says the Light Knight?"

"Yeah, sure. I'll do a logo," he said. "LK for Light Knight."

"He's indestructible, the Light Knight."

"Just like you, huh?"

"No, not at all like me." Tommy knew kids like him rarely lived into adulthood.

The bedsprings above his head creaked as Billy levered himself onto one elbow. His silhouetted head appeared over the edge of the top bunk. "Don't talk like that, d'you hear? You'll live as long as the rest of us." Billy settled back. Tommy knew he'd upset him.

"Sorry. Heh, Mom heard you say faggot," he whispered with glee. "You didn't know she was there, did you?"

"No."

"Billy?"

"Yep?"

"What exactly is a faggot?"

His brother sighed. "Tommy?"

"Yep?"

"Shut up."

~

Saturday was Tommy's favourite day of the week. Especially when the sun rose fat and yellow and his mother allowed him to play by the brook that ran along the southern border of Harvest Hill.

He scuffed up pebbles with the toes of his shoes and sifted through them for a suitable missile. About the size of a thumb tip would do. He found one, wiped it clean and slipped it into the cup of his weapon. A black cast-alloy Y with a finger-thick band of elastic, the slingshot was Billy's and he kept it well-hidden from Mom and Dad. The boys' shared secret.

His thin arms trembling with the effort, Tommy stretched the elastic and sighted between the forks. Looking upstream, squinting into the climbing sun, he could see the stone bridge that carried the main road out of Harvest Hill. Across the brook the Church of St Augustine dominated the skyline with its crenellated tower. Downstream the brook overflowed into water meadows cloudy with water fleas.

Tommy swivelled to face a stand of hawthorn trees and let fly the pebble. *Thwack!* White blossoms fluttered earthwards.

Perhaps the Light Knight should carry a slingshot. He looked down at the cardboard badge he had pinned to his sweater: a lighting-flash

LK. He'd ask Billy to add the logo and a slingshot to his illustration later.

He shielded his eyes against the sunlight on the water. A dead frog floated by, a flaccid star-shape swirling in the current. Then another appeared, its fragile body twisted in death.

Looking upstream, to where the green bridge crossed the brook, he heard laughing and cheering, and the soft plash of stones hitting water. Tommy ran, clambered the mossy parapet, crossed the road and peered down the other side.

Two kids were staring at the brook with their right arms raised. They were older than Tommy — about the same age as Billy — and one of them was a giant. At least six-foot seven. His hands and feet were oversized, and his heavy jaw jutted as though his lower incisors overlapped the uppers. Tommy thought he looked like a pike. The shorter kid had a high-domed forehead and buckteeth and looked a lot like Bugs Bunny. They both had close-cropped hair, leather biker jackets and stonewashed jeans. Bugs wore white running shoes, the Pike wore steel-toecap boots.

A fishing net and red bucket lay in the grass behind them.

With a suddenness that made Tommy start, they flung the missiles in their hands with whip-like viciousness. He stared at the patch of water they concentrated their energy on. A plump frog kicked in circles, and then floated motionless.

The boys cheered and high-fived, the shorter boy leaping to reach the other's hand.

The frog's body trembled over the washboard ripples.

The Pike moved as though he had splints strapped to his limbs. He dipped his hands into the red bucket and glanced up at Tommy. "What are you looking at, shit-for-brains?" The giant clasped a frog in his huge paddle-like hands. He tossed it into the water where it tried to swim across the current.

The animal died in a violent hailstorm.

Tommy shivered with rage at the boys' cruelty. Then the Pike turned to throw a stone at him. He saw the movement just in time and ducked behind the parapet.

When he straightened it was with a pebble in the cup of his slingshot and the Pike's head framed in the sights. The giant's ginger hair was shaved so close it looked like a helmet fashioned from suede shoe leather. Tommy wanted to punch a hole through it.

But the Light Knight showed the quality that set heroes apart from villains: *mercy*. He lowered his sights and fired at the bucket. It toppled and splashed Pike's jeans.

Tommy cheered: "The Light Knight, one – the Pike, zip!" Then he tucked the slingshot into his waistband, ran across the road, swung his legs over the parapet and dropped six feet to the grassy embankment. He hit the ground running.

It would have been quicker to use the road into Harvest Hill, but he had to hide the slingshot, somewhere safe from adult eyes. The boys usually kept it under a loose brick at a water outlet further upstream, but that was no longer an option.

The big boys' voices echoed under the bridge as they scrambled up the far side. Tommy wasn't worried. He had a head start and his escape route all planned out. He knew a spot where the brook narrowed to a few feet. Tommy would clear it with a running jump, duck the barbwire fence, dash through the field beyond, skirt the high wall surrounding the churchyard after tossing his slingshot into the nettles to be retrieved later, pass through the cemetery and emerge into the town square.

Bugs screamed from the top of the bridge: "You're dead!"

Tommy reached the narrow section of the brook and leapt. His feet thudded into the soft sandy earth on the other side. He threw a backward glance — saw the fleet-footed Bugs gaining.

Tommy sucked in a deep breath and grimaced. His chest felt full and tight. Sparks shimmered on the edge of his vision.

He clawed up a steep embankment and scrambled under the bottom strand of a barbwire fence. His head and shoulders were through when something tugged on his belt. He pushed hard but he was stuck fast. He twisted his body to see the slingshot snagged on the wire. The sound of running feet and stones scattering came closer. Tommy gave a desperate heave and the weapon jerked from his waistband. Leaving it, he jumped to his feet and ran for the cemetery.

He plunged through clumps of thistles, sent clouds of down into the air. His feet broke through dried cowpats, skidded on the slime beneath. Above the laboured scrape of his breathing he heard Bugs' pounding feet. Tommy's vision blurred and his knees buckled. He staggered, collapsed under a stained-glass window depicting a praying St

Augustine. The supplicant's eyes looked to the Heavens. Crows cawed from the surrounding ash trees.

Tommy gazed into a pale face framed by a cobalt blue sky. "You're dead!" Bugs turned to look back down the field. "Steve," he shouted. "Over here!"

The Pike trolled up the field, the slingshot dangling from one hand.

"I'vuh— I'vuh—" Tommy gasped and clutched his chest. "Can't breeve."

e Pike kicked him hard on the soles of his shoes. "What's up with him?"

Bugs shrugged.

"What did you fire at me for?" the Pike demanded.

Tommy curled into a ball. Everything was turning to shades of grey. "For killing frogs!"

The Pike raised the slingshot and drew back the cup. The overstretched elastic turned from brown to white. The pebble thudded into the ground scant inches from Tommy's head. The Pike reloaded and aimed at the birds perched in the trees.

"Fuh— Fuh— Faggot!"

"Steve, I think there's something wrong with him."

Tommy nodded.

"Damn right there's something wrong with him," the Pike said.

Bugs tugged on his friend's sleeve. "Steve?"

The Pike's lower incisors bared in a predatory smile. Malevolence glinted in the murk of his eyes.

Despite his resolve not to give them the satisfaction, the Light Knight wept. And felt the world fall away; the ensuing silence disturbed only by the flutter of crows' wings as they rose into a cloudless blue sky.

~

Billy rested his forearms on the parapet, dislodging powdery lichen into the water below, and watched the local bird population go crazy. Flocks of crows filled the sky. The air rang with their calls. They dived into the long grass and out again. Billy couldn't recall seeing them so agitated.

Tommy would have been fascinated. He could scan the skies for hours — well, minutes — with a pair of binoculars, or watch among the tree roots near the banks in the hope of glimpsing a rat. Or watch whirligig beetles draw crazy patterns on the water's surface, or scoop up frogspawn to examine the embryonic tadpoles wriggling inside.

Billy pinched the bridge of his nose to stop the tears. It had been more than four months since they found Tommy's body in the field behind the church, but it still seemed unreal. Like he expected his little brother to pop up from behind a bush or parked car with a mischievous grin and a cry of "Surprise! You didn't *really* think I was dead, did you?"

But they'd buried him under the watchful gaze of St Augustine on a warm May afternoon. Billy had watched the white coffin lowered into the ground and listened to the preacher give it the "ashes to ashes, dust to dust" bit. And you can't get deader than that.

The sounds of heavy footsteps snapped him out of his reverie. Billy looked up into the face of a green giant dressed in a ludicrous purple jumpsuit. He gasped. Then his brain caught up with his eyes. October the 31st Halloween.

"Been trick-or-treating?" he asked.

The giant slid the mask up onto his head. "No, I'm dressed like the fucking Green Goblin for my own amusement. Of course I'm trick or treating." He spat a mouthful of gum over the parapet. "I've had enough of candy. Got any coffin nails?"

"I don't smoke."

A thoughtful silence greeted his reply.

"You're Billy Knight, aren't you?"

"Yeah, that's right." Billy didn't need to ask the other boy his name. Everyone knew of Stephen Ellis in high school. It was kind of hard to ignore a kid as tall as Ellis. Besides, he had a bad rep.

Ellis' lips twitched into a sly smile. "I was there when your brother croaked." He laughed. "*Croak.*"

A frosted black stone lodged in Billy's throat. He swallowed, forcing it down.

Ellis narrowed his eyes and tilted his head to one side. "Weedy little kid, wasn't he?"

Billy's fists clenched. His breath hitched in his chest "I, um . . ." Lost for words, he put his head down and walked away.

"What happened?" Ellis called after him, "Your pa brung home the runt of the litter and your ma raised it?"

The frosted stone cracked. Ice spilled into Billy's heart and belly. He tasted it on the back of his tongue — ice so cold it burned. He turned to face his tormentor. Time slowed. Ellis moved as though encased in treacle, his mocking laughter sounding hollow and far away: "*Croak, croak!*"

Billy's hands found purchase on Ellis' lily-white cheeks; his nails gouged like fishhooks as he pulled the hateful visage towards him. With all the strength in his arms and neck muscles, Billy rammed his forehead into Stephen Ellis' face. Something splintered and gave. Billy reared back and without pause thrust his head into Ellis' face again. Blood spewed in crimson arcs from the giant's nostrils.

Time rushed in. Ellis choked and cupped his nose, smeared blood across his right cheek. His eyes bulged.

Billy clubbed him in the chest with an elbow and the giant toppled. Billy followed him down. He fastened his teeth on Ellis' face, exulted when the giant screamed like a little girl. Then Ellis grabbed him by the hair and slammed a sledgehammer fist into his face. Billy flopped onto his back, eyes squeezed shut against the pain. A persistent beeping penetrated the ringing in his ears. He opened his eyes to see a delivery van bearing down on them. Billy rose to his feet and staggered to the parapet. Ellis joined him and waved the van past The driver shook his head, doubtless bemused by the sight of teenagers playing superheroes.

Billy gazed through bleary eyes over the fields. The crows perched in the trees had fell silent. In the near distance, under the shadow of the old church, something stirred in the long grass.

His feet left the ground as a huge steel toecap connected with his balls. He fell to his knees. Then the giant dragged him to his feet and pitched him over the wall into the freezing water below, the blue-white shock jolting him out if his stupor. He stumbled to the embankment and hauled himself out.

Billy heard the wheezing snort of Ellis' approach. A fist connected with the back of his head and everything went white. He retracted into a foetal ball and covered his face as kicks and punches landed on his body and exploded in scarlet flowers of agony.

Then Ellis cried out and the blows ceased. Billy peered between his fingers to see crows mobbing his adversary. The giant flapped his arms at the raggedy black birds, swatted at them as they pecked and scratched his face and hands. Their sharp beaks cut diamond-shaped rents in his purple jumpsuit. A horde of creatures came swarming through the grass: mice, rats, otters. There was a silent rush of air, and a huge pair of eyes looked down from the parapet. The great horned owl stretched its neck and the tip of a rat's tail disappeared down its gullet.

The ground sagged, the besieged Ellis fell and the rodents swarmed over him in a brown wave. A mewling scream came from the boy's lips seconds before curved yellow incisors stripped them from his face. His frenzied limbs thrashed, but for every rat he displaced another took its place. Moaning, with furry bodies weighing him down, he crawled into the brook and submerged himself. The water ran red.

Billy edged away on his elbows and shoulder blades. Where Ellis had been standing the soil heaved with worms, like Medusa's head was buried there. Then order imposed itself on the chaos, and the worms arranged themselves into shapes as familiar as they were unexpected.

Billy climbed to his feet and blinked. On the grass, in neat letters, the myriad worms' bodies spelt out "LK".

~

The tower of the church glowed in the evening light. The Light Knight viewed it from the eyes of the owl, its great wings beating the air.

Killing the giant had brought no satisfaction. Ellis had only been a child. A cruel one, perhaps, but still a child. And therein lay a lesson for the Light Knight: he must rise above the level of petty vengeance. He understood now the code by which superheroes lived their lives, and why it was necessary. Power brought with it temptations that had to be resisted lest it spin out of control.

Billy had run off in a terrible lather, throwing glances every which way. Tommy gently steered the bird over the town of Harvest Hill to follow his brother home. He had many fond memories, but it was time to leave.

Although parts of him would remain.

He reached out and tasted damp earth all around, grains of dust clinging to his mucus-coated body; felt rough tree bark beneath his toes, his bushy tail curled round him for warmth; licked his lips at the strong scent of refuse; bumped the wooden slats of a stall; stamped a hoof; suckled a nipple; took cover under weeds where the sunlight did not fall on the water's surface…

Would he dissipate as he continued to spread through the food chain? He didn't think so. He rode tens of thousands now. They were like cells in an organism. He sensed no limits. Tommy envisaged plunging into dark ocean depths and steamy jungles, imagined traversing arid deserts. Where there was life, the Light Knight would expand.

And that's where he would fight his battles: where people carelessly shot, chased, harpooned and clubbed, or made homeless, poisoned, force-fed or experimented on creatures. He would make them part of the Light Knight, be their leader and protector.

Today Harvest Hill, tomorrow the world.

Raising Archie

The trilling dragged me though several layers of warm slumber. I sat up and swept the bedside cabinet with the flat of my hand before realising I didn't need my glasses to answer a phone.

Brenda turned to face me, concerned. Dead of night calls are not the norm in our household.

"Hello? Dave? What's that, mate? You've got a *what*? Okay. Well, I'm sure it can wait until tomorrow." I checked the glowing red digits of the clock-radio and corrected myself. "Later *today*. Goodnight." I put the phone down.

Brenda murmured, "What did he want, James?"

"Well, it's all a bit odd, really."

Dave had seen a listing on an auction website for some kind of big egg. No description to speak of, but a few left-clicks and £30 and one penny later, the egg was his. Now, apparently, an animal had hatched.

"He wanted to show me his new pet." I picked the phone up and dialled. "I'll be there in twenty minutes, mate."

"You berk," Brenda said, and rolled over.

I shrugged, unable to explain the contagious excitement, the sense of curiosity awakening in the marrow of my 39 year-old bones. A feeling that quickly dissipated in the frigid night air as I drove over to Dave's house.

All the windows of his semi-detached glowed in the blue-blackness. This, I thought, slamming the car door, had better be good.

Dave snatched open the front door, dragged me in then shut it behind me. I started to complain, but he spun me around. "You've got to help me find him! The little sod disappeared while I was on the phone to you. Whatever you do, watch you don't tread on him. He's grey and—" he made a fist —"about so big." He dashed up the stairs, leaving me blinking in the harsh light of the hall.

I sauntered into the lounge and found fragments of dull grey eggshell nestling in cotton on a glass coffee table. I examined a piece less than an half an inch across. The shard was both thicker and heavier than its chicken counterpart. I sniffed it and detected a faint scent that reminded me of schooldays. After a few moments, I identified the smell of chalk.

Dave had thoughtfully rigged a heat lamp. I angled the light obliquely across the glass table top and noticed a few motes of dust glinting on one edge. Encouraged, I picked up the lamp and, as far as the lead would allow, followed a dusty trail across the carpet. It ended in a small drift of whitish powder in an inner corner of the room.

I looked up. "Oh, very funny. Dave!"

He crashed down the stairs. "What, what, have you found him?" He followed my eyes to where a putty-hued face peeked from a ragged hole in the plaster cornicing.

"Stone me." Dave smiled. "Ah well. At least that confirms what he is."

"You are kidding me, right?"

Dave sat down on the sofa and watched the stone gargoyle do nothing, as stone gargoyles invariably do. "What do you think gargoyles eat?" he asked.

I shrugged. While I felt annoyed about leaving my warm, comfortable bed to witness such an elaborate hoax, I found myself humouring him just to see how long he would keep up the pretence. The hole he'd knocked in the cornicing alone demanded a level of respectful cooperation from me.

"How about coal, Jimbo?"

"Maybe. I saw on telly once that some birds nibble their eggshells, for vital minerals and stuff."

Dave plucked a shard of broken shell from the coffee table and offered it up to the gargoyle. When the piece wasn't snatched from his fingers, he rested it on the lip of the hole and sat down again.

I said, "The shell seems to be made of chalk, Dave. I don't suppose you happen to have any chalk lying around, do you?"

"Yeah, there's some in the middle drawer over there." He indicated the sideboard with his chin. "Pass him one, Jimbo. Go on."

I opened the drawer. Among a mess of staples, paper clips, rubber bands, pencils and biros lay a packet of blackboard chalk. "How convenient," I said.

"How do you mean, mate?"

"Never mind." I slid a chalk stick from the packet and offered it to the gargoyle.

A piece of eggshell was protruding from its mouth.

"How—" I looked at Dave.

He beamed. "You were dead right about the eggshell."

I placed the chalk next to the gargoyle and walked backwards to my chair without taking my eyes from the ugly stone head.

Dave rose and peered closer at the thing. While his head blocked my view I heard a distinct *crunch*. He jerked back and exploded with laughter. "Look at him go! He likes that."

I jumped up to stand beside him. The chalk, like the eggshell, had gone.

Dave said, "I think I'll call him . . . I don't know. What should I call him?"

I reached up and prodded the creature's face.

Stone.

Solid, immoveable stone.

"Dave, listen. Did you actually see— No, I meant to say, do you *think* you saw that thing eating?"

"Yeah, didn't you?"

"No!" I was growing agitated.

"Curious. I wonder if it only moves when it thinks it's not being watched. Me excepting, of course. I suppose he thinks I'm Mummy."

I clapped my friend on the back. "He's got your nose."

"Bog off. Anyway, what should I call him?"

"I dunno." Boredom was replacing agitation. "How about Archie?"

"Why Archie?"

"Why not?"

"Can't argue with that. He does look like an Archie, doesn't he? Yeah, Archie the Gargoyle, I like that. Nice one, Jimbo."

"Look, as much as I'd like to stay and look at a garden ornament you've embedded in your wall, and as much as I admire the trouble you've gone to in setting that little lot up—" I indicated the remains of the egg on the coffee table —"I'm going home."

I waited for Dave to relent. I'd played my part. Surely he could drop the act now?

"Okay, thanks for coming. I know it's late, but I just had to show someone. He is amazing, isn't he?" His ingenuous gaze met mine.

I shook my head and left.

~

Dave related his diet experiments. He'd invested in a cement mixer and tried various combinations of sand, cement and gravel. Although Archie liked sticks of chalk fed by hand, Dave guessed that an exclusive diet of chalk would not be healthy for a growing gargoyle.

I sat on an upturned bucket in Dave's yard and smoked a cigarette while he shovelled more sand into the mixer. "What's on the menu today, Mummy?"

"Two parts fine gravel and sand to one part cement with just a hint of silica and graphite for seasoning. I've told him if he eats it all, and *only* if he eats it all, he can have two chalk sticks as a special treat. I'm trying to wean him off the chalk. Isn't that right, Archie?"

Archie, squatting before a smaller bucket, reacted with stoic indifference. He was, I noticed, a slightly larger figurine than the one I'd seen a week before, more canine. He had a muzzle and pointed, upright ears. A rough tongue protruded from fluted lips.

"How long are you going to keep this up, Dave?"

He turned Archie's dinner a couple of revolutions before adding water from a hosepipe.
"Keep what up, mate?"

"This! I mean, what do the neighbours think?" As the local planning officer I was accustomed to disgruntled citizens complaining about their neighbours. "Do you take him walkies?"

"I take him out in the car, up Stretford Hills. He hates being watched and it's nice and quiet up there. Not too many folks about after eight. He's learning to fly!"

I looked at Archie's stunted wings and grunted.

Dave continued, his face becoming animated as he talked about his pet gargoyle. "I ride around on my bike and he follows, flapping his wings and trying to keep up. I wish you'd come and watch."

"Maybe I will someday," I said, meaning, *Not on your life, pal!* I wasn't buying any of it. But, hey, he was within his rights to be eccentric. Eccentricity was a noble British trait. Someone should have slapped a preservation order on him and paid him his dues for keeping old traditions alive.

I smiled as he tipped some sandy gruel into Archie's bucket and patted the statue fondly on the head. I enjoyed the role of passive observer, but the milk of kindness flowing through my veins was somewhat soured by the niggling question of why he had chosen *me* to take for a ride.

~

Three weeks later, I put the same question to my wife over our evening meal.

"Because he knows you'll humour him, that's why." Brenda forked the last scrap of cauliflower into her mouth and folded her cutlery on her plate. "Anyone else would have called in the men in white coats ages ago."

"That's a bit harsh, isn't it? Mind you, he's making a hell of a mess of his house. Archie's this tall—" I held my hand two feet off the ground —"and yet he still climbs—that is, Dave still *puts him* up in the corner of the lounge wall. The hole's massive. All the plasterwork's gone. It won't be long before Archie's arse pokes out the exterior wall."

She narrowed her eyes. "Have you asked yourself what Dave is getting out of all this?"

"I think it's a game to him, like chess or something. Every time I visit he plays it like Archie is real, alive. How the hell do you argue with someone when he tells you he keeps a grotesque statue as a pet?"

"Perhaps if you could find some incriminating evidence, like gargoyle moulds in his shed?"

"Do you think I haven't looked? There are no moulds, and if he had the necessary skills to sculpt one, I'm pretty sure he couldn't carve successively larger ones at the rate he'd have to. Archie gets a little bigger each week, like he's growing."

"Are you sure it's made of stone and not some sort of fibreglass or polystyrene?"

"It's stone all right. Dave's being very crafty about all this. Either that or . . ."

"Or what?"

I retreated under Brenda's scrutiny. "Nothing."

"He's taking you for an idiot, James."

"He wouldn't do that. Not deliberately. We go way back, Dave and I."

"Give him an ultimatum: either he stops messing you about or you call in the men in white coats."

"But he's a mate, and it's not like he's not harming anyone. I wouldn't expect you to understand. It's a bloke thing; we mates stick together."

"I'm telling you now, James—"

"Stop calling me James!"

"What?"

"I said stop calling me James. Please."

"But . . . but that's your name."

"Yes, I am aware of that."

Brenda took our plates into the kitchen. I knew she didn't understand my little outburst. I wasn't sure I understood it either. I'd set out on life's road as Little Jimmy, entered my teens as Jimmy and exited them as Jim. Somewhere in my late twenties, I morphed into James. People had called me James with a sort of mock seriousness, winking at my inevitable slide into middle-age. Only Dave called me Jimbo, and he did so without a trace of sarcasm.

I twiddled my thumbs and stared at the tablecloth, hoping I hadn't jeopardised my chances of dessert. Thursday meant sticky toffee pudding, my favourite.

Brenda switched the radio on in the kitchen. "All I'm saying," she said, raising her voice above that of Matt Monroe's, "is that sometimes you have to be cruel to be kind."

~

Dave and I were sitting in his lounge on a pleasant summer evening, the windows flung open to birdsong, ice-cream van chimes, and the clatter of lawnmowers as *homo suburbia* tamed squares of nature.

I waved a tin of lager at the statue in the corner. "He's looking a little cramped there, Dave."

"D'you think so? He seems happy enough to me."

"But are you being fair to him?" I persisted. "Think about it, his natural environment is up on a church roof or a cathedral somewhere, looking out over grand vistas. Baked by the sun one day, rimed with hoarfrost the next. This corner of your lounge, Dave, it's not natural for such a noble creature."

He took a thoughtful sip of his beer.

"And," I continued, "you have no way of knowing how big he's going to get. I mean, are gargoyles like poodles? Do they come as miniature, toy, and standard? What are you going to do if he keeps on growing? What is he now, three-foot, three-foot six?"

Dave sat up straight. "I know! I'll build a small church in the garden. Nothing fancy, just enough for Archie to sit on and feel at home."

"You cannot be serious?"

"Why not?"

"Because you'd never get planning permission for a start."

He smiled. "Well, I've got this friend who works in the Planning Department of the local council."

"No way, Dave. Forget it. You'd be asking me to compromise my integrity. People think they can just bypass regulations by bunging a planning officer a few quid. I deal with that sort of crap every day; I certainly didn't expect it from you."

Dave eased back in his chair. "No, Jimbo. You're right. Sorry."

"Yeah, well, a church in your garden's a stupid idea anyway." I took a photocopy from my top pocket and flattened it out on the coffee table. "Listen, I've been doing some research at work. There's this church in Llywny . . . Llywnyw . . . somewhere in Wales. It dates back nearly 500 years." I swivelled the paper so Dave could see it. "It's covered in carvings of masks, gargoyles, weirdy beasties."

"So?"

"So Archie would be among his own kind there." I pinned the photocopy down with my forefinger. "This is where he belongs, out there in the open. It would be perfect. Look, I'll leave this here with you. Think about it, mate. You're going to have to come to some sort of decision about what to do with him sooner or later. You've known that all along, haven't you?"

Dave shrugged.

"He's becoming reliant on you," I said. "You've done a great job bringing him up so far, but leave it too long and he's not going to be able to fend for himself in the wild. He needs to be among his own kind, Dave. Let him go. It's a kindness."

"It's just that I'll miss him."

"And, I'm sure he'll miss you."

~

The Church of St Eilfyw overlooked farmland to the east and north, the graveyard and a narrow country lane to the west, and a caravan park to the south. Once we had located the village of Llwynwygogog, the church had been easy to find. Three grotesque gargoyles topped a solid, squat tower thrusting into the darkening sky. Contorted faces peered at us from every surface.

I pulled into the lane leading to the caravan park and climbed out to open the gate, the salt tang in the air reminding me that we were near the coast. Archie will like it here, I thought, and then shook my head at the unconscious slip.

Once we were in the park, I lifted the rear door and reached for Archie. "Come on, Dave. Let's get this over with before it gets too dark to see. The last thing we need is for someone to come along and start asking us daft questions."

Or questions that would solicit daft answers.

I slid the stone effigy along the floor and tipped it over.

Dave appeared at my side. "Careful with him."

He took the head and I grabbed the feet.

"On the count of three," I said. "One, two, three, *lift*." Due to the confined space, I failed to raise Archie over the tailgate. There was the painful screech of stone dragging on metal and I was looking at a nasty scratch in my paintwork. "Oh, for crying out loud!"

Dave elbowed me aside. "Leave me to it, Jimbo."

"There's no way you'll get him out by yourself."

He huffed as if dealing with a wayward child. "Archie'll get out the same way he got in — by himself. Just bog off and leave us alone."

I bogged off. First I sought out the toilets and then took a wander around the park. Brenda had talked often about us getting a caravan for weekends away. Llwynwygogog looked a good place to stay — pleasantly pastoral, historical, romantic even — but the swarming gnats drove such thoughts away and *me* back to the car.

Dave had managed to manhandle Archie out on to the grass and was squatting before the stone effigy. I strode around to the back of the car to close the door when I saw a chip of masonry just inside the tailgate. A claw. I must have knocked it off the gargoyle on our abortive attempt to get it out. Still annoyed at the scratch in the paintwork, I slipped the claw into my pocket and banged the door down. "How long are you going to be, Dave?"

He looked drawn. I'm sure if the light had been better I would've seen tears coursing over his cheeks.

Embarrassed, I said, "I'm going to turn the car round and make ready to go. Come when you're ready."

Then, because it seemed the decent thing to do, I said goodbye to Archie.

I opened the gate, got in the car and headed back down the narrow lane. I pulled over on to the grass verge and switched off the engine. All was quiet. In my mirror I could just make out the silhouette of St Eilfyw's against the purple sky. A handful of stars twinkled.

Three, four minutes passed. I rolled the window down and stuck my head out. I was just about to holler for Dave to get his arse into gear when I heard a scream. The fuzzy hairs on the back of my neck stood on end.

A thick silence descended. I began to wonder if I had imagined the cry. Then came a rhythmic sound; hard, like leather on rock. I was out of the car and running toward the park when Dave came charging down the lane.

"Get going, Jimbo. Please, just get going."

I opened my mouth to argue, but the anguish on his face stilled my tongue. I spun around and jumped in the driver's seat. "What the hell happened?" I asked once we were moving.

Dave struggled for breath. "He wouldn't stay. I couldn't make him understand he had to stay. At first he seemed interested in the church tower. He flew up and had a sniff around the other gargoyles, but then he flew back down and started following me off the park. I turned on him and raised my arms. Shouted at him. *Yeaaghhh*! He just looked at me with his head on one side as if to say 'What's up with you?' He couldn't understand why I was leaving him."

"What was that noise I heard?"

"Probably me slapping him." Dave smiled through his tears. "I don't know who it hurt more, me or him. It is for the best, isn't it, Jimbo? I have done the right thing?"

"Yes, mate. You have. Don't forget your seatbelt."

We sped away. Game over. Checkmate to me. I'd only made one move in the entire game, but I had outmanoeuvred him.

"I hope the other gargoyles accept him," Dave said quietly.

A shiver went down my back. He was acting, of course. He *had* to be acting, because the alternative — that my friend had gone completely bonkers — was too frightening to contemplate.

~

The car headlights framed Dave's house as we pulled into the drive. I turned the engine off. "Any chance of a cuppa? I'm parched."

"Hm?" Dave blinked at me. "Oh. Yeah, sorry. I was miles away."

He walked up his drive and I followed. He stopped suddenly and peered into the bushes fringing the garden. "What was that?"

"What was what? I didn't hear anything."

Dave crossed the lawn in three strides and parted a red barberry. There, glowing dully in the feeble light of a street lamp, was Archie. Dave dropped to his knees and threw his arms around the gargoyle.

I ground my teeth. "How the hell do you explain that?"

Dave turned to face me. "It's Archie! He flew home!"

"On those little wings?" I hammered my head with my hands. "No, no, no. I'm getting as bad as you. He can't fly because he's a statue. We left a hunk of bloody rock in Wales two hours ago and now there's another one in your garden. It's not fair, Dave. You are not playing by the rules. I beat you fair and square. I'm sick of this whole bloody charade, this—this bloody farce!" I ran across the lawn and kicked the statue before collapsing, clutching what felt like five broken toes. "*Ya bugger!*"

Dave watched me without moving. "Game, Jimbo? I don't know what you mean." He nodded at the gargoyle. "That's my Archie."

I sat up. "It is *not* your Archie. You must have made it and put it there before we left. Come on, Dave," I said miserably. "Why not admit it? This has gone on long enough."

He shook his head. "I had no idea."

I pushed myself to my feet and hobbled to face him. "Dave. I want you to tell me truthfully now, do you really believe that you have a pet gargoyle and that he flew over 80 miles back to your house tonight?"

"Yes."

I grasped his hand and shook it. "Then that's it, mate. I can't deal with it. You're out of my depth. Brenda was right, you should be seeking professional help."

"Where are you going? I thought you wanted a cuppa."

I was limping down the drive. "I'm going home, Dave. I'll see you around." I fumbled in my coat pocket for the keys. Something hard dug into my finger.

I spun around. "Last chance, mate. Admit I beat you fair and square."

"It is not a game, I keep telling you."

"Oh, yes it is," I crowed. "And what's more, I've won."

I marched back with as much dignity as bruised toes would allow and flashed my trump card.

"What's that?"

"It's a claw. It came off the gargoyle we left behind at St Eilfyw's." I bent down to the statue in the bushes and examined its feet. "So, whereas that one is minus a claw, this one . . . *oh!*"

~

Within three months Dave's garden had become a trench. I left Brenda in his kitchen and ducked as a digger bucket narrowly missed my head.

"Sorry, Jim," the operator called down.

"No worries," I shouted back. "Where's Dave?"

He pointed to the pavement where Dave was facing down a clearly irate neighbour.

I ambled over to mediate. "Good morning, gentlemen."

"It would be a better morning if this lot packed up and went home!"

"Ah. You wouldn't be Mr Watkiss by any chance?"

The man eyed me warily. "That's me."

I turned to Dave. "You go and supervise the workmen."

He didn't need telling twice; Dave trotted off to a safe distance.

"This building is going to be an eyesore," raged Mr Watkiss.

"Well, you're welcome to your opinion, of course, but the fact remains that the occupant of this property has been given full approval by the local Planning Department."

"Aye, I know. I phoned them up. Fella there gave me some guff about exemptions for certain types of buildings."

"My card." I handed him my office number.

"What's this?" He frowned. "You! Listen to me, you smartarse. You're going to regret this. One phone call to your superiors and—"

"There won't be a phone call to my superiors, Mr Watkiss, from you or anyone else."

"Oh aye? We'll see about that."

"Is that your house over there?" I gestured down the street. "It's just that I've noticed it has a recent loft conversion that is not on our files." I let him absorb the ramifications before raising my eyebrows and politely asking if there was anything else he cared to discuss.

He stamped away, swearing under his breath.

Dave clapped me on the back. "I owe you one there, Jimbo. Thanks."

"Think nothing of it, mate. I had no idea compromising my integrity could be so much fun."

We surveyed the battlefield of his front lawn where he had been permitted to build a chapel. Fortunately for Dave, the planning officer who received his application had uncovered a little known statute allowing an exemption for building line infringements *if* the building was religious in purpose. I only hoped no one ever asked me more about it; I'd have to write the statute.

Brenda came out of the kitchen carrying a plate of beef sandwiches. Dave and I grabbed two each. "Thanks, Brenda."

She took the rest to the workmen.

"Your Brenda's been a real brick, Jimbo. S'funny, but I've never really got to know her that well. You'll have to bring her round more often. Does she know about . . .?" He tipped his head towards Archie, who was sitting by the back door with his eyes fixed on the construction of his new home.

"Kind of. She will, given time."

Dave sauntered off, humming contentedly.

I fished in my pocket for a stick of chalk and placed it in the gargoyle's muzzle. "Don't tell Mummy I'm feeding you these," I said, and chuckled as a rough tongue licked the dust off my fingers.

Give 'em Enough Rope

Dimly, through rasping breath, the beat of the drums and the baying of the crowd at the gates, a priest's voice droned in my ear. *Fiat voluntas tua, sicut in caelo et in terra . . .*

I twisted to face the hooded hangman, whispered from the corner of my mouth: "Any luck, Harry?"

He raised a thumb and folded two fingers into his palm. *Eight tenths sure*. Harry would need to draw out the spectacle to be certain we'd found our man. Not too long, though, or the rotten fruit and stones would start to fly. Somebody could get hurt.

I tried to ignore the thick cord chafing my wrists and the noose canting my head forward at an unnatural angle, and lose myself in the breeze drying the fear-sweat on my face. The gallows had been constructed in the cobbled yard of the Gristown watch house and the breeze smelt of dung and sweat from the stables.

Distraction is not something you find by looking for it. Had we placed the sandbags properly? Had Harry calculated my bodyweight and height? I started to pant. *Oh shit. Oh shit. Oh shit.* Any second now, Harry would release the trapdoor . . .

Any second now.

Any second . . . *now*.

Now.

"Christ almighty, Harry, just do it!"

He pulled the lever and I was standing on air. My posture pulled me forward, and then the noose bit my Adam's apple and snatched me backwards. My teeth crashed together with a noise like boulders splitting. My knees thumped the underside of the platform. I did the hemp fandango with sawdust dancing in the sun's rays.

My boots brushed the pile of sandbags.

I could feel the vertebrae in my neck separating. Straw-coloured sparks fizzled around the edge of my vision. This was going to be a close run thing. At least I'd remembered to keep my tongue in. I'd bitten the tip off the sixth time I was hanged. Or was it the seventh? *That's right, you daft sod. If you're thinking, you're living.*

I made a desperate scrabble with my feet for the bags. Harry had dropped several through the trapdoor ("To make sure the mechanism works," he said with a wink.) He'd also measured the rope to ensure I didn't have an ear torn off or my windpipe crushed by the drop. To be such an unsuccessful hangman, Harry had to be the best.

And I had to plant my feet on the bags or the jig was up.

A roaring tide flooded my brain. Thoughts moved like a spoon dropped in honey, sparkling and ponderous: *I've stopped swinging, so why can't I stand? Why is this . . . stand? Where's . . .?* A bubble of light burst behind my eyes, and then a thunderous mantle settled on my brow.

~

A muscle jerked in my leg and the weight eased on my throat. My feet were on the bags. It took a few seconds for my fogged brain to figure I had suffered a blackout.

Jesus.

I gagged a mouthful of foamy saliva. Harry unfastened the rope from the top spar and I collapsed to the ground; and there I lay, eyes closed and drawing shallow breaths, hidden from view by canvas walls and thanking the fates and other capricious spirits for my life.

Harry had a twisted back and one leg shorter than the other. I listened to his uneven footsteps clonk on the boards overhead. Then the rungs of a ladder creaked, a canvas drape flapped open and hands grabbed my ankles.

"You okay, Cal?"

I twitched a thumb.

He dragged me from under the gallows and strapped me to a wooden plank. The crowd at the gates had fallen silent. A horse towed my carcass into the stables. Wood squeaked on cobblestones. Feet shuffled in straw. A door slammed.

Harry patted me on the legs. "All clear, Cal."

I opened my eyes.

Three blurred figures stood over me. The first man was squat and misshapen, the second tall and thin, the third man fat and wearing a dress. I blinked and they resolved into Harry, a captain of the watch and a priest.

"Captain, this man is still alive!"

"It's all right, Father Bryan. He's meant to be." The captain slid two bolts home on the stable door. "I've posted two men outside, Mr Oates. We won't be disturbed."

I was tempted to say it was too late with a meddlesome priest in here (for what other kind of priest is there?). Harry cut the bindings on my ankles and wrists.

"That's the last time, Harry." I fingered the rope burns on my neck. "Never again."

His wheezing laugh sounded like the last grains of sand in a timer. "You always say that."

"Yeah, well, this time I mean it." Despite all our careful preparations and knowledge I had peered into Death's empty eye sockets. I had no desire to do it again.

I met my friend's gaze through the slit in his mask: Harry liked to preserve his anonymity, as much as a shortarse with a humpity back can. "Was it worth it, did you identify the Gristown Grendel?"

He blinked slowly. "Aye."

"You're sure? You have to be ten tenths sure, Harry."

"Beyond all doubt, Cal."

The priest eyed us warily. "What's going on? This man should be dead."

The captain removed his plumed helmet and squatted before me. "I'm Captain Phelps. The Commander of the Watch tells me you have information that could lead us to the real killer."

"The real killer lies there." The priest stabbed a fleshy finger at me.

"Please, Father, let them speak."

Harry cleared his throat. "The man you want stood at the back of the crowd. He had grey hair cut high over the ears and a red beard woven into three plaits. He wore a mustard-yellow coat and a black woollen cloak fastened with a gold brooch."

Captain Phelps' face contorted as if he was in pain. The priest turned away.

"Well?" I asked. "Do you know him?"

Phelps straightened up and loosened the collar on his tunic. "The description fits Will Connors."

I frowned. "The first victim was a girl named Beth Connors."

"She was Will's niece," the captain said.

The priest still wouldn't meet our gaze.

"Father." I tilted my head to one side, winced as something went crack. "Did Connors ever come to Confession?"

The priest drew himself up. "How dare you question me, you who have come to prey on Gristown-on-the-Marsh's grief like the crows you are! The Lord will condemn you for your mockery."

I glanced at Harry. *What's gotten him so worked up?* "Father, there's an evil bastard in your cosy little town and Harry here just identified him. Where's the mockery?"

"You let me say the Lord's Prayer over your tawdry little sideshow!"

"Oh." He had us there.

"Why wasn't the Council informed of this con trick?"

Captain Phelps said, "Mr Oates made all the necessary arrangements with the Commander of the Watch, Father. I was informed only minutes ago of the real nature of this, um . . ."

"Say it," the fat priest snarled. "*Con trick.*"

Phelps' gaze fell to the floor and the priest turned to me again. "How much is the Commander of the Watch paying you? What is it — half now, half after the arrest?"

My eyes went to the pouch of gold hanging from Harry's belt. Damn it if this priest wasn't making me feel bad about my living. "I'm a travelling performer — aye, an *artiste* — but I'm not ashamed. You expect me to starve for my art? You think there's job satisfaction in getting hanged?"

I clapped my hands to my cheeks, drew them down my jaw as though I could wipe away my exasperation. "Please, Father, this is getting us nowhere. What did Connors tell you in Confession?"

"That is between God and—"

"Not if he told you he'd killed children and dumped their bodies in the marshes, it isn't!"

"He confessed to no such thing!"

Phelps shifted his weight. "Then what *did* he confess to, Father?" His tone suggested that even God answered to the law when it came to child murder.

"He might have mentioned inappropriate—" the priest waggled his fingers —"*feelings* for his brother's daughter. That is all."

251

"That's all?" I looked at Harry. *Can you believe this?* He shrugged. It was all academic to Harry. He could read guilt on a man like it was written in a book. A fearful flicker of the eyes, a curl of the lip, an untimely sigh, a rub of the nose, they were dead giveaways to a man with Harry's talent. And what better place to observe them than at the hanging of some poor bastard wrongly accused of your crimes, when your "body talk" would be in stark contrast to everyone else's?

Enter Caleb Oates, the world's first and only professional hanged man. I hawked and spat a globule of phlegm into the straw. "Tell me, Father, did Connors tell you of these inappropriate—" I waggled my fingers —"*feelings* before or after his niece was murdered?"

The priest's mouth became a bloodless line in his doughy face.

"Father," Captain Phelps said, "three young girls are dead. You should have reported Will Connors' peccadilloes to the watch." He looked down at me. "What next, Mr Oates?"

"We wait until midnight, when I will arise and seek justice."

The priest's lips curled back from his teeth. "A travesty of justice, you mean. If you'll excuse me, I have important church matters to attend to."

"We'd prefer it if you stayed, Father," Harry said.

"What?" he snorted. "Why?"

Yeah, why, Harry? Personally I would have been happier to be rid of the miserable man of the cloth.

"My parishioners need me." Father Bryan looked to the captain for support. "I have a sermon to compose for the morrow."

Phelps shrugged his shoulders. "I'll fetch you ink and paper should you need it. But whether you like it or not, Father, you're part of this now." He drew the bolts on the door and left us.

I patted a pile of mouldering straw. "Take a pew, Father."

~

An eternity later, the stable door opened and Captain Phelps stuck his head in. "It's time to go, Mr Oates."

"And not a moment too soon," I muttered. "The atmosphere in here stinks."

Harry chuckled. "I like the smell of horse shit, meself."

I grinned at him. He knew I was referring to Father Bryan's constant bellyaching and sermonising, but Harry seemed to have taken a strange liking to the priest. They'd chatted a while about ropes. Ropes, for God's sake. Harry had shown the priest his noose so they could compare the fibres used in a hangman's rope with that in a bell-rope. The long hours just flew by.

Outside, Phelps introduced me to Constables Spooner and Kips. They regarded me with open suspicion. I had after all, been arrested and hanged for child murder, and mud sticks, even when it's fake. *You might have gulled the captain*, their eyes seemed to say, *but we ain't daft.* Moonlight glinted on their helmets, the silver badges pinned to their tunics and the pitted swords hanging at their sides.

Phelps led us through the gates and down a street flanked by tall narrow dwellings, with plastered walls criss-crossed by black beams. In other towns the walls are whitewashed, but here they'd left the plaster in its natural pink state. By day it might look pretty; by night it looked gloomy. Our footsteps echoed in deserted streets.

"Tell me, Mr Oates, how did you come to be in your line of work?"

I spared him a glance. He wasn't interested in me, he just needed a distraction. A small place like Gristown, where everyone knew everyone, Connors would be well known to Phelps. They could even be friends.

"I started out as an escape artiste, you know, chain me up in a sack and throw me in the river sort of thing. Tie me up and dangle me upside down over a bear pit. Unfortunately I was too good."

"How can you be *too* good?"

"People will only come to your show if they think there's a good chance you'll die. They sit at the front hoping the locks will stick. I met Harry and we devised a stunt where I pretended I was trying to escape the hangman's noose."

"Ah, I think I see."

"Aye, I failed to escape on purpose. Harry would cut me down and, after a few nail-biting minutes, I would come round and get the loudest cheer you ever heard. News travelled. Whereas Caleb Oates, Master Escaper played to a handful of people, the crowds flocked to see the World's Worst Escape Artist. We drifted from that into doing freelance work for the watch."

Phelps smiled. "Father Bryan was right," he said without rancour. "You are a sideshow act."

I sniffed. "I prefer to think of it as extreme performance art."

"And one which offers a beneficial public service," he said, smoothing my ruffled feathers.

"Harry will finish the public service bit."

He waved a finger. "Don't get ahead of yourself, Mr Oates. There has to be a trial first. Innocent until proven guilty."

"You won't need a trial, trust me. Connors will sing like a canary when he sees me."

With the watchmen hidden around a corner, I would knock on Connors' door and, when he answered, make sure he saw the rope burns on my throat before raising my finger to point at his chest: *Confess! Confeessss!* Stagey — and not funny unless you have a particularly cruel sense of humour — but it gets results.

Phelps gestured to a house on the outskirts of the town. Candles burned in the downstairs windows.

"It appears our Mr Connors can't sleep," I said, loosening the laces of my shirt. "Maybe he has a conscience after all."

"Sir."

The captain turned to face Spooner. "What is it, Constable?"

"This is Will Connors' house."

"He stands accused of the abduction, molestation and murder of Beth Connors, Cathy Bryant and Kate Croft."

"But sir, we drink with Will in the Bad Penny. Don't we Kips?"

"Aye."

"Ah, I see." Phelps' shoulders relaxed. "Look, lads, I know Will too, but it's inevitable that at some point in a watchman's life it will be his unpleasant duty to arrest—"

"No, sir, I wasn't meaning that. I meant we was with Will the night little Cathy Bryant went missing."

Phelps' eyes narrowed. "Are you sure?"

"Quite sure, sir. I won six pennies off Will. I'm not likely to forget a night like that." Spooner and Kips gave me a hard look.

"No way," I said. "Harry is never wrong." When that failed to move them, I added, "He was ten tenths!"

Phelps graced me a chilly smile. "Mr Oates, I appreciate you have risked your neck for us, but it would appear your friend got it wrong on this occasion." He rested a hand on his sword pommel. "I do hope he is where we left him, with the commander's money on his belt. Constable Kips, take this man and return immediately to the watch house."

"Stuff that for a game of soldiers!" I knocked Kips' hand away. His fist exploded into my nose and the cobbletones slammed into my back. Before I could regain my feet I heard a sound like tearing cotton and a cold blade pricked my throat. I peered along the length of steel into Captain Phelps' grim face.

"I'm a patient man, Mr O—"

Aaaagggghhhh!

Spooner drew his sword and stared wide-eyed at Connors' house. "What the bloody hell was that?"

A man's voice: "*No, no, no! Please! No, no, get away from me!*"

The screams raised the hairs on the back of my neck. The candles in the downstairs windows had been snuffed out and a queer blue light burned within.

Kips licked his lips. "It sounds like Will, but . . ."

I knocked Phelps' blade aside and rolled to my feet. Connors was making the sort of racket I'd expected him to make after he'd seen me. I reached for the door handle but stepped back when a body hit the other side. The door shook in its frame then burst open, spilling a red-bearded man to the ground.

Spooner rested a hand on the kneeling man's shoulder. "Will, it's me, Jim Spooner."

Connors grabbed the front of Spooner's tunic. "I—I loved them. B—Beautiful, so beautiful. I'm sorry, God knows, I'm sorry. Tell them I'm sorry." He shrieked. "*Tell them!*"

The three watchmen looked down at the man they'd respected and considered a friend, changed now into that most monstrous of felons, a child killer. With them distracted I slipped into the house.

My scalp prickled. The air in the hallway was charged like a gathering thunderstorm. A picture, its frame smashed to smithereens, hung from the antlers of a deer's head. A cold light flickered from an open door to my left.

In Connors' living room a heavy upholstered chair lay on its side. Candle wax and broken glass glinted on the floorboards. The air resisted my progress, as though I waded through syrup. My hair crackled. Sparks leapt off the backs of my hands. I pressed forward and my ears imploded.

Three little girls stood by the fireplace, flickering like deathly pale, blue-grey Will o' the Wisps granted human form. The unearthly light spilled from their eyes, from nostrils, from between their smiling rosebud lips. Their pretty dresses rippled through shades of brown and black; algae-slicked stones on a river bed.

One fixed me with her seraphic gaze and raised her hands to form a triangle above her head. A second inflated her cheeks and raised her arms at her side. A third drew a cross on her chest.

I tried to twist my head away, but my eyes refused to leave the spectacle as the girls went through the same pitiful charade. A pointed hat, a fat man, a cross.

Oh, Jesus. Oh, God, no.

"Mr Oates!"

I spun to see Captain Phelps charging into the room. When I turned back to the fireplace the girls had gone. My ears popped and air rushed into my lungs. A hundred questions sprang to my lips. Phelps summed them up:

"What in the blue blazes happened here?"

I whispered, "Connors had an accomplice."

"Who?"

My mouth drooped. "Oh God, he's with Harry."

I barged the captain aside and dashed outside. A whimpering Connors lay spread-eagled on the cobbles, blood streaming from his nose and mouth. Kips and Spooner had meted out some small town justice. I kept running.

Phelps shouted after me. "Where are you going, Mr Oates?"

"The watch house," I shouted over my shoulder.

I saw now why Father Bryan had been hostile towards Harry and me. Harry had read the situation straight away, that's why he had asked the priest to stay: to prevent him from alerting his partner-in-crime. "You're a clever bastard, Harry," I muttered, "but you made the mistake of thinking I am, too."

I prayed it wasn't a fatal mistake.

In the cobbled yard the sinister silhouette of the gallows stood framed against the midnight blue sky. A misshapen figure stumbled from the stables. It trailed a rope.

"Harry, you're safe." I ran to his side. "Where is he? Where's ...?"

Harry lifted his mask and the question died on my tongue. Blood oozed from his mashed lips into his beard. He peered at me though eyelids resembling hen's eggs and held up the coil of rope. "Sorry, Cal."

I grabbed the rope and wrung it in my hands.

"That sanctimonious bastard." While I had been dealing justice to his accomplice, Father Bryan had lashed my friend the hangman with the tool of his trade. I pictured the glint in the priest's eye as he meted out revenge: *An eye for an eye, Mr Oates.* My throat burned as if I'd been forced to swallow a hot coal.

Phelps ran through the gates, sword raised. "Father Bryan?"

"Gone," I replied.

Anger flashed in his eyes. "The girls would have trusted the priest. He picked them up for Connors to . . ." Poor Phelps. His ward had bred not one monster, but two, and they had found each other, fed each other's depravity.

He ran into the stables and emerged a minute later astride a powerful hunter. "Say hello to Molly," he said, and extended a hand. "Come, Mr Oates, there's no time to lose."

I vaulted up behind him and he spurred the horse into a gallop, its iron-shod hooves sparking on the cobbles. "Where are we going?" I yelled, threading the coil of rope around him and hanging on for dear life.

"If the priest crosses into the next shire he will be out of my jurisdiction."

"How far to the border?"

"Two miles."

Phelps guided his horse out of the town and onto the trackless marshes that lay to the west. The moon's reflection on the still grey waters shattered as the mare ploughed the reeking swamp, the gallant Captain Phelps' horsemanship paralleled only by his knowledge of the land.

It was a ride through a nightmare. The horse's rump constantly slammed into mine, leaving my buttocks sore and my plums tender. The stench of marsh gas made me gag. And every time I closed my eyes I saw the three girls, bright and unearthly. *A pointed hat, a fat man, a cross.* For comfort I pictured the evil priest taking flight, wading through the marsh with his cassock hitched up around his knees, his jowls wobbling and his heart hammering in his chest.

"We'll have you yet," I vowed.

Phelps brought us alongside a wide, relentless river; a ribbon of lamp oil under the night sky. "The border. Let us pray we bested the priest, Mr Oates."

We halted at a cart bridge, where a lone watchman stood sentry at the other end. A clay pipe jutted from his salt-and-pepper beard. When he saw us he picked up his halberd.

"You there," the captain hollered. "Has a priest come this way?"

The watchman removed his pipe and waved it airily. "He might have done."

"When?"

"Who's asking?"

Phelps, his nerves shredded already by the night's events, snapped. "Why, you impudent sack of pig shit, if you were one of my men I'd have you flogged, d'yer hear, *flogged*!"

"Captain," I shouted. "Look."

Upriver, a fat figure rolled down the riverbank and waded out into the water. Phelps turned to the watchman. "Seize that man. He must not be allowed to get away!"

"What's he supposed to have done?"

I dropped down off the horse and ran across the bridge. The grizzled watchman levelled the point of his halberd at my belly.

"Let me pass!"

"And you are?"

"Caleb Oates."

"What's your business, Caleb Oates?"

"Are you bloody serious, man?" I turned and pointed to the mounted captain charging up the river bank. "You heard what he said, you must seize the priest."

"Oh, I must, must I? Well, I'm sure he's a very fine captain and all that, but he's not *my* captain." The halberd twitched. "Now, I'll ask you again, what's your business?"

I looked upriver. The priest had made it into deep water. His cassock had inflated around his head like a toad's throat sac. The current was carrying him closer to the opposite bank. The captain would never reach him in time.

I studied the watchman. Shire authorities post men at the borders to deter smugglers. It's considered a soft duty, one that falls to some old duffer too slow for real watch work. I batted the halberd aside and swung a fist at his face. The wily fox saw it coming and ducked his head. My fist connected with his steel helmet. He replied with an uppercut to the chin. The cobblestones slammed into my back for the second time in one night.

Then he calmly ignored me to pass judgement on Father Bryan's swimming technique. "He won't get very far splashing like that. Long even strokes, that's the way of things in the water."

I growled through clenched teeth. "You bloody fool. He's the Gristown Grendel."

The watchman laughed and clapped his thigh. "That bloated frog is the Gristown Grendel?"

"Yes."

"The bastard what killed them three little kiddies?"

"The very same."

"I've got news for you, son. They hanged the Grendel earlier tonight."

I groaned. "Now there's a conundrum."

"Come on." The watchman grabbed my hand and pulled me upright. "Behave yourself. We'll fish him out when he comes under the bridge." He smirked at my surprised expression. "Your captain might know a thing or two about the marshes, but old Seamus here knows the river. Why get your feet wet when you can let the river bring him to you, eh?"

Now Seamus had pointed it out, I could see the way the current curved towards and then away from the opposite bank. Father Bryan's clumsy strokes would not get him across.

Captain Phelps' steed was also losing its battle with the river. The water swirled around the rider's knees. The mare's eyes rolled in terror. Accepting defeat, Phelps heaved on the reins. I waved and signalled for him to join me on the bridge.

"Here comes our fishie." Seamus leaned over the parapet and lowered his halberd so the priest would be able to grab the staff. "Bugger."

"What?"

He straightened up and regarded his halberd. "The water's low. He'll never reach this."

The temptation to simply spear the fat priest was strong. But I wanted him to stand on a scaffold alongside Connors, to feel the hatred of the people whose life he had blighted. I wanted to see the fear in his eyes when the noose went over his neck, and I wanted Harry to be the one to hang them. *An eye for an eye.* I ran back to where I'd dismounted and picked up Harry's rope. Seamus regarded it with a frown.

I shrugged as though carrying a coil of rope ending in a noose was a normal precaution. "It's all I could find at short notice."

Phelps galloped up. He understood our plan at a glance and looped the noose over the pommel of his saddle. "When Father Bryan has a firm hold of the rope, Molly will pull him up."

I tossed the free end of the rope over the parapet. It hit the water with a splash. The current carried it under the bridge and into deep shadow.

Father Bryan drifted towards us; a rotten lily pad revolving in the current. His eyes met mine and I saw neither remorse nor defeat. Anger blazed in my gut. It took a supreme effort of will not to grab Seamus' halberd and harpoon the arrogant bastard, and I would if he emerged from the other side of the bridge.

I scraped back my hair in frustration. It crackled between my fingers. The atmosphere had turned oppressive, like a thunderstorm was brewing. I blinked and saw the girls in the private darkness behind my eyelids: *A pointed hat, a fat man, a cross.* The peach-fuzz hairs on the back of my neck stood on end. My hearing dulled.

"Get away!" I staggered backwards. "Leave him. Let us do this our way!" Phelps and Seamus gave me a puzzled look. "Not you, I meant—"

Arrowhead ripples swirled around the priest's bulbous body. Dark shapes darted in to pluck at his cassock and tease his outreached hands. "Hey, what—" He smacked at small points of pale-blue luminescence. "Get away from me!" Then the priest's head jerked up to peer into the blackness under the bridge, his eyes bulging at something only he could see.

The slack went out of the rope. Seamus laughed. "Looks like we gone and caught ourselves a fishie!"

Phelps' horse started to drag the priest out of the river. It seemed to take ten minutes, although I knew it was more like ten seconds. Like a sickly moonrise, with his neck in a crude noose, Father Bryan's white head emerged over the top of the parapet. Air bubbled from between slack lips. One ear hung by a shred of skin.

"Dear God," Captain Phelps croaked, as the horse dragged the body to the cobbles.

The priest's sightless eyes stared into the void.

~

A cock crowed.

I'd been present at many executions, but while Harry is fulfilling our contract I'm usually sleeping under a canvas tarpaulin on our cart. This time was no exception. The priest's death had satisfied any thirst for revenge I may have harboured. There was a drum roll, wood creaked and Connors was dead: hanged by the neck.

The show's over, folks. The monster's dead. Return to your homes. You can sleep soundly in your beds tonight.

In the gloom I unrolled a scroll the good Captain Phelps had handed to me. It was from the Commander of the Watch. The burghers of Gristown had granted me a posthumous pardon. I laughed quietly, balled it up and tossed it aside.

After what could have been two hours, perhaps more, I was roused from a semi-slumber by Harry's uneven footsteps on the riding board. "C'mon Dobbin, look lively," he said, and the cart jerked into motion.

I waited for the rattle of cobbles to give way to hard earth and then popped my head from under the tarp. The morning had dawned warm and bright. The air had a sweet grassy smell and swallows flitted over the marshes. It was a good day to be alive. "Can I come out, Harry?"

"Aye, we're well clear of the town." He shuffled along the riding board to make room for me. As I clambered from under the sheeting I happened to glance back and saw three little girls sitting on the tailboard, their pale faces turned to the sun. I knew without asking that Harry had not seen them.

I tried to connect the killing of the priest with the picture of innocence before me now, but the pieces wouldn't fit. They'd had more right than anybody, and yet . . .

261

One of the girls turned her face to me. Her chin dimpled as she gave me a rueful smile. I shrugged my shoulders and she turned away.

"Are you coming up front or what?"

"What? Oh, sorry, Harry." I rubbed at the gooseflesh on my arms. Screwed shut my eyes, expecting the girls to disappear when I opened them. They were still there though, swinging their bare legs in time to the rocking of the cart.

I turned and stepped onto the riding board alongside Harry. A coil of rope hung from a hook. "That's for you," he said.

Glad for the distraction I picked it up. It felt smoother in my hands than our usual rope. Less fibrous.

"It's a bell-rope," he explained. "I acquired it at the church."

I raised an eyebrow. "Acquired, Harry?"

"I dropped a coin in the collection plate."

"That's all right, then. But why? I thought you carried a spare rope anyway."

"Ah, but that one is different. You see, Cal, a hangman's rope has to be made of a particular type of sisal that doesn't give when . . ."

Oh God. I closed my eyes, listened to the bees' wings buzzing in the grass verges and the crackle of pebbles under the wheels. When Harry starts talking about ropes it's the only sane course of action. I thought I heard one of the girls giggle.

"Anyway," he concluded, "that's no good as a hangman's rope, but it's fine for our act. It won't burn your neck so bad when I hang you."

"Gee, Harry. You're all heart. Actually, our act's something I want to talk to you about."

He turned his bruised face to me. "Go on."

"Um . . ." I wanted to stop our act, but I couldn't find a way to say it. I didn't want to tell Harry how close he had come to snuffing my life on the gallows yesterday. Professional pride? Protecting his feelings? I wasn't sure, and there was something else too, a niggling doubt about the rightness of how we made our living. I needed time to think before we sought out another commission.

"Nothing, Harry. It doesn't matter."

Except of course there was no such thing as saying nothing to Harry. People did most of their talking with their mouth shut.

He faced forward and jiggled the reins, then turned to me with a thoughtful frown. "I have a job and I do it to the best of my abilities. I don't pass judgement. Someone else does that."

"Before *and* after," I said with a rueful smile. I looked back. The girls were still there, enjoying their ride. Harry followed my gaze for a moment.

We turned back to the road ahead.

"It was a queer do with the priest, hanging himself like that," Harry said. "I don't feel cheated if that's what's troubling you? He was guilty, you know. I saw it written all over him."

"It's not that. It's just . . . Last night, I wanted the priest dead. I was ready to kill him with my bare hands if needs be. And yet when I saw his body all twisted and spent . . ."

Harry's beard curled up like a sleepy hedgehog. "We do what has to be done. It's all any of us does."

I saw a flicker out the corner of my eye. I raised a hand as a visor to the sun and saw the girls had alighted to skip along the grass verge. They left no prints on the grass, nor did they cast any shadows, and within a few heartbeats they had become part of the dazzling brightness.

AFTERWORDS

Tell someone you write fiction and the chances are they'll raise their eyebrows, do a little mouth-shrug and ask, "Where do you get your ideas from?" I'm never quite sure how to answer this question, hence the furtive mumbling and head-shaking that passes for my answer. The fact is, my ideas come from the same place the person asking the question get theirs. But whereas they might hear a song lyric, see a picture or watch a TV documentary, turn to their companion and say, "You know what . . ." or "This reminds me . . ." a writer will think *What if . . .?* It's a game anyone with an active imagination can play. You don't need to be smart. The following notes, I'm sure, will reinforce this.

SACRED SKIN

A relative of my wife told us his daughter Derryth had made a protective skin or suit for her boyfriend, something to do with her art class. With no more details than that, I started to mentally construct a sacred skin of my own.

As she inspired the story, I named the white witch in *Sacred Skin* after Derryth. I also think it's a lovely Welsh name, which fit my purposes nicely. Continuing with the name game, the possessed earl is named for my daughter, Heather, while I called the servant Simon because it seems like the sort of name a chamber maid might choose for her son — a bit of a posh name for a working class lad.

MEMORY BONES

A friend and I were chatting about immortality, and whether it would be a curse or a blessing. I took the view that it would be the latter and wrote *Memory Bones*, my first published story. It has been published several times now, including two appearances in zombie-themed anthologies. This strikes me as strange because I never really thought of it as being a zombie tale. Not that I'm complaining, mind.

As for the open ending, I have no doubts whatsoever about the contents of that drawer. If I was Dr Messinger I'd turn and run.

LONELY HEART CLOB

Clob is, of course, one half of the angel and devil partnership that sit on our shoulders whispering advice into our ears. The original intention was to have a saintly Clob as well as a naughty Clob, but good influences are boring so the one sitting on a cloud playing a harp was quickly dispatched, leaving the way clear for the horny little pig to guide our hero Leonard through life's social minefields.

A reader once remarked that Clob's pig form is clearly a reference to male chauvinism. I said yes, that's exactly what it is.

I was lying.

Clob's appearance is actually down to a record sleeve and a book cover. I think it was the third or fourth volume of the perennial *Now That's What I Call Music!* series that had a shade-wearing pig on the sleeve, while the book in question was Isaac Asimov's *Azazel,* which featured the one-inch high, red-skinned, demon-like figure of Azazel climbing into a guy's breast pocket. But if anyone asks, yeah, he's an anthropomorphic actualisation of male chauvinism. It makes it sound like I know what I'm doing.

THE DAMAGE DONE

This is quite possibly my sickest tale yet.

I had an awful dream where I was digging through the plasterwork of my house and found a child's fists in the cavity between walls. Ancient and dried up, they looked like little scraps of knotted chamois leather. As is often the case, the idea twisted and turned when I tried to set it down on paper.

Incidentally, *The Damage Done* marks my quickest ever acceptance. It took Gary Fry, the then editor of *Fusing Horizons*, about ten minutes from me emailing him this story to email me back with "I'll take it!" He is quite clearly a sick individual.

SHEEP

I first read about the Waldviertel in Donald James' novel *The House of Janus*, in which the Austrian forests are described as a place where the old ways linger and people still fasten spears to gates in case they should they come across a wolf. The character of Laura was based physically, in my mind at least, on Angelina Jolie, which is why she is wearing a tight-fitting leather suit and riding a powerful motorcycle when you first meet her.

I never claimed to be deep.

Sheep was written for, and subsequently shortlisted to appear in, an anthology where each story represented a particular horror trope. Alas, with the TOC just days from being settled, the editor emailed me to say my werewolf story had been displaced by a late submission from someone named Adam L. G. Neville. His story went on to be reprinted in both *The Year's Best Horror & Fantasy 2005* and *Best New Horror 2005*, the ever-so-talented bastard that he is.

I never claimed to be gracious either.

THE FALL OF AZALIEL AND LORCAS

At a loose end one afternoon, I rapped out a sentence about two WW2 soldiers trapped inside a tank. This didn't get the creative juices flowing so I made them angels in a brass bottle reconnoitring the snowy slopes of Hell — as you do — and winged it from there.

LIKE CAT AND DOG

The closing line of this story originated in a tiny 100 word piece I wrote called *Takeaway*. I then recycled it in a 2000 word story called *No Dogs Allowed.* After that story was published, I shamelessly expanded it to the 5000 word *Like Cat and Dog*.

Which spawned a novella.

Which — and this won't surprise anybody — has grown into a full-blown novel.

The first in a series.

THE EXCHANGE

Dreams are a fount of inspiration for story ideas, although more often than not, those ideas that seem so appealing on waking in the middle of the night look pretty rubbish when viewed in the cold light of day, or are sketchy at best. Or, before you have made notes (because, like, the dream is so vivid there's no way you'll forget it!) you, um, forget it.

The Exchange is based on a recurring nightmare, one where my daughter has fallen into deep water and I dive down to save her, unsuccessfully.

SOAPOCRYPHAL

Two trains of thought went into this story. First, I read a magazine article about how all the big corporations employ futurologists, people whose job it is to look at developing technologies and advise their employers on how to invest their time and money. Here's an example: a futurologist working for a car manufacturer at the turn of the century might have seen ways in which a mass-produced, personal flying car could be developed by 2010. However, figuring that legislation would make such things commercially unviable, the futurologist instead advised the company to invest in hydrogen fuel technology for when the oil runs out.

So I set about dreaming up a TV screen that could be tattooed on your body by extrapolating existing technology*. Can you imagine how intimate that would feel? This introduced the second train of thought: whenever a long-running soap opera character dies, the studio that produces the soap is inundated with flowers from grieving viewers. Clearly there are people whose perception of the border between fact and fiction is blurry at best.

Soapocryphal is what happens when that border disappears completely.

*Mark my words, Skinflicks will come along soon, and when they do, I want my cut.

THE UINTA INCIDENT

I wanted to write a giant monster story, something world-threatening in the mould of Godzilla or Mothra, and this was the result. The first draft featured just the middle portion, those scenes in the desert, ending where the earth trembles and the protagonists realise something terrible and awe-inspiring has been resurrected. The framing scenes were added much later.

SPEAKING IN FORKED TONGUES

A stab at comedic writing inspired by the title of the Tim Booth album, *Booth and the Bad Angel*, although I chose the name Jacob for the main protagonist because it resonated with a line from U2's *Bullet the Blue Sky*, "Jacob wrestled the angel, and the angel was overcome". The character Michael Halpin was named for the inimitable web-based critic Mick Halpin, because he offered me lots of encouragement through the online workshop Critters, and not because he engages in bondage sessions with ladies of the night. Well, not to my knowledge anyway.

THE BRIDGE

For several years I walked to and from work. As I set out at six of the morning clock, my journey to work was in the dark for several months of the year. The problem was, you see, is that I couldn't — *see*, that is. My night vision was the first casualty of retinitis pigmentosa and so . . . oh dear, there's no nice way of putting this, I was prone to treading on things soft and reeking. If there was any truth in the old saying "Muck for luck" I would have been a wealthy man. As such, I made it my habit, when walking home in the daylight, to memorise the positions of all the dog turds. I don't think this is quite what's meant when one is accused of having a shit memory, but there you go.

My daily journey took me on a footbridge over a dual carriageway and one black morning there was a perfect set of shining silver footprints ahead of me. A light snowfall had melted, apart from where someone had trodden and compressed the snow to ice. The effect was magical and it lifted my spirits. Then part of my brain — you know, the bit that says, "Did you just hear something?" when you're alone in the dark, or "Does this custard taste of strychnine to you?" (or is that just me?) — anyway, *that* part of the brain said, "Supposing the footprints end at the railings halfway across the bridge . . ."

THE *VENDETTA*

There are times, when writing these afterwords, I've been tempted to lie. This is one of them. The truth will make no sense.

It was on Newgale beach in Pembrokeshire. My daughter had a curved spade and I discovered that if I walked backwards, trailing the spade on its edge, it guided me to describe perfect circles in the wet sand. Which led me to speculate on what sort of demons you would summon on a beach in west Wales.

So I wrote a story where a fallen angel summons demons in the Mediterranean, using pentagrams on Frisbees made of ice.

I warned you it wouldn't make any sense.

JAPANESE MOTORCYCLE CLOB

I've owned lots of motorbikes, but the one that caused me the most grief was a Suzuki Katana 750. It was a big, heavy, low-slung missile of a bike. One day, one *very hot* day, the engine cut out and refused to start again. I had no choice but to push the bike home. Thankfully my parents' house was only two miles away.

However, I was wearing full leathers and biker boots which, while affording great protection against the wind and rain, flying insects and the occasional crash, were not made for walking.

And my parents' house is at one the highest points in Stoke-on-Trent.

And did I mention that it was a very hot day?

There are many words to describe my feelings right then. Unhappy is one. Knackered is another. Oh, and homicidal, that's a good one.

Years later I related this incident to a biker friend, who told me that another friend of his had suffered similarly, with the added ignominy of dropping the bike out of sheer exhaustion. Pushed beyond his limits, this guy then urinated on his stricken machine. I think I know how he felt. I might have taken revenge on my Suzuki in a like manner had I not sweated out all my bodily fluids.

PRETTY USELESS SAYS

I love playing computer games, have done since I was a child in the 1970s when the games were as basic as you can imagine. Anyone remember Pong? Nowadays my favourite genre of game is the first-person shooter. Many games in this genre feature combative online play. It was during one such session that I was routinely killed about a dozen times, in the manner described in *Pretty Useless Says*, by someone named Dion. And yes, his parting words were "man u suck dick".

I have not played a first-person shooter online since. Not once. Ever.

MARBLES

I wish I could pretend that a visit I made to Ephesus while holidaying in Turkey in 1990 inspired *Marbles*. Alas, callow youth that I was, I remember little of my visit to the ancient city port. It might as well have been a pile of breeze blocks for all I cared. It was unbearably hot and, thanks to illusions of artistic clever-dickery, my camera was loaded with monochrome film. As such, my photos of that day are as unclear as my memories.

I learned the true origins of Diana's multi-breasted appearance in Desmond Morris' excellent volume *The Naked Woman* around the same time that I saw a TV documentary charting the life of *Penthouse* magazine founder, Bob Guccione. The two collided in my mind and *Marbles* was born.

Conclusion: Breasts inspire me; bricks don't.

CUTTING THE CORD

This was written on the fly. In one sitting with absolutely no idea where it was going. An apple rolls off a table. What's going on here?

A year or so after it was first published, I was asked by Mark Deniz of Morrigan Books if I would contribute to an anthology of stories inspired by a favourite album of his, called *Scenes from the Second Storey* by The God Machine. The story he wanted me to write would be inspired by the song *Out*. I listened to the track, which starts quite light if melancholic before plunging into a drum-heavy riff, then read the lyrics about someone trapped and wishing to break out, and realised that I had already written this story. So *Cutting the Cord* was retitled as *Out* and I sneakily had another sale. Then Mark asked me to write an author's note explaining how the song inspired the story, proving beyond a doubt that when it comes to sneaky he trumps me every time.

THE RISE OF AZALIEL AND LORCAS

The first story featuring Azaliel and Lorcas was published in *52 Stitches* from Strange Publications. When I learned there would be a second volume, I leapt at the chance to write a sequel. Besides, I couldn't leave my angels stranded in Hell, could I?

The slight difference in tone between the two stories came about due to an upper limit of 750 words. As any writer knows, it's easier to write a longer story than a short one.

THE MIGRANT

Back in 2001 I wrote one of my first stories, called *Ricochet*. A soldier returns from WW1 only to find himself stalked while on a hunting trip in the Scottish highlands. It didn't quite work (the editor of *Weird Tales* magazine kindly devoted a full side of foolscap to explain why), so I broke it up to create this tale and, much later, another story called *The Devil's Fauna*.

The meat of *The Migrant* came from a TV programme that tried to determine the origins of Hitler's anti-Semitism. According to the documentary, Adolf Hitler lived with Jews in his student days, and he had a great deal of respect for his Jewish commanding officer when serving in the trenches of The Great War. So what happened on his return to civilian life in Munich to change him? Much of *The Migrant* — the bullet passing through Hitler's sleeve, him being blinded by mustard gas, his Iron Crosses for gallantry and his duties as a despatch rider — is factual. The rest . . . isn't, and is fired by my belief that the terrible events of The Second World War can and will happen again, as evinced by the first draft's closing lines:

"And from small acorns grew mighty oaks, and though the oaks were felled less than thirty years later, they sowed yet more acorns. Sometimes they find fertile soil, and sometimes not. It does not trouble me for I know that is the way of things. Men have not changed, and I am patient. Moreover, I am eternal."

Incidentally, passages from *Ricochet* also found their way into *Lonely Heart Clob* and *Japanese Motorcycle Clob*. Which just goes to show, you should never throw away a half-decent story. Just cannibalise it!

THE DEVIL'S FAUNA

I saw Stefan T Buczacki's *Fauna Britannica* and my brain conjured with the title. Imagine a book called *Fauna Satanica* that guided the reader around the Devil's bestiary. I'd buy it! Meanwhile, I had a sunken loaf of a revenge story on my computer, where a WW1 veteran is stalked on a hunting trip to Scotland by a comrade he accidentally shot during battle. The Reverend James Haplowe's *The Fauna Satanica* was the yeast that made the loaf rise.

I chose Glen Orchy for the location because it's the scene of many a 'happy' family holiday. Mum, Dad, my brother, sister and me, all cooped up in a little camper van. Oh what fun. We used to park on an idyllic spot beside the river Orchy, near to some spectacular waterfalls, and walk over the nearby mountains. At least I think they are mountains and not merely big hills. Footslogging up and down them left me completely knackered.

THE ARBITRATOR

Sometimes a story will need lots of careful coaxing to bring it to fruition. Other times an idea will pop into your head fully formed as if it has always been there and you had simply forgotten its existence. *The Arbitrator* was one of the latter. While out walking near my home, I crossed a brick bridge that passes over a brook. Within seconds I had the complete story in my mind, the characters, the setting, even the second-person narrative.

C IS FOR CLEAR

When I was playing with my then one-year-old daughter, my wife would often exclaim, "Honestly, it's like having twins!" Such as the time I cut doors and windows into a long cardboard box and wriggled inside, where I got stuck with my arms pinned to my sides and discovered I suffer from claustrophobia . . .

THE COLOUR OF LEMONS

If memory serves me correctly, this was the first story I wrote, way back in 2001. And it all revolved around holding an object at arm's length, closing one eye and imagining it being something far off and enormous. I do that a lot. We all do it, don't we? Yeah, course we do. And sometimes I hold my fingers apart so they frame a distant person's head, and then I squeeze so they explode in a squidgy mess.

Heh.

I forget what I was going to say now.

THE LIGHT KNIGHT RETURNS

Inspired by the excruciating and embarrassingly bad chorus of U2's *Elevation* (Google the lyrics if you are unfamiliar with the song), the first draft of this short story was novelette length. It took several years and lots of redrafting to arrive at the version in this volume. Those excess words dealt mainly with how young Tommy Knight came to be resurrected, which involved all manner of quasi-religious backstory concerning the games he played as the titular superhero. Even after several drafts the piece was overlong, overly complicated and would still be languishing in a folder labelled "Next stop, Recycle Bin" if I had not seen a submissions call for an anthology called *Harvest Hill**. The premise for this book was simple: every Halloween, in a Midwest town, something strange and wonderful happens. Simple, sure, but it gave me a license to remove all the extraneous material from *The Light Knight Returns.*

*It's a great anthology. I'm not just saying that because it's published by Graveside Tales, who also published the book you're holding in your hands (well, I am, sort of), but because it genuinely is very good. I kid you not.

RAISING ARCHIE

I doodled a few lines about a man buying an egg of indeterminate origin. What was in the egg — a dragon, a fairy, a two-headed Roc? I didn't know, and so the story sat on ice until the gargoyle idea, well . . . hatched. After that, the most difficult thing about writing this story was the title. Ask any writer and they'll tell you that titles are the bane of their life. This one laboured under the working title of *Statues and Statutes*. Yuck!

Matt Monroe playing on the radio was my idea of a cryptic joke. He sang the theme tune to the film *Born Free*, you see, with which *Raising Archie* shares some basic plot points. Well, when I say 'joke' . . .

GIVE 'EM ENOUGH ROPE

Caleb Oates' unusual career choice was a nod to one of my favourite James songs, *Johnny Yen*, which contains the classic line, "See Houdini and his underwater tricks, you were sitting at the front hoping his locks would stick". The story came about after I dreamed of a hanging where the victim would not die. It bothered me for several weeks until I sat down to write this story.

ABOUT THE AUTHOR

Mike Stone was born in 1966 in Stoke-on-Trent, England. Since losing most of his eyesight he has retreated from your world to travel the dark corners of inner space — or to put it more prosaically he thinks "What if?" a lot. The signs are clear to those that know him well, for his one not-so-bad eye glazes over and he is rendered deaf to all English except for "Would you like a cup of tea, Mike?" He will then engage with reality long enough to ask if there are any biscuits before drifting off again. While agreeing that this can be very trying for those around him, he remains unrepentant.

He is represented by Nat Sobel of Sobel Weber Associates, Inc.

Acknowledgements

Sacred Skin first appeared at bloodlust-uk.com, 2004: **Memory Bones** first appeared at stillwatersjournal.com, 2002: **Lonely Heart Clob** first appeared (as 'Clob') in Teddy Bear Cannibal Massacre, ed. Tim Lieder, 2005: **The Damage Done** first appeared in Fusing Horizons #4, 2004: **Sheep** first appeared at dredtales.com, 2006: **The Fall of Azaliel and Lorcas** first appeared in Fifty-Two Stitches, ed. Aaron Polson, 2009: **Like Cat and Dog** first appeared in The Beast Within, ed. Matt Hults, 2008: **The Exchange** first appeared in Northern Haunts, ed. Tim Deal, 2009: **Soapocryphal** first appeared in Fusing Horizons #3, 2004: **The Uinta Incident** first appeared in Worlds Apart #2, 2008: **Speaking in Forked Tongues** first appeared at downinthecellar.com, 2006: **The Bridge** first appeared in Triangulation: End of Time, 2007: **The Vendetta** first appeared in Strange Stories of Sand and Sea, ed. Esther Schrader 2008: **Japanese Motorcycle Clob** first appeared at tqrstories.com, 2007: **Pretty Useless Says** first appeared at dredtales.com, 2006: **Marbles** first appeared in Robots and Time, ed. Robert N Stephensen & Shane J Cummings, 2006: **Cutting the Cord** first appeared at everydayeirdness.com, 2009: **The Rise of Azaliel and Lorcas** first appeared in Fifty-Two Stitches Volume Two, ed. Aaron Polson, 2010: **The Migrant** first appeared at tqrstories.com, 2008: **The Devil's Fauna** first appeared at tqrstories.com, 2007: **The Arbitrator** first appeared at dredtales.com, 2008: **C is for Clear** first appeared at alienskinmag.com, 2003: **The Colour of Lemons** first appeared in Continuum SF #2, 2004: **The Light Knight Returns** first appeared in Harvest Hill, ed. Mike Hultquist & Douglas Hutcheson, 2009: **Raising Archie** first appeared at electricspec.com, 2006: **Give 'Em Enough Rope** first appeared in Tales of Moreauvia #4, 2012

ALSO FROM GRAVESIDE TALES

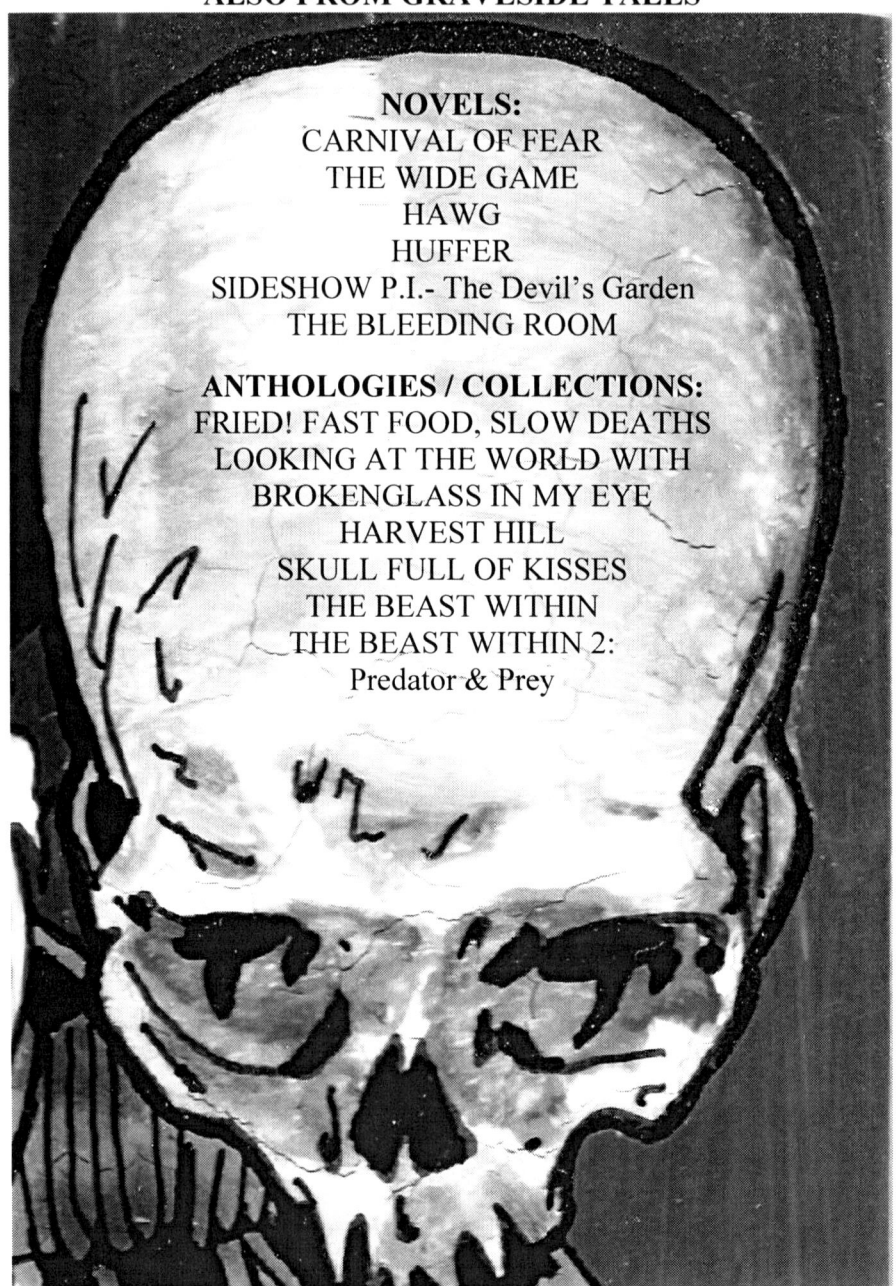

NOVELS:
CARNIVAL OF FEAR
THE WIDE GAME
HAWG
HUFFER
SIDESHOW P.I.- The Devil's Garden
THE BLEEDING ROOM

ANTHOLOGIES / COLLECTIONS:
FRIED! FAST FOOD, SLOW DEATHS
LOOKING AT THE WORLD WITH
BROKENGLASS IN MY EYE
HARVEST HILL
SKULL FULL OF KISSES
THE BEAST WITHIN
THE BEAST WITHIN 2:
Predator & Prey

GRAVESIDETALES.COM
http://amzn.to/gravesidetales

Lightning Source UK Ltd.
Milton Keynes UK
UKOW041419180413

209412UK00002B/47/P